W9-ACT-418

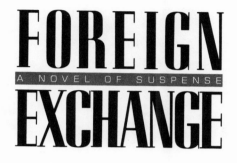

FOREIGN
A NOVEL OF SUSPENSE
EXCHANGE

Also by Larry Beinhart

No One Rides For Free
You Get What You Pay For

FOREIGN EXCHANGE

A NOVEL OF SUSPENSE

LARRY BEINHART

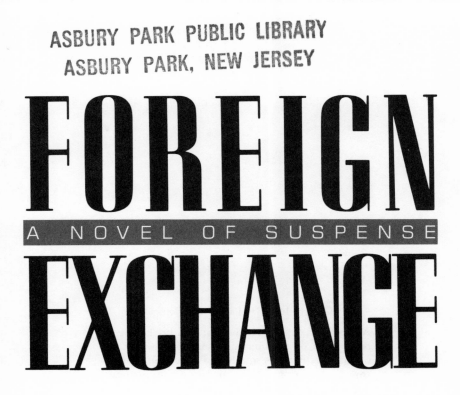

HARMONY BOOKS NEW YORK

Published by Harmony Books, a division of Crown Publishers, Inc., 201 East 50th Street, New York, New York 10022. Member of the Crown Publishing Group.

Manufactured in the United States of America

Library of Congress Cataloging in Publication Data
Beinhart, Larry.
Foreign exchange / Larry Beinhart.
p. cm.
I. Title.
PS3552.E425F6 1991
813'.54—dc20 91-7598
CIP

ISBN 0-517-57726-7

10 9 8 7 6 5 4 3 2 1

First Edition

This book is dedicated to
Anna Geneviève,
born November 22, 1988

ACKNOWLEDGMENTS

With thanks to all those who helped us on the way: Joy Harris at home; Karen Frankel at Nexus; Susie Chase-Motzkin, ski guru; Mike Meller in Germany; David, Mila and Dr. Slonim, Nika, Jaro and Jaroslav Prokopec in Prague; Saša Racz and Sandra Ferenčič in Yugoslavia; Micha Hajnàk in Budapest; Nancy Binkin in Rome; Yoshiro "Borro" Masaki in Japan; and especially IN MEMORY OF CHRIS COX, who died September 7, 1990, of AIDS.

FOREIGN

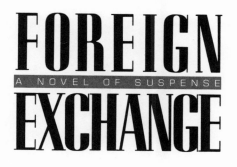

A NOVEL OF SUSPENSE

EXCHANGE

PROLOGUE

HOAR FROST

¥ = yen *$ = U.S. dollar* *ÖS = Austrian schilling*

DM = deutsch mark *FF = French franc* *£ = English pound*

SF = Swiss franc *KR = Swedish krona*

Hiroshi Tanaka took delight in brand names. They were his validation. His boots were Strolz, custom made in Lech, Austria, where the boot fitter measured him around the ankles, over the insteps, across the toes, then made a template of each foot—a craftsman as thorough as the tailor who cut Tanaka's suits in London. More important than the fit was the cost. Anyone who truly knew skiing knew that the Strolz was the most expensive boot on the market—ÖS5,500—$430 with the Austrian schilling at 11.62 to one American dollar. His LaCroix skis cost FF4,250, with the French franc running 5.6 to the dollar—$760; in schillings: ÖS10,000; and ¥97,280 with the yen at 128 to the dollar, which was the rate the day he bought them. Hiroshi took great pleasure in knowing where the yen was in relation to the dollar. It was creeping closer to that perfectly symmetrical barrier, ¥100 to $1, the four-minute mile of finance, the hymen of foreign exchange. The day it broke would be the day that the dollar went *yin*—passive, feminine—and the yen became totally, officially *yang*—masculine and dominant.

The thought of it stirred his crotch pleasantly. There was a direct connection in his mind between money and erection. That was not an ethnic slur, a personal aspersion, or even an artifact of sexism. There are many people, male and female, who have their genitalia tied to financial statements. Perhaps most. Certainly not all—certainly there are those who have sex for power. And out of anger. Fear. Duty. And love. The closer the yen got to 100:1 the larger Hiroshi looked to himself, when he pumped up and posed in profile in the mirror.

Unfortunately the yen had stalled at 123. In fact it was creeping back up, past 130, toward 140:1.

Never mind, no problem—he had something better than size. As in many other things, he had applied Japanese concentration, study, and discipline to Western technology. Ask Wendy. The American blonde, the nineteen-year-old American blonde who skied behind him. Hiroshi could make her scream, and scream, over and over again. First from pleasure. Then for respite and relief. Something no American boyfriend had ever made her do. She told him so and he had no doubt it was true. No—not even the black one she had gone all the way to New York City to find when she was in high school. An American high school in Danbury, Connecticut, where the children seemed to major in *party*, a word that loosely translated as excess alcohol, drugs restricted only by availability, and promiscuous sex. Hiroshi felt contempt for them. Hiroshi liked to feel contempt. It was the second best emotion, maybe the counterpoint emotion, of feeling rich. The "You are worse than I" implicit in "I am better than you." The American children in Wendy's stories partied as if they had been given a ticket that said, "Free ride forever." A whole generation, a series of generations, of an entire nation had made a Faustian bargain—though too illiterate, as a group, to know the hero from either Marlowe or Goethe—to party, on the assumption that their souls would never come due.

Hiroshi was Wendy's first Oriental.

Wendy was, by her own standards, a happy, healthy girl. She was off seeing the world, between high school and college. Skiing. Sailing. Hiking. Museuming. A taste of this, a nibble of that, a swallow of the other—an Austrian, a Brit, an Italian. Just as at home she'd sampled a jock, a nerd, an older man, a druggie. She told Hiroshi her party stories because they excited him. The idea of seven American high school girls, fourteen, fifteen, and sixteen years old, high and drunk and sloppy, playing strip poker, playing with boys drove her fifty-year-old rich Japanese lover insane. He would manipulate her with hand and tongue and Hitachi vibrator—$56, ÖS650, ¥7,168—letting her reach her orgasm limit before he would jump on top of her for his own release. It was true that he took a longish time at that also, but it wasn't unpleasant, and when he caught his breath he would always take her to Palmer's, that marvelous and ubiquitous Austrian chain of lingerie stores, and buy her a little something. Everytime she told him one of her party stories.

Wendy found herself in a bit of a quandary. It was true that she was in the relationship for the fun of it. And the novelty. At least to start with. That, she felt, was healthy. Her friends and her parents would have felt the same. But now she wanted a Burton board, basically a surfboard modified for snow, and as the T-shirts say, snow is just frozen water. She skied faster, if not better, than Hiroshi, and only stayed behind him because he sulked so severely when she didn't. And Hiroshi mostly liked the groomed blue runs because he looked so slick on them. In the bumps she could really blow him off. Wendy was a shredder—snow flew when she skied the bumps. She had happy feet. Plus teenage knees. So here she was, thinking about what element she would have to add to her next party story—a black basketball player of mythic proportions, the girl who pulled a train for the varsity football team, an all-girl five-girl daisy chain, tabs of acid and hallucinogenic bosoms—in order to score the Burton board, almost $1,000, ¥142,000, ÖS11,600, with import duties and resort prices.

Somewhere beneath those thoughts, unarticulated and not yet realized, but caused by those thoughts, Wendy had decided to break off with Hiroshi.

The decision was made instinctively, instantly, from the gut of her integrity. It had happened the moment she saw herself contemplating an exchange of sexual favors for cash or cash equivalent. Wendy was not one to delude herself that the difference between cash and cash equivalent changed the sexual favors equation. Her father was a tax accountant, and if cash equivalent was taxable, then it was real income, and if it was real income, then fucking for a piece of ski equipment made her a real whore.

Yet in a way she was richer than Hiroshi. Wendy had a gift for real pleasure, a sensuous delight in shopping and spending and having and consuming. For Hiroshi, all of these, earning, buying, owning, even gift giving, were just ways of keeping score.

Hans skied in front of them.

That was okay with Hiroshi. Not because Hans was another man but because Hans was hired help. He was their guide. Hiroshi paid the Arlberg Ski School, the most famous one in the world, the one that started it all, ÖS1,650 ($142) a day for him. Hans was highly trained. He had passed several difficult exams administered by the Austrian government and was entitled to wear the patch with the Austrian Eagle on it that said *Staatlich Geprufter Skilehrer*, state certified ski teacher, a serious title in a country in which skiing is universal. In addition, he was a *Skiführer*, which meant that he had passed another series of exams and was qualified in this land of avalanches, cliffs, and sudden storms to take tourists off-piste, away from the marked trails. Even with 135 kilometers of trails and 70 lifts, skiing the pistes was definitely not chic. Chic was the search for unmarked snow, fresh snow, your own snow, where you could make powder tracks. Chic was the *frisson* of danger—the more it cost the tastier it was—and that's the way Charles and Di did it and Andy and Fergie did it when they skied over the border at Klosters in Switzerland.

Hans was twenty-eight. He was a mountain boy, his horizons limited not by the peaks that hemmed in the valley, but by the narrow minds and the traditionalist society that surrounded him. Sons of farmers became farmers and something supplemental because when farmland is vertical and a big herd of cattle is eight cows, farming doesn't go very far. Shopkeepers inherited shops. Civil servants raised their *Kinder* civilly. The doctor's father had been a doctor and, by God, both generations cherished their titles and wore them like badges.

Sometimes a mountain boy had magic in his feet and steel in his thighs, a fondness for pain and total lack of fear. Then he raced. He'd start racing when he could walk. It got serious at puberty.

If he had a real shot at making the national team all *Österreich* knew it by the time he was fourteen. Most people have only seen a downhill race on television. They don't know it at all. The course must be seen in person and, even better, walked on or skied. If the snow is soft like snow, they pour water on it the night before the race so the course will be frozen. It will be ice. The sound of the edges of a racer's skis is like the sound of a train. They howl and clatter. When the racer loses an edge or catches an edge or misses his prejump or his feet can't move with a rippling series of ridges or he's just not strong enough or prepared enough to brave enough, then he's gone. A wild tumbling thing. Skis and poles scattered. Down the course. A body banging on a skittering cliff of ice searching for a soft obstruction to stop on before it meets a hard one and breaks. Stand next to the course. Watch them come. They come like race cars. All racers have broken bones, torn cartilage, reattached ligaments.

There are fewer skiers on the World Cup Tour than there are basketball players in the NBA or baseball players that make it to the major leagues.

So he charges down the hill, hell-bent for leather, to that moment of realization that he doesn't have the guts, or the commitment, or the skill, or the body, or the reflexes, or the eyes, or the right coach, the right diet, the right season, the right stars—something—and he will have to settle for humbler employment. If he still likes skiing and can say, "Weight on the outside ski" in another language, he can take the local exams and become a *landesskilehrer*, local ski instructor, more exams and try for his Eagle, other exams and become a guide. Each ski area has its own school, or schools, and its own way of doing business. The Arlberg Ski School is owned by a core group of the instructors, with shares divided in ways as mysterious and arcane as a medieval guild. An instructor's share depends on where he lives, how long he's been a member, what he teaches, and how much he works. He doesn't work if the customers don't like him. Like any other service person he counts on the same clients coming back year after year—and they do, asking for Kurt, or Rudi, or Luis, or Hans. When he works, an instructor makes about $500 a week. Which is not bad, but is not enough. So he has deals with the restaurant where he takes the class for lunch, with the bistro where he takes the class for après drinks, with the ski shop that he sends them to for outfits, and when he passes the shrines that dot the Catholic mountainsides, he says a brief prayer for a big tip.

Hans had grown up hard and narrow. Vision came to him in bits and flashes, denied almost as fast as he'd seen it. Perhaps he was bright, but he was taught that nothing would come from learning. He had some talent for skiing, but his father said it was for children and that Hans would have to learn that life was hard in the mountains and he would have to work, not play. He skied anyway, but came to racing late. All he ever broke was his left arm. He got back on skis when he was healed, as all the machismo in Tyrolia said he must, but a month after he returned he flew off a downhill course and caught a glimpse of the afterlife while he was airborne. He liked a little money. He liked how skiing kept his body hard, his face tan, his hair bleached, and how the girls liked that. He liked to get *bier* and schnapps and whatever drugs the tourists wanted to share and he liked to get laid. It was better than chipping ice off of cables before dawn in February or lifting boxes out of a delivery truck. Besides, he was a natural blond. Not something to waste.

The clouds broke at last. The sky opened, immensely blue, bluer than it ever got in the lowlands. The sun came from above; it hit snow and bounced back up. It was a number 10 sun block day. Wendy already had a stripe of fluorescent pink sun block on her nose. On her it looked cute and California. Hiroshi used Piz Buin. Hans skied easily, but not with precision. Then Hiroshi, more precise, but stiffer. Then Wendy, loose and looking for fun.

The Valuga is the mountain that towers over St. Anton. It can be reached by a series of three cable cars. The last a small one that goes to the very top, primarily for the view, because there is no way to ski down. There is, however, a way to walk around to the back of the Valuga holding on to a cable with one hand while you carry your skis over your shoulder with the other. From there you can ski all the way down to Lech.

Hans led the way. It wasn't that dangerous, there was something to hold on to. But it was still a thrill, an adrenaline tingle, because if the worst did happen, and you tripped, just when you were reaching for the next handhold, and you missed with your hand and didn't have the reflexes to grab something else, and you had the bad luck to be in a really bad spot, you were dead. In the literal sense of dead.

It had been a terrible year. The worst year for snow in living memory. Then, on February 10, it had begun to snow. It snowed for two days. And everyone felt their knees begin to twitch like teenagers on Saturday night. Snow, snow, thank God Almighty, snow at last. Then, at least in the valley, it rained for two days. Steady. Unceasingly. Over in France, in the Savoie, there were floods and death. Then it snowed again, for a day, and another, and another. Over in France, in the Savoie, more died in avalanches. In St. Anton and the rest of the Arlberg, and the Vorarlberg, the western tip of Austria, the high peaks were kept closed. All day long you could hear muffled blasts as the dynamitards set charges to knock down the loose snow and sometimes the rumbling thunder when a mountainside of snow avalanched down.

There had only been three days of super skiing all season. Now, even though this week-long dump of snow on top of nothing was going to be very dangerous, everyone waited, with baited breath, for the big snowfields up above the tree line to be opened. It took three days. Three days later there were tracks everywhere. Except on the back of the Valuga.

Now the last lift was finally open. They walked around, looking out onto the jagged vastness. All three of them filled with a kind of lust.

Powder.

Hans laid down a perfect trail of perfect curves in a perfect virgin snowscape. Here, high up, it was more than deep snow—it was deep and dry and light. Real powder. And that is what skiing is really all about. Next to it all other skiing is practice, or a technical event like racing, or simply what we settle for while we wait for the real thing to come along. Hiroshi, then Wendy each in turn laid down a parallel track. Hiroshi was precise. He tried to make his turns as perfect as his powder suit by S.O.S., made in Sweden,

$1800, KR12,075, ¥230,400, very hot colors and what the ski instructors in Val d'Isère were wearing this year. Wendy was ecstatic. She forgot about how she was going to break up with Hiroshi. She forgot about being tempted to be a whore. She forgot about what makes good girls into bad girls and how many pricks it takes to make a liberated woman into a slut. She forgot about going back to school and settling down and becoming an accountant so she wouldn't have to be dependent on a man but could co-join with a co-equal to "progenitate" and become propertied as her parents had done but as was, the media said, beyond the reach of so many of this generation. She forgot about the holes in the earth's atmosphere and the poison on the apples.

Powder.

Like a plunge into heaven. During the first two days of the storm it had been cold, about -10°C, about 0°F. Then, when it rained in the valley, it stayed below 0°C everywhere from the Galzig on up. Then the temperature dove—23°C, -10°F, and it kept on snowing. Which was magic. The colder the temperature, the lighter the snow. This was fluff, as fine as Colorado, as fine as the legendary high-desert powder of Alta in Utah. A skier who knows enough to let go of fear can drift down the face of cliff making his own cloud.

Wendy thought of Hiroshi as typically Japanese. Hiroshi did not. He thought of himself as an individualist. The typical Japanese was a member of the community first, of family, of company, of country, and an individual long afterward. Hiroshi was an adventurer. In his own mind he was a James Bond. Certainly he had that sense of ascendancy, the optimistic assurance that comes from the certainty of being racially superior that Bond had. It's something that comes with empire, territorial or financial.

They were off by themselves in a travel brochure. The sky was azure. The sky was morning glory blue, larkspur blue, cerulean, cobalt, celeste. Three sets of S curves. The valley and the towns far, far below, past the tree line, invisible. Jagged cliffs and snow above.

The grade of the slope eased. Hans stopped. They all stopped. Wendy was grinning. A big bubble of happiness. A pause to share this one perfect run with each other. Hiroshi accepted the tribute.

After all, it was his yen that had made this gathering, this perfection, possible. Hans accepted the silent accolades. After all, he had found this perfect patch of powder for them, virtually before anyone else. Which was his job.

There was a rumbling noise above them.

Neither Hiroshi nor Wendy paid any attention to it. They were catching their breath. Hans glanced up. Hans turned his skis down the hill, pushed with his poles, and took off. Then the other two glanced up.

There are scientific studies of avalanches. They will tell you that they occur on slopes over 35°. Depth hoar is one of the classical causes. Like the charming hoar frost that paints pumpkin fields for autumn postcards in New England, it is created by the crystalization of moisture from evaporation, hoar frost from dew, depth hoar from snow. These crystals have a cuplike shape and so fail to bond with the next layer of snow, leaving a layer of instability. The studies will speak of dry snow and wet snow. Dry snow avalanches usually occur during, or within several days after, snowfall. They may affect whole slopes even if wooded, and may exceed 100 miles per hour. Wet snow avalanches are slower. But the reality is that avalanches are at least as tricky as sex. They fail to happen when they should, then occur where they shouldn't. Like the big slide at the eastern end of town that took out the Shell station and twelve people back in '88. Or the one at the beginning of the '90 season, near Stuben, with less than a meter of snow on the ground and not more than fifty meters from a very well skied piste. It swept over a twenty-two-year-old girl. Fifteen people watched. Everyone joined in to dig her out. It took less than twenty minutes to find her. By then she was dead.

It is possible to outski an avalanche. It's been done on film. Charles, Prince of Wales, was almost caught in an avalanche while skiing off-piste in Klosters, Switzerland, in March of 1988. It buried one member of the prince's party, Major Hugh Lindsay, and threw Patricia Palmer-Tomkinson 1,200 feet, breaking both her legs. No one establishes chic quicker than the British royals, and being avalanched has had a certain snob appeal ever since.

■

The rumbling got louder. No. Bigger. It was a rumble the size of a mountainside. Low and deep and huge.

The run to safety was less than a quarter mile. There was a ridge and a flat. A skier could turn to the left, over the ridge and down, while the slide would—most likely—take the path of least resistance to the right, hit the wide, slight slope of the meadow, and roll itself to a halt.

Hans put his skis straight and wide. He bent, went into a tuck, his poles under his arms, hands way out in front, the way he had been taught way back before he found out how tough racing really was. Hiroshi did his best, in his stiff, precise way, to imitate. Wendy first felt fear, then an immense exhilaration. She too got into a tuck. Hans had the weight and the longest skis. He began to pull away from them.

Now the powder, which had been their delight, was their enemy, slowing them down, holding them back, like a molasses trap.

Hiroshi was fine for the first two hundred yards. Then his thighs began to burn. The burn was exactly midpoint between the knee and the hip. There was a secondary pain just above the knees. He looked upon the pain as a test. One of discipline. Something to feel and to go through. But still it ached and robbed him of strength.

Wendy, looser and younger, leaning back on her heels, planed her skis higher, and passed Hiroshi. He would have hated her for it, but he was centered in his pain, being very Zen. Wendy had never felt such exhilaration. She was moving faster than she had ever gone. At some point in her acceleration she had gone beyond herself, moving faster than she knew how to ski, leaving fear behind. Lost luggage bounded on someone else's plane.

Still, the avalanche was gaining.

Hiroshi's left leg trembled. He wished to stand, to stretch it, relax the muscle. It trembled. He caught an edge on the snow beneath the snow. The snow held the ski, the binding released, as it was supposed to. Hiroshi thought, as he felt it come off, that he could continue to ski on just one ski. But that wasn't true and it was only the hyperawareness of the moment that made it possible to have the thought, so very clearly, between the time he caught the edge and when he went tumbling. He lost both skis, then one pole. He rolled on his shoulder and head as he came to rest at the point where, one gasp later, the avalanche would roll over him, bury him, drown him.

Wendy was doing fine. Not as fast as the avalanche. Not even as fast as Hans, but fast enough so that in the convergence of time she would reach the ridge before the wall of snow behind her. The wall that had just covered her generous lover.

But that was not to be. There was a section of windblown hardpack under the powder. The backward lean that had given her extra speed in the deep snow was what now betrayed her. The hardpack slapped her skis upward and her position didn't give her the balance she needed to absorb it.

She fell. The avalanche rushed over her. She knew it. She hoped it would knock her out so she would die unknowing that she would die. It didn't. It just rushed over her and began to smother her. Caught with her skis and boots and poles on, she fought to find some way that was up and some tunnel to air. Every movement was hampered. The fear that she'd lost came back, wrapped itself around her and she whimpered. Time is elastic. Time is subjective. A downhill race lasts less than two minutes, finishing position is measured in hundredths of a second, and those two minutes are at least two hundred moments long. Anyone who has ever boxed knows that one round in the ring, three minutes, is longer than three hours with a book. Asphyxiation takes one to four minutes. If the subject holds his breath, like a drowning swimmer might, or has some air, like a person caught in a snowslide, he might last several minutes more. However few or many the minutes between her fall and her demise, Wendy, the nineteen-year-old girl from Connecticut, was a long time dying.

Hans made it over the ridge before he looked back. He was alone. He was sorry that the other two hadn't made it. But that was a mild feeling next to the exaltation that he felt. He felt high and strong and clean. He had played the greatest game of all, the one with the biggest stakes. The deaths of Hiroshi Tanaka and Wendy Tavetian were proof of that.

ONE

RICK'S AMERICAN LAUNDROMAT

According to my passport my name is Richard Cochrane. That's not true. My native home is Ireland. That's not true either. I'm an exile, an expatriate, a man without a country, a stateless person. Here in a white land. A snow-covered alpine country where they speak a language I barely understand in a landscape like none I've ever known.

But who cares? I have money in the bank. They have excellent banks here. But then, they do almost everywhere these days. I have a full-breasted young woman as my companion. Younger than me. Heavy breasted, round bellied, and ripe with child. My child. She says so. I believe her. Her passport says her name is Marie. That's true. Marie Laure. My passport says my profession is priest. That's not true. On the one recent occasion that anyone has actually read the slot by profession and looked at Marie's belly at the same time, I just grinned. The border guard grinned back. Then we both laughed. He was happier with the notion of a lecherous priest than of a false passport. The image harked back to a merrier age—Chaucerian, Machiavellian, Rabelaisian—when priests and even politicians were presumed to have penises. The alternative, the modern reality of false papers, would have just meant more work.

The truth is that I love Marie pregnant. Sexually. This is a surprise. All that roundness. I love to take her from behind and feel the fullness of her buttocks, that waddling wideness against my thighs, and my hand weighing the swollen tits and feeling the shape of her baby-holding belly. She's vibrant, and healthy, and womanly. There's no cancer-scary pills to think about, no age-of-AIDS rubbers, no Catholic rhythmic counting of days, no pulling out just in time. There is a free and mindless ejaculation, thoroughly primitive, into a completely technology-free vaginal canal.

I was very fortunate. I got dollars when dollars where strong. Artificially and excessively high because a strong dollar made Ronald Reagan feel good. I had the sense to realize that. But I was foolish enough to think that gold would be a good hedge. Fortunately, my banker, who carped about handling a mere $100,000, suggested that I simply put it in a variety of currencies—yen, deutsche mark, Swiss franc, and even British pound.

I was almost tracked down in the south of France.

We decided to move to the mountains. That was when Marie was with me the first time. I discovered skiing. And went into business. Marie left me. Not because of skiing or business. She had the hots for someone else. Someone younger. And I gave her every excuse. Fool that I used to be for French women. I was a pushover, a slut, for any female who did that thing with their *r*'s and their eyes, dropped their *h*'s and moued.

Four days into our first ski trip we needed clean underwear. Marie was going to wash out things in the sink. There is love, there is duty, but I'd come from the States and this seemed excessive. I insisted that we go to the Laundromat. The washing machine was FF50. Five ten-franc pieces. Even at the good old rate of FF7 to the dollar, that was $7.14 to wash one load. Another FF50 for one twenty-minute cycle in the dryer. A big load could easily take forty minutes. There was only one Laundromat in town.

That was the business for me.

Except that the owner had a "relationship" with the mayor. A family relationship. It was not possible to get a license for a competitive Laundromat. But the ski area extends far beyond the one town. In the advertising brochures the whole thing is called, in cosmic letters, L'Espace Killy (Killy did ski there, he did win Olympic gold in all three Alpine events—downhill, slalom, giant slalom—so he probably is a god). Connected by lifts and trails, and beyond the sway of the mayor of Val d'Isère, are the demitowns of Val Claret, Tignes le Lac, Le Lavachet, Tignes les Boisses, built almost entirely for skiers, with no history but greed in a hurry, ripe and open for coin-operated entrepreneurship. I not only established a Laundromat, I got laundry machine franchises in two apartment buildings. It was much easier if the businesses were owned by a French person, so Marie became my partner. It was her first nonjob source of income. To remember the delight on her face when she came to understand what it means to have business income with tax deductible costs and, even better, a strictly cash business with all those jingling, unrecorded, ten-franc pieces can still bring a bright, nostalgic smile to my face.

Given that Marie and I had made no promises. Given that my escape to her had been after years trapped with another woman in a molasses of misapplied fidelity, a tar baby embrace made of gratitude and of a guilt that was not even about the woman herself but about her son. And even that I had had to blow up my entire world to get out of it. Given that the joy of my relationship with Marie was its utter simplicity. For God's sake, we didn't even speak the same language. I didn't even know how to say "Did you come?" and she never once asked me if I wanted to buy a condo. She was still my girlfriend. And my partner. She came to Sardinia when I called her and when I was in hiding. She was my lover when I went around disguised in monk's robes. She protected my secrets. She asked for nothing.

So she deserved better than to find me with the two entirely too posh English girls on holiday who found me "rough," "roguish," "quaint." Not even I believed my story that it was merely a hunger for my native tongue.

I didn't understand that I was in love with her until she took up with Gerard, the ski instructor. Very much the coxcomb. More satisfied by making another man a cuckold than by getting laid. It made L'Espace Killy intolerable for me. I didn't care how many English girls there were. I didn't care about other women with cute French accents. Just the one. I didn't give a goddamn if my skiing was improving *avec rapidité* or about those ten-franc pieces clunking away into my machines. It made me insane to be in the same L'Espace with that woman with another cock between her legs and everyone in town, it seemed, aware of it.

There are those who will say it served me right.

There are those who will say it's the least I deserved.

Quite right, too. I left town. I left Marie the Laundromat and the machines and said I would trust her with the books. Even though I had taught her to cook them, even with her getting her hands on the cash before ever I saw it—*if* I ever saw it—and with her being the owner of record and myself being a stateless person traveling on a not quite real passport.

I went skiing. I had become, in a short time, addicted. I became a Byronic figure, noble, heartbroken, athletic, oft laid but never loving. To Chamonix and Courcheval to Verbier and Zermatt in Switzerland from which I skied over to Cervina in Italy, looking, looking always for a place that needed Laundromats.

Such was my condition when I arrived here.

A place like this is called a ski circus. *Circus,* from the Latin, means circle or circuit, like Rome's Circus Maximus, which was an oval race track. The lifts and the runs go from town to town to town, from Lech, to Zürs, to St. Christoph, to St. Anton. The tree line is about 500 meters above the town, at 1,800 meters, and the cable car to the Valuga goes to about 2,650 meters, a vast skiable landscape. Half of it is in the Arlberg, the other half, Lech and Zürs, are in a region called the Vorarlberg, which means in front of the Arlberg. Back in the days before the tunnel was built, when villages were truly the complete social unit, Arlbergians and Vorarlbergians were barely on speaking terms. Intermarriage over the pass was seriously frowned on. The Arlberg makes a reasonably valid claim to being the historical center of alpine skiing. A lot of good skiers ski there. It has a famous race, the Kandahar. St. Anton is named for Saint Anthony of Padua. I have been told that he is the patron saint of cows, a weather saint, and the saint who taught poor people to ski. Actually, he is the saint to pray to for finding lost things. The area is extremely Austrian and rather overfond of itself. But none of that is really to the point.

I was staying in a small *pension*, the equivalent of a guest house or bed and breakfast. It is the custom in these places for the woman of the house to take in the guests' laundry, make it look like very hard work, and charge the guests far more than they would pay at home. What the hell. The punters are on holiday, they expect a certain amount of ripoff, and the person scrubbing—or at least loading her machines, ironing, and folding—is their hostess. It's very hard to tell her to her face that she deserves less for handling your personal soil.

It happened that the Frau of this house took sick and there was no one to do the laundry. After recycling my cleanest dirty clothes one time too many, I asked my host for a laundry, and even hinted, for the sake of saving a few bucks, that perhaps I could simply use the laundry machine in his basement. He couldn't conceive of that. That was Frau territory. He said he would call the local laundry, they would pick up and deliver.

9	*Trikothemden*	*ÖS252*
8	*Unterhosen*	*96*
2	*Unterhemden*	*26*
2	*Unterhosen lang*	*36*
1	*Hosen*	*65*
3½	*Socken*	*42*
	Summe	*517*
+	*20%MWSt. (tax)*	*103*
	Total	ÖS 620

We are speaking here of T-shirts, underwear, sleeveless T-shirts, longjohns—one pair with a hole in the thigh so large that my foot went through it when I tried to put them on—one pair of jeans, three and one half pairs of socks. We are not speaking of delicate silken underthings, lace and pleats, suits of virgin wool, dress shirts of hand-loomed Egyptian cotton. We are not speaking of special handling, spot removal, dry cleaning, or tailoring.

At today's rate of exchange—ÖS11.60:$1—what we are speaking of is $53.44.

Fifty dollars for a half load of laundry. I had found my new home.

■

I was reasonably happy. I found an apartment. It was expensive. I found an Austrian, influential in the local community, and made a member of his family my paper partner. The beer was good. And reasonable. Alcoholic beverages were perhaps the only thing in town reasonably priced. The women tended to be blond, German, healthy. Friendly too.

In puberty, that most vulnerable and suicidal of ages, I was always able to make it through to the next morning by the thought of having sex with a new girl. No depression was so deep, so dark, so lasciviously sad that it couldn't be countered by the mere concept of new stuff. But in St. Anton my desire wearied at last.

The thought of another blonde, healthy and friendly, ready to play "bounce the mattress" and "bump in the moguls," was as exciting as one more glass of flat beer. When I did find myself in the act I seemed to hear a weary Peggy Lee, husky and cynical, singing "Is That All There Is?"

So I called Marie Laure. She answered the phone. Not Gerard. That was good. I said so. I shouldn't have said so. It pissed her off. So I said I was calling to make sure she was putting my share of the Laundromat money aside. Marie Laure hung up on me. But I felt better. She was a brunette, with dark and magic eyes.

The next day there was a knock on the door.

I opened it. She was standing there. A duffel bag on her shoulder. I was glad to see her. "You couldn't stay away," I said. "Could you?"

She swung the duffel off her shoulder in an arc and at me. Ten kilos of ten-franc pieces bashed into my midsection. It was like a giant blackjack.

" 'Ere. 'Ere is your mon-ee," Marie said.

I just smiled and smiled. I took her hand and pulled her into the apartment.

Later on I asked her about Gerard.

" 'E is a jerk," she said.

"So am I," I said.

"Oui," she said, "but that is different."

"He's a lot younger than me. And better looking," I said.

She looked at me. She had always had the knack of speaking

paragraphs with a glance. This glance was a brief lecture on how funny men were about what they thought women thought was important and how sad it was to be a woman and have to bear such knowledge.

I pulled her closer, insofar as that was possible. Then I entered her. I wasn't bored at all. I wasn't sad. "*Je t'adore*," I said.

"I know that," she said, challenging, but her hips were moving. Heavy hips, not chic at all, round and muscle solid.

"*Je t'aime*," I said.

"Tell me in English," she said.

Aimer, "to love," is also "to like," and though *je t'aime* sounds terribly romantic to Americans, I think it sounds insufficiently definite in French. "I love you," I said.

"Oh, yes," she said, her eyes moist, and she held as tight as she could. Her mouth was wide and hungry, kissing me. I repeated the phrase and Peggy Lee sang not a word.

TWO

MY SON

My first child was born in a snowstorm, the first of the year, in November 1990. There were other things going on in the world. The Berlin Wall had just come down. Czechoslovakia was declaring itself to be free. But things like that don't seem so important when you're dealing with the essentials of life, like birth and an early snow.

It made everyone anticipate a good season. Which we needed after the last two winters. The Austrians said, "*Zu-per.*" The English called it "bril." Which is short for *brilliant*, an adjective applied with such indiscriminate verve that one begins to hope that it means "I promise not to speak when we next meet." The Aussies said, "Another pint of lager, mate."

The promise of November was to be broken. It snowed once again in December, when the baby was a month old, then it stopped. Giant storms came in from the Atlantic, battered England, scoured France with hurricane winds, drenched Belgium, headed for the mountains—where they were wanted and belonged—and then they split, north and south, leaving a big unwanted circle of warmth and sunshine across the Alps. Until the big storm of February. The one that brought the avalanches.

In a commercial sense St. Anton was one of the luckier alpine resorts. It was high enough that the snow we got in December was a base that lasted for the next two months. What little subsequent precipitation we had was snow, not rain. Hundreds of smaller, lower ski areas had nothing. Even such high giants as Val o'Isère actually closed. There was talk of putting the French ski instructors on welfare. Poor Gerard. But what snow we had was limited, and once you left the few pistes with snow-making equipment you had to cross patches of rock, grass, and cow shit to get from snowfield to snowfield. The instructors and the ski bums got out their rock skis, the repair shops went into overdrive. I was the only person I knew virtually unperturbed by how bad conditions were. I was so elated with the baby that what I skied on barely mattered. The laundry business was far better when people fell in the mud than when bright, clean white snow was everywhere.

The grandmothers-to-be wanted to come for the birth. Marie's father was not so eager. He referred to our happy fetus as *le bâtard*. I asked Marie if she would like to get married. That is not to say that I proposed.

"Would *you* be happier if we were married?" is what I said.

"To who," she said. "To Rick Cochrane?"

The point *appeared* to be: how married would we be under an assumed name? Which I might have to change again? But what she *really* meant was "I might marry you when and if *you* want to marry me, enough to get down on your knee and beg me and make me believe it is something *you* want. Don't do me any favors." At that point I did not inquire into what she really meant and was pleased to take what she said she meant as the excuse that it was.

"What shall we name our son?" she said. She was certain it would be a boy. She had that knowledge As a Woman. She knew it because it was Part of Her. Herr Doctor Ochsenboden agreed with her. He deduced it from the strength of the heartbeat. So did Fraulein Glütz, the midwife with the umlaut. She knew from the way he kicked.

If it had been a girl, the name would have been easy. Anna Geneviève. One name for each grandmother.

Naming a boy was more complicated. Marie's father was named Gerard. No way. My father's name was Michael. Which might have been all right, except we were excluding her father, who was pissed enough about *le bâtard* already. We got books. Baby name books are apparently among the great staples of the publishing industry, along with cookbooks and Bibles. Yet the number of names we couldn't agree on was enough to fill six of them in four languages. I had a yearning for simplicity—like Mike, Jake, Tony—and for Americana, revealing to myself that I somehow, someday expected to be able to go back. She wanted something romantic, different, perhaps Celtic or Gaelic.

I think, perhaps, if we had been married, we would have had the grandmothers come. God knows, they were ready enough to set up residence. Marie said she didn't want to be the focal point of a baby watch. We all have our own ways with anxiety.

It doesn't matter how cool you are. It doesn't matter how perfectly normal the doctor says the mother's condition is. None of that matters. I don't think there is such a thing as birth without fear. Not fear of the pain or the mess—that is something the woman goes through, God bless her—nor is it what she fears. The fear is of what is inside. Does it have two of everything it's supposed to have two of? And one each of all those things that people are designed with one of? Two arms, two legs, two eyes, two ears, two kidneys, two lungs, two buttocks; one anus, one mouth, one nose; ten fingers, ten toes. Is its brain enclosed, does its heart have holes, can it process food, cleanse its blood; can it yell, excrete, feel? Can it think?

All in all, then, I was relieved not to have my mother there. Because in addition to birth fear, I had another fear. Would they follow her? The way most flown felons are caught is by going home. I knew that from the days when I used to chase them. It didn't matter how heinous they were. The baby-rapers, the cop-shooters, serial killers—they all go home to see Mom. Or their woman. Or the hood. This was the inverse. I did not in fact know how closely watched she was. If there was a permanent wiretap and mail search on her home in Brooklyn. If there was an army of agents, or even one fanatic, obsessed with nailing me, waiting to follow my mom overseas. It would be too literary and ironic to be taken and extradited as my first child was being born. And I felt too distracted by the coming birth to arrange for my mother to break whatever surveillance she brought with her. How do you ask a woman in her mid-sixties to fly halfway round the world, then jump out of a train heading south from Paris into a waiting cab to the Gare du Nord, then onto a train to Charles de Gaulle; change her clothes, her hair, her passport in an airport bathroom; and catch a plane to Zurich, where she will begin a new set of evasive maneuvers. Not that she wouldn't do it to see her first grandchild.

I wrote her and asked her to wait until after the birth, when we were certain that the mother was up to it and the father could cope. My letters take about two weeks. They go through Rome. Not via the Italian postal service, where the letters are lost as frequently as delivered and the delivery date is selected by lottery. They go through the Vatican post—the Church is an independent country in Rome—then by Vatican diplomatic pouch to New York, where they are passed by hand, or messenger, to her friend Father Guido. It's a lot of favors and seems like an excess of precaution, yet it's been a long time and I have had no trouble. So we continue.

I was making Marie lunch. Marie was timing the minutes between contractions. She was calm, I was pretending to be cool. When the sun came out it hit fresh fallen snow like a trumpet's blare of jubilation. It was so happy that I opened a window to feel the warming air and the freshness of it all.

"I am glad you are not skiing today," Marie said.

"I'm not. Look at that powder."

"It's dangerous, the first snow of the season."

"Nothing would happen to me," I said. "You bring me luck. You and the baby."

"He is almost ready to come out," she said. "And you will not ski until 'e does. You would do something like breaking of the leg and then someone else would have to help me and I would be very angry with you."

I went around behind her and put my arms around her. I felt her breasts and that big full belly. Our child kicked. Marie held my hand to the kick.

"I am glad I'm here," I said. "Not skiing. I'd rather be here with you."

She leaned her head back against me. If it hadn't been true when I'd spoken it was true then.

The intervals between contractions were decreasing. While it is overwhelming for the new parents, it is simply a signal to the doctor and midwife. Over and over again, in fractured English and less fragmented French, they had explained to us that we were not to come over to the birthing center—which was one room attached to the Sports Injury Clinic—until the contractions were coming every five minutes.

I helped her on with her shoes and her jacket and her hat. I helped her down the stairs. Then I made her wait while I ran back up for the duffel bag of stuff and her mittens. Inside each ski town, obscured by all the tourists and the business, is a tiny town of intensely ordinary people. Once you begin to participate in that town, particularly if you stay through an off season, you know a remarkable number of them. Of course, they know you are not really one of them. Where was your family in the eighth century when St. Boniface was defining the boundaries of the bishopric and when the Duchy of Bavaria was incorporated in Charlemagne's Frankish kingdom? Where were they in 1552 when Maurice, elector of Saxony, invaded? Did they repulse the Swedes at Ehrenberger Klause in 1632 and the Bavarians in 1703? What do you and yours know of the Pragmatic Sanction, the infamous Treaty of Pressburg, the ceding of the South Tyrol and Trentino by the Treaty of St. Germain? What secrets do they harbor from the Anschluss and the days of national socialism?

We had been told to walk the eight blocks to the birthing center. Both the motion and the position would help the baby. There was a foot of snow on the ground. The best that could be said was that it was packed down hard. Pregnant, wide, and prone to overbalance, Marie clung to my arm. Every yard of the journey, someone seemed to appear to say "Good luck" in one language or another.

Franz of the Gendarmerie, the federal police, was running across the street with his large and ill-tempered German shepherd, Rudi.

Rudi is one of the few dogs in town. Austrians don't seem to like them very much. That may say as much about their national character as the French obsession with canines says about theirs. Or it may not, Franz stopped to pump my hand and give the mother-to-be a kiss on the cheek. He apologized for running off. But there had been an accident near the pass. Two cars over a cliff, he said, and Rudi was needed. Rudi's job was searching for bodies.

Halfway there, between contractions, tears of sentiment overwhelmed Marie. She held me close. "We can name him Michael," she said, "for your father."

"What the hell," I said, "we can even name him Michael Gerard after both of them. Then maybe your father will stop calling him *le bâtard*."

"You are sweet," she said, "but I don't think so."

Even into the delivery room we kept discussing the names. Jean-Claude because he was a ski baby. Sean because of my Irish passport. Phillipe for her grandfather, who she adored. Even Guido, for my mother's friend. Or possibly even name him after me, after my real name, though I don't like Juniors or people named the Second unless they are going to inherit something that comes with a throne or at least a coronet.

My love gave birth in a squatting position after just four hours of labor. She yelled, but not excessively. She sweated and strained and impressed the hell out of me. We were lucky; the baby was in the right position and seemed to be moving easily. I saw Marie's vagina stretch wide and there was the matted, wrinkled, wet, hairy head of my firstborn, centimeters away, up the vaginal canal. Stunningly real. Poised at the demarcation point. Waiting for the final push and the starter's gun.

"Push, push," said Fraulein Glütz, the midwife with the umlaut, in German.

"Yah," nodded Herr Doctor Ochsenboden. "Looks goot."

Fraulein Glütz inserted her fingers into Marie's vagina and smeared lubricating jelly all around the stretched labia and the emerging head. I kept saying, silently, to myself, "Holy shit, holy shit."

Marie pushed. What a pusher. Push, push, push. One, two,

three. Out came the head of my baby. Ugly. So ugly. It is another of the subtle biological differences between the genders that men clearly see how ugly a newborn is and women find them beautiful. But I was counting and the count was good. Two ears (check), one head (check), two eyes (at least two eye formations—they were closed, check), one nose with two nostrils (check and check), one mouth (check). Then Fraulein Glütz blocked my view as she reached in to help slide the shoulder out.

"Is goot, is goot," she said. Doctor Ochsenboden looked over her shoulder so that he could accept his fee in good conscience. "Is goot, is goot," he said, and nodded at me.

Then they were pulling the baby out, with the mess and the cord. Two arms (check), a bunch of fingers including two thumbs (check), a chest, a belly (check, check), two legs (check).

Then my eyes fell between its legs. "Oh-my-God!" I said to myself, as I saw my fears come true. My mind raced forward; the years of our future flashed before my eyes, like the endless hallway from a horror film—our flawed child, Marie's heartbreak, the extra care, medical and psychiatric, and the constant explanations. "Oh-my-God! My son has no penis!"

"Yah, ve vas mistaken makin,'" Doctor Ochsenboden said. "You hev girl baby."

"Is goot, is goot," Fraulein Glütz said.

"Oh," I said. "That's what it is."

T H R E E

LAUNDROMAT BLUES

I met Arlene Tavetian at my Laundromat.

I didn't know who she was, but I instantly knew so much about her. She was an American. East Coast. North of Washington, south of Boston, not inner urban. I knew she was—on the whole—a nice person, who tried hard to do the right thing. Not a person I would have known in most phases of my life and in those times when I might have met her, I would have passed right over her. Not unattractive. Well maintained, certainly past thirty-nine, but significantly under fifty. She looked married, not single or divorced. It gave me a warm feeling to see her, as if something more solid than nostalgia had walked into the room, an artifact of normalcy, the kind of person I used to imagine existed when I tried to picture who it was that watched a measured portion of prime-time TV back in the U.S.A.

She had a load of laundry that wasn't hers—unless I had radically misjudged her. There was an entire collection of G-string underwear. Two sets, really. One in the dainty hues—rose, fawn, mist, jade, sandalwood—silk and satin, from Palmer's most likely, and the other in hot neons, phosphorescent red, green, orange—colors for playing strip disco or neo-LA. The jeans had artistic rips and patches. The T-shirts were the type that teenagers wear to carelessly demonstrate to an envious world that there is a time in life when breasts are gravity defiant.

She came in full of organization and competence. But it all

collapsed when she tried to figure out how much change she needed to operate the machines. I figured she was in sad shape. A woman like that could walk into any Laundromat in the world, from Darien, Connecticut, to Casablanca, and come out with clean clothes. I offered to help.

She apologized for being so befuddled. She was glad, very glad, that I spoke English. She insisted that she knew how to do wash—I believed her—but she was confused by the currency. "The machine seems to require seventy schillings."

"Yes," I said.

"But that's over five dollars," she said. "I'm not wrong, am I?"

"Quite right," I said. "About five dollars, five cents."

"That's not right," she said.

"Twenty percent of it is tax," I said. "Like VAT, or sales tax."

She started to cry. Her mascara cracked and her makeup ran. She tried to choke it back but she couldn't. "My daughter's dead," she said to apologize for her display. "My daughter's dead."

"The American girl. In the avalanche?"

"Wendy," she said. She looked at me. With her daughter's name spoken she stopped fighting it and the tears fell with simple clarity. She stood there, for several minutes. Not sobbing. Just crying. I had a daughter. A perfect baby girl. Her name was Anna Geneviève. She was home with her mother, nursing, or napping, probably. She had come out as ugly as ET. I mentioned that once and never again. Marie Laure thought that the baby was born into beauty. To question that was to raise doubts about my baby love. Marie Laure had fallen in love with her daughter. Right there in the delivery room. A love that practically swept me out, but left me no room for jealousy, and gave me a new role to play.

"Would you like to sit down?" I asked Wendy's mother.

"I thought," she said, "that I should give her things away. To Goodwill or whatever they have here. That's what I would do at home. But I couldn't give away her clothes unless they were clean," she said. Of course she couldn't. And in Austria they probably wouldn't accept them. Everything is perfect in Austria.

"Why don't you sit down," I said. I led her to a chair. I took the clothes and tossed them in washer number six, which always seems to do a slightly better job. I didn't separate the whites from the colored and used nonchlorine bleach. I held back some of the Palmer's stuff. "This should be hand washed," I explained. "I think you could use a drink or a cup of coffee or something."

"No. No, thank you very much," she said. But she had to explain again, to me or to herself, "My daughter is dead."

"I know just the thing," I said. "A cup of hot chocolate."

"I don't want to be any bother," she said.

"Of course not," I said. I went across the street to Johann's Café. The temperature was dipping, the air had a snap to it, and the wind was picking up. Johann put a dash of schnapps in the chocolate and the obligatory cream on top, ÖS34. She thanked me and told me her name. I said it was no bother, that I was sorry for her pain, and that I was Rick Cochrane.

"It's good to speak to an American," she said.

"I'm not really American. I just spent a lot of time there."

"You sound American," she said.

"How's the chocolate?"

"It's very good. Hits the spot." She tried a smile.

"I could take care of putting the clothes in the dryer and then bring them over to wherever you're staying. Or drop them off at the church. They do that sort of thing, so you don't have to see the stuff."

"You're very kind. But. . . . She was just nineteen. She was a beautiful girl. She didn't do drugs. I swear it. She was a good girl. Smart. She was a wonderful skier. I don't understand how this could happen. . . ." Arlene was ready to cry again, but she stifled it. "I did her laundry, washed her clothes, folded them, ironed them from when she was . . ." Then she started to cry again, holding her hands not more than eighteen inches apart, the length of a baby from head to toe. ". . . and we went shopping together and I taught her to sew. She was a good student. She was going to Amherst, in a year."

I saw Arlene Tavetian again, the next night, at the Rasthaus Ferwell. She looked terrible. She was with a man who I assumed was her husband. After I had discreetly pointed them out to Marie, I tried my best to ignore them.

It was an evening for kitsch, an Austrian invention. By virtue of its location and lack of pretension, Ferwell is one of the few spots in St. Anton with genuine charm. It's off in the woods, three kilometers from the road. It can be reached by car or taxi, but it's better to cross-country ski or hike in, or, as we did, take a horse-drawn sleigh, riding all muffled under blankets. The Rasthaus itself is small. One of the two rooms has two tables, the other has four. The walls are hung with antlers and other rustic artifacts. The menu specializes in game: venison, mountain goat, rabbit. The restaurant is heated by an Austrian stove, another local invention, widely celebrated in the Middle Ages, at which time it was a tremendous breakthrough. The medieval fireplace was a disastrous affair, sending more heat up the chimney than into the room (which fireplaces still do) and more smoke into the room than to the outdoors (less likely with modern flue design). The Austrian stove is a closed ceramic box that sends all the smoke up the chimney, keeps most of the heat in the house, even, like the stones in a sauna, radiating warmth after the fire is out. The stove can be set into the room and is usually covered in cheery, decorative tile that is easy to clean. As far as I know, aside from ski resorts and Mozart, it is Austria's greatest contribution to civilization.

We unswaddled our baby and adored the miracle of her while Arlene Tavetian stared at us. Such a hardy child. Not even three months old and she didn't mind the cold ride at all. She had sturdy legs. Slightly bowed and made of roll after roll of baby fat, but she already loved to hold my fingers, stand up and wobble. That was terrifically funny.

"My downhill racer," I said.

"*Jamais,*" Marie said. "Ne-ver."

"Why not?"

"Because the women racers, they have legs bigger than their hips. Which is not nice in a girl. Because they ski into trees with their faces and then they are not so pretty. And because they chew tobacco."

Arlene Tavetian kept staring at us.

It was a good meal, though heavy, as most Austrian meals are. In the middle of it, Anna got hungry—something she did at least every three hours, around the clock—and Marie gracefully opened her blouse and put the baby to her nipple. It left her one handed and I cut her food for her. We decided to skip dessert and even coffee. When I asked for the check, Arlene's companion got up and came over to our table. He apologized for intruding. He was, as I thought, the husband, Robert Tavetian.

"I want to thank you," he said, "for being so kind to my wife the other day."

"It was the least I could do," I said.

"She's extremely grateful," he said.

He looked at Anna, who looked engorged with contentment. To judge by the results, breast milk contains something very like heroin. When Anna was hungry for it her craving was something painful to see. When she was presented with the nipple she jumped on it like a dog on a bone. Once she began to suckle, all pain would leave her. When she was done, her eyelids would fall to half mast, her head would hang heavy and wobble, for all the world like a junkie on the nod.

"That's your little girl," Robert said. "They're so incredible at that age. And yet—yet it gets better. My wife, she's upset." So was he. He'd been cored, like an apple, and didn't know he was wrapped around his own emptiness. "I—I asked the restaurant to let me pay for your dinner."

"That's not necessary," I said.

"That's very kind," Marie said. Americans assume that there is a great prairie out there that keeps spewing up food. No matter how many meals you give away, no matter how many cattle you slaughter, there's still more acomin'. The French assume a finite number of meals in the universe, every one of which can be rated, any one of which you might get overcharged for.

Robert looked over at Arlene. He had been sent on an errand that he knew was more than he should be asking from a stranger. His wife looked back at him. He looked helplessly at her. She rose and came across the room to look at him until he was forced to ask whatever it was she wanted him to ask.

"Maybe you can help us," Robert said. "It's so hard here. They really don't speak a lot of English, not most of them, and I hardly ever know whether they really get it when I talk."

"Get to the point, Robert," Arlene said. She was pale beyond the disguise of makeup, and tired, and as full of grief as I've ever seen anyone.

"My wife," he said, "is . . . sort of obsessed."

"It's not an obsession to want to know. I just want to know . . ."

"There's nothing to know," Robert said. "What you want is to—is to have just some more of her. And there is no more to have. She's dead, Arlene, dead."

"Please," Arlene said, "Rick—it is Rick, isn't it? I just want to know."

"What is it you want to know?" Marie asked, cradling Anna in her arms, speaking as one mother to another.

"That's your little girl?" Arlene asked Marie. Marie nodded. Arlene sat down, leaned forward and gazed at our little girl. Arlene was having a breakdown or was very close to it. Anna looked plump, juicy. The kind of baby that makes people want to bite baby's bottoms. "Ask your husband to help us," Arlene said.

"I don't know what you want . . . but . . ."

"Look," Robert said, "my wife wants to know how my daughter spent her last days. That's all. How she lived. Was she happy? We heard that she had—that she was going with an older man. And that he was . . . Asian."

"Tanaka," I said. An avalanche death is big-time news in a small town. What there was to know, everyone knew, some of it accurate. "Hiroshi Tanaka. The man who was skiing with her when . . ."

"You see, you do know things," Robert said. Arlene stared at Anna. "What it is, is you're an American . . ."

"I spent time there," I said. My passport says I'm Irish. And a priest.

"Whatever. You talk like an American and I know I can relate to you. But also you know these people here. You're part of the community. You can get around. Please, for the sake of my wife's sanity, could you just—I don't know—find out how my daughter spent her last little time on earth?"

"I think you should do this," Marie said to me. "If it was my Anna and it was in a place strange to you, you would want the same thing."

"Marie," I said, "between helping you with Anna and the Laundromats and maybe, if I'm lucky, getting in a little skiing someday . . ."

"Poof. Poof on you and your skiing. And the Laundromat. You are more than that. When I met you, this is not what you were. So there," she said to me and turned to the pained father. "Monsieur Tavetian, you have come to the right person. He will help you." She turned back to me. "A mother," she said, "is entitled to her grief as well as her love."

I went along with Marie's request to examine the final days of Wendy Tavetian, daughter of Robert and Arlene, accountant and housewife, because the downside risk was virtually zero. All I had to do was listen to gossip. Easy enough to do in a small town. If it had been a wrongful death involving serious criminal, financial, or political matters, it would have been a serious error for me to get involved. Anything that brought me too much official attention could be a mistake.

FOUR

DIRTY LAUNDRY

When tourist girls want to score a ski instructor, Luis is usually their first choice.

The big boom in skiing took place in the sixties. Where once the position of ski instructor was a high-turnover job for kids, like lifeguard or tennis pro, it slowly became a reasonable career even for a mature man with a family. So the instructors began to stay on the job. Once upon a time many of them looked like they had stepped out of a ski poster, blond and firm and tan with a twinkle in the crinkle of their blue-on-blue eyes. But that was twenty or thirty years ago and most of the full-time instructors are now distinctly middle-aged, with middle-aged faces, middle-aged bodies, mortgages, and middle-aged wives.

Luis, who is actually a Spaniard with seven names, is exactly what the girls think they are buying when they book their one or two weeks in the Tyrolian Alps. An actual ex-Olympics alternate, blonder and more Teutonic, in a pleasant beach-boy, circa 1969 surfer way, than any of the Austrians. But that has been Luis's situation for many, many years and it's hard to get his motor running. He'd much rather discuss financial plans. He reads the exchange rates every day and loses money trading in Eurocurrency futures. He's convinced this not-quite-yet-existing version of money will replace the dollar as the leading international denomination of exchange.

I like Luis because he taught me the invisible key to slalom racing. Not that it made me a racer, but it was a true teaching. It is to always look two turns ahead. The feet deal with the gate you are in and where they are is already history. The hands are leading the shoulders into the coming gate. The eyes are up ahead, at the turn after that, commanding the body to prepare. It is easiest to understand this in the gates, although it applies to any skiing and becomes extremely obvious with all difficult skiing, in the bumps, on the steeps, in the woods. The future arrives very rapidly on skis. If where you are is where you're at, you're already stuck in the past, facing the wrong way when the moment that has just become the present knocks you on your ass.

"Yes, I think I met her," he said.

"She'd been here almost two months," I said. Which is a long time by ski area standards. Certainly long enough to have stumbled on Luis.

"Do they ever have bad years in the Rocky Mountains?" he asked me. Again. Luis has decided that being beautiful and a great skier is not enough. He should be in business. He says he wants to package tours from Los Angeles. "That would be a good time for me to start."

"It always snows in the Rockies," I said. "Plus the dollar's down because General Motors fell asleep for twenty years and let the Germans skim their cream while the Japs gutted them from underneath. That's not to say there's not a ton of money still in the States. But they won't come for the snow. What about the ski guide, Hans Lantz? Did he make a mistake taking them the other side of the Valuga?"

"I don't know, Rick. It's always possible to make a mistake about the conditions. Would I have skied there? With clients? I don't know."

"So what do you remember about this girl? This Wendy?"

"She was American," he said positively.

"I want to know who she hung out with. What was she like? All that stuff. For the parents."

"Tell them nice things, Rick. Oh, she was a very good skier. Attentive in ski school. Quick to learn. Dressed nicely. Did not fuck around too much. Yes?"

"Do you remember her?" I asked him. "Did you pass her on?"

"Oh, really, Rick," Luis said. But that is exactly what he does. At the start of each week he has three or four girls hanging on to him from ski school. That's the day group. Then there is a second group that seems to appear in the evenings from the disco crowd. Luis, who is very polite and keeps tabs on who is the loneliest and the horniest of the other instructors, manages to introduce each of the girls to someone else. "You know about her and Tanaka? Tell me, Rick, what do you think of package tours for the Japanese? Is that a permanent trend?"

"Was she going out with anyone else? Who'd she hang out with?"

"I am remembering that I think she went out—maybe once, I think—with Kurt."

"Which Kurt?" I asked him. There were at least three in the ski school. "Tall blond? Short blond? Or short and losing his hair?"

"Tall Kurt," Luis said.

"Ah, married Kurt," I said.

"Well, yes," Luis said. "But he was having a terrible time with his wife. He was very unhappy."

"Did she stay with him? Or recirculate?"

"You know, I have been thinking about the avalanche. It is sad, of course, that this girl is dead and this Japanese and I am sorry for them. But I think it is good that we have the avalanche. It is important to remember that what we do on the mountain—it has risk, it has death. It is good to be reminded that the mountain can strike. Otherwise we might as well all go to Disneyland."

"She was a little too American," tall, blond, married Kurt said. "This is for you and me only, Rick. I am with my wife again. She is very stormy."

"What do you mean a little too American?"

"We would never leave each other," Kurt said, in reference to his wife. They were both locals and therefore very Catholic. "But she went to visit her mother, in Pettneu." He made it sound very distant. It is the next town down the valley, about three kilometers away. "So, you understand. Anyway, she is back but it is still a little stormy."

"Yeah," I said. "I won't tell anyone about Wendy."

"Well, I took her out. Over to Kris's apartment. We drank some wine. Then she jump into bed. Nice body. Not too big"—Kurt cupped his hands in front of his chest—"but pretty good. An athlete, I think. But she did it like an athlete. I think that she is keeping score in her mind. Like she is rating me on form and distance like a ski jumper," he laughed, but it was not a happy sound. Jumping is for Norwegians and Finns.

"You went out again?"

"No," Kurt said. "She left right after. But I saw her with the Japanese. He had a lot of money. I think he was buying her things." He said this to let me know that women didn't leave him over any lack of size or competence, but only for money.

"Did she have any special friends?"

"I didn't know her, Rick. Just that once. We did it, like she was taking a sample, then she was done."

A ski bum is not a bum in the sense of being unemployed. He or she is *underemployed*, forsaking career and taking less than minimum wage to clean, to serve, to labor, so long as the job allows ski time and includes a discount season ticket. The going rate is about ÖS1,000—$90—a week, plus room and board, which is not as bad as it sounds since rooms are more precious than gold and food rather uniformly overpriced.

Wendy, Bob Tavetian told me, had come to Europe prepared to work. That was unusual. I could count the number of American ski bums in St. Anton on my fingers. It is not that foreigners are barred from doing dirty work for even less than Turks will work for—Australians and Kiwis are ubiquitous. A bewildered English-only speaker can hardly say, "*Sprechen ze* English?" without a ski shop technician, chambermaid, waiter, or bartender offering a cheery "Goo' day, mate," like Crocodile Dundee peddling Australian holidays in a television commercial. My ski bum at the Laundromat, Anita, is a strapping young lady from Melbourne, solid as a brick and sweet as the day is long. It may be that Americans simply don't have a global vision—they think that it's all in the U.S.A. and they stay there. It may be that skiing in the States is an upper-middle-class sport and in America upper-middle-class kids just don't do jobs that involve labor and dirt.

The closest thing to a requirement for a job is bilingualism, and that too is rare in America.

Wendy had not prearranged employment from home and she had not arrived with a working visa. It's not unusual, but, as Anita discovered, it is difficult. Anita arrived at about the same time as Wendy. It took Anita three weeks to find a job cleaning a *pension* in St. Jakob, sort of a suburb of St. Anton, if a town averaging two blocks wide and half a mile long can be thought to have a suburb. She called and the Frau said she could start right away. The job included a room, so she jumped at it without discussing wages. After a day of scrubbing toilets and changing sheets, Anita asked the Frau how much she was getting paid.

"We must see first," said the Frau, "how good you can clean."

"Never," I told Anita when she told me her story, "deal with an Austrian unless you settle the price up front and what's included."

"Easy for you to say," Anita said. "I was desperate. *Am* desperate."

"I will not tell you the full extent of my humiliation," I said, "but I will tell you how I learned this. When I first came to St. Anton I went to a *pension*. It included 'English breakfast.' I've been in England. A real English breakfast is a weighty affair. Even in France an English breakfast is a serious meal."

"Oh, God, yes," Anita said. "Bangers and grilled tomatoes and eggs."

"Right, and toast, and cereal, and tea."

"And jam, and butter, and cream."

"So, this was Haus Kurt Ebner," I said. "And each morning Frau Ebner very kindly said, 'Would you like an egg, Mr. Cochrane?' 'Oh, yes,' I said, 'I would like an egg.' And Frau Ebner would serve me an egg. A good Austrian egg, soft boiled to perfection. She had a special machine for it that just boils eggs, with that sleek, form-follows-function, we-also-build-Porsches, Germanic design. I stayed there for three weeks. When I got my bill at the end, there was an extra ten schillings a day for each and every egg."

Anita laughed. I said she could have the job.

"How much does it pay?"

"Fifteen hundred and a room."

"Great," Anita said. "I'll take it."

"You didn't get the point."

"What?"

"The egg is not included."

"Oh," she said, and thought about it. "Oh, bloody hell. I'll bloody well starve. A pizza and a beer is a hundred and fifty."

"But you can make extra. Lots of people don't want to sit and wait. For that matter they don't want to separate and fold. Plus they want stuff ironed and all that. All of that we charge extra. All the schillings that go into the machines, that's mine. All the rest, where you do the work, we split. Plus, when the punters want to do their laundry, at the hotels and *pensions* and they ask the chambermaid, if the girl doesn't have access to her own washer, she's going to come here. She charges the tourist double, triple, whatever's going. There's lots of room because what a Frau charges 250 schillings, 350 schillings for, it costs 120 schillings in the machines. So the ski bums can make a couple extra schillings. They don't always want to do the work either, so they ask you and then you split with them."

"Yeah," she said, "I could go for that."

"It's very entrepreneurial," I said.

"It's very American," she said.

"That's what it says over the door—" I said, "Rick's American Laundromat. But in New York, last time I saw New York, all the Laundromats were run by Koreans."

"The first place to look for a job, particularly if you don't speak good Deutsch," Anita said, "is Down Under."

Down Under is a restaurant and disco run by an Aussie named Paul. He's a smart businessman and steals good ideas wherever he can. All the tour operators have resort reps. They help the tourists get into ski school, rent equipment, fight with their hotels, find a laundry. In imitation of Dick's T-Bar in Val d'Isère, Paul got the reps for the British tour companies to make Down Under their local—"Every day at 4:00 P.M. your rep will be Down Under. Stop by with any problems or just to have a friendly drink." In imitation of The Underground, a St. Anton bistro, the staff is English-speaking. The Brits, Australians, and Americans love it. You can see them breathe a sigh of relief every time they walk in the door. Rather than resent it, the Germans and Viennese think it's clever and quite exotic.

"You wouldn't wait till closing time to chat her up," Paul said.

"Yeah, she came here looking for a job."

"You didn't give her one?"

"Down Under is the first stop for a pretty girl looking for a job, now isn't it? Clean kip, good grub, you can speak the king's English and still get better tips than at the Krazy Kangaruh. We fill up fast."

"So where'd she go from here?"

"Dunno, mate. But I'll tell you what. She came back, a week or so before she died, asking again. During the storm. Did a lot of business. What with people drinking instead of skiing and then coming in after the avalanche, because if the mountain is falling down on people they want to be in here chatting about it and having a drink rather than out there where it's falling. How's the Laundromat business?"

"Great during the storm. Everybody doing their laundry. Not much to do here if you're not skiing. She come here much?"

"Fair amount. Her boyfriend, the Nip, he was a good spender."

"I hope he didn't run a tab."

"Not a chance," Paul said. "American Express. Platinum Card all the way."

"Typical Jap?"

"No. No, he wasn't. Quite Western. He was hardly here with a group all packing Nikons and clicking away, now was he? You're not just dropping in and passing the time of day, are you, mate?"

"I had the misfortune to meet her mother. The dead girl's mother asked me to see what I could find out about the final days. She asked me in front of Marie and the baby. Marie pulled some motherhood solidarity shit on me and I can hardly say no to her, can I? She's the one breast-feeding."

"How is the babe, then, anyway?"

"Fine. She feeds every three hours. Marie hasn't slept since she was born."

"Gets a bit rocky, that. I know how that is. Went through it a couple of times in Sydney. Best thing for you is out of the house. Drink?"

"No thanks," I said.

"See, that's one of the things that makes it hard for people to believe you're really Irish. You don't have the drink in your hand enough, now do you?"

"That's what keeps people from thinking I'm Australian. So what did you say to her when she came back the second time?"

"I said I'd put her on the waiting list, is what I said."

"Did she have any friends that you know about?"

"Well, mate, there's Carol—bosom buddies I think those two were. Carol's American too. I've got her washing dishes. She'll be in tonight. You come in, go to the back and chat with her. You ever done this kind of work before?"

"Me? No. I just got boxed in."

"I don't like Japs particularly. Greater Southeast Asia Co-Prosperity Sphere I think it was that they were going to have if they'd won the war. Would've made a Jap port out of Sydney, now wouldn't they? Maybe they still will."

"What about this one? Tanaka?"

"A little on the arrogant side. But so are a lot of Germans and the French, of course—not exactly egalitarian, like your people and mine. But aside from that, dressed well, spent a lot of money, drank old Scotch, didn't make no trouble."

"Sounds boring," I said.

"There's a Jap around. Another one," Paul said. "He's also asking about Tanaka."

Skis pulled out of a Finnish bog have been carbon dated as being four to five thousand years old. There is a picture of a skier on a rock in Rodney, Norway, from 2,000 B.C. Peasants from Scandinavia to the Sudtirol had been putting boards on their feet to get from here to there, even to slide down hills for the fun of it, for a long time. But that didn't count because they were poor people in the backwaters of Europe and skiing did not become a "sport" until the British—those snow-starved, Alpless islanders—made it a sport at the turn of the century. It was the Edwardian Age, the days of Pax Britannica, the pound sterling ruled, and whatever a British gentleman did set a standard for those lesser people who had to get by with marks, francs, kroner, florins or forint, dollars and dolares, dinars, drachmas, lire, lei, or lev. The English came to the Alps for recreation—they hiked, they climbed, they sledded, they skied—and for the first time people realized how to make something lucrative from these scenic but otherwise totally impoverished peaks. The automobile was rare, any major snowfall blocked what roads there were, neither the airplane nor the bus tour had yet been invented, so they came by train. There were lots of alpine hamlets with slopes and snow. But St. Anton was on a main rail line and thus became one of the first great ski resorts.

It's the same track that carries the Orient Express—Paris, Zurich, St. Anton, Innsbruck, Vienna, Istanbul.

"We met," Carol said, "on the train."

She sniffled, stifled a sob, and dropped a glass. The door banged open. A waitress—one of five that hustled in and out, dumping dirty glasses and grabbing refills—spun through the swinging doors into the kitchen. Every time one of them opened the door we got a blast from the Bulgarian rock band doing a very creditable cover of Donna Summer's "Love to Love You Baby."

"Oh, shit," Carol said, about both grief and broken glass.

"We became friends, like, instantly," she said. "This is my first time in Europe. And there I was. Like, I hardly made it from the airport to the train with my skis and my suitcases and all this stuff. It was my first train ride too, you know. Two cute American girls. Well, one really cute and the other not so cute." She pushed a stray clump of hair off her damp forehead with a wet hand. She was right. Wendy had been the attractive one. "She was my best friend. Here. Maybe ever. We would have been friends like forever, if you can believe that. What a bummer. For her parents, too."

Somebody stuck his head in from the bar. "Glasses, darling, we need glasses!" he yelled. The Bulgarian rock band had reached the important part of "Love to Love You," the stylized sighs and moans of disco orgasm. Kitchens, like laundries, are hot. Carol's skin was damp with sweat, the tank top clung to her awkwardly, her jeans stuck to her skin. She was thick and probably strong, but she just looked meaty. I thought of the German word for meat, *Fleisch*.

"Why shouldn't I believe that you and Wendy would be best friends?"

"Look at me and look at her," Carol said, as if it were obvious.

I have been in the waiting rooms of dentists in America. I have seen the covers of *Cosmopolitan* and *Mademoiselle* and I know there are specific codes about whether a pretty girl should hang out with an equally pretty girl, or a less pretty girl, or a truly plain girl, or even a girl who is overweight, has a slight mustache, fails to use deodorant, and has no fashion sense. It is a burning issue because it will determine the kind of men they will attract, in what combinations, and dictate the options of what can be done with such men once they have approached.

"I saw a picture of her," I said, "in the newspaper."

"I saw that," she said. "But you couldn't know Wendy from that. I mean you had to see her . . . her total presence. Like her clothes. She had the kind of body that they actually make clothes for. Not"—she gestured at herself—"this."

"Glasses, darling, clean glasses," a voice yelled through the door. The Bulgarian rock band had two girl singers, "Ohhhhh, ohh"—harmonizing their orgasm.

Carol opened the dishwasher. Steam and the odor of dish-washing detergent rushed up at her. Her tank top got even wetter. As it molded itself to her, I realized that she was one of those women that had one breast noticeably larger than the other. She cursed and began furiously pulling glasses out of the machine and stacking them on trays to be taken away.

"You mean you shouldn't be friends because clothes fit her?"

"You don't get it," she said.

"No."

"Didn't you ever notice that some people are right and some are wrong."

"Right and wrong?"

"And there's not a whole lot you can do about it, you know. Even though everybody tries. There are some people just naturally look good in the right clothes, and whatever they pick, that's the right clothes. You put me in ski pants and I'm a cow. You put Wendy in ski pants and guys are skiing into trees. Not because she wants them to. Just because that's the way things are. She was a natural blond. She was a cheerleader. She got good grades without being a grind or a nerd. She was good at skiing and tennis and swimming. But she wasn't a snot or a snob. And she was my best friend."

"I like your T-shirt," I said. It was one of those standard wiseass ski resort T-shirts—JUST BECAUSE I SLEPT WITH YOU LAST NIGHT DOESN'T MEAN I HAVE TO SKI WITH YOU IN THE MORNING—but I wanted to lighten things up. "Where did you get it?"

"The last guy I slept with gave it to me," she said. "He thought it was funny."

Three waitresses came in, one after another, leaving trays of dirty glasses, picking up the clean ones. There was a bus load of Swedes in the other room and the beer was flowing very fast. The disco simulation of Donna Summer sex takes about six minutes. It's quite impressive. But the Bulgarians had finally worked all the way through it.

"Some things must work out for you better than her. I mean you got a job here. Paul said she tried to get one. She didn't, you did."

"Oh, wow, lucky me," Carol said. "Wendy, if she'd taken a job here, which she was not going to do—no way, José—she would've gotten a bar job or waitress and been out there with people, and with tips, not back here with suds and slops."

"Why didn't she want to work here?"

"Hey, look, to some people working Down Under is a primo supremo job. Even back in the steam room," she said, sorting glasses. Some went straight into the dishwasher. The ones with cigarette butts and other sodden debris had to be dumped and rinsed first. "I'll never find, you know, true love back here, but I can ski every afternoon, which is what life is really about. 'What's love got to do with it?' I get free food. It's mostly bar snacks, but I'm from the world of Burger King and Dairy Queen. So it's just the thing with Paulie, and back in the real world I've put out for worse than Paulie."

I almost missed the beat. "Uh," I said, "so Wendy wouldn't put out for Paul?"

"And, like, I do?" She'd sensed an attitude and gave me attitude back.

"Hey, I didn't mean to offend you."

"Wendy would've handled Paulie if she wanted to handle Paulie. You don't understand. Wendy had it together." The Bulgarian band had moved on to "Staying Alive"—BeeGees, 1977. Pop Europa is a time warp of white teen Americana. "Well," Carol said, "I have my own way of dealing with Paulie."

"How's that?"

"I lay there like I was like dead, you know. I'm not a video game. You turn me on and I start to go *ping, ping, ping* all over the place."

"But Wendy just said no?"

"I wish you understood, I wish you could meet her. You know, I diet and get fat. Wendy could live on candy and beer and look perfect. Wendy knew she had it. So she didn't have to put out. Unless it was what she wanted to do. If Wendy wanted to go with Paulie, she would've—and probably blown his mind. If she wanted to."

"Like with Kurt, the ski instructor?"

"You mean tall, blond, married Kurt?"

"That one."

"That's exactly what I mean. Wendy thought it would be fun to make it with one of the ski instructors. But he was, like, not worth it."

"What do you mean, 'not worth it?' "

She sighed like I was an idiot, then layed it on the line for me. "A lousy lay. She didn't even stay the night. He didn't cut it, she cut out. I wish I was more like that. Now with Hiroshi everything was different. It was, like, you know, something to do. He was, like, Japanese, and older, and had lots of money and was into stuff."

"What kind of stuff?"

"Like, interesting stuff," she said defensively, as if I'd suggested something perverse. "Like, money and getting exactly the right clothes, and he was even into art and the differences between being Japanese and American and Austrian and stuff. He was fun, too. He knew he had more money than us and he was generous about it without doing, like, mind games. Well, that's, like, not entirely the whole truth and nothing but the truth, but he wasn't a pig about it. A lot of older guys who have a lot of money are pigs about it. So it was, like, really good for her to have Hiroshi taking care of her—especially compared to working here."

"Like, what do you mean?" I asked her.

"About being pigs about it?"

"No, I mean what kind of games did he play without being a pig?"

"You really wanna know this?"

"Yes," I said.

"Right. And this is for her parents?"

"Yeah."

"Sure, and you're gonna tell them the truth, the whole truth, and nothing but the truth."

"Does anybody?"

"Wendy did."

"To her parents?"

"Nobody tells the truth to their parents. Even if they have okay parents. Which Wendy had—she said so. She liked them. Particularly her dad. Her mom was a little obsessive-possessive. But they were no way Parents from Hell."

"What are Parents from Hell?"

"You know, daddies who come to your bed at night, mommies who drink all day—there are lots of different kinds, you know—Parents from Hell."

"Did you have parents like that?"

"I'm older than Wendy, you know. I'm a nurse. When I go back to the States I can get a good job anywhere emptying bedpans and passing out pills. It doesn't pay much, but a lot of nurses—they feel good about themselves. So I'm out of the house and that's all settled. You know? So you want to know about Wendy?"

"Yeah, you were telling me about Wendy and Hiroshi."

"What do you want? You want some dirt? Some exciting stuff?"

"I want whatever was happening."

"Okay, well, I'll tell you. Like, Hiroshi wanted to get it on in a threesome. That's like what every guy in the whole world wants. I don't get it. Do you get it? It's not like every girl wants to watch her boyfriend get it on with another guy. So Hiroshi knows that Wendy and I are like really, really tight. I mean we're tighter with each other than with anyone else around this place. So he keeps trying to set it up. Wendy—she's never done that before. Wendy—she's into doing stuff that she's never done before. Which I think is kind of wonderful. So one night we got pretty stoned, drinking, and let Hiroshi take us both home with him.

"Can I watch," she said, "while you tell Wendy's mom about this? Oh, shit, that was a mean thing to say. They're probably in real pain. I should just tell them that Wendy was the greatest."

"Yeah, you probably should."

"You think so?"

"They're at the Schwarzer Adler. You can tell them that. But, in the meantime, why don't you tell me about Wendy and you and Hiroshi."

"It was really just Hiroshi's thing," she said. "We were willing, but it didn't work. I mean we got all undressed and naked and stuff. I was more into it, I think, than Wendy. I mean my body—some people like it, but it's like almost gross it's so big." The Bulgarian rock band was doing Billy Joel's "Vienna." "Wendy's body was, like, just right with those cupcake tits that never give you trouble when you're shopping for clothes, and she had that good skin, that was smooth and no hairs in the wrong places. Anyway, so Hiroshi's, like, oooing, and *oh*ing and candlelight and stuff. I'm touching Wendy, you know, and she's touching me. But, like, you know, she doesn't get it. Even though she's drunk, she doesn't get it and she's touching me like I'm a chair or something. So what ends up happening is I go down on Hiroshi and Hiroshi goes down on Wendy. Which is probably the right way to organize this. Because when he went down on her, he was really, really good. Much better than I could ever be."

At an earlier time in my life I would have envied the dead Hiroshi Tanaka. Salacious thoughts would have dominated my reactions. But I seem to have given up possession of my head and my heart and my genitalia as well to the mother of my daughter. Nothing stirred between my legs. I wondered how long that would last.

"Paul said," I said, "that she'd asked him for a job, just before she died. How come? If Hiroshi was taking care of her?"

"Wendy wasn't *into* Hiroshi taking care of her. It was just something that happened to her, like having parents or being born in the U.S.A. He had the apartment and he liked paying for things."

"It sounds like he was rich," I said.

"I don't know," Carol said. "Aren't they all rich now, the Japanese?"

"Maybe."

"Wendy said she was, like, hip to his game. She never asked for any of it. Once he got her to ask, then he had her, so she wasn't going to ask, but it was getting real tempting. She wanted a Burton board and she wanted a new pair of skis. Wendy was always real careful with her stuff, but this year's been shit for snow—rocks everywhere—and the bottoms of her skis were shredded, I'm talking serious P-tex time, repairs every night. Hiroshi would've bought her new skis like a shot and she knew it. That's maybe why she was talking to Paulie about work. If she started asking for skis maybe she was, like, getting into something she didn't want to get into, it was getting into a place where it would be out of hand."

"So she was going to leave him?"

"You probably got the wrong picture—like, totally wrong. Wendy was really sweet and together. She just wanted to get out there a little bit before she got, like, you know, married and pregnant and yelling at her children that they better study or they'll end up at Burger King. And if she was a guy, you would really understand and say, 'Hey, wow,' 'That's cool,' 'A ski bum screwing all those snow bunnies,' 'Wish it were me.' So I hope you understand, because I don't want to be saying bad of the dead."

"Yeah, I think I understand," I said.

"She was just taking a break from the real world. Before she went back to college to become a cog in the American dream. She always knew just how far to go, to take things. That's why it's so weird that she bought it, you know."

Carol even had a copy of Wendy's key to Hiroshi's apartment. Because, she said, sometimes when Hiroshi was away she stayed there to get away from the slave quarters, the rather unkempt and undersized premises that Paul provided. She gave it to me.

It was beyond the call of duty, but being handed the key made it just too easy to pass up.

It was a frosty night; the wind was blowing, tossing crystal sparks of snow around—just a touch of mean. I like the winter. I like the mountains and the clean air. It's a good life, being a petit bourgeois in a petit bourgeois country with time to ski and a newborn who'd turned into an infant who was turning into a baby. She could suckle, she could grasp, she was learning to sit up, and she certainly knew how to fill a diaper. She started with black muck, the consistency of beach tar. Then it became the color and consistency of Grey Poupon. Back in America Grey Poupon is advertised as the mustard carried by people who ride in Rolls-Royces. It was almost odorless, Anna Geneviève's, much to my surprise. And relief. But as soon as she had anything but breast milk, her shit would smell, I was told, like shit.

I could hardly wait to take her skiing.

The real little ones ski without poles and with their own technique. Adult technique is very complicated. The kids just put their skis in a V and lean left or right. From the flats to black runs, they ski exactly the same, a bundle of clothes, a cap and goggles, arms out, legs spread, animated teddy bears in a department store window's Christmas display.

We have very few apartments in St. Anton, only a couple of apartment complexes, and no high rises at all. The tallest building, the seven-story Alte Post, has a chalet-style peaked roof and is also one of the oldest structures, dating back to the eighteenth century. This makes us very proud of ourselves. In France the ramshackle barbarousness of the real estate developers would make an American blush. Even the great Chamonix has lost its charm to unplanned traffic and unrestricted growth. The Italians are offhand. The Swiss have new resorts that look American. We are not like that. We have no developments, our establishments are small, we respect our Tyroleanisms by law and, even more, by community pressure. Pitched roofs, timber trim, plaster fronts are rules with no exceptions. Facade paintings are semioptional. When the tourists come they are entitled to their Austrian charm.

When there's snow on the ground and snow on the roofs, it works. When there's no snow—as in the first half of this season—it doesn't. The hollow heart is revealed. It is merely a place where someone passed a law defining what charm is, and the inhabitants, being Austrian and at least as law-abiding as Germans, thoroughly and charmlessly obeyed it. The old is so well kept it looks new. The new consists of such stolid and standardized imitations that the only way to tell the difference would be with a carbon-dated core sample. The sole exception is the shabby *pension* across the street from the Spar supermarket. Its half-submerged basement is a winter barn. You have to stoop to see the cows through the small ground-level window, but even standing absolutely upright you can smell their hide, their piss, and their shit. It is the only indication that there might be a real life that has nothing to do with Kevlar and carbon fiber multilaminates, Thinsulate, Hollofil, Gore-Tex, plastic boots, and cable cars.

Hiroshi's apartment was in a small, brand-new but traditional-looking complex up the hill to the left of the Galzigbahn, near the Krazy Kangaruh. It had ten apartments, a sauna, a plunge pool, and a solarium. It was ski in, ski out. Everything for the athlete and sybarite. Once I figured out which apartment was Hiroshi's I walked around the building twice to see if there was any light on in the window or any sign of activity whatsoever. I stepped in drifts higher than my boots and got some snow down around my ankles, but all was quiet.

Then I went up to the second floor, where the apartment was. I knocked at the door next door. A fair and British type came to the door, slightly fey—whether he was homosexual or just public school I couldn't tell. I told him in a quite straightforward way that I was inquiring about the girl's last days. He told me that he had just arrived, after the now notorious avalanche. I asked him if anyone had moved into the now vacant apartment next door. He asked if I thought it was dangerous on the mountain. I told him that this sort of thing was very rare. He, of course, remembered that he'd almost lost one or two of his royals that very same way in Klosters. He spoke as if he were a royal cousin, some once or twice removed. I doubted that he'd even been buggered by a cousin twice removed, but I didn't say so and the conversation remained polite. He was kind enough to inform me that the apartment next door seemed to be quite unoccupied, and if I was interested I might be able to pick up the lease from a Herr Himmner in Innsbruck or through an estate agent on Mumble High Street, London. He invited me in to use a pencil and paper if I needed to write it down. I thanked him, but I said I would remember, my wife always remarked about how good I was about remembering. He nodded. He closed the door.

I went to Hiroshi Tanaka's apartment. I knocked. There was no answer. I opened the door with the key that Wendy had given Carol. There was a light switch by the door. I turned the light on. Ski house furniture tends to the utilitarian and disposable because skiers tend to be drunk and disorderly and abuse it. This stuff was very good. Real Tyrolian antiques. I also expected it to be neat. A stereotype, I suppose. I think of the Japanese as living in tiny spaces, cheek to buttock with their own family and separated only by paper walls from the next, people who have to stow things as neatly and ingeniously as submariners, keeping their surfaces as clean as a sushi bar. This place looked like it had been ransacked.

I checked the bedroom next.

"And who are you," said the Japanese man sitting in the armchair beside the bed. He spoke in bad German, even worse than mine.

I told him I was a cousin of the family of the landlord here to check on conditions because there was a security deposit. I spoke in German as rapidly as I could in the expectation that our combined incompetence with the Teutonic tongue would confuse the situation sufficiently to distract from the fact that even though I had the key I was engaged in an act of at least illegal entry.

"*Sprechen ze English?*" he said with a certain desperation.

"Yeah," I said before I thought about it.

"Ahh," he said. He was slender and intense, with thick glasses. "An American."

"No," I said. "Richard Cochrane, County Clare, Irish Republic."

"I was definitely expecting an American," he said.

FIVE

GLACIER

"Mike," he said, "Mike Hayakawa," and held out his hand in a frank, straightforward manner that promised a firm and manly handshake, which he delivered. Then he gave me his card. It was an essay. In addition to his name—Mikio Hayakawa—in English and Japanese, his position—field executive with the international division of the Musashi Trading Company—a list of offices—Tokyo, Frankfurt, Los Angeles, London—it had all four prestigious addresses, phone and telex and fax numbers.

I didn't have a card. I explained that I was there for the parents of the poor dead Wendy, who, I was given to understand, had virtually lived in this apartment.

"I too," Mikio "Mike" Hayakawa said, "am here for a family in mourning."

"It's very sad," I said.

"A terrible tragedy," he said.

"Struck down in the prime of life."

"By a force of nature."

"Yes," I nodded, solemn as a Lutheran mortician.

"Nature is a great and terrible thing. This is something we Japanese have a feeling for."

"We feel it here in the mountains too," I said.

"Ah, yes," he said, as if giving real thought to a comparison between the Austrian experience and the Japanese.

"I was wondering if you found anything that belonged to the girl," I said.

"Most of her things," he said, "have already been given to her parents by the police. There are one or two items that clearly belong to a girl. I suppose they are hers."

"You speak English very well," I said, "like an American."

"You too," he said.

"I spent some years there," I said.

"Me too," he said.

"Bit of a mess," I said, referring to the apartment.

"Yes."

"He was a messy man," I said.

"Hiroshi Tanaka was a very well organized person. Everything in its place."

"Like a sushi bar," I said.

"Like a well-organized home or office," he said. "Perhaps something that belonged to Hiroshi Tanaka was given to the girl's family in error."

"You really, really sound American," I said. I looked around the apartment again. "I guess you must be going through it for the family."

"I think someone else must have done this. Perhaps to steal something," Hayakawa said. "You don't sound Irish at all. Of course, I don't know what Irish people sound like, except in the movies."

"Oh, really?" I said with a stage brogue. "What are you thinking there was here for them to steal? A pot of gold belongin' to the wee people?"

"Yes," he said, "they spoke like that. In *Darby O'Gill and the Little People*. A Walt Disney film, I think."

"Yeah, well now, I'll tell you what I think you remind me of," I said, still with a brogue you could put in the hole in the sole of your shoe to keep your sock from touching ground—it was that thick. "You remind me of a movin' picture from the grrrreat war—World War II, it must've been—where there's a Japanese fella who's interrogatin' some American who's heroic and bare chested, and this Jap officer—he appears so civilized, they're all astounded by it, until he explains that he went to UCLA."

"Actually, it was UC Berkeley."

"Good school, Berkeley."

"Too many hippies," he said. "They weren't very serious. You sound like some of the students from New York—that's what you sound like. Yes. I think someone took something."

"Not something belonging to the girl?"

"Maybe it got mixed up with the girl's things. If you were to come across it," he said, "I would be very interested."

"Of course you would," I said.

"The family would certainly be prepared to show their gratitude," Mike said. "With the yen so strong we can afford to be generous."

"So this is a family heirloom we are looking for?"

"Mr. Cochrane," he said, coolly, "I come to the home of a family friend. I see that it is in a condition in which he would never leave it. I conclude therefore that someone came here looking for something. If so, it belongs to the family. I am trying to be polite and discreet. If you have knowledge of this situation or are a participant in it, I offer you a reward. If not, I do not know what we have to discuss."

"This thing," I said, full of foolish and habitual curiosity, "is it bigger than a breadbox, or smaller than a video cassette?"

"I am not playing games, Mr. Cochrane. If you know something that I don't, you may help me. If it is the other way around, I have no reason to help you. Do I?"

"This thing you're looking for," I said, at my most juvenile. "It wouldn't be a black bird, about so high? It wouldn't be . . . the stuff that dreams are made of?"

"I like that movie. That was the best part of Berkeley, everybody was movie mad. But I am not interested in sarcasm or jokes. Do you really expect me to believe that you are from the family of the girl?"

"Hey," I protested, "don't you know who I am?"

"Who?"

"I own the Laundromat. Rick's. Short for Richard."

"The Laundromat opposite Johann's Café?"

"The only one in town," I said. "Ask anyone about me."

"That place is a ripoff. Eleven hundred yen for one load of wash. Back at Berkeley it was a buck and a quarter."

"That's right," I said.

It always pleases me when someone gets it. We all have one simple discovery that to us is the key to life. For Ronald Reagan it came when he was a young sports announcer in Des Moines, Iowa. By adding creative color to the tersely coded box scores that came in on the teletype, he announced the Chicago games as if he were actually seeing them live. On one occasion the line went down in midgame. Ron had two choices—tell the listeners out there that he was not actually at the game, was never at the game, and that the teletype that he depended on had failed, or make up a game. The second choice seems to be by far the most dangerous. It was the sort of lie, however harmless—letting the batter foul off ball after ball after ball for the eternal six minutes until the wire came back—that would inevitably catch up with him, because it was impossible that the game he made up would be the same as the one that actually took place. And it was not. The great discovery was that a good story was a good story and *reality did not matter*. This lesson served him well through an acting career and two terms as president. There are people to this very day that think that he cut the size of the federal government, cut federal spending, cut the deficit, and made America strong again—just because he told them so. Even though the irrefutable public record is that he increased the size of the government, increased spending, increased the deficit beyond anyone's wildest imagination, and turned the United States from the greatest creditor nation in the world into the greatest debtor nation—incidentally making Japan the world's new economic superpower. But he was right—he made up his stories, told them to us on TV, and *reality did not matter*.

George Bush's primal lesson must have been something more subtle, yet much more ordinary—almost Japanese—"The nail that raises its head gets hammered down." He proceeded to accumulate all the right credits—Phillips Academy, Yale, Skull and Bones,

Phi Beta Kappa, Navy combat pilot, the oil business in Texas, congressman, ambassador to the United Nations, head of the CIA, chairman of the Republican Party, subservient vice-president—without doing a single thing that anyone actually remembers: When he became president he sent troops around the world to administer this lesson to other foreign leaders. My great revelation came late in life—had it come earlier I might have been a tycoon rather than merely a ski bum and proud new father—my revelation was that the self-service Laundromats had not come to Europe.

I could see Mike relax as he understood the class of person he was dealing with. "That's how I can afford to ski with next to no work," I added.

"Pretty cool," he said. "You must make out like a bandit."

"What do the Laundromats get in Tokyo?"

"In Japan we all have our own laundry machines. I have an Aisaigo Day Fuzzy machine," he said with great pride.

"That's nice," I said. "What happened is, I ran into the girl's mother there, at my Laundromat."

"You do not know what an Aisaigo Day Fuzzy machine is, do you?"

"It's a washing machine."

"It uses fuzzy logic!"

"Don't we all?" I said.

"It has fuzzy chips," he said. "It reasons intuitively and approximately. It can determine the size of the load, how dirty the clothes are, how long to wash, to rinse, to spin. It has six hundred different cycles. I got one of the first twenty-five thousand made. It cost eighty-three thousand yen."

"How much is that?"

"Five hundred twenty-five dollars. I was able to get it because Aisaigo is associated with my company, Musashi Trading Company."

"I meant in schillings."

"Six thousand three hundred thirteen schillings. America has nothing fuzzy yet. Japan is first with fuzzy."

"Does that include the twenty percent VAT?" I asked.

"What?"

"The tax. We got a twenty percent sales tax here."

"I don't think it includes the tax. We are not selling it in Austria anyway. Yet. It is just in Japan."

"Wow! Six hundred wash cycles. I don't know what I'd do with six hundred cycles. Anyway, I'm sitting in a restaurant with my new baby and my wife and there's Wendy's mother again. Hysterical. My wife is now part of the International Sisterhood of Mothers, so here I am, trying to find out if Wendy's last days were happy or miserable and pick up any clothing or whatever she might've left behind."

"How old?" he asked.

"A couple of months, almost three months."

"Congratulations," he said. "It's a very special time."

"You have kids?" I asked.

"Yes, yes." He nodded eagerly. "I have a boy three years old and a girl one and a half years. Would you like to see pictures?"

"Yeah, sure," I said. I was learning that there is a big club in the world and the birth of my daughter had entered me in it. The Parents, like the Mafia or Freemasons or Moonies, has recognition signs, a secret language, and obsessive concerns with certain special subjects. The boy in the Fuji film photo already looked like his father—big nearsighted eyes and a slightly domed forehead. The little girl was all plump babyhood, twinkly and round and solemn all at once, formally dressed in some sort of Japanese baby robe and tiny obi.

"I miss them. Very much," their father said.

"Cute kids," I said, as I now understood that I had to do even if one had looked like a dwarf Godzilla and the other like a Ninja Turtle.

"You have picture of yours?"

"Not yet," I said, feeling vaguely guilty. "Where are yours? Back in Japan?"

"You should," he said. "Very good to have. Do you have a camera? I have a Minolta. I think Minolta is the best and Minolta Corporation is very closely related to my company, Musashi Trading Company. Yes, they are home with their mother." He took the photos back. "You must know many people. Perhaps you could do me a favor while you are going about your own business.

I too am interested in the final days of my friend, Hiroshi Tanaka. Anything you might find out about him and you could tell me, it would be very good."

"Obviously you have something in mind. I mean you think something is wrong."

"I tell you, Mr. Cochrane . . ."

"Call me Rick—everybody calls me Rick."

"Okay, Rick. Call me Mike. Reminds me of America. All first names. Very good. I don't know if anything is wrong. A man dies in an avalanche. Surely that is an accident. I spoke to the police and they said that it was an accident. And who would have any reason to kill Tanaka? No one. He was a good man. But then I see that this apartment was searched and I do not know why. Perhaps the police might talk to you more than to me. Frankly, many Europeans are prejudiced against Japanese. Either because they think they are better than us or because they think we are better than them. I would appreciate any help."

Franz, the gendarme, lives four houses away from me. Nobody in St. Anton lives very far from anyone else. Nobody lives in a home that is just a home. Land and housing are too valuable for that. All homes are also hotels or *pensions*. Sometimes it seems we are all the staff of one big but decentralized cruise ship. Just as no real cruise ship is the The Love Boat, we, the inhabitants, are not quite as bright and cheery and neatly packaged as we would be if we were acted. Only our cops live up to their clichés. I don't know if it's true of all Austria, but in St. Anton our gendarmes, who direct traffic and silence drunken Swedes, look like—dare I say it?—the spitting image of cinema Nazis.

Franz, for example, looks ready for a remake of 1939. He's six, one and 215 pounds, he has hands like hams and thin mean lips, his pallid eyes are a merciless Teutonic gray, and even when he strolls his stride holds a hint of a goosestep. Yet he's generally easy and pleasant to deal with. I deliberately ran into him the next day. All I needed was a time-to-kill expression on my face and a let's-chat attitude to be invited into his kitchen. His Frau, who runs their *pension*, brought out homemade schnapps, sausage, cheese, and bread. Franz asked me about the baby. His Frau sat a yard away from us, poised tentatively on the edge of her chair, prepared to stay only so long as it appeared that we were speaking of women's subjects.

"She's great," I said.

"My grandson is just three months older than your little girl. We must have them meet soon, eh?" Franz has three children. He is so proud that the first grandchild is male, you would think he had personally reached in and matched up the XY chromosomes.

"Yeah, Franz, they're ready to start dating. By the way, is there anything odd about this thing—this avalanche and the Japanese guy and the American girl?"

"There is nothing incorrect," Franz said as his Frau disappeared. It was not a woman's subject and there was work to be done. "They were not in an area that was officially closed, their guide was a *Skiführer*, fully qualified."

"I've never skied with him," I said, "but I'm sure he knows his stuff."

"Of course he knows. He is qualified. He is a *Skiführer*."

"Yeah, I understand. But everyone makes mistakes. I mean when an airline crashes the verdict always seems to be 'pilot error.' I'm not questioning Austrian standards of ski guide qualifications. But anyone can make a mistake."

"This is possible. Also it is possible that no one could know that this avalanche would happen in this place at this time. All the time when we ski we make this judgment. Usually we are right."

"Do you know anything about Hiroshi Tanaka? I'm not doubting the guide."

"About Tanaka," Franz said, "he had money. What tourist doesn't? He liked young girls. He could afford them."

"There's another Japanese, down at his apartment, claims the place was broken into and something stolen."

"What was stolen?"

"He wouldn't tell me."

"There is no report of theft. All is correct."

"Well, he thinks something is missing. He thinks it might be in the stuff you gave the girl's family. You gave her family her clothes and things."

"It was Martin gave the mother the things of the girl. But I saw those things and they were all girl things. Clothing, makeup, cosmetics. It was correct to give them to the mother. A mother's love for a child is a powerful thing and must be respected. If this Japanese thinks something is missing, he must report it to the police."

"That's what I told him," I said. "I told him I only do laundry. This is the guy." I gave Franz the card that Mikio Hayakawa had given me. "He's sitting there, looking for something and waiting for someone."

"For what?"

"That's all I know. Find any drugs in the apartment? Anything like that?"

"No drugs," he said.

"Well, at least that's something I can tell her mother."

"Tell them this snow, five days of snow in February on top of nothing, there will be avalanches. Tell them if you ski off piste there is some risk, even for the Prince of Wales."

That's what I told Marie.

That's what I told the Tavetians.

Nobody was satisfied. The Tavetians because they were full of grief and in the grip of the most powerful of all human hungers, the hunger for meaning. Their child had been taken from them at random. Act of nature, Act of God, cosmic accident, chance. That doesn't cut it. That does not suffice. I once heard a twenty-six-year-old woman dying of cancer claim that her disease had come because she failed to express her anger at her husband. Death demands a reason and all of reason's comforts—guilt, blame, and some parameters to put a limit on grief.

"Tell us about how she lived," Arlene Tavetian said.

"Let it go," Bob said.

"Please tell me," she said to me.

"She was a happy and healthy young woman," I said. "A good skier. Pretty. Desirable. Likable."

"Rick, please," Arlene said. "When my father died, the priest who did the funeral didn't really know him. So he said all those nice things you're supposed to say. I sat there and I got so angry. Who the hell was he talking about! My mother kept shushing me. That was nobody he was talking about. A generic dead man, like generic detergent. Why didn't he say that my father drank too much, which he did—at least it would have been about him. At least we all would have known who the hell it was we were burying. Why didn't he say he sometimes hit my mother. He could say he was a good man overall, but not every moment of every damn day of his life he wasn't. Please, I want to know who I'm burying. Some truth, please, even if it's ugly, even if it's painful—at least it would be real. Please tell me."

"I don't know what to say, Mrs. Tavetian," I said.

"I would rather you tell me she fucked her way across Europe . . ."

"Arlene, please," Bob said.

". . . than tell me," Arlene went on, "she was a . . . a . . . a pretty nonentity. A nothing. Who did she love? Anyone? Who did she like? Who did she hate? What did she care about? Did she care about anything?"

"She cared about being alive," I said. "She had something. I don't know what exactly. Maybe just femaleness. More than cuteness. More than prettiness. But everyone remembers her presence. Paul, at Down Under, he wanted her, but she said no. He hired her best friend—that's Carol—figuring it would bring Wendy around. Wendy was collecting experiences. Which for my money is right on, and exactly what she should be doing. She made it with a ski instructor . . ."

"Which one?"

"They're interchangeable," I said.

"Which one?"

"His name is Kurt. He's going bald, has a wife with a tough mouth and a mean streak. He wasn't good enough for her, so she moved on. I don't know too much about how she felt about the Japanese guy, but at least he was an interesting guy. She had to be learning something about the world from him."

"Thank you," she said. "That was certainly a lot more informative."

"You're welcome," I said.

"Now find out," she commanded, "who killed her."

Bob Tavetian looked at me, pleading.

"Mrs. Tavetian," I said, "the mountain killed her."

Marie wasn't satisfied either. But she hadn't had more than four hours' uninterrupted sleep in three months and wasn't satisfied with anything. More precisely, she wasn't satisfied with anything I did. She was deeply satisfied with her daughter. Watching the baby grow was her primary satisfaction and sole joy. When Anna first arrived her existence seemed ephemeral. When she slept, she slept so still that each of us, in turn, without saying anything, so as not to alarm the other, would creep close and fearfully touch her to be certain that she was breathing. Now she almost snored, snoring adorably of course, as only an infant can. She'd even gone briefly yellow before her liver had fully kicked in and there had been two days of anxiety. But she turned pink again and began putting on weight from her cheeks to her toes.

I went skiing.

The Greens had enough political clout to eliminate helicopters from St. Anton last year, much to the regret of the serious skiers and the ski guides. Helicopters were still available on the other side of the pass, in Lech. But due to ski school politics, far too Austrian and arcane for me to understand, *Skiführers* from the Arlberg Ski School in St. Anton acted as if the Lech copters didn't even exist. So we drove all the way down to Galtur, near Piz Buin, the peak for which the sun block is named, where profit is also still running a hair ahead of the environment and they continue to offer heliskiing. We flew up to the glacier in the wide Silvretta range on the southern border with Switzerland. Where we could make fresh tracks. Where it was quiet. Far from a woman who was irritable with lack of sleep. Far from a hysterical mother wanting answers about a dead daughter.

As soon as we were in the air I experienced a sudden panic. That was new to me. I'd been in choppers before and I've always known about how dangerous they are. But it used to be just brain knowledge. Now it was gut fear. Who had built the thing? Were the workers drunk or on drugs? Who supplied the rivets, the steel, the plastic? Who did the maintenance? Was our pilot quietly crazed or prone to strokes? I didn't like being in the air. If something happened on the ground at least I had a chance. Even against an avalanche. Hadn't my guide, Hans Christian Lantz, outrun one?

I concentrated on my breathing and set my face in the hope that my fear didn't show. A new fragility had come upon me with fatherhood and mortality stood beside me.

As soon as we touched down it was all right again. I was safe, on solid ground.

"How come, after all this time," Hans asked while we were putting on our skis, "you hired me?"

"Oh, I heard in town that you were good," I said. We spoke in German. Like most of the officially multilingual ski instructors, Hans's English was limited to about fifteen phrases—five for skiing, four for drinking, three for eating, two for intercourse, and one for oral sex. "That you really knew the mountains."

"That is true," he said. "But that is not why you hired me."

"No?"

"No. I have a certain charisma now," he said. "I am the man who outskied the avalanche. *Ja.* I am right?"

"Actually," I said, switching to English, "if you think about it, that's not exactly a recommendation. It's great for you, of course, but who would want to be one of your clients when you want to try it again?"

"You are making fun," Hans said, but since I'd spoken in English he wasn't nearly sure enough of what I'd said to know if he should be offended.

"Fun? No," I said, switching back to German. "Like with Toni Sailer—I want to ski with him, but I wouldn't want to do a downhill with him."

"*Ja,* I understand," Hans said. He liked the comparison. Two people in history have won all three alpine Olympic events. Toni Sailer was the Austrian who had done it. "Austria has the best skiers in the world. We invented modern skiing. There"—he pointed off in the distance—"in St. Anton, by Hannes Schneider. We are related." Let the Austrians claim skiing. If the French did not have Jean Claude Killy they would still have Paris, Italians without an Alp would still have style, Germans have deutsch marks, and the Swiss have banks. Take skiing away from Austria and what's left? An old waltz and the shabby birthplace of Adolf Hitler.

The first thing he tried to do was blow me off.

It's what they all do, in varying degrees, particularly to another male who shows testosterone signs. They call it evaluating your abilities. In spite of my age, and my station in life as a Laundromat mogul, I am just as juvenile about it as they are. While I generally won't die to prove my abilities, I have to be pushed awfully hard. Fortunately for my machismo most glacier skiing is relatively gentle. If there were groomed pistes they would be graded blue and red, intermediate skiing.

Hans took off. The snow was deep, which is what we were there for. It was also a little heavy, but he still laid down some perfect rhythmic turns. The kind they photograph for postcards. I matched the track, although I had to give it all my concentration and Hans was just fucking with me. So he tried some straight running. Which was fine. Except that if he really wanted to dump me he would lead me into something hellacious and completely unexpected.

Just as I was thinking that, he pulled up.

"*Ja,* you pretty good skier," he said when I caught up to him. "We can have some fun."

"Great."

He skied. I followed. I had to admit he knew his stuff. He found great snow and I felt perfectly safe. Twice he stopped and had us skirt a slope because he thought the snow was avalanche-prone. The third time we stopped he took a pair of binoculars out of his pack. He looked out across the mountains, searched, focused, found something, and then handed them to me.

"You see, up there," he pointed toward St. Anton and I thought I recognized the Valuga way in the distance. "From there, that is where the avalanche came. You see, almost the whole mountainside, it came down for us."

What looked like a shadow might have been the area he meant. I certainly couldn't tell and I don't think he really could either. But it was clear that he liked talking about his avalanche run and he assumed that I wanted to hear about it and that I was after a vivid vicarious thrill from seeing the site of sudden death, even at this distance.

"See the point there? That's where we were. There is a ridge you can't see from here, behind the mountain. That was safety.

Anyone who could ski to that ridge before the avalanche, they could live."

He was proud. Like a matador. Why not? If Hemingway was right and courage is grace under pressure, then surely retaining your skill while a mountainside that wants to be a runaway freight train is rushing downhill at you certainly qualifies. If Hemingway was right, we also must assume that fishing and suicide are the zenith of human existence.

Hans turned and headed down a new slope. It was both south facing and open to the wind. The result was a crust on top of soft snow. Crust is the trickiest of all snow conditions. If it's thick enough to support your weight then you ski it very gently, weighting your skis evenly, skidding your turns with as little force as possible and almost no up–down motion. Breakable crust, and it can switch from one to the other instantly, requires exactly the opposite approach. You must crash through and jump out of it. And you must have faith, a belief that your skis will perform as they should in spite of every effort of the conditions to trap them. They will perform. I've seen other people do it lots of times. I've even done it myself sometimes. This time my faith faltered, or I rushed a turn, or caught an edge, jumped too hard or not hard enough, or some damn thing, and went down.

Hans waited patiently for me. He was pleased. He'd found one of my limits.

I brushed the snow off of my face. I picked up my hat and tried to shake the snow off of the wool. I clomped back up the hill, found where I'd buried my ski, dug it out of the snow, cleared the binding, scraped the snow off of the bottom of my boot, and stepped back in. I took a moment to catch my breath, then skied down to Hans.

"It is good to test yourself," he said. "It is often hard to do that in today's world."

We skied down to Galtür, mostly in better stuff than the breakable crust. A cloud covered the sun and a chilly wind was coming through the valley, so we ate indoors.

As usual in Austrian cafés the accumulated smoke was thick enough to make a nonsmoker feel like a rat in a cage designed to determine how fast lung cancer can be created through passive smoking. The menu had the standard ten Austrian lunch dishes: eight varieties of sausage, Tirolergöstel—a sort of home fries with bits of ham—and the yeast cake called *Germknödel*.

If we had been back in St. Anton we would have gone to a restaurant where Hans had a deal. The standard ski instructor deal is that the instructor eats and drinks for free in return for bringing his group in. If the instructor brings in good-size groups and doesn't drink up all the restaurant's profits, there are sometimes cash considerations. The shortcomings of this system from the point of view of the client quickly become clear. If you ski with the same instructor regularly, you eat lunch at the same place every day, which is not a spot chosen for its cuisine or its ambiance or its scenery. And his deal, not snow conditions or crowds, determines where you will ski because your instructor will choose a route that gets him to his free lunch by noon. If the client takes the instructor outside his usual territory or insists on a restaurant where the food is good, then the client is expected to pick up the *Skiführer*'s tab. I was buying. I ordered a bottle of wine. I did the pouring and let Hans do the drinking. When we finished the first bottle I ordered a second.

"Hiroshi Tanaka always skied with me," Hans told me. "We understood each other. He understood the warrior spirit. He was in business, but he said that in business one must proceed as in war. One must study strategy, tactics—one must study one's enemies as if life itself were at stake."

"The Laundromat business isn't like that," I said. "What business was Hiroshi in?"

"I often think," Hans said, "it would be good to live in a country with a war. You Americans were lucky. You had Vietnam. You could test yourself."

"Some test," I said.

"It is not the winning or losing—it is the personal testing. 'Man is a rope stretched between the animal and the superman—a rope over an abyss.' Did you ever hear that? . . . We must put ourselves to our ultimate to supersede. *Ja?*"

"Oh, *ja,*" I said, and poured out some more wine. "So you liked Hiroshi?"

"Yes. Liked and admired. He was a strong man." Hans leaned forward and I could smell the wine on his breath even through the wine on my own. "He liked winning. But it was important that the contest be worthy. His final contest . . . it was worthy. Against the mountain. If he knew . . . he would have understood."

"If he knew what?"

"That he was in a contest," Hans said.

"You think that's how he thought of it?"

"Yes. The best kind. A contest to the death."

"What about the girl?" I asked him. "Wendy?"

"A bimbo. *Ja?* Good American word. Bimbo."

"You get it on with her?"

"Look at me," Hans said, and straightened himself. "I am very Austrian, very Aryan, *ja?*"

"*Ja.*" He was about two inches taller than me, six, one, 190 pounds, blond, with the sort of sun-squint wrinkles around his eyes that the various Marlboro men have. He also had crooked teeth with tobacco stains.

"I have all the women I have need of. So I make it a rule. No fucking of the women with the clients."

"Never?"

"Maybe, sometimes I make a special exception."

"With Wendy?"

"She was the kind that likes the money," Hans said. "We meet lots of them here on the mountain. They do chasing of the gelt. Until they get married. Then they come after us to get a good fucking." He pumped his arm, then made a dismissive gesture. "No more does that matter. I am not just a mountain guide. I have money now. I am more than this. I don't need this."

"So Wendy didn't go for you?"

"She was looking at me, I know this. But Hiroshi was my friend. Did you know that he had samurai ancestors? We discussed this often. He died a samurai death."

"And Wendy? What kind of death did she die?"

"What are you asking me?" Hans said, suddenly suspicious.

"I'll tell you what I'm asking you. I'm asking you how come you make judgments like this based on an accident. Something fell down a mountain. Three people were standing underneath.

All three ran away. On skis. One got away. Two didn't. Good death, bad death—to me it's bullshit. You got a rush because you came close to dying and survived. Hey, I can dig it. I've been there. It gives you a rush. But it was an accident. Not an act of courage or nobility."

"To perform well when you are looking face to face at death—that is the ultimate test," Hans said. He was angry, and surprised, that I didn't worship him. I knew because he bunched the muscles in his neck and wrinkled his forehead. "To ski pretty on the baby slope for the girls to watch—that is nothing. To ski well when the avalanche is behind you—that is courage."

"It was an accident. You were luckier than they were." I shrugged. "And you're a better skier. That's all you can say."

"What if it was deliberate? What if I knew it would happen and still I faced it? Would that change your mind?"

"Deliberate?"

"It does not matter. It is the act, the pure act that matters," he said, and I didn't know if he was clarifying the rhetorical nature of his statement or backing away from having almost confessed something. "Come. We ski."

Once again the helicopter scared the hell out of me, and when we landed I was relieved to be on solid ground, even if it was actually a glacier, which is, technically speaking, neither ground nor solid. A glacier is formed when the winter snowfall exceeds the summer evaporation. The snow melts and when it refreezes it becomes ice. First it becomes granules called firn. The edges melt, the granules merge and recrystallize, now as a solid block of ice. Ice is normally brittle, but under great pressure it is a plastic material that flows. Not very fast, but it does flow a few centimeters a day. Slow enough for me to feel it as solid ground.

Although someone had made the mistake of reading excerpts from Nietzsche to Hans, I had to admit again that he was a good guide. He knew the mountain. As we skied, the cold, clean air and the exercise burned the alcohol out of my system. We seemed to be past the testing and he kept things at a level where I was comfortable. We avoided the crusty wind pack. It wasn't Colorado powder, but it wasn't tricky either, and when we stopped to look back at our tracks it made us look good. We did some cruising and we skied some steeps that looked more frightening than they were.

"You like to get some air?" he asked. "I'll show you my favorite jump."

"Okay," I said. Somewhat foolishly. Getting air between your skis and the surface is fun. But it's for kids. Kids who like to crash and burn. I'd recently seen an American kid wearing a T-shirt with a drawing in the romance comic style that showed a skier, a kid, who'd just gone off a major cliff, skis cocked up in a stylish freestyle move, poised in midair, his thought bubble saying, "Time to burn."

"When we get to it," he said, skating to pick up speed, "go for it!"

I didn't go for it with quite as much enthusiasm as he did. I didn't skate for the extra speed; I didn't get into a tuck as early as he did. He was a bigger, better, younger skier than me. I saw the lip before he took off. It was lovely. As perfect as if it were built as a launching pad for stunts.

Hans hit it perfectly and I saw him get air. He flew.

I hit it less perfectly. And with less conviction. He had warned me. "Go for it," he'd said. Which was something I should have done even without his warning. It is necessary to ski with complete conviction and commitment to whatever you are attempting. To ski half assed is to die half assed.

What he hadn't told me was that we were leaping a crevasse. The upper layers of a glacier are not under pressure. They are not plastic, they are brittle—and when different pieces of ice underneath flow at different rates, the surface cracks. These brittle surface layers, and therefore the crevasses that they form, are 30 to 60 meters deep. Since we are talking about a place on top of a very high alp—not an urban area with elevators, cranes, fire department rescue services, and so forth—even 100 feet is, for all practical purposes, a bottomless pit.

I didn't feel like that figure on the T-shirt, hanging in space with time to reflect, time to act, time to burn. I felt like I was going to die.

I almost made it. I lunged forward and the tips of my skis hit the far side. Hard. Then they popped off. My momentum carried me forward and I went face-first into the snow on the edge. I grabbed at it. I dug my hands into it, even encumbered as they were with ski poles.

Then I started sliding. Then it was sheer. The dream of falling appears to be universal—it comes early and is one of the standard nightmares of childhood. Free-fall.

Thirty feet down, I landed. I landed in deep snow. I landed feet first and face second. I was wet and in deep, but I was unbroken and substantially more alive than I'd anticipated. I looked up, wiped the snow from my eyes, and spit it out of my mouth. Hans was looking down.

"I gave you fair chance," he said.

"Fuck you, you motherfucker," I said, in English. Then in German I asked him: "How are you going to get me out of here?"

"You guessed, didn't you?"

"Guessed what?"

"You goaded me into admitting it," he said, shaking his head.

"Just get me the fuck out of here."

"But I gave you fair chance."

"Fair chance, fine—what are you talking about?" I said, beginning to realize what he was talking about. With a sinking feeling, almost as bad as the falling feeling, but not as dramatic, it came to me that Hans was a serious wacko.

"Like I gave Hiroshi," Hans explained. "He was a samurai. You too should die bravely." He gave me a sincere look and started backing away.

"*Wait a minute!*" I yelled.

"*Ja?*"

I looked around me. Without a pick and crampons there was no way I was going to get out of that pit by myself. "You gotta get me out of here. I have a baby. Her mother—she's going to worry about me. She . . ." I almost said that Marie knew who I was skiing with, but this Nietzsche-quoting Austrian asshole was crazed enough to go after her too. ". . . she doesn't know who I went out with. But lots of other people do. Including Franz, the gendarme. And Luis at the ski school."

"I gave you fair chance," Hans said. As if that settled everything.

"You set Tanaka up? You set the avalanche?" I asked him, to keep him talking, to keep him there.

"*Ja.* I did," he said with some pride. "So you see, it was not an accident. I was daring the fate. I was making the risk. I was testing myself. It was true courage. Not luck. Do you admit that now?"

"Sure, Hans, sure," I said.

"Then good-bye," he said.

"How did you set off the avalanche?"

He turned and disappeared. I yelled and yelled. But he didn't come back.

SIX

PAST LIVES

I have a past life.

In that I am very lucky. Most people live one time, as one self. In that past life I was in a different country. I was in the embrace of discontent. Angers as obscure to me then as they are to me now drove me into constant conflict, as if conflict was both my nourishment and joy. I lived in New York City. To Europeans New York is a large part of the definition of America. But to Americans, New York is as far from America as Baghdad. I wasn't always a Laundromat tycoon. I had other professions. The essence of them was conflict.

I also had a different family. I lived with a woman and her son, Wayne. My affections for Wayne were immense. The relief at disentwining myself from his mother was equally immense. It still astonishes me sometimes that I walked away from all of that, like a snake dumps its old skin, like a caterpillar comes out of a cocoon, and got to be something different. Wayne and I still maintain a relationship by mail. Any knowledge I have of his mother is through the son. He's fifteen now.

I had a favorite story that I used to tell Wayne. It involved a grizzly bear and a trip to the Rockies. This was before I'd ever lived in the mountains. In this story, which can be drawn out as long as the teller likes, the storyteller, alone, unarmed, is finally cornered by the exceptionally large, especially enraged bear. There is no escape. The teller drags the story out until the impatient listener finally asks, "What did you do?" or "How did you get away?" The storyteller then says, "Nothing I could do. That bear—he done killed me."

That was the joke. There was no way out. That crevasse—it was going to kill me.

I had actually landed on a snow bridge. It was fairly wide, but a quick exploration showed me that in either direction the only way for me to go was down. Fifty to a hundred feet further down. Even if I survived the additional fall, that was hardly the direction I want to go in. I had my Pieps. One of the rules of skiing off-piste, let alone on the glacier or in the backcountry, is to carry an avalanche beeper. It both broadcasts and listens on 457 KHz. The closer you get, the louder the signal. It's a fairly straightforward application of a miracle of modern technology. Its major shortcoming is that it is not an air-raid siren. No one will hear it by accident. They must be looking for you and, since the effective broadcast range of the beeper is only fifty to seventy-five feet, they have to have a fair idea of where to look. Nonetheless, I turned it on. Then I looked for a way up. Up was a sheer wall. What I needed for it was very obvious and available in any mountaineering shop: pitons, a pick, crampons, rope, and other people.

This is not to say that I did not try to find a route out.

Down below, in a place I couldn't see, I had a child—Anna Geneviève. For the first month she had been virtually an inanimate object with eyes and a mouth, her face still fetal, her expressions gnomic at best. She only cried for a reason and she could only conceive of three reasons—cold, hunger, and gas. Feed me, swaddle me, help me squeeze that stuff out. In honesty, I concluded that only a mother could love a newborn or refer to one as beautiful, and that was just as well because it was only out of motherhood, out of something innately feminine, from the bonding of breast-feeding, that anyone could give an infant the care that a newborn needed. At least, so it seemed to me from the love and patience and concentration that Marie lavished on our daughter. Who was born serious. I believe that we are born with a great deal of our nature—the obvious things like intelligence and hair color, but also temperament and capacity for laughter, energy level, hunger, greed, and aspiration. Like dogs. Anna was born so serious that I asked the doctors if this was a permanent condition. If it had been, I don't know that we could have lived together. They assured me, several times, that no infant comes out grinning, let alone snickering, and it takes time before they learn how.

Then, after five weeks, she smiled.

Shortly thereafter some of her gurgles could be interpreted as laughter and within a week of that she was truly burbling.

I had never been suicidal. But looking backward from this now, I could see that I had some sort of need to put myself so far out on the limb or so deep into turmoil that the animal instinct to live would come out and assert itself. I didn't need to do that anymore—not now that Anna Geneviève could laugh. So what the hell was I doing in this crevasse?

It gets cold up on the mountain. Unforgivingly cold.

Frostbite is a result of the body's defense against hypothermia. The body withdraws the blood from the extremities to keep the core at a survival temperature. It can occur whenever the ambient temperature falls below freezing, 0°C, 32°F. Wind and wet skin hasten heat loss from the extremities. I once went running on an early spring day. Deluded about the temperature by bright, enthusiastic sunshine, I just wore nylon jogging shorts. They did nothing to block the wind or protect me from the evaporation of my sweat. My dick began to freeze. It shriveled, turned white, and lost all feeling. Thank God for Marie. She treated it immediately with the warm, moist bath of her mouth. This is not an erotic memory. I remember it only as "the day my dick froze," although freezing was so mild and treatment so prompt that there were no permanent aftereffects. Aftereffects of frostbite even following treatment, presuming there is treatment, can be as severe as infection and tissue death, requiring amputation. Lack of treatment can lead to gangrene. General hypothermia is defined as depression of the inner-climate body temperature. Mild hypothermia, like mild anything else, is not a terrible problem. Warmth, food, rest, and it goes away. Extreme hypothermia is critical and often fatal. When the body cools below 34°C (93°F) metabolic temperature control becomes unstable and, if cooling persists, is lost. That is followed by coma, cardiorespiratory failure, and then death.

I had heard of people making igloos for themselves. Tiny enclosures, the smaller the better, coffin sized, dug into the snow, which would act as insulation. But I didn't know how long that would work. And if it did, what would I then be waiting for? I was certain that once I lay myself down to sleep I would never wake. Only movement would keep me alive. It would keep the blood circulating. So I began to try to make my way back up.

I tried to go at it methodically and slowly. Not frantically and full of panic. First I zippered all my zippers all the way up, snapped the snaps, tucked the cuffs of my jacket into the cuffs of my gloves. I loosened the buckles on my ski boots to allow maximum circulation and made sure the built-in gaiters on my pants were down over my boots and left no gap for snow to sneak in. Then I inspected the sidewalls visually, looking for a route up, a handhold or a foothold. I didn't find one.

My skis were nowhere to be seen. The closest thing I had to tools were my ski poles. They were metal; they had points. Surely they were worth something. I began to use them, trying to uncover or carve fissures and ledges that would allow me to climb. On my first attempt, I got almost five feet up before my foothold, and then my handhold, gave way, and I slid back down.

There is something about cold that seeps in and saps courage.

Cold is a killer. It's easy to forget and underestimate cold. Until you are surrounded by it without shelter or relief. Then it is more vicious than Hitler's armies, more relentless than Napoleon's troops.

I once knew a very high Buddhist teacher. He taught, as oracular obscurantists invariably do, that the longest journey begins with a single step. He was a thoroughly reprehensible bisexual who had AIDS, and knew it, and went around inserting his penis into other people anyway. Nonetheless, the one-step concept has some validity. There is always enough strength to take one step. Just take the one. The second step, and even the need for a second step, does not yet exist. And never will. Of course if you race slalom on such a basis, you're fucked before you're through the first gate.

I stood up. I got my ski poles and this time I broke them up. Something I should have thought of earlier. It gave me seven spikes. Four from one, three from the other, for no reason except that I am not a professional ski pole breaker. They would function as my pick and my pitons. That took me probably a half hour. I had also decided not to look at my watch. Not to know how long anything took, or how long I'd been there, or how soon the dawn. Knowledge of time would only bring delusions of hope or despair.

Then I began to climb again.

I only got a foot, perhaps two, further the second time. Then I fell again.

By the time I stood up, it was growing dark.

More slowly, and with smaller steps, I began to climb again. This time just to keep moving, with not much hope of climbing out. I don't know how long I would have lasted. Perhaps not until morning, perhaps for days.

Clouds drifted in and it grew darker still. It meant a new storm, new snow to cover me. I heard the wind. It got louder and louder. It roared. Then a light, like a headlamp beam, flashed against the sides of my crevasse. Then there was barking. I looked up and saw Rudi, that mean and unsociable dog, at the edge, looking down, barking at me. Then the source of the light appeared. A helicopter passing over the crevasse.

I'd been found.

The chopper moved out of my line of sight and landed. A few minutes later, Franz, the gendarme, appeared. He threw down a rope ladder. It is not as easy as it should be to climb a rope ladder if you are very tired and wearing ski boots. With great and weary gratitude I stumbled up.

Franz was urging me to move faster. Rudi was barking. The chopper was making noise and wind. When I got near to the top, Franz grabbed me and pulled me up.

"It was deliberate," I said. "That motherfucker tried to kill me."

"*Ja, ja, ja,*" he said, in a hurry. He shoved me along toward the chopper. I wanted to go slow. "Come on. Wind is coming."

"What? What?" I asked him. I wanted to tell him about Hans. I wanted to have dinner and a beer. I was a bit out of it. Tired or relieved or mild hypothermia, it was hard to tell. He shoved my head down as we moved under the blades. "Did you bring the beer?" I said.

"Stay!" he said to me, while he helped his dog into the chopper.

Then he turned to me and pushed me along inside. It was loud. Not a conversational place. The pilot seemed to be in a hurry. It was windy. I could tell because clouds raced heavily in front of the moon. The second I was in, he lifted off. "Well, we found you, and you are alive," Franz yelled in my ear. "He called on the radio"—he pointed to the pilot—". . . to tell Marie Laure that the father of her baby is alive and well." He pulled a sausage from his bag, cut it in three parts, gave one piece to Rudi, one to me, and took one for himself. As it went down I could feel how much my body craved the fat. The cells sucked it up and threw it on the internal fire; it put heat in my flow of blood and slowly spread through me.

"If you hadn't found me, I wouldn't have made it."

"*Ja, ja, ja,*" Franz said, and put a blanket over me. "Shut up—it's too noisy." My stomach jumped as the chopper lurched down the mountain in the dark, but when Franz pulled out more food—good Austrian bread and rich Austrian chocolate—I ate greedily. That's three things they do really well—bread, chocolate, and mountain rescue. It made their faults seem minor.

The first thing I did after we landed was call Marie Laure and Anna Geneviève. They were napping, already secure in the knowledge that I was safe. Since any sleep at that stage of life, for mother even more than child, is such an achievement, my adventure paled beside it and my call was merely an annoyance. Irritated, I climbed into Franz's car. The heater was going full blast.

Franz started driving and headed for home. I bitched about Marie. He pulled out the schnapps. "She's a good girl," he said. "You should marry her."

He passed the bottle. I took a sip. "How did you find me?" I asked him.

"The helicopter pilot," he said. "He remembered where he put you down. We could see your tracks—also, Rudi could follow your tracks. Also, when we got close, we picked you up on the Pieps. It was easy."

"He tried to kill me—you understand that?"

"Oh, sure, *ja.*"

"This is a crazy man. Psychotic. You understand? He led me to that crevasse and then skied away and left me there to die. Not only that—I think he killed the Jap and the girl. He either set that avalanche or knew that it was coming, though I don't know how he did it."

"How did he do it?"

"And he's proud of it. You shouldn't let German kids read Nietzsche. This superman shit is not good for them."

"We are not German, we are Austrian."

"So what are you going to do about him?" I shook. My body kept doing that. "It's a game with him. That's another thing. And he's getting to like it. He tells his victim, 'Follow me but watch out for the cliff,' then he leads you to the cliff. Only he knows it's coming and you don't, so you go over and he stands on top, saying, 'Oh, I gave you fair warning, ha, ha. What a great game. I'm alive and you're dead.' He's going to do it some more. Did you arrest him yet? You better get this guy."

"Have another schnapps," he said, and passed me the bottle. "Why did you go skiing with Hans? Alone?"

"He thinks he killed me for a reason. According to him I goaded him into telling me that he killed Tanaka and Wendy Tavetian. But I didn't goad him and he didn't even really tell me. He wanted to tell me. He wants to brag. There were guys in Vietnam used to cut ears off the people they killed—and wear them, you understand. He wants people to know he's a killer. He didn't really confess until after I was down in that crevasse and he was pretty damn sure I wasn't ever coming out. Right now he makes it a game. You and him against the mountain. I bet, in his mind, he doesn't do the killing. No, it's the mountain doing the killing—the avalanche, the crevasse."

"How did he do the avalanche? You think he did the avalanche?"

"Oh, shit," I said. "My skis. My skis went down that crevasse. My good skis, not my rock skis. Practically brand-new. With bindings, we're talking about five thousand, six hundred schillings!"

"Those Dynastars?"

"Yeah, new Dynastars."

"They're not so good," he said.

"You just say that because they're French."

"Austrian skis are better—even so, you paid too much."

"Really?"

"*Ja,*" he said very seriously. "Five thousand, six hundred schillings is much too much. You should go to Sporthaus Glück—at least twenty percent less." It was his cousin's shop. He passed the flask.

I drank and I shivered as Franz drove back to St. Anton. The road twisted, a sheer drop always on one side. On the other, enough snow loomed above us to bury anything that passed. Where the engineers were certain that the snow would slide they had built half tunnels, awnings of cantilevered concrete, over the road. This was not to say that the mountains lacked sufficent originality and whimsy to avalanche in places that the road builders hadn't prepared for.

We finished the flask in silence.

He dropped me home. I forgot to even say *danke schön* or *gute Nacht*. Franz said, "*Gross Gott.*" I shoved my ski boots off and dropped my jacket. Then I picked up Anna Geneviève and held her in my arms. She smiled at me. She was mildly hungry, so she tried suckling on my finger. She knew better and perhaps it was just a hint. Then I made a face at her and she laughed.

"Hold her head up," Marie Laure said, although Anna was quite strong enough to hold it up herself now. "I was worried about you."

"I'm all right. It was all right," I said, sipping the hot chocolate she'd made for me. She told me with a look that she knew that wasn't true. "You saved me, I guess, by going to Franz and telling him to look for me."

"You need someone to look after you," she said.

"Do you think we should get married?" I asked, gazing at my daughter.

"I called your mother today," Marie Laure said, "and told her she could come."

"That made her happy, I bet."

Then my daughter started to cry. She was well wrapped, as she likes to be. So the best guess was that she was hungry. I gave her to her mother, who exposed her breast and put the infant to her nipple. She ate and fell asleep, but as soon as we went to bed she woke again. Marie tried to nurse her even though her nipples were sore. The milk didn't have its normal soporific effect and Anna was crying and restless.

"*You* do something," Marie said, never angry at the baby, but angry at me.

An American tourist who'd once seen me carrying Anna through the town asked me if I knew the football carry. I said no.

"I was carrying my own baby," he said, "in Riverside Park. Except my baby was crying. Wailing away. Disturbing the peace. There was this black guy. Nice, mellow-looking black guy. Well dressed. Not threatening. 'Is that your first?' he says to me. I said yes. 'Don't you know how to carry a baby?' he says. I say, 'Of course, I do.' He says, 'No you don't. You carry them just like a football. Let me show you.' It's a black guy. It's Riverside Park. Am I going to hand him my firstborn son? Not even if it's Bill Cosby, I say to myself.

"Then I realize it *is* Bill Cosby. I'm standing in Riverside Park and Bill Cosby wants to teach me how to carry a baby. So I said, 'Sure. Show me.' He crooks his arm, takes the baby, puts him with his head at his elbow and feet toward his hand, arms and legs dangling down, and the kid shuts up. Happy as a clam. Then Cosby hands me my son back and I try it. It's easy, comfortable, kid can't fall out. You know what I think? They like the view of the ground. America, it's amazing. Me and Bill Cosby in Riverside Park, and I learn to carry my son like he's a football."

So I put Anna on my forearm, legs and arms dangling down, view of the ground, and began to walk. She got quiet. I walked for a while until I thought she was out. I went back to bed and gently, gently put her down, and began to slip my arm out from under. She wailed.

"You cannot stop so soon," Marie Laure said, furious.

"Right," I said, and lifted my daughter and put her over my arm and went back to pacing. Riverside Park, I knew it well. New York. America.

SEVEN

DAMAGES

By the time Franz went to arrest Hans Lantz, the mountain guide was dead.

It was an apparent suicide. The corpse held a long-barrel .22 in its right hand, an expensive target pistol by Beretta. The bullet had entered the right temple at the appropriate angle. It was clearly a contact wound. There were powder burns and the skin had exploded outward around the entry point. There was a note.

Sort of a note. A page had been torn from a book of poems and attached to the table in front of him by the expeditious method of stabbing a hunting knife through the paper and into the wood. It was a short piece and the last two lines had been circled with the slash-pointed calligraphy pen that lay beside it. It was not a Pentel, but like it, and also made in Japan.

MORPHINE

Groß ist die Ähnlichkeit der beiden schönen
Jünglingsgestalten, ob der eine gleich
Viel blässer als der andre, auch viel strenger,
Fast möcht ich sagen viel vornehmer aussieht
Als jener andre, welcher mich vertraulich
In seine Arme schloß—Wie lieblich sanft

War dann sein Lächeln und sein Blick wie selig!
Dann mocht es wohl geschehn, daß seines Hauptes
Mohnblumenkranz auch meine Stirn berührte
Und seltsam duftend allen Schmerz verscheuchte
Aus meiner Seel—Doch solche Linderung,
Sie dauert kurze Zeit; genesen gänzlich
Kann ich nur dann, wenn seine Fackel senkt
Der andre Bruder, der so ernst und bleich.—
Gut ist der Schlaf, der Tod ist besser—freilich
Das beste wäre, nie geboren sein.

"*Morphine?*" I said. "Is that morphine? Are we talking about drugs here?"

"'Sleep is good, Death is better,'" Franz said, translating the circled lines, "'the most best is never to be born.' This is Heine, Heinrich Heine. I don't think it has anything to do with morphine."

"It says morphine," I said.

"It is a *bildlich.*"

"A what?"

"Metaphorisch."

"I would have thought MTV was more his style," I said.

"You have to tell me everything that he told you, word for word," Franz said. "It is the quote of a romantic teenager. They teach this in all the schools. But, *ja,* I agree. From Hans I would expect a quote from the disco at Krazy Kangaruh. AC/DC or Madonna. Yet every person is entitled to their choice of last words.

"Two days ago you were all over town asking questions about him. Do you want to tell me why you went skiing with him? Alone?"

I told him how Arlene Tavetian had come to the Laundromat, then run into us at Rasthaus Ferwell, how Marie had pressured me to help the bereaved mother discover her daughter's final days. "I just figured that if I spent a day alone with Hans he would talk. About the avalanche, the girl, whatever. They were regular clients,

Tanaka and the girl. Besides, it was an excuse to get out of the house and up on the mountain."

"I tell you, Rick, you have a knack for this. You go around asking questions and the first thing you find out is that someone else is asking questions, all the way from Japan. Then you find out that someone stole something from the dead man's apartment. Then that the accident was a murder. Maybe you were a detective back in Dublin. Richard Cochrane of Royal Dublin Constabulary? Eh?"

"They call them the Gardia back home."

"Gardia. Oh, is that what they call them? So, you really are Irish?"

"Was it really a suicide? Why should he kill himself? He got away with one killing. He didn't know you pulled me out of the crevasse. Odds were nobody was going to find me till spring. You really figure this is a suicide note?"

"*Ja*. Definitely."

"It's not like he wrote something in his own handwriting and signed it, is it?"

"Perhaps I did not translate it well for you," Franz said. "It is a poem they teach us in grade school. They tell us that it is a poem about escape from earthly woe. Personally it was not my interest. But it is what they teach."

"I don't believe it. Hans was full of himself. He was really strutting. This guy felt no more guilt than Klaus Barbie. None. However he killed Tanaka, he was proud of it. Like he was proud that he dumped me down that hole. According to him, it was some kind of contest. And Wendy, Hiroshi, and me—we lost. It made him the great skier. It was going to make him popular with the girls. Trust me. This guy only liked other people's death. Not his own."

"I like things simple," Franz said. "We have a forensic specialist in from Vienna. A specialist in the pathological evidence of suicide. There is nothing in the forensic evidence to contradict suicide."

"He didn't kill himself."

"You would have to imagine someone very clever and complicated to make it look like Hans Lantz shot himself when he did not. Who is this person? Why would they do this? Where are they?

No. I like this better. *Skiführer* has clients killed *by accident* in an avalanche. Then has another client fall, *by accident*, into a crevasse. Filled with guilt, he kills himself."

"If he was feeling so guilty, how come he wasn't the one who called for help for me? How about that?"

"Afraid," Franz said. "Afraid to admit so much incompetence. Rather than face it, he killed himself."

"Who are you trying to kid?"

"It's been a bad season. We have maybe four, five months to make our money." This is a litany that Austrians recite to justify everything from ÖS24 for a cup of coffee to the practice of putting a 200 to 300 percent markup on phone calls from hotels and *pensions*. Franz's own additional income, the incomes of his various in-laws, cousins, and friends all come from the winter season.

"So you don't like the idea of a ski guide psycho killer knocking off the punters. That's quite a nightmare for our guests."

"*Ja.*" He nodded. "Like the great white shark in *Jaws*. Chase the tourists away. But our great white shark is dead. I like things quiet. Everyone making money."

"He talked about having money. That he didn't have to work as a guide anymore. He had something else going. Did he have a lot of cash around? Did you check his bank account? Did you look under the mattress? Maybe someone paid him to kill Hiroshi Tanaka or Wendy Tavetian."

"For now, it was an accident. Both them and you. And a suicide."

"Bullshit," I said. "I know that's not true. I don't know why you want to cover it up, but I'm going to see to it that it's not covered up."

"Don't do anything to embarrass me," he said.

"I know you saved my life . . ."

"*Ja.*"

". . . but fuck you, Franz. That son of a bitch tried to kill me. He killed two other people, at least, and maybe there's someone else or something else involved and more people are going to die. So I don't buy your version and I'll go over your head or to TV news or whatever if I have to."

"You know, Rick, I'm a good Catholic. I don't think you were ever a priest. A big investigation, maybe someone will look at your Irish passport. You're a nice guy and you got a nice baby and a nice girlfriend and mostly you don't cause anybody any trouble. But if you are in the middle of trouble, trouble will fall on you."

"Hey, Franz, don't push me around. Loosely speaking, what's good for me is good for you. But for the same reason, I can take you down with me."

He shook his big head slowly no with an expression more in sorrow than in anger. "What is good for me is everything smooth and quiet. My interest in your Laundromat only makes me your friend when everything is smooth and quiet," Franz said. Technically, one of his sons is my Austrian partner. He lives in Vienna. I've only met him twice. He's the one who gave Franz his first grandson. Franz's Frau accepts the son's share rather than making me ship it all the way to Vienna. "Why don't you go home?" he asked me, sounding merely curious.

"There are no Alps in Ireland."

"I think you cannot go home."

"I have a good business here. A home."

"What is it? Drugs? The IRS? It isn't politics—you don't have politics. Did you kill somebody? Americans are always killing people."

"Do you really think he killed himself?"

"Yes," he said, very emphatically. "Maybe somewhere you were a policeman like me. Maybe in America. Are American policemen like they are on television? Do they say things like 'I'm going to get to the bottom of this!' 'We'll get him, no matter what it takes?' Mike Hammer, *bang bang*. Hunter, *bang bang*. Starsky and Hutch, *bang, bang, bang*.

"Anyway, I think in America there is plenty of murders, *ja?* Here, in Austria, there is no murders. We have the lowest murder rate in the world, of any developed country. We have the lower murder rate than Japan, even.

"Suicides, *ja,* we have suicides. So, an American, maybe he automatically thinks, he sees a dead person, a bullet wound, it is murder. Austria, we don't think this. Here it is important to be correct. We are interested in order. What is important here"—he sort of joked—"is what are we going to do about the Swedes."

The St. Antonians are distraught over the Swedes. They speak about them in a collective negative that I have never heard one group of white people apply to another group of white people before. The problem is that the social improvers of Sweden have pushed the price of a litre of beer up to $5 and a bottle of Vodka to $30. So it's worth it for them to come all the way to Austria—thirty-six hours on a discount group bus—to drink. Austrian drinkers, who tend to be slow, steady alcoholics, starting with a beer at breakfast, another at ten, some schnapps and beer at lunch, then some genial conviviality from the end of work until bedtime, claim that the Swedes don't know how to drink and that's why they get out of hand. They sing, yell, and curse. They battle in the clubs and in the streets. The Austrians don't mind the fistfights, but they hate the noise.

"This is for you," Franz said, handing me a ski bag with ATOMIC written on the side. I opened the bag. "They were Lantz's," Franz said. "Much better than French skis." They were Atomic 733SLs with ESS bindings, top-of-the-line stuff, and they looked brand-new. "You lost yours and he'll never use them."

EIGHT

THE SHORT MAN

"Hi, Tony," the little guy who walked into my Laundromat said.

"My name's Rick," I said. "It's on the sign over the door."

"I like the Rick's American Laundromat thing," he said, "but you're Anthony Michael Cassella, from New York City. West End Avenue and 96th Street, as a matter of fact."

"You got the wrong guy," I said.

"My name's Chip Sheen," he said, holding out his hand and smiling in a sociable way, "and I'm with the IRS."

NINE

FRENCH COOKING

The smells coming from my apartment were so good and so distinctive that they stopped me in the street. I stood there and simply breathed. It was not sausage in any form, it was not *schinken,* it was not schnitzel. It was *beurre* and *vin rouge* and shallots, it was a slow waltz of sauté, a sense of sauce. It was nothing Teutonic. It was all French.

Marie Laure was finally up and about. Perhaps a miracle had happened and Anna Geneviève was sleeping in five-hour shifts. Or perhaps Marie Laure had finally relented and decided to accept household help. It made me very happy for two reasons. First and most obvious was that I would have a good meal. Second and more important was that it meant she was ready to travel. Chip Sheen knew. No bluff, no denial was going to stop him. All he had to do was ask the Austrians for extradition.

The point was not that the U.S.A. had a tax extradition treaty with Austria, but that my status in St. Anton rested completely on false papers. One phone call to the Irish embassy in Vienna, a cross-reference to my passport number would blow me out of my fictions in a matter of minutes. Franz, the gendarme, was certainly not going to stick his neck out to protect me. Neutrality is written into the Austrian constitution.

Once the gears started to turn, they wouldn't stop. Once I was caught up in judicial processes my life would turn into a nightmare. A series of indefensible positions that would leach my life away in legal processes, attorney's fees, holding cells, hearing rooms, courts, and, in all probability, prison.

The only sensible thing to do was get out before they got on to me. I wasn't happy about having to cut and run, but I was hardly in despair. Most of my assets were liquid. My liabilities were minimal. The actual machines were on a lease deal secured by themselves. That left two property leases—the commercial one for the Laundromat and the apartment lease. The apartment lease was the one dead loss. The season was practically over and subletting it for the spring and summer was an exercise in futility. The lease on the Laundromat space was really an asset. Selling the share of the Laundromat that was in my name would be relatively easy. The place was a cash cow. Paul of Down Under wanted it. Heidigger, who owned the laundry that had charged me that first $52 and inspired me to stay in St. Anton, would be delighted to get his hands on the place. Even if it was just to shut it down. It wasn't a real possibility because he was involved in a three-generation feud with the family of Franz, the gendarme. But I could use Heidigger to motivate Franz to buy me out. There were others. The only problem would be to make the deal fast, before the IRS put some kind of lock on the property. Once I turned something into cash, one thing I knew how to do was launder it.

So I put a cheerful face on and opened the door. "Hello, Marie, hello, Anna," I called out.

"Antony!" my mother cried.

She came running out of the kitchen with my daughter in her arms.

"Oh, Antony," she said, "what a *bellisima bambina.*"

"Uh, what are you doing here?"

"I didn't think I would be so moved by seeing her."

"How did you get here? And why are you speaking Italian?"

"She really is beautiful, Antony. And so strong. What a grip."

"Mom. Were you followed? By a little guy, about twenty-five, thirty? Gray eyes, sandy hair, slight Midwestern accent, altogether too happy?"

"And I am so happy to meet Marie Laure. What a wonderful girl. You're very, very lucky. Luckier than you know. This apartment is very nice. Marie Laure showed me how the couch folds out. I can stay. What a nice girl. I really like her, Antony."

"Did I ever teach you how to spot a tail, Mom? I mean, did you even check to see if anyone was following?"

"What are you talking about, Antony?"

"Why don't you sit down and tell me what you're doing here, Mom? Not that I'm not happy to see you . . ."

"What does it look like I'm doing here . . ."

". . . but it really is an incredibly awkward . . ."

". . . I'm here to see my grandchild."

". . . time. We were just going to . . ."

"And to help of course. It's been . . ."

". . . pack."

"Pack?"

"Yes, Mom. Pack."

"What are you talking about, Rick?" Marie Laure said, coming out of the kitchen. However nice she had been to my mother, her voice had that sleepless edge when she spoke to me.

"Rick—who's Rick?" my mother said.

"It's okay, we can go back to Tony," I said.

"You didn't tell me you had to pack," my mother said to Marie.

"I don't have to pack," Marie said to my mother.

"Because if you have to pack, then I certainly can't stay," my mother said.

"Exactly," I said.

"Of course you are staying," Marie Laure said.

"Umm, Marie, my beloved," I said.

"Open some wine for dinner," Marie Laure said. "Something good, something French. Then help your mother unpack."

"I don't need any help unpacking," my mother said. "I thought you were going to pack."

"Exactly," I said.

"It will be very nice to have your mother here," Marie said. "I am looking forward to it."

"I can help. I want to help," my mother said. "With the baby, with the shopping, with whatever I can."

"We're moving," I said.

"Ridiculous," Marie said.

"A man from the IRS showed up at the Laundromat today," I said.

I shouldn't even have had to explain what that meant. It was, unfortunately, an open-and-shut matter. Right or wrong, and it was mostly wrong, if the IRS could put their hands on me, they had me. It had been a setup, a very good one. A hatred of prison and a horror of legal fees was what had kept me on the run—if a life as alpine, lucrative, as full of love and sunshine as mine could be called "on the run." I thought I had made a remarkably good adjustment to fugitivehood. I saw no reason to renounce it. I thought both my mother and the mother of my daughter would agree with me wholeheartedly, without even a discussion.

"I am not moving," Marie said.

"You shouldn't," my mother said to her.

"I have a baby to take care of," Marie said.

"She's absolutely right," my mother said. "It's about time you dealt with this."

"How come you're taking their side?" I asked my mother. "You just met them, both of them."

"If you are moving, you are moving by yourself," Marie said.

"Don't worry—he's not moving," my mother said.

"And if you move," Marie said, "don't bother to come back."

"He's very smart. He'll figure out a way to deal with them," my mother said.

"Mom, me and my lawyers have been trying to figure it out for six years."

"You haven't tried hard enough," my mother said. "Fix it, make a deal."

"*Exactement,*" Marie said. "You have a family now."

"Antony," my mother said, in that tone of command that hadn't really worked since I was ten, "it is time that you grew up. You must take some responsibility."

"*Exactement,*" Marie said.

"Talk to the man," my mother said.

"The IRS doesn't deal," I said wearily. At least, not in my case. I was on somebody's enemies list. Forever. Or until the Republicans were gone. Which, considering how things looked in 1990, would be longer.

"Nonsense," Marie said.

"Everybody deals," my mother said, with a rhythm and a gesture from her Sicilian childhood.

The baby started to cry. My mother rocked her. But the baby kept crying. Marie Laure went to my mother, took Anna, and put her to the breast. It was a big swollen breast, luscious and full of milk. Too bad I wasn't allowed to play with it. Anna Geneviève became very happy very quickly, in her greedy way.

"I'll give it a shot," I said. "But you better be ready to pack."

"*Jamais,*" Marie Laure said.

"You'll fix it," my mother said as she walked me to the door. Taking my arm and speaking very quietly she added, "She's a nice girl, Antony—you should marry her."

The IRS, like the old FBI, possesses several powerful myths. The first is that of incorruptibility. This is not true. Agents have been and continue to be bought. Not with the frequency of Mexican police, but it does happen. It wasn't going to happen in my case.

Another is that there is a certain degree of fairness. Also not true. The IRS prefers the easy opponent. They will fight the odd tax battle all the way to the Supreme Court, but, like any other government agency, they have limited resources. They do not want to spend 11 percent of their legal budget on any single case. Therefore they fight less vigorously if they expect their opponent to mount a major legal defense. Major does not mean the sort of defense you or I could put up, no matter how inflamed we were. Major refers to the type of legal resources that Fortune 500 corporations routinely employ.

The usual mess with the IRS involves underpayment. It's an argument over accounting practices. What income is what type of income and what deductions are allowed. They are not saying you failed to mention your income or manufactured false deductions. If they win, as they usually do to some degree, they claim an additional payment, plus interest, plus penalties. While the actual amounts are administered at various levels of pain, the matter can be settled by simply paying money. This was not my problem.

The much more serious mess is tax evasion. You implicitly agree about the amount due. Why else did you avoid payment by failing to report your full income or by falsifying deductions. At their discretion, this can be treated just like underpayment. Then all they want is payments, interest, and penalties. But if they want it to be a criminal offense, it is. With prison sentences as well as fiscal penalties. What determines the difference? That's an excellent question, as my accountant once said to me. It depends on whether you're Lockheed, Al Capone, General Electric, or the mayor of New York, who your lawyer is, and if your moon is in Sagittarius. That was not my problem.

I was accused of destroying my records after the IRS had requested an audit. This naturally put me in line to be penalized for underpayment since I could hardly document either my income or expenses. It set me up to be charged with false reporting and nonpayment. The logic is that if I destroyed the records I had a reason. The only reason the IRS can conceive is that I was destroying evidence of tax evasion. Each destroyed document is one count of obstruction of justice.

Obstruction of justice, like perjury or contempt of court, is a crime that sounds innocuous. Compared to rape, armed robbery, assault with a deadly weapon, murder, kidnapping, fraud, and burglary it sounds like some sort of technicality. But it is a crime against the justice system and, like all systems, its very first duty is to itself. It is more important, in some ways, to punish the perjurer than to catch the murderer, because if society does not believe that there is a certain amount of truth in the witness stand, then the system fails and there is no court to control any murderer. If Admiral Poindexter lies to Congress, if Ollie North destroys records, they are guilty of obstruction of justice. They are guilty of preventing the system from operating. Such crimes are taken very seriously indeed. It takes hundreds and hundreds of thousands of dollars in legal fees and political clout on a presidential scale to stay out of prison.

Obstruction of justice was not my problem.

My problem was that I had crossed some very powerful people. Some were out of office because of me, some were still in office. All of them still had major political muscle. They had promised to set me up. They succeeded, as I had known they would, though with more success than I had anticipated. They were the sort of people never to go back on a promise. Unless it was expedient. Then they'd go back on a promise sooner than Ronald Reagan could forget the name of the head of the Joint Chiefs of Staff. But the likelihood of my making them back off was subminimal. Operating out of Rick's American Laundromat, it was nil.

My mother did not understand that.

Marie Laure wasn't prepared to even hear about it. And if she understood it, it didn't matter. Motherhood had turned her—I hesitate to say unreasonable—less flexible. Leaning toward adamant.

Anna Geneviève would line up on the side of the breast that fed her.

So even though it was an exercise in futility, I went to see the man.

"Sure we can deal," Chip Sheen said.

"We can?"

"Absolutely, guy." He had sandy hair, slate-gray eyes, and a quick mechanical grin that snapped on and snapped off. "Would you like a beer? Gee, I love this Austrian beer. And they serve it in such big glasses—not like back in the States."

"What kind of deal did you have in mind?"

"What kind of deal did you have in mind, guy?"

"Oh, I was thinking about something along the lines of the IRS realizes I was framed, that I paid all my taxes, and the whole thing is dropped."

"You'd still owe Social Security for the last six years. You haven't paid in a dime."

"Hey, I'd be happy to pay my Social Security."

"Then there's the income tax you owe the Austrian government. And the Republic of France. You don't report every schilling and franc that gets dropped in your laundry machines."

"Bullshit," I said. Certain that even if he knew it, he couldn't know how much, or prove it. "And why should you care?"

The grin snapped on. "You mean I don't know by how much and I can't prove it," he said. "I do know that it's a cash business and that you or your wife . . ."

"We're not married," I said.

"She seems like a really nice girl. And you have the baby now. You should marry her."

"Thanks for the advice."

"Anytime. It's always you or her that empties the machines, guy. So it's axiomatic that you're stealing from the government. I just wanted you to know that I know and that I could let the Austrians know. Just so you know how much of a box you are in."

"Thanks," I said. "We were discussing a deal. To get me out of the box."

"Yes, we were. But it's important to understand what a terrific, inescapable box it is so that you can appreciate the deal. Otherwise, you might not, guy."

"Do me a favor," I said.

"Sure, guy, what can I do for you?"

"Don't call me guy, guy."

The grin snapped off. But he decided to be pleasant. "Sure, gu. . . . Of course. But what should I call you? You didn't want me to call you Tony. And I don't want to call you Rick, because I know you're not Rick. You understand what I mean, guy?"

"Call me Tony," I said.

"Nah, the heck with it," he said, "I'll call you Rick. It would confuse everything if I start calling you Tony. Until we get back to the States, of course. I mean here. Here they all know you as Rick, and if all of a sudden you became Tony, it would be very strange."

"Are we going back to the States, Chip?"

"My real name is Chester. Call me Chip. I like Chip a lot better."

"I will," I said. "I'll call you Chip."

"That's great. We're going to get along just fine."

"What's this about going back to the States, Chip?"

"Oh, I assumed you wanted to. I mean isn't that what all expats want? Go home and have all the things they miss? Burgers and fries and apple pie? Macy's, the Mets, CBS, and Monday Night Football? Gosh, America's full of great things. Bargains. Have you been shopping here? Do you know what I paid for a banana? I paid eleven schillings for a banana. That's a buck a banana. And jeans. Hey, I don't know about you, but when I want to relax, when I want to kick back and just be one of the guys, I like to have my pair of Levi 501s on. Back home I can go to Jack's House of Discount and get me a pair of Levi 501s for twenty-one ninety-five. A pair of jeans over here is seventy-nine ninety-five, eighty-nine ninety-five, ninety-nine ninety-five. Gosh, you must miss the US of A."

"Gosh, Chip, I hadn't thought about it like that."

"Wow, if I'd been away from home as long as you, by golly, I would."

"I like to ski, Chip."

"See that? Even skiing is better in the US of A. I mean we have more snow in New Jersey than you guys do here in Austria." He laughed. He thought it was funny.

"Yeah, it's been a bad year."

"If you like skiing, America's got the East—Vermont, New Hampshire, Maine, even New York. Why, they had two Olympics in Lake Placid, New York. Two of them. Then there's the Rocky Mountains, right from Idaho down through Wyoming to Colorado and New Mexico and Arizona. Then there's the Sierras. You can ski in California. In California you can ski in the morning and drive to the coast and surf in the afternoon. Or you could go up to Canada, which is practically some more United States."

"What do you want, Chip?"

"And they don't go around killing people in avalanches. No-sir-ee-bob. Not in the US of A."

"What's the deal, Chip?"

"We were speaking of avalanches."

"We were?"

"Sure, we were. And you're messed up with this thing with Hiroshi Tanaka."

"What thing with Hiroshi Tanaka?"

"Oh, heck," he said. "Here I thought we were together on this. Here I thought we were going to make a deal. Here I thought we were going to help each other. Darn it."

"Do me a favor, Chip. No, two favors."

"I don't know that I want to, Rick. Now that you don't want to cooperate."

"Oh, these are favors you'll want to do."

"I will?"

"Fuckin' A," I said. "First, stop using baby words. *Darn* and *heck*. It makes you sound like an asshole. Enough of that shit. Then you can tell me what the fuck you're talking about."

"If I want to express myself without recourse to foul language . . ."

"Then don't say *darn* and *heck*. It makes me think you're a Mormon."

"What's wrong with being a Mormon?"

"There's nothing wrong with being a Mormon."

"I hope not," he said, "because I am a Mormon."

"I'm happy for you."

"No, you're not," he said. "I know that. I understand that. I accept it. But I will have you know that Mormons are very nice people. We believe in honesty and hard work and integrity. If a Mormon gives you his word you can be pretty darn sure that his word is better than a New York bond!"

"Do you ever get the feeling that you're talking to someone who is having a different conversation than you are? Does this happen to you a lot?"

"So I don't use filthy language," he said, and something far away was happening behind those gray eyes. He had the body of someone who does his Nautilus or calisthenics with dedication and regularity—to be fit, not to bulk up—and those toned-up muscles gave a slightly too emphatic push to his gestures. "It's a pledge I took. That doesn't mean I'm not one of the guys. That doesn't mean I don't sit back for a couple of brewskis now and again. I'm a little defensive about being a Mormon. You can understand why."

"Chip, it's been nice knowing you," I said. "When you decide you want to tell me about this deal, you call my lawyer."

"Rick," he said, "sit the fuck down and listen."

"That's better," I said.

"Did that sound right?"

"Abso-fucking-lutely," I said.

"Good. But be straight with me."

"Gosh, I'll do my best," I said.

"What's your involvement with Hiroshi Tanaka?"

"None," I said.

"Oh, darn," he said. Truly upset.

"There you go again, with the baby words."

"Rick, I'm not effing around. I will go to the Austrian tax authorities and point them at your little laundry. I will start extradition. You can run but you can't hide. Not with the girl and a new baby."

"Don't forget my mother," I said. "My mother just arrived."

"I didn't know that."

"I guessed that you followed her to me," I said.

"No. Not at all."

"Don't tell me you came all the way from Washington . . . ?"

"Yes, Washington."

". . . all the way from Washington just looking for me."

"I wish you wouldn't keep denying that you're involved with Tanaka. It makes it all very difficult."

"You know, I'm getting sick of telling this story, but I'll tell it again. There was a girl killed in that avalanche. She had a mother. Her mother met me, by accident, in the Laundromat and . . ."

"Sooner or later, everyone comes to Rick's," Chip said. He giggled. "At least everyone who's dirty."

". . . she wanted to know more about her daughter's life and death here. I agreed, under pressure from my wife, to find out what I could."

"That's what you say," Chip said. "But I saw you going to Tanaka's apartment right after he died. Then you go skiing with Hans Lantz, who tries to kill you. Why would Hans Lantz try to kill you? If you're not involved with Hiroshi Tanaka."

"How do you know he tried to kill me? What do you know about Hans Lantz? What the fuck is going on here?"

Chip pointed to himself. "I'm the investigator." He pointed at me. "You're the criminal." And back at himself. "I hold the cards. I ask the questions."

"You're a Mormon. I'm an Italian New Yorker. You couldn't figure your way out of a paper bag if someone bent it double. If you want me to play, you better talk to me."

"I'm the one that has you in a box."

"Who the fuck cares? That's the point, you know. Who the fuck cares? I disappeared once. I can do it again. It took you six years to find me, and I wasn't hiding. I got money in the bank and you don't know which bank and the account is numbered and you don't know the number and I have cash in my pocket and I can be out of here in a New York second."

"What about your cute new baby?"

"What about her?"

"You wouldn't leave her."

"You don't know that. She wouldn't be the first girl I've left. Maybe I'll take her with me. Maybe I'll send for her later. But you, you give a shit. You care. You got some kind of point system back in your office. 'Hey, Chipper closed two more cases than Harold this week. Chipper gets two gold stars. That makes him officer of the month. Oh, hooray for Chipper.' I know what feds are like. I know what bureaucrats are like. I even have a pretty fair idea of what a Mormon is. And they don't drink beer. They don't even drink coffee."

"That story about the girl's mother—is that true?"

"I swear by the bones of Joseph Smith," I said. Smith invented Mormonism.

He nodded reverently. Maybe he was a Mormon. "About the beer," he said. "A guy's got to fit in with the guys a little bit. Otherwise they think you're a Holy Joe."

"I won't tell the elders," I said.

"What do you know about Hiroshi Tanaka?" he said.

"I don't know shit about Hiroshi Tanaka except that he was an okay skier, had lots of money, claimed that he was descended from samurai, and liked young pussy."

"That's almost more than we know," he said. "You may still be the man I need."

"Who's we?" I asked. "You're not IRS."

"I am if I want to be," he said.

"What's the deal?" I said.

"Tanaka had something. I was after Tanaka and he had some material that was important to us."

"What did he have, Chip?"

"This other guy—this other Japanese that's been hanging around Tanaka's apartment—maybe he's got it. If he's got it, could you get it from him?"

"You got warrants or something? Are the gendarmes or the *Polizei* working with you?"

"They're financial records," he said.

"A book?" I said. "A big book?"

"Why? Did you find a big book?"

"No, I didn't find anything—I haven't been looking."

"It could be a big book, but we don't think it's a big book. It's computerized stuff. It'll be in a computer format. If it were the printout—you know, hard copy—it would be a big book. But it wouldn't be a printout. It would be on a disc."

"Floppies? Regular five-and-a-half-inch floppy discs?"

"No. Not those."

"Those new little ones—what are they?—three-and-a-quarter-inch, like for a laptop?"

"Not those," Chip said. "Probably an optical disc."

"An optical disc?"

"It looks a lot like a CD. The other possibility is that it might be on tape."

"On tape? Like a cassette of the Stones to put in my Walkman?"

"No. Big tape. For a main-frame computer. Like one-inch videotape."

"These are pretty heavy-duty records."

"They're very complicated," Chip said.

"Whose financial records are these?"

"What do you mean, whose financial records are these?"

"Well, I mean are they the records of the Medellin cartel? Are they records of all the cocaine traffic between Colombia and Miami? Are they the Sicilian Mafia? The new memoirs of David Stockman?"

"These are really important records," Chip said.

"If I don't know what they are, how am I going to recognize them?"

"You wouldn't understand them anyway. They're all in code."

"Coded financial records?"

"If you find them," he said, "I can clear your problems with the IRS."

"Everything?"

"Just about. Do you know where the records are?"

"They claim I underpaid by forty-six thousand dollars. Do you know what the interest and penalties on forty-six thousand dollars is? Accumulating and compounding for six years? I owe over a quarter million dollars."

"Is it a mistake?"

"Absolutely," I said.

"Then I'm sure we can clear it up."

"The twenty-two counts of tax evasion? You know I really reported everything I earned."

"I think that can be arranged. One hand washes the other." He demonstrated. "How soon can you find the records?"

"Soon, Chip, soon. You know what I'm really worried about, Chip? The obstruction-of-justice charges."

"We can clear that," he said. "If you get the records."

"All four hundred sixty-six counts?"

"Yes. You solve my problem, I'll solve yours."

I told Marie Laure and my mother what Chip Sheen had said. They were very pleased.

That meant they didn't get it.

My mother nodded sagely. "There is always a deal," she said in a tone of parental vindication. "There is always an arrangement."

It was a tone of voice that is one of nature's primary ways of driving human children from the warmth and safety of familial shelter into the cold cruel world to become adults. "What are you," I said, "a *consigliore* in a Godfather novel? Was it you who taught Mario Puzo *il via siciliano*?"

"It will be good to go to America," Marie said. "It will make Anna Geneviève very 'appy. She wants to visit her *grand-mère* in Brooklyn and New York City where 'er mother and father first became lovers."

"Anna Geneviève couldn't care less at this point," I said.

"What do you say, *ma chérie,*" Marie cooed to Anna, "do you want to go to Manhattan?" The baby made a sort of noise. I admit that. "Anna Geneviève understands everything," Marie Laure said. Human beings have a powerful anthropomorphic urge. No one and no thing, from equipment to infants, is safe from the need to impose feelings, ideas, and ideals that are just like ours. A car won't start and it's sullen. A cat rests—people see smug self-satisfaction. A dog cocks its head—it's the face of puzzlement. Our daughter was born with the knack of looking like she possessed enlightenment. I took her and I looked into her blue eyes. She looked back and I fell right into the anthropomorphic delusion.

"You're right," I said. "She looks like she knows everything." I would have preferred to debate with her directly, but Marie Laure was her official spokesman. It's nice to debate gender roles and try to demolish them like they do in America, but they seem to be more deeply rooted and less superficial than we all had supposed. That's what the babies tell us. "We have to look at this so-called deal," I said to her mother. "We have to ask some questions."

"Where do you want your daughter to grow up?" Marie Laure said. "Should she grow up in 'iding? Or in a good place? That is the important question."

"I would like it if she grew up somewhere near me," my mother said. "If you want to take my feelings into account."

"Okay, Mother, you were right," I said. "It was worth talking to this guy. If only because it means we have a chance to deal with things in a measured and rational way." As far as I was concerned my conversation with Chip Sheen had only changed things a matter of degree. Our sojourn in Austria and my incarnation as Richard Cochrane, lapsed Roman Catholic priest of County Clare, Irish Republic, was over. The reality was that I only had two options—run now or play for time and run a little later. Time to get a decent price for the Laundromat. Then we would disappear. There are lots of Alps—Swiss, French, Italian, Yugoslavian, German. Even Lichtenstein has Alps. There are lots of borders and lots of crossings. There are names and passports for sale. The reasons that I'd kept this identity and the papers that went with it lay somewhere between laziness and if-it-isn't-broken-don't-fix-it. If it looked like Europe was too small to hide in, what with two generations of women to take with me, possibly three, there was Australia, New Zealand, Chile, and Argentina. I'd been dying to ski Portillo and Las Leñas. There was Sapporo in Japan. Maybe it was about time that someone started to ski Nepal and Tibet.

■

But the women had been talking in my absence. They were united, mother and mother. They had cast me in a snowball Western movie—a frostbitten John Wayne riding out to clear my name so's my family could stand tall. Confronting the league of mothers directly would just harden their position. I know something of women. They would dig in, it would become the long and bloody business of trench warfare. It was best that they be led, gently, to discovering the truth by themselves. "Don't you even want to know the details?" I said.

"I 'ave faith in you," Marie Laure said. "You can do this. That is all I need to know."

"What does he want you to find?" my mother asked.

"That's a good question," I said. "There are better ones, but that's a good one to start with. Chip Sheen was after Hiroshi Tanaka, who died in an avalanche. That avalanche might have been deliberately set. The man who led him into that avalanche more or less admitted that to me, then tried to kill me, then he died. His death certainly looks like suicide but I wouldn't bet the laundry on it. Plus there's a girl who's dead. Let's not entirely forget Wendy Tavetian, because Ms. Tavetian set off some powerful feelings in people and maybe has more to do with this than we know. Anyway, Tanaka died before Chip Sheen could get to him." Anna Geneviève looked bored. I put her face down, one hand under her belly. When I did that she stretched herself out straight, arms and legs extended. I swooped her through the air—a game called Flying Baby. My mother looked nervous. As if I would drop Anna Geneviève. I put her on my arm, on the football carry, and just rocked her.

"Now Sheen is looking for something that belonged to Tanaka," I said. "He is very reluctant to tell me what. When I ask him if he has warrants or is working with the gendarmes, then he doesn't answer that question and says he's looking for 'financial records.' Whatever the contents are, the dingus itself is either computer tape or an optical disc. Which looks like a CD but is used for computers. Next question."

"Where will you look?" my mother asked.

"That's a funny next question, to my way of thinking," I said. "I ask myself things like: 'What's going on here?' 'Is there just one criminal psychopath or am I stepping into something truly serious?' 'Being a new father, earning a living, doing a little skiing, making sure that strangers can get their clothes clean—isn't that enough for me to do this month?' Those are good questions."

"Where will you look?" Marie Laure asked.

"Chip Sheen thinks that 'the other Japanese' might have this thing. Now he doesn't bother to say whether or not this other Japanese has a legit claim to the dingus. He also fails to mention the Musashi Trading Company. Anyway, I already know that the other Japanese, Mike Hayakawa, is also very cagey about saying what this dingus is and he also wants me to look for it. That means he doesn't have it. He thinks that maybe the Tavetians have it. That it might have been with the girl's things. Franz, the gendarme, says no, not possible, only the girl's things were passed on. All is correct. But maybe Arlene and Bob Tavetian do actually have it. None of which I mentioned to Chip Sheen, so I can take a week to discover it for him and look like I'm doing something.

"But an even better question," I said, "is, Who is Chip Sheen?"

"What do you mean?" my mother said.

"Is he IRS? Could he turn me in to the IRS? Yes. But is he IRS?"

"It's good to see you at work again," Marie Laure said. "I like to see you think." She moved close to me and put her head on my shoulder. From my neck to my waist, I felt the soft human warmth of her wash into me as if I had a special set of receptor cells just ready and waiting for that moment. It was the first time she had touched me in a womanly way since Anna's birth. "He is a very smart man." She said it to my mother, but I heard her in all the places where the message was really sent. I wanted her desperately.

"But the best question of all," I said, "is, Is it a good deal?"

"You tell me, my smart man," Marie said.

"It's a great deal," my mother said. "All you have to do is find this thing, and everything gets fixed."

"Yeah," I said. "Find one little thing and a quarter million dollars in interest and penalties—gone! Twenty-two counts of tax evasion—gone! Four hundred sixty-six counts of obstruction of justice—gone!"

"It's too good," my mother said, the way she does when she figures out the plot before the hero and tells the television about it.

"Right. And it's too easy. A real cop, he would tell me he might recommend leniency to the prosecutor who would tell the judge I was a cooperative and valuable guy. But no promises." I had to make them understand that Chip Sheen was willing to give away the store because it wasn't his to give. "Even if this dingus is so important that they're willing to drop all the charges against me, they don't say so on the first date. Also, if he really is any kind of government agent, he's got to consult—he's got to get three, four approvals. Nobody takes that much responsibility on their own."

"Once you get the thing then you can make him give you a letter or something that will make him live up to the deal," my mother said.

"*Mais oui,* of course," Marie Laure said.

Anna Geneviève fell asleep.

"What I have to do is string this guy along. To keep him from turning me in while we figure out some kind of game plan of our own." Please understand, I said silently, that all I can get for us is time—time to get where we're going next. Which is not at all bad. We have a good life. A good way to make good money—in any currency—clean air, safe streets, scenery. With a little better paper, a moustache, and some window dressing we can make it a permanent fix and have it on some other mountain.

"This is my man. Enough of the laundries," Marie Laure said. "I am tired of the laundries. I like 'im when 'e is a detective."

"I like him when he makes me a grandmother," my mother said.

TEN

LOVE DREAMS

I dreamt that night of America.

Wayne took me by the hand. We were in Central Park. By the Shakespeare Festival Theatre. Blossoms were falling. We stepped carefully around the beggar with running sores and tossed some money to the scabby one. He muttered, "Tourist fuck" when he clutched the coins. We stepped off the curb and out of the park.

"Hi, sweeties," a guy said to us. I didn't say anything.

Wayne was small, like when I left. He clutched my hand tighter. A full-cleavaged woman in a red dress, high-heel sneakers, and Tina Turner wig turned her face from us.

"You were supposed to be here, Pops," Wayne said.

"I left you a condominium."

"Fat city, Dads, fat city."

"Look," I said.

"Look at MTV," he said. When he faced me, he'd grown. He was bigger than me and needed a shave. He was at least sixteen. And very gay. Then he laughed. "Do you remember what I'm supposed to do with my life?"

"You wanted to be a fireman?"

"Stick it up your ass. I never did," he said, and walked away. It was true. He never did want to be a fireman and he never had that much attitude. He went off with some boys.

Then his mother said, "Come on up. Just for a cup of coffee. I've changed. Let me tell you about it."

She put her hand in my pants and did fun things with my penis, which responded avidly even though I kept trying to say, "But I'm married now." She bent over, raised her skirt, lowered her underwear. She had a more photogenic vagina than I remembered from real life and a shapely ass. Even if it showed her age, which I could see with mean X-ray eyes.

"Do it," she said. "Enough of the responsibility shit. Do it to me."

It sounded inviting and it had been a long time since my penis had been anywhere except hanging in my pants. The doctor had said Marie would be sore for two to three months. I could see where that would happen. And, being the late twentieth century semiliberated male that I was, I knew I had to accept the noninsertion rule until healing took place. There are so many other fun things to do and we had had so much fun doing them before, that it never occurred to me that birth would be the death of sex. But it had been. Her body currently belonged to another process. Her love belonged to another person. I understood. I sympathized. And it made my sexuality feel as welcome as a cockroach at the embassy ball.

So I took my erection in one hand and with the other I stroked the first serious offer. The lips spread easily and inside they were coated with that thick moisture that is so symbolic of welcome. I put the tip of my cock up against it, just feeling the moist heat, ready to savor the insertion.

"You know New York is impossible these days," she said, "with the homeless, the crime, the AIDS, the crack addicts—the hospitals are overwhelmed. You can't walk down the street to the drugstore. We have to move to the suburbs. But don't worry about it now—go ahead and come first."

That woke me up. I had my erection beside me. It was alone. Marie Laure was across the bed, Anna Geneviève between us.

It was dawn. The lifts wouldn't start until eight. I put on my ski clothes and boots and grabbed my skis anyway. I decided that it was time to learn something about real backcountry skiing. Downhill skiing requires a stiff boot and a binding that nails your heel to the ski. Cross-country skiing requires a flexible boot and a binding that holds the toe down but lets the heel rise and fall for a gliding stride. Now they have special skis, bindings, and boots that will function both ways.

That may be what it's really about. Getting out into the mountains. No lifts, no pistes, no tracks, no crowds. No restaurants, no bars, no sex, no lies, no cops, no *federales,* no relationships, no property. Just being. Puritanical, cold, and in love with your own virtue. My mind is not a steady thing. It knows a story is just a story. That everyone mostly thinks they're right. People need to be right. My mother, Marie, me, Anna Geneviève—four corners of one circle, and we each are certain that we're right. Franz, the gendarme, his dog Rudi, this Chip Sheen, all the cops think they're right. Hans Lantz, killer and suicide, thought he was right. He told me so.

In the meantime, I put my skis on my shoulder and walked up the mountain. That's for eighteen-year-olds. An hour walking uphill in ski boots is worth two Jane Fondas plus one Jazzercise. Sweaty and panting, I sat alone in the sunshine at the top of the Kandahar. Moonlight is a fragile thing. Most places it is washed away by the first sun that comes along. But in the valley there is an overlap, a slow crossfade, where, in the shadow of the mountains, the moonlight stays briefly brighter than the beginning of the day.

I had a chocolate bar for the sugar rush. I put my skis on, the almost-new Atomics that once belonged to Hans Lantz, and charged down the hill. It was a good run. But not as good as I hoped it would be. Not as good as I wanted it to be. I had started thirty years too late to ever be a world-class skier.

By the time I reached the bottom I knew what I was going to do.

I found Mike Hayakawa in The Underground. He was drunk and thought it was a *Karaoke* bar. And who's to say it's not. There's a microphone, there's a piano if you want to play, and sometimes there's a piano player to keep you company if you can't. I've heard lots of people sing there. The quality varies from fair to worse, but it's a friendly place and I've never seen anybody booed off or removed by force. There are seats around the piano. If anyone likes the song they sing along. Singing loud and in public is one of the things that people like to do when they're far from home and drunk.

Bob Tavetian was at the bar.

Arlene Tavetian was at a table. With Kurt, the ski instructor. The one Wendy had fucked. Arlene was drunk. Arlene was putting the moves on him. Kurt was going for it.

Hayakawa was singing Bob Dylan's "Lay, Lady, Lay." He sang with heart. He knew all the words. He was very sincere and it made him look particularly Japanese.

Bob Tavetian saw me looking at Arlene. He saw that I could see what was going on. A man might not give a damn where his wife lays her body down, but no man likes to be seen wearing horns. It's not the sex—it's the looks you get, and the sign you wear on your chest, loser where winner used to be.

Hayakawa sang "Ballad of a Thin Man" which is the one about a Mr. Jones who doesn't know what is happening here. Tavetian finished his drink and came over to me.

"She can't help herself," he said. "Wendy was her baby. Her only baby. It hurts more than she can stand."

"Don't Think Twice, It's All Right," was Mike's next song. He was very serious about it and drank as steadily as his singing would allow. He drank Johnny Walker Black. I drank beer. I can't say he had a good voice, but nobody ever said Bob Dylan did either. Then he started to sing "Blowin' in the Wind." I would have thought it was a song that was owned by a particular time and place—memories of Martin Luther King, marching against the war in Vietnam and for the Pill. Yet everyone in the place—Aussies, Kiwis, Austrians, Americans, Swedes—seemed to know it and have some feeling for it. Two full tables, one of Brits and the other of Germans, sang along.

When he was done I crossed through the applause to the piano. Hayakawa looked up, like he'd been waiting for me. "That's my favorite," he said. "Which one do you want to hear next?"

"We have to talk about Hiroshi Tanaka," I said. "And money."

"Okay," he said. He stood up and stepped away from the microphone, staggering slightly. With a generous gesture he offered it to whoever wanted to share their music next. I took him by the arm and led him between the tables toward the door. Behind us an Australian had taken over the piano. He sang "The Dock of the Bay." A lot of people seemed to know that one too.

Like two inept conspirators, we stumbled through the night and the cold looking for a spot to converse. We went around the corner to the empty square in front of the post office.

"Hey, Rick," he said with a drunk's smile. "Laundry man, my ass—I know better."

"This dingus that you're looking for. I'm going to help you find it."

"You know where it is?"

"The key question is not where it is. It's what it's worth."

"Don't worry about a thing—it's worth a lot."

"Would you like to name a figure?"

"Musashi number one," Hayakawa said, holding up his forefinger. "Musashi take care of everything. Not to worry. No problem."

"Mike, old buddy, old pal"—I put my hands on his shoulders, looked him in the eye, and matched my beer breath to his whiskey breath—"it's time to cut the shit. You have to name a number. An actual cash figure."

"How about one million," he said.

"Dollars?" I asked, just to be sure.

"Oh, no. Yen."

"Mike, you're not even in the bidding."

"Bidding. Are there other people bidding? Then you have the piece?"

"That's what? Seven thousand dollars? I'm sorry, Mike, I made a mistake. We have nothing to talk about." I started to walk away.

"Okay, Rick," he said. "Not yen. One million . . ."

"One million what?"

"Deutsche marks!"

"Done," I said. It was about $666,000. Not bad.

"Good," he said, and sat down in the snow.

I hauled him back up and propped him up against a telephone booth. "Are you too drunk to know what you're talking about?"

"A Musashi man is always ready for business. Day or night. Drunk or sober. Work hard. Play hard. We are all one for Musashi and Musashi is number one for the world."

"And you can commit one million D marks?"

"That's our slogan," he said. "But it doesn't really translate. You have to hear it in the original. *Musashi no motoni warera ha hitotsu. Musashi ha sekai no nambah wan!*

"Can you commit that much money? You, Mikio Hayakawa?"

"Worth every dime," he said, and slowly sat down again.

I squatted beside him. "Now—what am I looking for?"

He fell asleep.

It was too good an opportunity to miss. I searched him. If Mikio "Mike" Hayakawa was a false identity, he'd really loaded up on it. Everything was in that name—international driver's license, VISA, Eurobank card, company Diner's Club and American Express Platinum cards, six golf club IDs from three different countries, company ID, medical insurance, personal checks. Swiss Air, Lufthansa, Pan Am frequent-flyer cards. He had about two thousand dollars in travelers checks on him, half in D marks, half in schillings. There was stuff in Japanese that I didn't understand. He had enough receipts for me to believe he was turning them in to be expensed. I took his keys out of his pocket. They looked familiar. I assumed he was staying in Hiroshi Tanaka's apartment.

I got a taxi. The driver and I loaded him into the cab. Handling his body, I realized that he was hard and lean. He awakened briefly when we lugged him out of the car and into the apartment, but by the time I paid the driver he was passed out on the couch.

I tossed the place.

The second most interesting thing in the room was a *manga,* a thick erotic comic book. Presumably for adults. I didn't know if it was Hayakawa's or the dead man's, if it was escapist dreaming like a Harlequin novel or had a more specific utility, like *Penthouse* or *Hustler*.

I flipped through it. If it was typical, indicative of the Japanese mind, it would make Freudians twitch and anthropologists want to play with their theses. The female sex objects were more Occidental than Oriental. The sex was assaultive—either voyeuristic or heavy-duty S & M—the girl-women tied and whipped and stabbed. But, like those few Japanese films I've seen, the sex, the violence, and the combination of the two seemed ritualized, formalized to the point of being aphysical. In the West we make a lot of noise during big moments like orgasm, torture, and death by violence. Particularly in comic books. In the *manga* they were marked, at most, by a profound sigh or an eye-widening gasp of recognition. The leading lady was little more than a girl, her pubis as hairless as an infant's, her lovemaking semiabstract and, judging by the expression on her face, predating the discovery of female orgasm. Although I prefer my sex hairier, wetter, noisier, and more mutual, I can't say the comic was dull. There was one page torn out. But the story appeared to be simple enough that it probably didn't matter.

One side of the closet held Hayakawa's things. Two suits, some ski clothes and casual wear. There was a *gi* for one of the martial arts. And a black belt to tie it closed. The other side of the closet belonged to the dead man. I don't know why the difference was so completely and immediately obvious, but it was. Perhaps clothes that are hung unused, without the intent to be used agitating them, acquire additional inertia and solidity in their storage. Hiroshi Tanaka had been an avid skier. His ski wear had been the best that money could buy. There was a shelf of ski books and ski magazines. He wore sandals in the house and had a variety of them, including the kind that have a surface of rubber spikes that point upward at the feet. Most of the rest of his clothes had been packed in boxes. They sat there waiting for someone to decide what to do with them.

Mike Hayakawa was not representing the family. Had he been, he would have sent the personal effects to some home somewhere. But I already knew that. Just as I knew that what he was looking for was not a family heirloom.

I found an address book. But it was Hayakawa's. I leafed through it.

The most interesting thing and the really significant discovery was the police envelope with the cataloged personal effects. It contained sets of keys to places other than the St. Anton apartment. It contained Hiroshi Tanaka's wallet. Credit cards. Receipts. A collection of business cards. I took the receipts and business cards. A surprising amount of cash. DM10,000, ÖS23,000. Combined, that was about $8,900. It surprised me that neither the police nor anyone else had seen fit to consider it found money. The address on Tanaka's license was different from that on his business cards, though both were in Vienna. I took the license, a business card, and the keys. I left the money.

I turned around and saw Mike looking at me. He was half asleep and all drunk, but he knew I was searching the apartment. That was all right. I knew how to handle that.

I went into the kitchen, opened the refrigerator, and took out a mineral water. Then I went back to the living room, opened the bottle, and poured it on him. He sputtered and tried to jump up. I pushed him down.

"You lied to me." I sounded terribly offended.

"What?"

"You're no friend of the family." *J'accuse!* "Did you even know this guy?"

"Sure I knew him," he said defensively.

"What'd you do? Meet him once?"

"No, no. We met several times. I was assigned . . ."

"Assigned what?"

"Never mind."

I got in his face. "You want me to help you?"

"No. I don't know. How can you help me?"

"This is what I do, asshole. I find things. I fix things. The Laundromat is but a recent affectation."

"A what?"

"I'm a detective. Gumshoe. A dick. Now, lemme guess—you were supposed to get something from Tanaka."

"No . . ."

"An optical disc."

"Yes. How did you know?"

"And he was supposed to give it to you." I stopped being the bad guy and became his friend.

"Yes," he finally admitted with a sigh.

"What? The day he died?"

"Yes," Mike said.

"But when you came to look, after he was dead, it wasn't here. But the place had been searched. Turned upside down, right?"

"Right."

"So you made up that bullshit story, friend of the family, and who here knows anything about Japs, one looks like another, so no one argued with you."

"Yes," he said, amazed. "That's how it was."

"Then—then you did nothing," I said. A funny thing happens, sometimes, when you're questioning someone. It's like when you're really hot with a new girl. Suddenly you tune in, you get it, you read their face like it was a book. "You couldn't figure out what to do next. You just sat and waited."

"What else was there to do?"

"Shit," I said. "Did you call his office? Did you go to his home, in Vienna? Did you call in the team?"

"I—I have never done anything of this nature. I must succeed. I must. But how to do this. I don't know how to do this. I was sent. By Musashi Trading Company. This is very important. I must succeed. You will help me?"

"Can you really come up with a million D marks?"

"Yes. I swear it."

"You'll tell me everything you know about him and about what you're looking for . . ."

"I don't really know."

"What don't you know?"

"What it was. I was sent to get something—something vital, something valuable. Yes, it was on a disc. But I don't know what."

"Could it have been financial records?"

"I don't think so," he said.

I didn't either. "Doesn't matter," I said. "You'll tell me what you do know and we'll find it."

"Could you give me a towel," he said.

"No," I said to Marie Laure as emphatically as I could through my hangover. "It does not mean that I'm a double dealer. It does not mean that I'm going to cut and run . . ."

"If you do . . ."

". . . not *necessarily*."

". . . you will be running alone."

"It's what you call an option."

"It's what you call *le cop-out. Le bullshit. Le crap américain.*"

"It's what you do when you're walking into a trap," I said. "You look for two ways out."

She picked up her daughter in one hand and held her close. She picked up my coffee in the other and hurled it at me.

"Goddamn you!" I yelled.

She glared at me and my raised hand, held our daughter as her shield, and dared me to strike back. My mother walked into the kitchen. She didn't have her glasses on.

"I smell coffee," she said. "Could I have some." Then she peered around. "Oh. Oh, dear. Am I interrupting?"

"No, Mother, you're not interrupting. I like coffee in my hair. This is the way we discuss things now."

"To have been with a lot of women," my mother said, "does not mean that you understand women."

I grabbed a dish towel, dried my hair, face, and shirt. "I was just explaining to . . ." I groped for the proper word. I wanted an aspirin very badly. Two. And my coffee.

"To me!" Marie Laure said. "But 'e doesn't know who I am. His girlfriend with the baby? Maybe. 'Ow does 'e introduce me now? This is uh, oh, *la je ne sais quoi*, the mother of my daughter."

"That's not what we were talking about," I said.

"He was talking to the Japanese man. He made a deal with him. For money."

"Don't sneer," I said. "It's a lot of money. If you're going to sneer at money, you don't sneer at a million deutsche marks." I picked up Marie's coffee and rather stealthily took a sip. I know she uses sugar in her coffee, I know I hate coffee with sugar, so I don't know why I expected to like it. I didn't.

"How much is that in real money?" my mother asked, her practical streak showing.

"Deutsche marks are real money. D marks are considered hard currency these days. Six hundred sixty-six thousand dollars. But that's only half the story. The rest of the story is that if I'm going to find the dingus for anybody—for Mike Hayakawa, for Chip Sheen, for you, for her"—I gestured at either my daughter or the mother of my daughter or both—"I needed someplace to start. The man from the IRS—he's no help at all. This guy from

Musashi—he's useful. He's the one that actually had a deal with Tanaka."

"And then?" Marie Laure said.

"Then, if I find this optical disc, then I see if Chip Sheen is on the level. If he is, that's great. We all go to America. Maybe Aspen, maybe Jackson Hole."

"Wyoming," Marie Laure said, recognizing the name.

"That's a long way from me," my mother said. "This is my first grandchild."

"Maybe New York," I said. "On the other hand, if Chip is not on the level, then we have another exit. A backdoor." I had to at least get them to consider the alternative. "A very rich six-hundred-thousand-dollar backdoor that will get us out of Austria into new identities, pretty much anywhere we want."

"You see," Marie Laure said, enraged, to my mother.

E L E V E N

VIENNA

There are many reasons to go to Vienna. Music. Museums. Shopping, shopping, and shopping. I went because that's where Hiroshi Tanaka had his home and his office. If I'd know that everyone was coming with me I'd have stayed home and gone skiing.

"Of course I want to go to Vienna," Marie Laure said.

"I'm not going for pleasure," I said.

"I 'ave to shop for baby clothing. Anita will watch the Laundromat."

"Do you want to take the train with me?"

"Of course not—we will take the car," she said.

"I'm not going to have time to do things with you. I'm going to try to get into this guy's apartment."

"You don't have to spend time with me. I have Anna for company."

"Well, I'm glad you're not leaving the baby at home, but I don't know if she'll be much fun to dine with."

"I speak of your mother."

"My mother?"

"Of course."

"What are you going to do when you want to rest? Never mind when the baby wants a nap, when you want a nap. And my mother . . ."

My mother, who apparently never misses a cue anymore, appeared with her little blue suitcase, her day bag, and said, "I'm ready."

". . . and my dear mother, who is not as young as she used to be, wants to rest, what will you do then?"

"We will go to our 'otel room," Marie Laure said.

"Of course," I said.

"I am packed," she said. "The baby is ready. Will you 'elp me take our things to the car?"

But of course they weren't ready. Neither was I, now that I was taking the car and the family. There is a law of family time ratios. The length of time it takes to leave the house is multiplied sequentially by the number of people involved. If it takes one person five minutes, then it takes two people ten minutes, three people thirty minutes, four people two hours. Forgive me if I exaggerate. An hour and a half after my train was scheduled to leave—in which I would have traveled at leisure, enjoying solitude, reading the *International Herald Tribune*, perhaps the London *Times* or the *Economist*, sipping a glass of wine—I was finally behind the wheel with one Anna beside me and the other in the baby seat in back. My mother has never appreciated my driving. I have never appreciated hers. The only alternative was for me to ride in back with the baby, but the baby is only truly comfortable close to the breast. I used to be a tough guy. Really. I worked the mean streets of New York. I messed with wiseguys, guys doing time, and violence-prone drug abusers.

"Where are you going?" Mike Hayakawa cried.

I didn't really hear what he said. My window was closed, the heater fan was on, the baby was crying, my mother was warning me to drive carefully, and Marie Laure wanted to know if I'd brought enough cash. But I did see that he was running toward the car, waving. So I said, "Wait a minute!" to everyone inside and I rolled down the window. Mike slipped in the snow, crashed into us, and repeated himself.

"To Vienna," I said. "My favorite city. To get you know what."

"I am going with you," he said.

"You are not," I said. "Everybody, this is Mike Hayakawa. This is my mother."

"Hello, Mrs. Cochrane," Mike said politely. He even bowed a little, but he was jiggling with impatience like a man who has to urinate twenty minutes ago.

"You know, you could use a little more Oriental composure," I said.

"It's not Cochrane, it's Cassella," my mother said.

"Ma!" I said.

"Sorry," she said to me. "That was my maiden name," she said to Hayakawa, thinking quickly.

"And this is my daughter Anna. And Marie Laure, her mother, the woman I love."

"I'm very pleased to meet you. Ohhh, she's so cute," he said to Marie Laure.

That had become true. Her head had lost its point. In skulls, roundness is considered attractive. She drooled from time to time, but not that often and with a certain restraint. She wasn't one of those steady spit-up babies. Each day she filled out more. Her wrists looked like they had rubber bands around them. So did her ankles. Her belly was round and full and healthy, which looks as good on babies as it looks bad on adults.

"Anyway, Mike," I said, "I have to say good-bye. Everybody, say good-bye to Mike now."

"I cannot let you out of my sight," he protested.

"Not even for toilet functions?"

"I know what you took from Hiroshi Tanaka's things."

"Yeah? So? Remember you want me to find the dingus. The CD. Whatever it is. It isn't here. So maybe it's there. In his office, or his apartment. That is why I have to go there. That's in Vienna. I need the address. That's why I took the license and business card. Then I need to get in. That's why I took his keys. You could've done it. You didn't even think of it. Now that I've told you about it, maybe you should do it. I don't mind. I'd just as soon stay home." I opened the car door. "Vienna's perfect. I hate Vienna." I got out and dug in my pocket for Hiroshi Tanaka's keys. "So take the keys, guy. You go!"

"No. We are a team now. We go together."

"There's no room. I'm sorry. Much as I would like to, I won't kick my mother out of the car to make room for you."

"This is too important. Much too important. I must stay in touch all the way. I have spoken to the home office. Those are my instructions and I will follow them."

"Hey, they know what we are doing all way over there in Tokyo?"

"Yes. In London too. They have approved my association with you. Rick, I told them that you are an American detective. They were impressed by that. Forgive me, I did not think they would be impressed by an Irish detective. Everyone knows America is still number one with detectives. It's because you have so much drugs and violence."

"Did you learn this in Berkeley?"

"I am sorry if I have offended you."

"Not me," I said, "I'm Irish."

"But people in Tokyo only know America and detectives from television and movies. So I thought that was the best thing to say."

"I understand," I said.

"Since there is so much mysterious death already, we think it is good that there is someone who understands violence."

"Sure," I said. "I'll tell you all about it when I come back."

"I have a car. I will follow you," he insisted.

"Why not," I said. "Bring anything of Tanaka's that I didn't already take."

"Thank you, thank you," Mike said. "You will wait for me. I will only be five minutes."

The Japanese might have entered the auto market from the low end—smaller, cheaper, better gas mileage. But by 1990 everyone had figured out that the really good bucks were at the top end and to go after BMW, Mercedes, and Jaguar. Honda developed the Acura; Toyota, the Lexus; Nissan, the Infiniti; and Musashi had the Élégant. There probably weren't more than fifty of them in Europe and, import restrictions there being much tougher than in the States, they went for over $45,000 in Germany and $55,000 in Austria. Hayakawa had one. Twenty-five minutes later we pulled out. Me and the three women. Mike behind us. Whoever was following us behind him.

■

The A12 from the Arlberg Tunnel east toward Vienna is a brand-new superhighway. There is something terribly sleek about it as it runs through the Alps, an elegance to the half-cylinder tunnels and cantilevered causeways that cover the road to protect it from avalanches. I'd been over here for a while, so I don't notice it anymore, but my mother was shocked by how rich and new and clean it all looked. She was fresh from America, where even the interstates have potholes—fresh from imperial New York, where the elevated expressways are falling down and the bridges are being closed due to neglect. She wanted to know if it was all like this and why. And if, as it appeared, the Austrians were actually so much richer than Americans.

They are and they are not the only ones. So are the Germans, the Swiss, the Swedes, the Danes, and of course, the Japanese.

We'd left so late that after an hour and a half it was time for lunch. We stopped in Innsbruck, the capital of the Tyrol, which has been the site of two winter Olympics. In a year with good snow it is an enchanting place. In a wet and gray winter it still has a terrifically touristy automobile-free medieval center, a bad Chinese restaurant, and an excellent old-fashioned whorehouse.

Marie Laure, my mother, my daughter, myself, and Mike Hayakawa went to the old town to eat something typical and charming. We found an inn with an Adler—Eagle—in its name and even a Goethe *Stube*—a room where Goethe once sat. It's the equivalent of a "Washington slept here" in the States. Goethe lived for a long time a long time ago and got around a lot. Everyplace he stopped, from Heidelberg to Rome, has been marked. I suspect that it's been done to make the German tourists feel comfortable, as if other groups recognize the Teutonic people for something besides having a lot of money and committing genocide. It had a classic Tyrolean menu, but fortunately it had a broader range of dishes than the usual St. Anton standard.

We hadn't decided where we were going to stay. I mentioned that a decent hotel room would run ÖS1,500 a night, per person, double occupancy more for the single person in the single room. This was a way of complaining about going on a mission with an entourage of females. James Bond always liked a mission with women around, but that was Pussy Galore, not his mother, infant daughter, and a postpartum wife.

"Yes," Mike said, "Austria is a very good bargain."

I looked at Marie Laure, she looked back at me. Then she smiled and I did too. We both laughed and she took my hand. "A good bargain" is how the French boys translate a phrase that means good in bed. It's been a pet phrase and a running gag in our lives for some time.

My mother, who was reading the menu, said, "I don't think it's a bargain at all. I think it's very dear." She was quite serious.

"Oh, I'm sorry," Mike said, sincerely embarrassed. It's a faux pas for someone with yen to talk about the cost of things to someone whose reference point is dollars. "It must be difficult for you."

"That's all right, Mom, let me order for you," I said, knowing that she would order strictly by price. I have days like that too.

"How do the people who live here afford it?" my mother asked. She comes from that generation that regards Americans as the richest people in the world and Europe as a place to send CARE packages. So did I, to a lesser degree. Schilling shock cures it fast.

"They have a very strong work ethic," Mike said enthusiastically. "They have a homogeneous population and a sense of the common good. There has not been a major strike here for many, many years. Technically this is achieved through the Parity Commission for Wages and Prices."

"I didn't know this," I said. "Ski bums are not included. There we deal in straight exploitation."

"The federal chancellor and all the important ministries are involved—the Austrian Trade Union Confederation, and the representatives of the employers and of the farmers. They settle all claims about wages and prices. The most interesting part, I think, is that their recommendations are not binding. Yet everyone follows them. This is like Japan. In Japan an agency like MITI, the Ministry of International Trade and Industry, does not rule by making laws, like an American government agency, but by leadership and suggestion. This is only possible if both sides believe they are on the same side ultimately and are willing to give priority to the economy as a whole."

"But what do you do," Mother said, "when the bosses say everybody has to work more for less, but they give themselves bonuses. The people with money—they don't give a penny more than they have to. If you don't watch them, they'll rob the pension fund."

"That is American thinking," Mike said. "It is one reason why America's time is passing."

Marie Laure got up to go to the *toilette.* I took the baby. She woke up and started to cry. I gave her the pacifier. Anna Geneviève sucked experimentally. She was not fooled. She spit the rubber out and wailed for reality. With a sigh Marie took her back.

"I like the Austrian spirit. We will invest here," Mike Hayakawa said.

"Who's we?" I asked, as the hardworking waitress, aware of her importance in the scheme of Austrian tourism as a whole, slammed our dishes down in front of us.

"Musashi Company," he said. "We will invest here."

"In Japan you all work for the common good?" my mother asked.

"I am very lucky to be with my company, Musashi," Mike said. He was fervent about all of this—evangelical for Japan, Inc. "I know that I will have lifetime employment. If I want to buy a house, they will make a house loan. Even if I want to join the golf club, they will make me a loan to join the golf club. So I know that what is good for Musashi Company is good for me and what is good for Musashi Company is good for Japan."

"Did you study this in college?" my mother asked.

"University of California, Berkeley," he said. "I studied economics and sociology."

"Do you know who is following you?" I asked him.

"You mean the Little Dragons? Taiwan, Hong Kong, Singapore? Yes, the Japanese way is widely imitated."

"No, I mean the blue Ford that followed you from St. Anton."

He looked shocked. As I had intended. It made me feel better. I ordered an extravagant dessert, then suggested that Musashi Company pick up the check. "I'll take it off my fee," I said.

■

I had a pretty fair idea of who was following us. But I didn't expect to be accosted by him in the men's room.

He was standing at the urinal in the classic pose, face forward, hands low and in front. He was watching the door through the mirror over the sink. When I came in he turned around abruptly. I jumped back, expecting a spray of urine. But he was completely zipped up. "I'm glad you finally came in here," he said. "It's been a strain standing here. There was one guy kept staring at me. He must have thought I had a bladder problem."

"That's one description of guys who hang out in men's rooms."

"Oh, come on, I don't look like one of them."

"Send in the clowns," I said.

"Okay, now, enough of that. I want to know what you're doing!"

"Having lunch."

"Don't get wise with me, Cassella! I can have your ticket punched. Right now if I want to!"

"Hey, whatever agency you're with, Chip—didn't they teach you how to tail someone?"

"What do you mean?"

"What do I mean? I mean my mother spotted you behind us!"

"No. You're joking, aren't you?"

"I never joke about *trade craft*. But it doesn't matter about my mother. She's Sicilian—she doesn't get nervous about stuff like that. But the Jap—he spotted you too, Chip, and he's squirming."

"I want to know exactly what's going on here!" Chip said. "Are you on our team or not?"

"Am I on your team? Who is your team?"

"America's team, darn it."

"Tell me something, Mr. America's team, what am I looking for? Don't tell me it's financial records. I know it's not."

"There are some things I'm not at liberty to disclose."

"And you want to know what team I'm on. Maybe I'm on the first team that tells me what the fuck is going on."

"Let me warn you of one thing," Chip said, waving his finger in my face. "I see you have your whole family with you. If you try to make one move over the border . . ."

"What border?"

"Any border, any airport, any train. One move, Mr. Wiseguy, and I will shut you down, round you up, and take you away. The closest you'll get to snow will be the prison exercise yard, back in the States."

"Back off, Chip. Now listen to me. We're going to Vienna . . ."

"All of you?"

"Just listen, dammit. I'll be staying at one of two *pensions*, probably. The Schwarzer Adler or the Marie Louise. They're listed in the phone book. So in case I lose you, you'll know where to find me. And my wife and baby and my mother."

"What about the Japanese guy?"

"Does one of the Musashi companies own hotels in Austria?"

"Yes. Five Star. They just acquired the Imperial Eagle. It used to be a Hilton."

"That's where he'll be. Come to think of it, that's where I'll be too, if I can get him to put me on his tab. Can we put it on your tab?"

"You're going a little too fast here, guy."

"You ask me what team I'm on. The other guy—I assume Tanaka is the other team—he's ready to pay my tab, and you're not. You just want to blackmail me, push me around, take my laundries. Then you say you want me to be on your team."

"I . . ."

"Well, goddammit, I am. I'm on America's team. Because I'm a goddamn red-blooded, dyed-in-the-wool American." I try to talk to people in terms they can understand. "Now, I have to work with the Japanese because he was close, in some way that I have not figured out, to Hiroshi Tanaka. With him, I have access. I got Tanaka's keys from him. For Tanaka's office and apartment in Vienna. So just relax."

"Can I trust you?"

"Of course you can, Chip. Two Americans in a foreign land—you bet!" I said. I shushed him abruptly. I opened the men's room door and looked out. I shut it quickly and turned back to Chip. I shoved Chip into the toilet stall. "It's the Jap!" I whispered urgently. "Get in there. Don't let him see you. As soon as it's clear, I'll come back and tell you. Remember Pearl Harbor!"

I left the men's room. I left the restaurant. Mike Hayakawa had picked up the check. Everyone was already waiting for me outside the restaurant. I found the blue Ford and flattened the tires. It impressed Mike no end. He thought it was something right out of a TV show. The next time I spoke to Chip I would tell him that vandals must've done it. Or Hayakawa.

TWELVE

TRUST

My mother liked Mike Hayakawa. She thought he was polite, well educated, and intelligent. She likes people with strong opinions. I asked her how Guido was. Guido is her closest male friend. I don't know exactly what their relationship is except that he does the cooking. He's a priest and I initially did not like him for that reason. But he was the one that helped me leave America, disappear, and end up with the ridiculous passport that I now carry.

Guido had been sick, she said. But she wouldn't be specific. Just sick and had not felt up to coming with her.

It was a long and grueling drive. My left knee ached. I'd hurt it skiing but it only bothered me when I was in the car. It was late when we arrived in Vienna, so I didn't really appreciate the hotel.

The Imperial Eagle looked like a wealthy woman of forty who had been recently widowed—it had just had a complete makeover. To pursue the metaphor any further would be sexist and in the worst of taste. It existed for businessmen with serious expense accounts and the name of the game was service. I was not the only man in the hotel in jeans, but I was the only one in jeans who was not associated with a camera on a professional basis. These people wore very serious clothes. They were not there for vacations or frivolity—though they knew how to enjoy themselves with brandy, a cigar, and an escort service after a hard day of *der Schilling machen*.

I was the only man in the hotel with a wife and baby and a mother. Mike got us a suite with his Musashi card. Japanese was featured in all the multilingual signs and services. A sign at the reception desk pointed out that they were happy to accept travelers checks in yen denominations.

By the time we entered the room the phone was ringing. It was Chip. He was calling from a phone booth somewhere near Linz. He accused me of letting the air out of his tires to escape. I told him that was ridiculous and that in any case I was exactly where I'd said I'd be so that he had nothing to worry about. I told him it was a very nice hotel and he should come and stay there too. It was far more, he said, than his expense account permitted. I told him not to worry—that there were many excellent *pensions* in Vienna at a price he could afford. Even if he didn't have yen.

There was a thorn-free rosebud and a chocolate on each pillow. A maid entered by force and insisted on turning down our covers. Complimentary fruit was set out in a bowl. There was a minibar with a wide selection of beverages to be charged at three to five times their value. I had a half bottle of wine for $30. Marie, a nursing mother, had a *mineral Wasser* for $7.50. My mother couldn't bring herself to have anything at that price. I heard her in the bathroom drinking a glass of tap water. God bless her.

The sheets were soft and so clean they glowed dimly in the dark. It was nice to lay there in that broad expanse of mattress with Marie Laure and Anna Geneviève, so small, so serious, between us.

The phone woke me in the morning. It was Chip. The baby woke up and began to wail. That woke Marie Laure. She glared at me as if it were my fault.

"I'll take it in the living room. When I get in there, hang it up."

She glared at me ferociously when I handed her the phone. When I picked up she slammed the extension down.

"What time is it?" I asked him.

"It's six."

"Asshole," I said. "Okay. Here's today's schedule. I'm going to get up in two hours. At eight. Then I'll be down for breakfast at nine. Then we go to Hiroshi Tanaka's office. It's on Josefstädterstraße, number forty-eight. We should be there around ten. Rent a different car if you're going to hang out out front, and get a moustache or something."

"I'm downstairs," he said.

"Well, don't be," I said.

"How do I know you're going where you say you're going?"

"What are you going to do, sit in the coffee shop for three hours? This is his place. Maybe he's not smart enough to have the house detective on watch for you or someone like you. But maybe he is. Just do what I tell you and if we're both lucky we'll both go back to the States."

"I'm going to wait down here. I have sunglasses and I'm combing my hair differently."

"Chip, don't do that. Eat some breakfast, have a good shit, get the *Herald Tribune,* and go sit in the park and read." I hung up on him.

"Why do you treat them that way?" Marie Laure said, standing in the doorway.

"What way?"

"I want you to clear up this mess you have and I want you to have your real name and to be able to go where we want, even to Brooklyn. You are very rude. Like they are idiots or clowns."

"To keep them off balance. If I treated them nice they would think I was afraid of them. They're dangerous. Or one of them is. One of them probably killed Hiroshi Tanaka, Wendy Tavetian, and maybe even Hans Lantz."

Breakfast, included in the price of the room, was sumptuous. Fit for a German appetite. Prepared in a country that has not yet heard of cholesterol. There was coffee, rich Viennese coffee, or decaf, and a selection of teas. Fresh juice, fresh fruit, stewed fruit, eggs however you wanted them. There was ham, sausage, schnitzel, wieners, bacon. There was butter, cream cheese, yogurt, and eight varieties of cheese. There were four different kinds of cold cereal plus packaged cereals, nuts, raisins, mixed dried fruit, and sunflower seeds. There were three different kinds of rolls, four different breads, a selection of jams, marmalades, and honey. There were grilled tomatoes, hollandaise sauce, béarnaise sauce, waffles, American pancakes, syrup, and seven miscellaneous.

Mike Hayakawa ate sparingly. I made something of a pig of myself.

"How come," he asked, "you're dressed like a Catholic priest?"

"I am one," I said. I wore my ancient Irish tweed sports jacket over my clerical collar and black dickie. I reached in the pocket and took out my passport. He'd never seen it. It looks real. It is real. Sort of. He read the entry for profession, then reread it and looked upstairs as if he could see Marie Laure as he'd seen her at lunch in Innsbruck, lush swollen breast coming out of her blouse, the nipple bursting with milk to feed my daughter, her dark eyes full of woman's knowledge of both having babies and making them.

Oh, I was impatient for that vagina to heal so I could spread her legs and slide inside again, my chest pressing against her heavy breasts—I wondered how much they would change from birth and nursing; I wondered if it would matter to me—and her hands on my back and on my buttocks, pressing me into her, taking me into her, into the passage through which our daughter had traveled. Would it feel different in there to my cock? to my mind?

"The idea of clerical celibacy came relatively late," I said. "Originally married men could become priests and priests could marry. The rule forbidding priests to marry after they were ordained wasn't proclaimed until 325. Then there were two classes of priest. The premarried and presumably sexually active. The unmarried and supposedly celibate. Marriage, as a Catholic rite, is indissoluble. So in 385 Pope Siricius made the somewhat bizarre decree that married men who were ordained had to remain married but had to stop having sex with their wives. This is in contrast to the rabbinical tradition, which makes sex a duty to health and marital well-being. They suggest Friday night.

"In any case, clerical marriage wasn't actively attacked until 1089 under Pope Urban II. To prove they were serious about it, the Pope and his council said that priests' wives could be sent into slavery. But even after that, celibacy was honored more in the breech, if you'll pardon the pun, than in fact. John XII and Benedict VII were both murdered by jealous husbands who caught them flagrante delicto.

"Innocent VIII was the first pope to acknowledge his bastards.

Pope Sergius III was the father of Pope John IX, Pope Sixtus IV of Pope Julius II. Sixtus was also the first pope to license the whorehouses of Rome and he imposed a tax on priests who kept a mistress. Alexander VI, who was Rodrigo Borgia, had ten illegitimate children. A celibate clergy is an idea that seems indivisible from the Catholic Church, but history, theology, and the study of comparative religions all suggest that it is a questionable practice."

I sound very authoritative doing that. Enough so that Mike looked at me with the suspicion that I might really be a priest and that it was the detective part that was an act.

"Tell me of the pagan rites in your country, my son. Does the Buddha require his followers to forswear their manly nature? Must the Shinto comport himself as a castrato?"

I had spent three months in a monastery cell next door to a Capuchin monk named Luther who was dying to have a sexual relationship with a woman, but he was the unfortunate sort of fanatic that wanted to change the world to fit his dick rather than simply break a rule and be happy. When Marie visited and we went down to the beach he would spy on us, then take long cold showers during which he wept. When she was away he eagerly shared the results of his research with me, particularly the more salacious tales of papal profligacy.

"Your mother," Hayakawa said, "is a very nice person. It is good to see elder people who are vigorous and involved in life."

"I like her too," I said.

"She is an Italian-American from Brooklyn," he said, looking at my passport.

"Yes, but she doesn't conform to the stereotype, does she? Neither do I."

"That's true," he said, and handed me back my passport.

I looked at the selection of pastries. There was one in particular with lightly glazed blackberries that I found terribly attractive. "We'd better get going," I said.

"Okay," he said. "You never dressed this way in St. Anton."

"Look around you. What should I wear—jeans and a T-shirt? ski clothes? This is a cheap way to look respectable. I don't have a pinstripe suit and a power tie," I said. "But I'm glad that you do."

Vienna was re-created in the nineteenth century by its last emperor as a monument to empire and all the statues are larger than life. They tend to be static, stolid, and sturdy, as compared, say, to the statues of Rome, which are so often languid, frolicking, and, no matter how rippled their stomach muscles, ready to eat grapes off the vine. A lot of Vienna's statues are female nudes. They have that pornographic perfection that one expects from a *Penthouse* or *Playboy* spread, their granite tits even harder and more upthrust than silicone enhanced flesh. They are stockier than the current Western standard, but it's all muscle, as if the sculptors of Vienna, en masse, had fallen in love with a gang of German masseuses. There is also, as in today's men's magazines, an ongoing lesbian motif. Constantly sculpted two together, they touch in ways that are either suggestive or possessive. Whichever they are, lesbians or masseuses, surely a pair will someday come to life when the right man falls to his knees before them crying, "Pummel me, beat me, hurt me. Teach me what true love really means."

There were two pair of these females on either side of the entrance to Hiroshi Tanaka's office building. They held up the portico with casual strength and teamster solidarity. Across the street, Chip Sheen gazed at them intently. He had changed his car to a minimalist green Opel from Hertz. He also had sunglasses and some sort of tweedy golf cap. He gave me a sidelong look, then he made some sort of recognition signal, flicking his nostril with his thumb. He'd seen it in a movie.

"What now?" Mike asked, as if I knew.

"Wait here," I said. "I'm going to go up and reconnoiter."

"What should I do?"

"Just wait."

"Rick," he said, grabbing my arm, "why are you dressed like a priest?"

"Because priests are always going where they have no business being."

■

"I'm Father Cochrane," I said to the severe but very well turned out woman at the front desk. I spoke in English with a slight brogue.

"Yes, *Pater,* how can I help you?" she said. She spoke excellent English, but not colloquial English. The slight bar of language kept a distance between us.

"I'm here to see Hiroshi Tanaka."

"Oh, dear," she said. "I'm afraid that won't be possible."

"He made it very clear I was to come and see him on this very day."

"He's dead, Father."

"Oh, well then. The poor man. How did it happen?"

"An accident. A snowfall while he was skiing."

"A snowfall? He was caught in a storm?"

"No. I'm sorry. *Lawine.* The snow slide."

"Dear me. And he seemed so alive, so vital."

"Yes, he was."

"I hate to be indelicate at such a time, but the orphans are depending on me."

"The orphans?" She seemed faintly surprised. The shortage of orphans in Western Europe is even more severe than in white America. Even in the home of Holy Mother Church, babies are in such short supply that childless Italians shop for them in South America.

"Ah, yes. In Dublin," I said. No one in Europe knows much about the place, except for the The Troubles of course, because it's a poor place and therefore neither promising nor threatening. "I met the late Mr. Tanaka in St. Anton, in fact, and although he was not of our persuasion I prevailed upon him to promise a contribution. I thought it was very kind of him."

"He was a good man, *Pater,*" she said ritualistically. There was an 85 percent probability that she was of "the father's" persuasion. It's a very Catholic country.

"Since it was to be a corporate contribution—that was my understanding—perhaps I might speak with his successor. After all, the orphans are as needy now as they were before the sad event."

"That would be Herr Schwardtfager."

"Might I . . ."

"He's out of town at the moment. You could speak with him next week."

"Tell me, my child, what's your name?"

"Helga. Helga Kaltenbrunner."

"And a melodic name it is. I just had a marvelous thought. Perhaps I could arrange to talk to everyone here at your lovely company. What I'm thinking of is a memorial contribution in the name of Hiroshi Tanaka. What a blessed gesture that would be. Think of a plaque on the chapel—which needs a new roof as chapels so often do—the Tanaka chapel . . ." It was almost working, but her eyes glazed every fourth beat with the effort of keeping up with the language. I carried on. ". . . Or even a small new wing to the orphanage itself. The Tanaka wing. It would be betterment of cross-cultural understanding and the ecumenical impulse . . ." But to hustle, to manipulate, you use words to get past words, to touch emotions, knee-jerk reactions, desires.

"I would have to take that up with our managing director," she said, definitely not buying it. I was a fisherman without his hooks, a hunter without a gun, a con man without a line.

"That would be . . . ?"

". . . Herr Schwardtfeger," she said.

"Thank you," I said, as I picked up a piece of their stationery and wrote it down. "You're a lovely and mature woman, Helga, but you've got to learn to take more responsibility on your own. I'll call next week."

"I came up with a lovely scam to talk my way in," I said to Mike Hayakawa.

"Yes?"

"It didn't work," I said.

"Oh," he said.

"But I learned a lot."

"Good," he said.

"We can get in. But we'll only have ten, twenty minutes. Which is plenty if we know what we're looking for and where it is. If we're just looking for the great unknown, hoping we stumble on it, we're in deep shit."

"But we have the key," he said.

"Their alarm system," I said, "is right out in plain sight. It requires a key and a number code. See the video cameras." I pointed at the stone lesbian on the left. She had a camera over her shoulder. Across the street, Chip Sheen tried very hard to look like he wasn't staring at us. "Inside too. Are they taping or just watching? Maybe they have round-the-clock on-site security. Maybe not. What we do have is a key. What we don't have is the number code. Unless you're holding out on me?"

"No."

"They have a lot of expensive electronics to protect. Fax machines, copiers, PC's. Everyone up there has a PC. It looked like about ten employees. They're consultants and executive search. Offices in Amsterdam, Frankfurt, Los Angeles," I said, looking at the piece of stationery I had picked up from Helga's desk. Tanaka's business card had only listed the Vienna address. "What the hell do they consult about?"

"I really don't know," Hayakawa said.

Chip Sheen held a paperback book sideways so that it looked like he was pointing a disguised microphone in our direction. I reached over, turned the ignition key, then put a cassette in the tape player. Bruce Springteen sang, "This gun's for hire."

"You're so full of shit," I said. "What's going on? What game are we playing? Who the fuck are you?"

"I might ask the same of you. You're not Irish."

"Who cares? Since when is it a crime not to be Irish? This is bullshit," I said. "If I don't know more, I'm going to quit." I opened the car door.

"Rick, wait."

I closed the car door.

"What?"

"That car, across the street, I think he's watching us."

"Yeah," I said. "Same guy that followed us in the blue Ford."

"How did he find us?"

"Easy," I said. "He's after the same thing we are. He came to the same place. Tanaka's office. Now, let me in on things, or I take a hike."

"Please be patient," he said. "This is not the sort of thing I expected to be doing. I am an economist. I am here to help place Musashi Company investments. We must be positioned in Europe before 1992. Suddenly this meeting was demanded of me. I was only assigned to Frankfurt six months ago. Three weeks ago I was called back to London to the office of Yoshiro Masaki, who is the head of all European affairs. He sent me to meet Hiroshi Tanaka. He told me I was to get something from him. I was to bring it . . . I was to get instructions in Vienna once I received it and then bring it where I was told. It was a vital thing. I think perhaps Yoshiro Masaki's job depends on it. Maybe mine too."

"You told my mother yesterday that Musashi takes care of its own, that you had lifetime employment."

"Things are not that simple. If Masaki does not deliver this item, this computer disc, then he will be dishonored. Even if it is my failure it is his dishonor because he selected me. Then he must resign."

"So this lifetime employment thing is bullshit."

"No. He could remain in his job. But he will resign because he has failed Musashi Company. You don't understand anything in the West. All you care about is self. Your job. Your money. There is no substance. I would go mad if I had to be an American. If it were the sixteenth century and he were a samurai perhaps he would commit seppuku."

"What if he doesn't resign?"

"He will be placed in a job of diminished responsibility. Some office where he passes papers across his desk and everyone looks at him and knows his failure. Who can live in such shame?"

"And you?"

"I must not fail. I will go on without you. Give me the keys. I will go to Hiroshi Tanaka's house and search it. Then I will wait for the night and go into the office."

I tossed him the keys and got out of his car. He was genuinely shocked. He gave me a pleading look. Then he gathered his determination and drove off.

Chip Sheen, across the street, was on the verge of panic. Who was he to follow? Me or Hayakawa? I made as discreet a gesture as I thought he would understand, telling him to stay put. When

I was certain the Musashi Élégant was out of sight, I turned around and sauntered across the street to Chip Sheen. I opened the door and got in on the passenger side.

"What the hell is going on?" he said.

"Who are you really with?" I said.

"I think it's time you answered some of my questions."

"You know the Jap spotted you again. Do you know that?"

"I changed cars and everything," he said.

"Some people are just not good at some things. What are you good at?"

"You're going to start listening to me. You're getting me really riled."

"You know what, I already had this conversation. Thirty years ago. In the playground behind P.S. 11. *'Who's gonna make me'—'I am'—'You and what army?'* "

Furious, he pulled a gun out of his shoulder holster. "I am," he said.

"Be calm. Don't be stupid," I said. "Put the gun away."

"What are you doing?" he asked me. He didn't put the gun away. He held it with a fondness that made me very uncomfortable.

"I'm going to rejoin Mike Hayakawa," I said, telling the truth, "and I am going to convince him that I'm his friend. That he should trust me. That way I can get him out of my way and search for the dingus."

"I don't trust you, Cassella."

"I hate to say it, Chip, but it's mutual." I tried to speak to him as if the gun in his hand didn't exist. "I want to trust you. I want to believe that you'll clear me with the IRS. But you won't even tell me what agency you're with."

"I told you, I'm IRS."

"Yes. Would you please put the gun away? I'm a father now. I can't afford to die."

"You should keep that in mind," he said.

"I will, Chip," I said humbly. "Now, can we drive to Tanaka's apartment or do you want to let Hayakawa search it alone?"

"How are you going to get him to trust you?"

"I'm going to call the cops. Then I'm going to trip the alarm or pretend to trip the alarm. Tell him that he did it. Then I'll either hustle him out of there or protect him from the cops, whichever seems more practical."

"Hey, that's pretty good."

"You like that?"

"Yes, by golly, I do."

"Will you put the gun away then? Please?"

"Sure," he said, putting it away. "I just had to make sure you had your priorities straight. Also, I don't like being kidded, you know. No hard feelings?" He put his hand out.

"No hard feelings, Chip." I shook his hand. He looked very gratified. "That was a pretty neat gun. What kind was it?"

"A Glock-17," he said. "Made right here in Austria. Nine millimeter, NATO standard ammunition, state of the art construction—polymer, a patented space-age plastic, just nine-point-five-oh ounces fully loaded. Seventeen rounds, one in the chamber, sixteen in the mag."

"And that paperback you were reading. What did it have, a microphone inside?"

"Hey, how did you guess that?"

Tanaka's apartment was on Prinz Eugene Straβe near Belvedere Palace. I turned on the radio, Glenn Frey was singing "Better in the U.S.A." "Drive past it, then stop at the first pay phone you see." There was a café on the corner. He stopped there.

"I still don't trust you," Chip said.

"I can understand that," I said.

"So I'm going to wait down here. Make sure you don't double-cross me."

"That's a good idea," I said.

"I'll be waiting and I'll be watching," he said.

Inside the café I called the police. I told them that there was a suspicious-looking man in a red Opel parked on Prinz Eugen Straβe near Belvedere Palace and that they should be careful—I thought that he had a gun. When they had taken that report I hung up. Then I called again and told them that I was a neighbor of Hiroshi Tanaka and that I had seen strangers enter his apartment.

Then I went upstairs to join Mike Hayakawa.

He jumped when I opened the door. He really wasn't built for surreptitious entries. "What are you doing here?" he said.

"I like this place," I said, standing in the doorway. "A lot. Did you find the dingus yet?"

"I just got here," he said.

"Did you turn off the alarm?" I asked him.

"Alarm?" he said. "I don't hear any alarm."

"Silent alarm," I said, which it was. "Like the office. Hooked up directly to the police or security service." I went to him, took the keys, then went over to the box by the front door, and reset the alarm. The door was still open. So now it was ringing wherever it was connected to.

"I did that," he said.

"Two full turns around?" I asked him. It had been on long enough. I turned it off.

"No," he said.

"You blew it. That's why I followed you. I knew you'd end up in trouble."

"Shouldn't we get out of here?"

"Let's look around," I said as I closed the front door. The foyer opened onto a living room. The living room faced out on the formal gardens. Light streamed in the windows. I looked down to the street. The call about the man with a gun had really got the police moving. Chip Sheen was surrounded, machine pistols pointing at him from both sides. I turned back to the living room. The furniture was elegant but comfortable—Old World Viennese, like the apartment itself. If I ever got rich and gave up skiing, this was where I wanted to live.

"I'm getting out of here," Hayakawa said. He looked panicky.

I grabbed him and held on. "Never run," I said. I held on to him.

"I don't want to be arrested," he said. "I cannot afford to be arrested."

"Easy. Take it easy. There are already cops downstairs. You run right into their arms, they'll really be suspicious. Trust me."

"Let me look," he said.

"Don't look," I said. "Cops are like dogs. They smell fear. Do something Zen and calming. How many bedrooms?"

"What do you mean how many bedrooms?"

"What'd he have, one bedroom, two, three bedrooms?"

"I don't know," he said. "I just got here."

"Just follow my lead. Act like you don't speak a word in *Deutsch*. Except maybe *Ich spreche keine Deutsch*. Don't panic. Look sure of yourself. Do you have your passport? They'll be upstairs soon," I said.

"You think so?"

"Teutonic police are efficient. One of the great ethnic secrets of New York City is that while the police department appears to be ruled by Irish-Americans it is actually run by German-Americans."

"Is that true?" he asked.

"Maybe," I said as the local Teutonic police pounded on the door and demanded we open up.

"Trust me," I said. "And remember—you can buy and sell this country. Be arrogant."

"Are you sure?" he said.

I opened the door, put on my most Fatherly smile and best brogue. "No need, no need at all for that pounding on the door," I said. There were three of them, and they entered with guns drawn, Belgian FN35 automatics. Their leader, a sergeant, put his gun to my gut. The other two brushed past us. They saw Hayakawa. One pointed his gun at him, the other kept moving.

"Who are you? What are you doing in this apartment?" their leader barked in *Deutsch*. His gun was pointed at me.

"*Deutsch* is it?" I said in *Deutsch*. "My Japanese friend and I are here at the invitation of the apartment's owner. Hiroshi Tanaka."

"Where is the apartment's owner?" the sergeant barked.

"Actually, we believe he is out of town at the moment. Skiing, I believe."

"Put your hands up," the second *Polizei* barked at Mike.

"Put your hands up," I said in English, in a hurry, because Mike forgot that he didn't understand. "He doesn't speak German," I said. "Only Japanese and English."

"Is there anyone else here?" the sergeant asked me. The third man had disappeared down the hall.

"No. What is the problem?"

"Passports!"

"Give him your passport," I said to Mike, in English, while I reached for mine. I don't think Hayakawa had ever had a gun pointed at him before. It didn't make him happy. "Now, sergeant," I said, "I don't know the reason for this, but I will have you know that we are respectable people. I am a cleric from Dublin and my friend here is a representative of a major multinational corporation. We happen to be good friends of the owner of the apartment. Such good friends that he gave us the keys"—I drew them slowly from my pocket—"hearing we would be in town, and practically ordered us to stay here rather than . . ."

"Shut up," he said. "You," he said to Hayakawa, "what are you doing here?

"*Ich spreche keine Deutsch,*" Mike said. Unlike his English, which sounded quite colloquial most of the time, his German had a heavy Japanese accent. It was very convincing.

"He doesn't speak German," I said, as if the sergeant couldn't understand Mike saying it.

The sergeant stomped over and examined Mike's passport. He came back to me. "You set off the alarm!"

"Ah, dear me," I said. "I'm hopeless with electronics. At seminary they had microfilm machines. I was forever breaking them. If I touch an automobile it seems to self-destruct. It's a terrible curse. I'm sure it was something I did wrong. Hiroshi explained it was turn to the left, then turn to the right. Or was it two turns to the left, with the very odd little key here. You see the one."

"All right, *Pater,*" he said. "Sorry to bother you."

"No problem," I said. "*Gross Gott.*" I made a vague sign of the cross.

"*Gross Gott.*" "*Gross Gott.*" "*Gross Gott.*" "*Gross Gott.*" Everybody said "God is great," and I said it back, piously, as the door closed behind them.

"Thank you, thank you, thank you," Mike said.

"That's okay," I said.

"I don't know what I'd have done if I'd been alone."

"Gone to jail for breaking and entering," I told him. Gently. He sat down. "You want to go back to the hotel? I can take care of things here."

"No," he said resolutely, "my instructions were to stick by you."

Which he did. It was a great apartment. The paintings appeared to my untutored eye to be originals. The ceilings were a full fifteen feet high. The kitchen was as well equipped as Braun, Krup, and Toshiba could make it. The bedroom was sexy. The VCRs and TVs were Sonys. In addition to the wide selection of erotic tapes, polycultural and multilingual, there were complete collections of François Truffaut, Francis Ford Coppolla, Martin Scorcese, and John Huston. I switched on the VCR to see the last film that Hiroshi Tanaka had watched in bed. It was *Across the Pacific,* Huston directing the old gang from *The Maltese Falcon*—Sydney Greenstreet, Mary Astor, Humphrey Bogart. The Japanese were the villains. I wondered if Hiroshi and Wendy had found that titillating.

I started looking through the CDs since this thing was supposed to look like one. "No," Mike said, "it's bigger." I put on Clapton. "Layla." It was an incredible sound system. "After Midnight." "Cocaine." America might die, but rock 'n' roll is forever.

The other bedroom had been made into a study. A home office. It had a desk and a computer, two phones, one to a fax.

The bookshelves could have belonged to Tom Clancy. Someone was either researching high-tech thrillers or they were in the business of military aviation and aerospace. *Jane's Military Aircraft. Jane's Aviation Armament. World Market for General Aviation Aircraft: Avionics & Engines. Export of Aerospace Technology: Proceedings of the Goddard Memorial Symposium. Aircraft Weaponry of Today. Aircraft Industry Dynamics. A Competitive Assessment of the United States Civil Aircraft Industry,* from the U.S. Department of Commerce. *The Japanese Commercial Aircraft Industry Since 1945, Government Policy, Technical Development & Industrial Structure.* Trade magazines. Computer publications. There were titles in German and French. There were volumes of U.S. government publications. Procurement manuals. Bid specifications. Aviation. Missiles. Helicopters. Satellites.

"Oh," I said, "we are in deep shit."

"I thought you knew that," Hayakawa said.

"How would I know that?" I said.

"When I said yes to six hundred sixty-six thousand dollars," he said.

"I thought that was shuck and jive," I said.

"No. I was quite sincere."

"I should learn to be more trusting," I said.

It was late when we rode back to the hotel in Hayakawa's leather-lined version of Japanese luxury.

He was ferociously disappointed. "Where can the disc be?" he said.

"Are you going to tell me what's on the disc?"

"If I told you that I didn't know, would you believe me?"

"Why don't you call your office and find out."

"We must get into Hiroshi Tanaka's office," he said.

"I could do the office," I said. "If it was New York and I had some time to recruit some specialists. You're talking about a high-grade burglary—you understand that. Like something out of the movies. With a team of specialists. The alarm guy, the wheelman, the lookout, the safecracker."

"You must find a way," he said. "You must."

"There's one slim possibility."

"What is it?"

"I don't even know if it's worth trying."

"Tell me! I will decide."

"The big problem is the alarm," I said. "There are several problems, but the big one is the alarm. It requires a number code. We don't have it. You saw the response time of Austrian *Polizei.* So that gives us . . . ten minutes, if we're lucky, once the alarm goes. More like five."

"I understand this," he said impatiently.

"But we don't know where the optical disc is. So we need a hell of a lot more than five minutes."

"I understand this," he said. "You told me this."

"So the trick is to be inside before the alarm is set. If you trip it on the way out, it doesn't matter. You still have five minutes and all you need to do is leave."

"How do you do this?"

"Well," I said thoughtfully, "maybe you go in with the cleaners. Maybe it's even easier. You hang around, wait till Helga goes to the john or for coffee or whatever, and just ease on in. Find the broom closet or an empty office and stay there until they shut the place down. Or if someone is working late. Maybe Helga goes home promptly at six. So the front door is open and unguarded."

"I see," he said.

"It's a one-man job," I said.

"I understand," he said, not happy.

I turned on the radio. There was a commercial for Sony, then the *Theme from Peter Gunn*. Stand-up bass and saxophones. Jazz for a rain-swept street reflecting neon lights while a hooker with a heart of gold hikes up her skirt, shows her leg, and says she's never heard of crack, she's waiting for a good-time gambling man who looks like Peter Lawford and sounds like Cary Grant. When the next commercial came on I said, "Okay. I'll do it."

"Thank you," he said. "Thank you again."

THIRTEEN

SYMBOLS

Vienna is perfect.

The boulevards are wide. The sidewalks are immaculate. Traffic flows. Nothing is in disrepair. The lawns, the shrubs, the trees are groomed. The shops are full. There are lots of shops. Pedestrians never cross on a red light. There is a great deal of that which means capital Culture—public sculpture on imposing architecture, famous paintings, museums, and live music from dead civilizations.

Vienna has several images.

A living operetta: waltzing cavalry officers in gorgeous uniforms at balls with long-gowned ladies, high-hatted strollers, and an emperor.

Fervent dreamers in cafés: Freud and revoltingly subconscious sex, subversive literature in the bookstalls, twelve-tone music, Art Nouveau, utopian theories with cream, coffee, and Sacher tortes.

Postwar intrigue: After World War II Germany and Austria were jointly occupied by all the Allied powers and divided into four zones. It happened that the capital cities of both countries were deep within Russian sectors. They were additionally divided, Berlin into four zones—French, British, American, Soviet—and Vienna into five, the fifth being the jointly run First District. The mark of this unwieldy arrangement—immortalized in Graham Greene's *The Third Man*—was four men in a jeep, one from each Allied force, patrolling the streets. The Cold War had begun even before the old one was done and anyplace where the East and West were so closely entwined became a center of the trade in information, in contraband, papers, and people.

In 1955 the Soviets agreed to end the occupation. They demanded two guarantees—there would be no repeat of *Anschluss*, the uniting of Austria and Germany, and an independent Austria would be permanently neutral. This was agreed to by treaty and neutrality was written into the constitution of the new Second Republic. This did not put an end to the business of espionage. Neutrality and geography guaranteed an ongoing boom for the Viennese spy. Switzerland was neutral, but deep in the heart of NATO. West Berlin was deep in the heart of the Warsaw Pact but had Checkpoint Charlies every which way you cross. Austria was the only neutral with borders both ways. To the west it touched Italy, West Germany, and Switzerland. To the east were Czechoslovakia, Hungary, and Yugoslavia—countries that had once been administered from Vienna as part of the Hapsburg Empire.

Even though we were being followed, spy capital was still not my personal image of Vienna. I think of the city as the Mall Without Walls. Move over, Rodeo Drive; sit back, Fifth Avenue. We were on Kärntnerstraße, heart and soul of a city of shops, a pedestrian street that runs from the Staatsopern on The Ring to Stephansdom, the church at the very center of the Old City. So I said, "Let me buy you something," to Marie Laure. I was thinking most specifically of Palmer's. Satin things that clung and hung off of nipples. French-cut underwear with the wide legs that could be pushed aside. Perhaps an overpriced dress that would make her feel feminine, womanly, adored.

"I know what I want," she said.

Instead of a lingerie shop we entered a *Kinder Kaufhaus*. In a matter of minutes we'd spent ÖS4,200 on a McLaren stroller. I didn't understand the appeal. It didn't matter. I enjoyed spending the money. I was happy that I was in a position to get things for my family. There are many different definitions of manliness, a wide variety of activities that make a male feel masculine. Climbing a mountain. Winning a wrestling match. Mugging a mugger. Earning a million dollars. Having sex with women who look like

Viennese statues. Striving, battling, competing, scoring, winning! Then there's buying Änsa baby bottles, deciding if the baby's pajamas should be pink or blue, and picking out crib toys in nontoxic primary colors.

Our watchers waited outside for us. I almost asked them to carry our packages. But it would have embarrassed them. And I wanted to pretend that we were alone.

"I didn't buy all that stuff because I feel guilty," I said.

"Why did you say that? Everything was okay."

"All right," I said, "everything is okay."

"Now it's not," she said.

"Look, I know you were mad at me because I didn't show up for dinner last night."

"Or telephone. I was not mad. I was worried."

"I didn't want to call from Tanaka's apartment."

"You think I am wrong to say you should telephone? Talk to your mother. Your mother, she says I am right. She too had worry. She says you were always like this. Always irresponsible."

"Let's get something straight—the only reason I'm dealing with these people is for you." I held on to her. "No. Don't look at them. Listen to me. I don't think I can pull this off. I don't know how the system works. I don't have the language. I don't have contacts. And no backup."

"I back you up," my not-quite-wife said.

"If I were alone," I said, "I would tell them to fuck off. I'd sell the Laundromat and head for higher ground. I'm doing this just for you."

"Just for me? What about your daughter?"

"I know you think you speak for Anna. But she might like Argentina or New Zealand. Or Australia."

"What about for you? Anthony Cassella did not like people who changed their names."

"That was in America."

"What does that mean?"

"That means someone who changes their name to deny who they are and where they come from. Like from Guiseppe Ciccolini to Jonathan Charles, Jr. Or Isidore Lipshitz becomes Burt Lancaster."

"Was that Burt Lancaster's real name?"

"No. I was trying to make a point. That it's different."

"Is it?"

Why do I suddenly question what I know to be true just because a woman says, "Is it?" with a flick of the eyebrows and a bit of reverb in her voice? "Let's let it go," I said. "Let's just try to enjoy the day."

"All right," she said, "we will try."

But she did not throw her arms around me or kiss me in a manner that suggested that she was overcome with lust. So I was certain that she did not understand and that more explaining would make her understand and love me again, without reserve, the way she loved our daughter. "Let me explain. First of all, I was on a job. We spent eight hours taking that place apart. I'm the man in the middle. Both of them—Hayakawa and Sheen—know more than me. I have to shake both of them. Assuming this thing is found, I have to be the one to find it. I have to be alone or at least in control of the situation when I find it. I'm not going to let Chip Sheen take it off of me with his gun. That way he gets a big 'Attaboy!' at the Bureau or the Agency—wherever it is that he works—while I end up without our deal with the Justice Department and I don't get Hayakawa's Japanese money either. I can't let Hayakawa find it first. Then I have to get it away from him. He wants it real bad. More than half a million dollars' worth. That means someone is going to get hurt. Him or me, or both of us. Even if it's him that gets hurt, that doesn't mean that's the end of it. Those things have a way of escalating. So if I'm searching that apartment with Mike Hayakawa, I don't turn my back on him for a second. Because that's the second that he finds the disc and it's in his pocket before I see it and it's 'Oh, so solly, search is over, going back to To-kyo, too bad Mr. Cochlain. No money for you.' Then it's me and you and Anna against the IRS and extradition, without an extra six hundred thousand dollars to flee or fight. If I fight, a million D marks might just be enough for legal fees and back taxes. You get it?"

"First you say to just forget it and enjoy the day. Then you tell me the whole story all over again."

"Right, right, sorry. Let me buy you something else. Like a dress."

"I want to go to a museum."

They had a lot of Flemish paintings at the Kunsthistorisches Museum. There was a point in history when the Netherlands was ruled by Hapsburgs. Which is confusing because what Americans call Dutch are actually Flemings and what is now Holland was once shaped very differently and included Belgium, but it wasn't either country at that point anyway.

Peter Paul Rubens impressed me.

This was carnal knowledge. Those great soft women lying there, fleshy and open, creatures of sensual appetites. Like my Marie used to be. Not very long ago. And surely would be again. I put my arms around her from behind, put my hips against her hips. I looked for a staircase or a screened area or a hidden nook, where, like lust-crazed teens, we could, at the very least, dry hump. And if we were lucky, do something truly dirty and daring.

We were not, alas, on the same wavelength.

We met the two Annas at Café Central, a Viennese coffee shop that is both typical and famous, a period piece from the days when Vienna was the center of an Empire and a place of intellectual excitement. My mother looked out the window and said, "What is that nice Mike Hayakawa doing out there?"

"Oh, he's following us, Mom."

"Oh, that's terrible, standing out in the street like that. Ask him in."

He tried to look away when I approached, he tried pretending not to see me, then he tried to pretend that he was there because he liked leaning against walls to read the *Herald Tribune*. "Come in out of the rain and have a cup of coffee," I said.

"It's not raining," Hayakawa said.

"Yes," I said. "I'm trying to make it less embarrassing."

"This is embarrassing," he said.

"Did you enjoy watching me neck with Marie at the museum."

"A Japanese couple would never behave like that in public," he said.

"You should see Paris. Or Rome," I said. "A park in Rome on a Sunday afternoon is a soft-core orgy. A voyeur's dream." An ongoing theme in the *manga* at Tanaka's apartment was peeking and peeping. "Voyeurism seems to be a Japanese fetish, or was that just Hiroshi's thing?"

"I'm sorry," he said. "You have my deepest apologies. I am here because, as you know, I have been instructed to stay with you."

"I don't mind," I said. "Did you enjoy the Rubens?"

"Do men really like women," he said, "who are so . . . fat?"

"While you were following me," I said, "did you notice anyone following you?"

He turned around reflexively. "No," he said. He didn't see them. Neither did I, at that moment. "Was someone following me?"

"You know who keeps spotting you," I said, as we entered the café, "my mother. She's the one who said we should invite you in. I would have left you out there."

"Hello, Mike," my mother said, beaming. "Are you enjoying Vienna?"

"It is a very cultural city," Mike said.

"Sit down and join us," my mother said. "If you must keep track of my son, it's easier to do it this way."

"Thank you, Mrs. Cassella," he said. "You will be here for several minutes, won't you?"

"Yes," she said.

"You won't go away, will you?"

"No," my mother said. "We'll be here."

"Then you will excuse me. I must use the men's room. I will be back shortly. Rick, you must explain to me what you do about that. It is by far the hardest part of tailing a person."

The other two were better at following people. My mother didn't notice them at all. I was aware of them, but I didn't get a good look at them. I assumed that Chip Sheen had brought in the backup team. But it could have been a whole new set of players.

If they hadn't been to Vienna before, then the day would have been a treat for them too.

Wandering back to the hotel after coffee, we crossed the Judenplatz. *Platz* means square. *Juden* means Jew. "This was the center of the Jewish quarter," my mother said. She was keeper of the guidebook.

"You will go tonight," Mike Hayakawa asked me, "to Tanaka's office?"

"Tonight," I said. "They close at six. I'll be there around closing time."

"I am part Jewish," Marie Laure said to my mother. It was something that I was aware of, but rarely had reason to think of. "I was raised as a Catholic, but my mother was considered to have Jewish blood. When the Germans came they took my *grand-père*. Grandmama—she took my mother and they went to Algeria. That's where my mother met my father. So your granddaughter—she too has Jewish blood."

I took my daughter—that beloved, innocent, and fragile person—from her mother's arms. Forty-five years earlier they would have taken her. They would have put her on a train. A special train. In a cattle car. To an extermination camp. Because of who her great-grandfather was. She curled her hand around my finger. She looked at me. With complete trust. That war—the last great crusade where right was right, wrong was wrong—had seemed so faded and far away in the new Europe of the mighty Deutsche mark, with the Berlin wall falling down, communism collapsing from Budapest to Moscow, and 1992 coming. A war that they made movies of in black and white. A war so good that the actors who had played in it—the John Waynes and Ronald Reagans—thought they'd actually been in it. It had nothing to do with me. Suddenly it did. History telescoped. The past collapsed forward. Who would take my beautiful, precious Anna Geneviève and kill her? Who are the madmen who murder children?

The answer was—possibly—any Austrian over sixty-five. There were ambiguities. Hitler forced the *Anschluss,* but they truly cheered him from the Tyrol to Vienna. Most soldiers were probably draftees, just as most people just go along to get along. But they served, they knew, they participated, and were the first to agree that the Aryans were a master race.

"In Europe today they forget what America means. But my family does not forget," Marie Laure said. "I want to be able to go to America. I want to go with you. I want Anna Geneviève to visit her grandmama," she said to me.

Mike Hayakawa drew back and said nothing.

"What do these people think of their president?" my mother asked me.

"I don't really know," I said.

The story of President Kurt Waldheim, once Wehrmacht Oberleutnant Waldheim, is a strange one. He had been Secretary General of the United Nations from 1972–82 and Austria's representative there before that. For obscure, unfathomable reasons that reek of international intrigue but could as easily be casual carelessness, it was not until he ran for president that his war record crept out from under the rocks. While it was clear that he was not Adolf Eichmann, it was also clear that he was a knowing participant in an army unit involved with the deportation of civilians to concentration and death camps, reprisals against civilians, deportation of Jews from the Greek islands, mistreatment of Allied POWs, and handing over civilians to the SS. Also, as each revelation came out, he lied like a Nixon, each lie requiring another to cover the last.

"Black people can use the word *nigger* with each other," I said, "and they do, all the time. But a white person can't. That's what I feel like if I ask an Austrian about Waldheim."

"There's a joke in America," my mother said. "You've heard of Alzheimer's disease? That's where you forget everything. Then there's Waldheimer's disease. You just forget you were a Nazi."

"What does the book say about this place?"

"'The Judenplatz,'" my mother read from her Berlitz guide, "'housed a synagogue until fourteen twenty-one, when it was dismantled in a pogrom and its stones carted off.'"

More than the palaces—the Hofburg, the Neue Burg, Schönbrunn, or Belvedere. More than Stephensdom or The Ring itself or the Opera—that synogogue is the perfect icon for Vienna, a thing that is not there, symbol of what was and now is not—Gustav Mahler, Sigmund Freud, Franz Kafka, Theodor Herzl, Anton Bruckner, Arthur Schnitzler, Ludwig Wittgenstein, Victor Adler, Arnold Schönberg, Max Reinhardt, Martin Buber, Bruno Bettelheim, and the Nobel prizewinners in physics, Hess, Rabi, Pauli.

What is Vienna without them? Vienna is perfect. A great place to shop, if you don't mind buying retail.

FOURTEEN

THE THIRD MAN

I had lied.

The alarm at Hiroshi Tanaka's office was very simple. There was no number code. The key turned it off. It was a good lie. It did two things for me. If the disc was in the office, I would be alone when I found it, in control of its destiny and value. If it was not there, Mike Hayakawa still owed me one, for being the guy who went in while he stayed safe at the hotel, in the bar, drinking Scotch. He wanted to wait downstairs. I convinced him that it might draw the cops.

I arrived at the office a little after six. I stood in the street and watched the lights go out and saw Helga exit between the stone lesbians who supported the portico. Then I telephoned from the booth on the corner. No one answered. It's not foolproof. Sometimes switchboards are shut even if someone is in the office. But it's one more sign.

I went upstairs. I looked, I listened. It was quiet. It was dark. I opened the office door with the set of keys from Tanaka's apartment in St. Anton, then turned the alarm off. I was inside.

Then the cops grabbed me.

Two of them came through the door. They had flashlights. They had guns. I put my hands up. One shone a light in my face. The other went behind me. He pulled my arms down and put plastic ties around my wrists. They were tight enough to be uncomfortable. Once they were secure, the one in front punched me in the solar plexus. It knocked the wind out of me and I went to my knees, gasping. Then the one behind me kicked me in the ass, knocking me down to the floor. I managed to land on my shoulder instead of my face. They kicked me several more times. But not in the kidneys, testicles, or head. They didn't want to harm or mar me, just hurt me.

When they stopped, a third man was standing there. He didn't wear a uniform. He was a big man, heavy, about sixty, and leaned on a cane. "You are a pain in the ass, Cassella," he said. In English. "You're smart. I can use that. But you're stupid, and that's going to get you hurt." American English.

"I'm too old for this shit. I'm a father."

"Take him away. Throw him in the jail," the third man said in German. His hair was cropped short and shot with gray. It was a tough gray. He knew it.

The two *Polizei* stood me up.

"What do you want?" I asked him.

"What is it *you* want, Cassella?"

"What do I want? I want some snow. I want to make a little bread from my Laundromats, without bothering anyone. I want to teach my daughter how to ski. I maybe want to have another baby."

"Bad answer," he said.

One of the *Polizei* whacked me across the back of the thigh with his flashlight. It was four D cells long and at least that heavy. Police don't carry them to light up the world, they carry them because they're good for beating on people.

"Fuck you," I said. I meant ouch. Then I asked, "What's the right answer?"

"You tell me," the third man said.

"I hate this game," I said.

"The next time he'll hit you in the kneecap." The two uniformed *Polizei* said nothing, in English or German. Grabbing, holding, and hitting were their things—not speech.

"I know what I want to do," I said very reasonably. "I want what you want."

"That's better," he said. "Now try this—'I want to serve my country!' "

"I want to serve my country," I said.

"Try 'I want to go back to America!'"

"Okay," I said, "I want to go back to America."

"Did you sic the cops on Chip the other day?"

"Me? Would I do that?"

The other *Polizei* hit me across the other thigh with his flashlight. It was all very fascist and cruel.

"I assume you did. You've been making things very difficult for him. He's a nice, sincere kid."

"And a Mormon," I said.

"That too," he said. "If you cooperated with him, you wouldn't have to contend with me."

"It's hard to have a lot of faith in him," I said.

"I understand," the third man said. "But you better learn to get along. He holds your future in his hands. Maybe your life. Do you see what I mean?"

"Actually, I don't. We could do a lot better without the heavy mystery and the secret secrets. If I knew what was going on, maybe I would cooperate. Maybe I could cooperate. Pardon me for being frank, but all I've gotten so far is a lot of bullshit. Now you can beat me up some more, though I hope you don't, but it would probably be a lot more practical to break out the brandy and cigars and sit down and discuss this in a frank, open, and informative manner."

"Sure," he said, amiably. He turned and walked toward the inner offices. He had a heavy step with his good leg and a stiff movement with the bad. He gestured for me to follow him. The *Polizei* shoved me along. We entered the rather grand corner office.

"Was this Tanaka's office?"

"Exactly," he said. He sat, with a grunt, in the chair behind the desk. There was a chair facing the desk. He indicated. I sat. here was a humidor on the desk. He carefully selected two cigars. He put one down, clipped the other, moistened it, lit it, then got it going with noisy signs of pleasure. "You like skiing. A lot," he said.

"Sure," I said.

"Fine," he said. "Break his kneecap," he told the cops. As if they'd been waiting for the command, one cop whipped his arm around my neck from behind, the other raised his flashlight. "Wait," the third man said. The raised flashlight stopped in midswing. "What I wanted to explain was control. I am in control. I am running things. Do you understand that?"

"Yes," I croaked through the choke hold.

"I don't think you really get it. We used to do some shit in Vietnam. You throw someone out of a chopper, the other guys know who's in control. You cut off an ear or a finger, they get the picture. I want you to understand that I'm a person who will go to extremes. I've been called a control freak. And I like to win."

If he liked control and winning he should have hated Vietnam. But he didn't seem to remember it that way. So I didn't say anything. Except "Yes, sir."

"That's good," he said. "I like the 'sir.' Maybe you are getting it. You understand that I'm trying to be a gentleman about this. I have threatened you, but not your family. Your mother, your daughter, your girlfriend. Gosh, she's pretty. I know you think so. You were practically coming all over her in the Flemish section. I can reward you too." He smiled. "It's okay. Release him." One of the *Polizei* snipped the cuffs. "Thanks, boys," he said. He took an automatic out of his shoulder holster. It looked like a Glock, like Chip's. He chambered a round, took the safety off, then put it on the desk in front of him. He nodded at his *Polizei*. Like good Dobies, they trotted off.

"What do you think, Cassella. You think the disc is here?"

"Well, it's not in his apartment in St. Anton. It's not in the Vienna apartment. I thought this was a good bet."

"So did I," he said. "You might as well search it. Maybe you'll see something we missed. Did you want the cigar?"

"I'll take one," I said. "Will you tell me what the disc is?"

"Sure," he said. "It's a source code." He gave me the cigar.

"Of course. I should have realized. Source code. That's heavy-duty stuff."

"Don't be sarcastic with me, Cassella. We don't know each other well enough for that yet."

"What do you want from me?"

"I want you to find the disc," he said, and offered me a light.

"Which I now know to be a source code."

"Correct."

"Am I allowed to ask some questions here?"

"Certainly. You would be a fool not to."

"Who are you?"

"Let me be frank. I'm an old-time spook. An intelligence officer. A spy. In your situation, I am your case officer. Your handler. Your control. Welcome to the CIA."

"That's a hell of a line," I said. "Does that usually blow them over. How about what does the CIA need me for? Doesn't the CIA have its own clowns? Well trained, well paid, with medical plans, pension funds, and loyalty oaths? Guys who will sit still to be polygraphed and have their urine tested? Fine Americans like Chip Sheen?"

"Yes, we do. But not a single one of them happened to be a German-speaking ski bum in St. Anton at the time that Hiroshi Tanaka bought it, who also is a trained and very talented investigator. Don't be modest—I've checked. There are people who truly hate you. You're very good. You upset a lot of equations."

"It didn't matter in the long run, did it?"

"No. I guess it didn't."

"But you did have a man in place. Chip Sheen was there."

"He sticks out like a sore thumb, doesn't he?" the third man said. "I lost my train of thought there. What was I saying? Oh, yes. Ski bum, in St. Anton, has languages . . ."

"My German sucks."

"It'll do. You don't have to pass for a native." He paused and picked up the list, " . . . Investigator who I can control because he's under indictment, who is not known to any of the opposition and who is trusted by Mike Hayakawa. Don't you love how he does that Mike thing? So American. So trustworthy. So helpless. Fucking Japs do that all the time. That small and humble act. Little island, few resources, learning from us, depending on us. Voom! Badadadadadada. The next thing you know, Pearl Harbor. So we put 'em down. We put 'em in their place. Bombed 'em back to the Stone Age.

"Humble. You wouldn't believe humble. You should've been there before Nam, when the yen was three hundred sixty to the dollar. Service. You could get a pedicure, a full sashimi special, and your cock sucked—all at the same time, for ten bucks. And they gave good value for your money. Now ten bucks won't get you a cup of Tokyo coffee. They learn. Don't underestimate 'em. They learn from success and failure. Their success was that we underestimated 'em. So they made sure we did that again. Keep on bowing. Radios! Bowing. Cameras. Bowing. Televisions. Little things. Their failure was that they hit us head-on. Got us united and our backs up. So not this time. This time it's commercial—Toyota, Datsun, Honda, Isuzu, Mitsubishi, Mazda, Suzuki. Microchips. Computers. No guns, no killing, but ruthless just the same. War, just the same. Don't kid yourself that nineteen ninety is not an extension of nineteen forty-one. It's the same master plan from the same master race.

"So there you have it. You're on the inside. It's like God handed me a double agent. I don't overlook God's gifts. I'm no Holy Joe, like Chip Sheen, I'm a whiskey-drinking, cigar-smoking, pussy-loving son of a bitch. But when the good Lord hands me an advantage on a plate, I say, 'Thank you, Lord.' "

"So you want me to find this thing, make sure that Mike Hayakawa doesn't get it, and that you do."

"No, son, not at all. You don't appreciate the full dimension of this thing. But you will. You will truly enjoy this."

"I will?"

"Now I believe that Mike Hayakawa—do you know that his father was mentioned as a war criminal? We never tried him, but he was part of the military-industrial combine that drove Japan to war, used slave labor, abused POWs. His father sent him to California to learn to be American so he could learn to use America against itself. He has made you a very substantial offer. I believe the figure was six hundred sixty-six thousand dollars. Am I right or am I right?"

"You're very close."

"Don't fuck with me, son. I'll hurt you," he said.

He knew the number. It wasn't a guess. He'd been listening to me and Hayakawa. He hadn't found me breaking in. He and the *Polizei* had been waiting for me. There were microphones back home and in Vienna too. Probably in the Musashi Élégant, maybe in the hotel as well.

"Do right by me and you will do very well for yourself."

"Yes," I said. "That's the number."

"You wouldn't want to forgo that, would you?"

"If it meant a choice between the money and my country, I would take my country, sir! Particularly with what you have on me, sir!"

"Well said, Cassella. I didn't think you were capable of such heartfelt insincerity. It's a sign of maturity. Or a stint in the military. Well, I have a very pleasant surprise for you. Your job is to get that money."

"It is?"

"Oh, yeah. I want you to find the disc. I want you to give it to Mike Hayakawa. You might as well get your money while you're at it. But you better make damn sure that he doesn't get away with the disc. Your job is to set him up. So I can catch him dirty."

FIFTEEN

FRIENDS

Mike Hayakawa was waiting up for me.

He had the hotel staff tipped and alerted. The sober uniformed doorman told me to head for the Amadeus Mozart Bar. As I crossed the lobby the chirpy bellman told me that Mr. Hayakawa was expecting me. The very responsible spectacled fellow at the front desk hailed me and informed me of the same. He also handed me a note. It told me where to meet Mike in case the entire staff of the hotel had it wrong.

If they'd only beaten one leg I would have had to pretend not to limp. Since they had both been whacked, I had to pretend not to hobble. The bar hostess showed me her cleavage. Then she showed me to Hayakawa's booth. By then I was certain both were wired.

"Did you get it?" Mike said.

"No," I told him. His face fell. "I'm sorry." I had searched. I hadn't done any better than the third man. I now had a name for him. Lime, like Harry Lime. It was a code name. I was Apple, as in the Big Apple; Chip Sheen was Peach; Hayakawa was Cherry. We were a bunch of fruits.

"I know that if it had been there you would have found it. But I don't know if you would have given it to me. You are a trickster, Rick."

"Call me Tony," I said, building trust. "That's my real name. Anthony Cassella. The Upper West Side, by way of Brooklyn."

"Put 'er there, Tony," he said, and held out his hand. "Have a drink with me."

Why eighteen-year-old Scotch should kill the pain any better than eight-year-old or even twelve-year-old is a minor mystery. Not as significant as mother love or the female orgasm, but still worth noting for its transubstantial nature.

"What do we do now?" he asked.

"I'm sorry I have failed," I said.

"You have not failed. It was logical and it was necessary to look here. But if it was not here, you couldn't find it here. What do we do next? That is the question."

"We go back to St. Anton. And start again," I said. Unless I could convince Marie Laure that our best option was to disappear, change some names, get new passports, and head for higher ground.

"How do we start again? Where?"

"Let me ask you something," I said.

"Ask me anything," Mike said.

"Why is this disc so important to you?"

"Why is success important to any man? It is a matter of ambition, respect. Honor. Duty. These words sound very strange in English. In Japanese I would say *taimen, giri*."

"Yeah, they don't use words like that much anymore. Everyone is too cool. But when you think about it, who did?"

"What do you mean, who did?" he asked.

"Gunga Din? Rudyard Kipling? Don Corleone? The Light Brigade? Somebody said, 'England expects every man to do his duty'—I remember that from somewhere."

"Lord Horatio Nelson," Hayakawa said. "He sent that message by signal flag at the Battle of Trafalgar when England was a great island empire."

"That meant they should either kill somebody for a bigger empire or die for one. Same when Don Corleone said it. In World War I, I bet they used *duty* and *honor* a lot. Kamikaze pilots—they believed in duty and honor."

"The will to kill. Ready to die. Without that, no greatness," he said. I couldn't tell if the voice he was speaking from was that of a college sophomore drunk on a Japanese version of Nietzsche or the standard credo of economists at Musashi Trading Company or the rattling tail of a psychopath.

"Maybe," I said, "honor is to die when it won't help and duty is to kill without mercy. Maybe we're better off without them."

"That is very sad," he said.

"Yes, it is."

"That," he said, "is the real tragedy of America."

"I've always wondered what the real tragedy of America is."

"It is not that you have become a debtor nation or that you have fallen behind in technology and are declining in your place in the world. That is not the tragedy. The tragedy is that you have lost your sense of mission, of honor, of purpose. To die for what you believe in—that is purity, that is *chuhgi*."

"How did you like Berkeley?"

"Japanese work very hard in grade school and in high school. That is where the competition takes place. College we . . . fuck off!" He giggled. "If you get into the right college you are set. It doesn't matter what you do there. That is the myth anyway. It's not quite true. Sure, if you go to Tokyo University you will be on the fast track. Nissan, Toyota, Musashi, Mitsubishi, Fuji, Hitachi—you will be with an A-1 top-level corporation. But if you impress the right professors and make the right connections, you will be on the inside lane of the fast track."

"So did you fuck off at Berkeley?"

"Not as much as I wanted, and I have to tell you that fucking off at an American college is a fuck of a lot more fun than at a Japanese one."

"Why's that?"

"Japanese girls are not as liberal as *gaijin*. American women are much more . . . experimental." He giggled again. "There are no drugs in Japan. The rock and roll is all from the States. College was very tough—I was a stranger in a strange land. How do you like being a stranger in a strange land, Tony, my friend?"

"It's all right," I said.

"But you are a sportsman. And you have Marie Laure." He had even more trouble pronouncing it than I used to have. "And you are not Japanese. We Japanese are a unique people. We are. We think differently, feel differently than anyone else. All this is proven scientifically. To be away from family—from the company, which is like family, away from Japan—is hard."

"How does your wife feel about you being away."

"She is very good. She is taking care of the children."

"What does she feel about you seeing other women while you're out and around the world."

"She is a Japanese wife. She understands these things."

"Wow," I said.

"Wow?"

"I've never met a woman who understands these things."

"Japan is a much simpler place than the West," he said. "Women have their place. But a man does not expect as much from a wife. We have our duty to provide. She has her duty to run the home. We are to have children, she to raise them. The woman has the home, the man has the world. American women expect much more. When they are young, in college, that's great. It is overwhelming for a Japanese man, but it's great. When she grows older, I think the American girl grows unhappy because she cannot have all she wants for as little as she wants to pay. Which is the American disease. To have everything and have it at a discount."

"You think so?"

"You know more about America than me. Do you know any happy American women?"

I thought about that. It was a three-Scotch question without a doubt. The answer was "No."

"Ah-hah! I case my rest."

"You are drunk," I said.

"Yes. I case my rest," he said again, heard it, and laughed.

"Do you know any happy Japanese women?" I asked him.

"Happy? I am not sure. But I know something even better. I know many Japanese women who do not complain."

"I'll drink to that," I said. "As one sexist pig to another."

"Ah, sexist pig. So nice to hear you say that—such memories it brings back of Berkeley. Do you know, Tony, my friend, that I used to know one girl who was very politically correct. American girl—she used to like it from behind. She used to yell, 'Fuck me, you sexist pig. Your prick is a tool of oppression. Fuck me.' Ah, Berkeley—there was nothing like it."

"Is that a true story?"

"I don't know," he said sadly. "I read it in *Penthouse*. You know—the letters that people send in about their great sexual experiences? Mostly they start by saying 'I never thought that I would write to *Penthouse*, but . . ."

"I bet," I said, "that they have writers who write those letters."

"You think so?"

"Yes."

"That would be very sad," he said.

"What's a source code?" I said.

"Your mother is a very extraordinary woman. Isn't she?"

"Yes," I said. "I've never heard of a source code."

"She's intellectual, understanding, broad-minded."

"A very civilized woman," I said.

"Where is your father?"

"He's dead," I said. "And yours?"

"Dead. Cancer. Probably from radiation poisoning. From Nagasaki. But he didn't die until nineteen fifty-five."

By the time I reached our suite I was very drunk. Thereupon more noise was made than was strictly required in such an inhospitable setting. No one had informed me that my daughter had been making a difficult night of it, full of sounds and short of sleep, reducing Marie Laure to a state both raw and fragile. She accused me of being inebriated and thoughtless. I accused her of being something equally vile—sober and censorious. She said that she was carrying the burden alone. I said that she carried exactly as much as she wanted and not to lay that shit on me. The baby woke and started to cry. Marie Laure said I had done that, when clearly it was she. "You wake her, you take her," she said in what used to be a very charming French accent. She placed the squalling brat in my arms. I rocked her and made coo-coo noise that left her less than impressed. Poor tyke—she turned and gnawed at my bosom. It lacked both sustenance and comfort. I made an announcement to that effect and thrust her back upon her mother, who enuciated very clearly a revisionist view of our relationship in which she hated me.

Having slept with hatred more than once in states ranging from sober to drunk to stoned, I know that a couch with its lumps brings more rest and comfort than a mattress shared with a woman and rage. I blessed my Oriental friend's expense account that had provided us with a living room. Far better than sleeping in the bath. But the fight followed my flight.

It woke my mother, who emerged, as old women will, with a robe wrapped around worried pajamas. My mother, like many Americans, defies her age in looks, in vigor, in interests. But in the middle of the night, rheumy-eyed, without her teeth, worried and wrinkled, she was cronelike. There stood the triad of women—infant, fruitful, and ancient. I was certain I was faced with female solidarity and that my mother would take Marie Laure's part.

"What's going on?" my mother asked.

" 'E's drunk," Marie said.

"I had to be. It was business."

"You are a liar," Marie said. "No one 'as to drink."

"The Japanese guy thinks I'm his friend. He thinks I saved his butt. I have to cement that. I have to make him sure that I'm his friend. That means drinking with him tonight. I'm sorry. But that's what it meant."

"You are just wishing you didn't have to be responsible for us," Marie Laure said.

That wasn't true, but it was just true enough to make me shut up for a moment.

My mother fixed Marie with her gaze and spoke as if in judgment. My mother, as Mike Hayakawa and others have noted, is normally a broad-minded, intellectual, literate, and very rational person. Civilized. Somewhere in her genes or infantile memory there must have been a crone, a hill woman full of folk wisdom and Sicilian doom who spoke through her now. She said, in a vendetta voice, "My son is behaving correctly. Keep your friends close, but your enemies even closer. How else will you know when to strike?"

In the morning I apologized. She did too. But I had a headache and hangover and it didn't make me smile. She was tired and had evidence that my mother had allied with me against her.

So Marie didn't grin either. Which was a damn shame because we both knew that we were in love, with each other as well as with the baby. Something truly stupid was going on and I wasn't bright enough to stop it. After breakfast and coffee it hadn't gotten any better. Nonetheless we agreed to sightsee and shop for at least the morning before going back to St. Anton, since, it appeared, my business in Vienna was unsuccessfully concluded.

She took an awfully long time getting ready. How long can a woman take dressing and hairing and making up? The answer, as every man knows, is twenty minutes longer than we would possibly imagine and ten minutes more than we can stand. Knowing that this is sex-role typing or the sexist equivalent of racist thinking doesn't stop it from happening exactly that way.

"How the fuck do you take so long?"

"If you have such a rush, you can leave without me."

"I want to be with you—that is the point."

One of us carried the baby and two of us carried the attitude as we emerged from the hotel.

"What is your problem?" I said.

"It is your problem," she said.

Mike Hayakawa, who was coming toward us, realized what he was walking into. He politely stood aside, as if by seeming to ignore us our privacy was guaranteed.

"I am not a plaything. Like all of your others."

"No, you're not. And I treat you differently too."

"You have no commitment."

"I put the laundries in your name. Two great Laundromats. Come the nineteen ninety-two Winter Olympics, the one in Tignes alone will make your fortune."

"Is it money we are talking about?" she asked. "It is not money we are talking about," she answered.

"Well, it's certainly not sex that we are talking about. We haven't talked about sex since the baby was born."

"You want to have sex? Do you care if it is 'urting me?"

"That's not what I mean. I mean I am totally faithful to you even though we don't have sex. And sex is not a matter of intercourse, is it?"

"You want *le pipe?* Would you like me to suck you while I am nursing? Or while I am changing 'er diapers?"

"How about just treating me like a decent human being."

"Because you are not a decent human being and I cannot trust you."

We were deep in fear, angst, and rage. Truth didn't matter anymore. Or love. Or caring. I don't know what did matter. Scoring points. Venting tension. Exposing pain.

"Okay, you don't trust me. Maybe I should give you something not to trust me about."

"Like what?"

"Like maybe I should get some affection from somewhere."

"Fuck you, Anthony Cassella." In her rage she turned from me. I wasn't having any of that. We were going to have it out. So I grabbed her arm. She wasn't having any of that. So she tore herself away from me. Without looking or realizing where she was going. Then she was off the curb. She stumbled and in trying to keep her balance her feet went out in front of her so that she was stepping out into the street.

Austrians are very Germanic. That is to say, orderly. Cars stop at red lights. People cross when the light says WALK, and only at the crosswalk. Drivers depend on this obedience and proceed as if traffic rules were laws of nature. On the positive side, it means street traffic really moves. On the negative side, it means that if someone does break a rule, the cars are usually going too fast to stop. So perhaps the driver who hit Marie should not be blamed. He put on his brakes as soon as he could. The skid marks were there afterward to prove his effort. Nor is Marie to blame, for running from me, or tripping. Perhaps I should be as generous with myself. Perhaps I should embrace some guilt. Who knows?

When the car struck her, she was already turning around—she saw it coming.

When the car struck her, the impact traveled through her. The kind of thing they demonstrate in high school physics by striking one pool ball through another. The same thing that happens when your croquet ball is against your opponent's and you put your foot on yours to hold it in place, then hammer it in order to make the other ball fly.

It was a law of physics that sent Anna Geneviève flying out of her mother's arms. All I could do was watch and wish I were dying instead.

Mike Hayakawa, who was not involved, started moving as soon as Marie stumbled. Not expecting what was to happen, but to help her. So he was already in motion. He changed course. Like the most glorious receiver in the history of American football, he was running, reaching for my daughter, his arms outstretched in front of him.

But she was out of his reach. Falling toward the street. Car coming.

Mike dove for her. In his perfect Japanese businessman's suit, he slid on the Viennese pavement. He caught her as gently as could be. Rolled over away from the oncoming car and held her to his chest.

Marie was alive. She'd been knocked against a parked car, then fallen to her knees. She staggered over to her baby. And to Mike. I ran to them. She held her baby tight.

"I'm sorry, I'm sorry," she said over and over.

"No, no, it's my fault," I said.

"I'm sorry," she said again.

"Are you okay?" I asked.

The driver of the car rushed up. "You were not crossing in the crosswalk," he said. "All was correct. I am not responsible."

"Yes," Marie said to me. "Is my baby okay?"

The driver said, "You should not be crossing when cars have the green light."

"She's fine," I said to Marie. "Are you okay, Mike?"

"Sure," he said. "I'm fine."

"You're a hero," I said.

"You bet," he said, as happy and proud as he deserved to be.

SIXTEEN

PHOTOGRAPHS & MEMORIES

When we arrived in St. Anton there was an ancient Citroën CV6 parked in front of the *pension* where we have our apartment. It was classic black and red. Inside was an irate *grand-mère*.

The conversation that ensued was in very fast, very colloquial French. The gist of it was that she was angry that her daughter and granddaughter had not been there to greet her. It did not matter that they had not known she was coming. Her granddaughter was beautiful. Her granddaughter had all her parts. Her granddaughter was not as well looked after as she ought to be, but now that would be rectified. Oh, this was the father of her granddaughter—not a terribly interesting piece of information. And this was the other grandmother—far more interesting. Negotiations would ensue. How come the father of her granddaughter had not yet taken her bags inside, and which room was hers?

The politics of government are actually more rational than the politics of people. Yet it is governments who employ officers of protocol to decide who sits next to whom at dinner and who gets to sleep where, because experience has taught them that even diplomats grow undiplomatic when they think another occupies a more advantageous piece of furniture. We had no professional assistance and war seemed imminent.

The final accommodation was to rent two additional rooms in the *pension*, one for each grandmother. That gave us our apartment back, but not, somehow, our privacy or peace.

People of a certain age—and we were all of a certain age since we were either below puberty or parents—have a certain rigidity of needs. Best hours for dealing with others, for eating, for being alone. Favorite foods, favorite irritations, a variety of required noise levels and silences, necessary television programs, sources of news and forms of entertainment, tasks they need to do and tasks they cannot bear. The variety of different coffees alone was enough to destroy harmony. I prefer German coffee, which is similar to American coffee in the way that a Mercedes is to a Buick. It's exactly the same except that it costs twice as much and it's a lot better. Geneviève, *la grand-mère,* preferred French coffee. It had taken me years to wean Marie Laure to the Teutonic format and now suddenly we were back to that black and bitter brew, much like espresso but not quite as extreme a statement, relieved only by heated, not steamed, milk. Anna, the elder, wanted decaf, instant preferred. But if she had real coffee her preference was the Italian style—that is to say, cappuccino, with the milk steamed, not heated. Marie Laure, as pure as any California girl, had forsworn coffee altogether for the sake of caffeine-free breast milk and was drinking only herbal tea.

Not that I had a great deal of time to contemplate this.

As I carried Geneviève's bags in from the Citroën the phone rang.

"Hi, guy," Chip Sheen said.

"Be careful what you say," I said.

"Why?"

"You're tapping the phone, aren't you?"

"Yes," he said.

"See what I mean?"

"I thought Mr. *Lime* had a word with you," he said, very irritated.

"Yes, Peaches, he did."

"I want a little respect. Mr. *Lime* warned you."

"Who is Peaches?" Marie Laure asked.

"I think we need to sit down and have a meeting," Peaches said.

"About what?"

"This is not a secure line. We need a face-to-face."

"Of course it's not a secure line," I said.

"Who is Peaches?" Marie Laure asked. "And why do you need a secure line to talk to her?"

"Mr. Lime said I should have a face-to-face with you and plan your next move. If you don't come up with something I'm to call him and he says he will lower the boom. I'm talking about making *applesauce*. Cored, boiled, and mashed."

"I thought it meant you wanted to eat me with sugar and cinnamon," I said.

"What is that supposed to mean?" Chip said.

"What is that supposed to mean?" Marie Laure said.

"It has to be alone," Chip said. "Shake off you know who."

"You mean Cherry?"

"Who is he calling *chéri?*" Marie Laure's mother, who had also wandered into the conversation, asked.

"I don't know," Marie Laure said, "but it is someone he calls Peaches."

"Yeah, it would be a good idea to be alone," I said.

"Good, when can we meet?" Chip "Peaches" Sheen asked.

"And why do you need to be alone?" Marie Laure asked.

"*Pourquoi seules?*" Marie's mother asked. "*Pourquoi une tête-à-tête?*"

"How soon can we do it? I need to get out of here," I said.

"*Quel dommage,*" Marie's mother said.

Marie just sat down and sighed. Anna Geneviève made some new baby noises.

"Right now is fine," Chip said.

"Same place as last time," I said.

"Oh, God," Marie Laure said.

"*Mon Dieu!*" her mother said.

"I want to know who Peaches is," Marie Laure said as I hung up the phone.

"I'm sorry. I never got around to telling you. We all have code names. That was just Chip. He's Peaches. There's also Lime, Apple, and Cherry." As my mother walked in I said, "We're all fruits."

"Oh, no," my mother said.

"That's better," Marie Laure said.

"*Je ne comprende pas,*" Geneviève *la grand-mère* said.

As I opened the door to leave, our hero, Mike Hayakawa, was raising his fist to knock.

"Am I intruding?" he asked.

"Not at all," I said. "You're welcome, I'm leaving."

"What are we going to do now?" he asked.

"I'm going grocery shopping," I said. "Why don't you go in and meet Marie's mother."

"We are defeated, are we not?"

"Stay for dinner," I said. "You're our honored guest. One of them anyway."

"You're going to the supermarket?" he said, worried that I might be going somewhere that he should be following me to. Which I was.

"Look, you can't follow me every minute of every day. I'm not going to let you follow me to bed. You can't keep up with me on skis. And I can lose you if I put my mind to it. So relax. You saved my baby. I owe you. You can trust me. Two things I promise you. One is that we are not yet defeated. And two"—I looked him square in the eye. I was my most Caucasian sincere—"if I find the disc, the very first thing I do is put it in your hands. Trust me."

"Okay, Tony," he said. "I'll trust you."

"Great. Go make nice to the grandmothers."

With Cherry diverted I made my way to Peaches. There was no reason that Cherry couldn't have come along since I had nothing to report. No ideas. No plans. It was just that it would have changed a double game into a triple and I was already having trouble keeping my prevarications straight.

Peaches made me call his boss. He had a portable scrambler built into a genuine pigskin attaché case that interfaced with any phone system in the world. It was very James Bond.

"I want action," Lime said, his voice distorted by being deconstructed and then imperfectly reassembled. Something like Darth Vader without the rolling elocutions.

"What do you want me to do, jump up and down in place?"

"Understand something. You are a wanted fugitive. I am holding off your extradition and arrest. I am giving you a week to find this thing . . ."

"Where do you suggest I start?"

". . . or I will let matters proceed."

"It's a dead end," I said.

"You'll think of something . . ." Lime said.

"I can't do anything . . ." I said.

". . . because you're cunning and because you're motivated . . ."

". . . if there is nothing to do."

"Because you know that I can see to it that it's a long, long time before you see your new baby girl again."

"You motherfucker," I said to the dead telephone line.

"You shouldn't speak like that to Mr. Lime," Chip "Peaches" Sheen said. "He is working for America and America is God's chosen country. I can't understand people who don't respect that."

I went to the supermarket to cover the lie to Hayakawa and because we needed food. It was almost closing time and all the best bread was already gone, which annoyed me no end. There were no good bananas either, and since everything closed at the same time I was too late to hit one of the other two markets. When I got home Cherry was still there. My mother had convinced him to stay for dinner. I was a preoccupied and sour host.

When we finally got to bed, Marie Laure moved close to me. "I love you," she said with great warmth. "I don't want anything to happen to any of us."

"Are you all right?" I asked, politely inquiring about her bruises.

"Yes, I'm fine," she said.

I put my arm around her. Her body was warm and womanly against me. I stared at the ceiling as if the plan I didn't have would appear there. I wanted my woman and my child and to go from day to day free of worry. No more than everyone else wants. I was in a box and inside that box I was wrapped in chains and those chains had weights on them.

In the morning I went down to the laundry. Machine number 5 was acting up. The mounting bolts that hold the section that actually spins have thick rubber washers that act as shock absorbers. There is something asymmetrical about number five and it destroys them far more frequently than it should. Once that happens, it's metal against metal, bouncing almost a quarter inch per spin. With fifteen pounds of laundry soaked with ten pounds of water it sounds like Soviet tanks are on parade through the center of town. I fixed it and collected the money from the change boxes.

Anita was handling everything else with reasonable competence.

I didn't particularly want to get back to the House of Women, though I should have with Marie in a loving mood. I spent the afternoon skiing. We were back to rocks and gravel again. I tore up the bottoms of my beautiful Atomic 733SLs. I skied until they shut the mountain and chased me off. I skied like they were going to take it all away from me tomorrow.

Then I went to Down Under for a drink.

Paul was sitting alone at a table in back. He looked unusually bitter for an Australian. He failed to say "Goo'day, mate."

"What the hell's the matter?" I asked.

"What's your poison, mate?" he said.

"Wine," I said. "Something light and white."

He gestured for the waitress. "You got it sussed," he said. "One good Sheila and a kid. That's the way to go."

"What happened, have your heart broken?"

"I wish it were my heart. You can break my heart any day," he said to the waitress as she appeared with a Williams and a beer. "Can't you, love? And I bounce right back."

"Yes, Paul." She said to me, "His heart hangs between his legs."

"Oh, God, it's true," he said, full of rue. "Bring the lad here some vino."

"Do you want to tell me about it?"

"Not really," he said.

"Okay. Tell me about Wendy and Tanaka," I said.

"You're still on that?"

"Yeah," I said, "I'm still on that."

"What were you? In love with her?"

"It's gotten complicated," I said.

"It does do that. You won't believe this story."

"What story?"

"Never mind. It was Wendy that I wanted. She had a certain appeal. More than an appeal. There was something very like a schoolgirl about her. Like, she would be bald as a peach once you got up under her dress. Yet at the same time she knew what it was all about. Twisty little fantasy there. She was as tasty as her pal Carol is dull. The two of them together were like a pastry next to the dough. I only took on the dough because I thought the pastry would follow along. Like I said, mate, the wandering cock will get you in trouble. Stick with your Sheila and keep your willie in your trousers. Do you know what happened to me?"

The waitress showed up with my drink and another Williams for Paul. He downed the pear schnapps in a swallow.

"Maybe I should talk to Carol again," I said.

"Wendy stayed over often enough. She might even have left some of her stuff here. There was this Belgian girl . . ."

"Belgian girl?"

"Arrived last week. Pear-shaped tits, didn't wear a bra. Lean. Beautiful tits. Rick, she had beautiful tits. Do I repeat myself? Yes, I do. It took me a week to get into this one's pants. Just luscious. Worth the wait, too. That's what I thought. Never mind."

"So I should go ask Carol about anything Wendy might have left."

"Carol's a pain in the arse. You want to look around Carol's room, come on—I'll let you in. I'm 'er landlord, aren't I? I've got the bloody key. Come on," he said. When he got up, I followed him. Staff housing was around the back of the club. "Yvonne, her name was."

"The Belgian girl?"

"With the tits," he said.

"I didn't imagine she'd left 'em behind."

"We fooked our brains out," he said. "Just fooked our bloody brains out. Up and down, sideways, backways, sitting, sliding, and standing up. Bloody lovely it was," he said as he opened the door to Carol's little room. It was fairly neat. There was a bed big enough to get laid in but not to spend the night. A chest of drawers. A closet. There was a window. If the room had a saving grace, that was it. I started going through the place. There was a truly cheap painting of an alpine scene on the wall. Paul sat on the bed. "You've done this kind of thing before," he said.

"Could well be," I said.

"So there we are, me and Yvonne, from Belgium. And do you know what she says to me?"

"No, what?"

"I'm talking about after fook number four. When my dick is bloody well raw, isn't it, from trying me New South Wales best to make her satisfied. Do you know what she says?"

"No," I said, working my way from the bottom drawer up.

"She says, 'It's fun to fook a white man again.'"

"What's that mean?" I asked.

"Exactly what I says, exactly," Paul said.

"So what did she say?" I said, up to the next drawer, finding nothing of consequence.

"She says, 'I've had nothing but black men for the last six months.' 'And where've you been?' I says. What do you think she says?"

"I don't know. What did she say?"

Paul lifted the pillow from its place at the head of the bed and held it up as if it were the Belgian girl. He spoke in a falsetto, "'Rwanda, I've been in Rwanda.'"

"What's wrong with that?"

"It was just two weeks ago I saw it on the telly. They did random blood tests in Rwanda. Random tests. Thirty percent positive for the AIDS virus."

"Oh, shit, Paul," I said, looking over at him. He was hunched over the pillow, hugging it. At the head of the bed, where the pillow had been was a packet of three-by-five snapshots. The packet was folded open and Wendy Tavetian looked out at me from the top photo.

I picked up the package. There was Wendy in an urban landscape. A city I couldn't place. There was Wendy with another girl. There was the other girl, alone. Where Wendy had her appeal, this one was truly stunning. In this humble snapshot she looked ready for *Elle* or *Vogue*. She had the cheekbones and the slightly almond eyes and the lean languid provocative look. She had the big moist lips that have become the primary secondary sexual characteristic of models since they got too slender for breasts. There were several photos of Hiroshi Tanaka with the two of them.

"What the fuck are you doing in my room," Carol said, banging the door open.

"It's my fooking room," Paul said, "in my fooking building, and if you don't like it, get yourself another job."

"I'm looking for anything that'll tell me about Wendy Tavetian. I'm sorry if I invaded your privacy," I said, trying to be conciliatory.

"Get out, get out, get out," she yelled.

"I'll get out when I feel like it," Paul said.

I lifted him up. "Come on, Paul," I said. "She has a point. Let's go."

He more or less nodded and more or less came along. I had the pictures in my pocket. As we left, Carol threw herself on the bed weeping. It occurred to me that if Hiroshi Tanaka didn't have the disc where he was when he died, perhaps it was where he'd been before he got here. That was a tale that would be quickly told by his passport and described, very probably, in the photographs.

SEVENTEEN

BUDAPEST

"What was Hiroshi Tanaka doing in Czechoslovakia?" I said.

"I don't know," Mike Hayakawa said.

"What was he doing in Poland?"

"I don't know," Mike Hayakawa said.

"In East Germany?"

"I don't know," Mike Hayakawa said. "If I did, I would tell you."

Complex visas with logos in a variety of colors marched through Hiroshi Tanaka's passport marking his travels through all of Eastern Europe, up and back, Moscow to Berlin to Bucharest, right up to the week of his death. The photos of Hiroshi, Wendy, and the unknown girl had been taken in one of the East Bloc countries. I didn't know if they mattered but they were all I had to narrow the field. I didn't show them to Hayakawa. I said, "Do you have his address book?"

"Yes," he said. I knew he did. I'd seen it in the apartment the night I brought Hayakawa back there drunk.

"Give it to me," I said.

"What was Hiroshi Tanaka doing in Hungary?" I asked.

"I don't know," Chip Sheen said.

"What was he doing in Romania?"

"I don't know," Chip Sheen said.

"Aren't you supposed to know? Who does know?"

Chip hooked up the Porta-Scramble and put me through to his boss in Vienna.

"So you're crossing The Line," Lime said. "Parting the curtain."

"I thought the curtain was down. Last year, nineteen eighty-nine," I said, "they changed the world. That's what they said on TV."

"You have a lead?"

"I have his passport. I have his address book."

"I told Peaches you were cunning," Lime said. "All you needed was motivation."

"Have all those places really changed?" I asked Lime. "Or am I going to end up in a totalitarian prison?"

"What's in the address book?" Lime said.

"Do they have due process? Lawyers? Bail? Or do they send me straight to the Gulag?"

"Which country are you going to?"

East Germany, Poland, Hungary, Czechoslovakia, Romania had all stopped being communist. Even if you'd been hiding out behind false papers and a snow-covered alp you had to know about it. Every TV crew in the world showed up the day the Berlin Wall came down. Gorbachev became everyone's best friend because he was letting it happen. Lech Walesa taught everyone that you don't pronounce Polish names remotely the way they are spelled and opened the Gdansk shipyards to capitalism at a time when no one in the West could compete with the shipyards of Japan and Korea anyway. Czechoslovakia made the cover of *Life* even though that was the issue in which the editors picked America's cutest baby. A group of Romanian cleaning ladies had their pictures front page, top, center of the *New York Times*. It was the morning after the revolution and they were literally sweeping up, brushing the bloody stones with old-fashioned brooms made of twigs. The Hungarians didn't get any major photo ops, but they regularly received a kind of honorable mention in every other country's story for sort of starting the whole thing by opening their borders and letting East Germans go to Vienna to shop, that being one of the two things that all East Europeans want to do with their newfound freedom. The other is to find an ethnic minority to persecute.

"It's hard to believe anything could change that fast," I said. "The question is, Has it changed so much that American spies are welcome now?"

For forty-four years we all knew what the shape of the world was. For forty-four years we were eyeball to eyeball, over two million men at arms on each side, poised for the moment when someone would take the dare and cross The Line. The tanks were lined up. The artillery. The armored columns. The bombers and fighter support. The missile-bearing nuclear subs and the carrier fleets playing ocean chess, jockeying for position. Spy planes and satellite recons. Defectors, defectors in place, microwave listening devices, phone taps, wire taps, radio taps. Disinformation and assassination. Billions upon billions into building better weapons, maintaining them, deploying them, lobbying for the contracts to build them, encouraging other countries to arm so that the arms industries could export product and amortize the cost of the Cold War.

"I went to the travel agency," I said. "I asked what I need to cross the borders. A passport, they said. Just a passport. No visa. No special appointment. Just show up at the closest Checkpoint Charlie and cross over." I had also showed the photos to the women at the agency and asked if they could tell where they'd been taken. I didn't mention that to Lime. "But all those people, who used to run the police states, who ran the Cold War, they have an investment. Did they just fade away? Have they all disappeared?"

"Which country you going to?" Lime asked. "I want to see the address book."

"The TV said the Cold War is over. But the Pentagon is still in business. The CIA is still in business. I bet the KGB is still around and the Hungarian KGB and the East German Stasi and whatever the Czechs have and the Poles. Where do spys go when the Cold War is over?"

"Did you show the address book to Peaches?"

"No," I said.

"Let him see it. I want a copy."

"That's my edge," I said. "I don't want to turn it over."

"Why is everything with you a problem?" he snapped. "I

thought we taught you that we're in this together. I can have you deported tomorrow."

"Okay," I said. I'd wanted him to work for it so he'd think he'd achieved something. "I'll give it to Chip."

"Put him on the phone," Lime said.

I handed Chip Sheen the phone.

He listened intently, his eyes narrowed, his brow furrowed, he said, ". . . East Bloc . . ." and beneath his trousers his loins girded to do battle with any remaining unbelievers. ". . . Cover, we need deep cover," he said. ". . . Okay . . . shallow cover. . . . I remember the tradecraft courses. They were my favorite. . . . Yes, I know . . ."—he glared over at me—". . . I can handle him."

I snickered. It was rude and I was wrong to do it. Chip flushed.

". . . Annulment," Chip said.

I figured that was the new jargon for *terminate with extreme prejudice, sanction, wet work.* Lime must have suggested that was excessive because Chip said, ". . . only if *necessary.*" Lime must have told him it shouldn't be necessary to annul me because he looked frustrated. Then he listened some more, gave me a hard look, and handed me the phone back.

"I'm giving you Peaches as backup," Lime said. More like a keeper.

"You mean little Chip here," I said. "Or Chester or whatever his name is."

"You know who I mean."

"I have to tell you something, I'm having trouble with the funny names."

"You think you're a tough guy, a wiseguy," Lime said. "And I can see where Peaches is a real tempting target. But if I were you, I'd be careful, even respectful. He's a true believer."

Mr. Lime rushed us passports by courier. The courier had a green-and-red woolly ski cap. We had a code phrase to greet him. "Hey, that hat looks like a mango." He was to reply, "Mangoes are out of season." The counter countersign was, "By the fruit you shall know the tree." It was hard to tell with Lime, if he had a military man's insistence on doing the absurd to prove he could enforce obedience for its own sake or if he had a sense of perverse humor.

Chip handled the exchange. He insisted that I handle the *dry cleaning*. This was a piece of *tradecraft* that meant tailing him to the *brief encounter* to make sure that there were no *minders* watching him. As best I could tell, he was *sterile*. We received Canadian passports. They are real faves in the *Co*(vert)-*Op*(erations) world because Canadians are exactly like Americans except that they are cloaked in a certain obscurity that gives them an image of enhanced political innocence, a North American version of Norwegians. Mine was in the name of Andrew Applebaum. The photo was me. Which meant that Lime had had it standing by. He went up a notch in my estimation, from sadist to competent sadist. Chip became Charles Pêchier.

I let him look at the address book. If you were a tourist in Central Europe it was very thorough. It listed hotels, favorite restaurants, car rentals, banks, Amex offices, cambios, taxis. Beyond that it was useless. Not a single business contact. Not a friend. All that time, all that effort, all that money, all the traveling—Berlin, Prague, Budapest, Bucharest, Mariánské Lázně—and he kept everything he was really doing—the names, addresses, phone numbers—in his head.

Marie found me studying the photos. She was not amused.

"Who is that girl?" Marie Laure asked. In three of the twenty-three shots the subjects were nude. They had been shot on a balcony either in a tall building or on a house on a hill—a cityscape was behind and below them. There were patches of snow on old-fashioned roofs and smoke rising from chimneys. The first two shots were Wendy and another girl, nipples erect in the cold. Tanaka had gotten into the third. Marie Laure was referring to the unknown female with the swaybacked butt and oral-sex pout. The same people appeared with their clothes on in several of the other photos.

"I don't know," I said. "We see three people. Sometimes they appear one at a time, sometimes all together. I think there were two couples. I think there's a fourth person. That's who I'm interested in."

"I don't think so," she said, disbelieving my focus, not denying the fourth person.

"Who is the person who took the pictures but never has his picture taken? It's wintertime. Some people are messing about, naked. They run out onto the balcony—you can see the giggles and the goose bumps if you look closely. They didn't ask some stranger, 'Hey, come snap this picture.'"

"You 'ave to look very close for that," Marie Laure said.

"And they have their picture taken. It's taken by someone that is playing with them. But is never in the pictures—not even in these private moments. A very careful man."

"Where are you going?" Marie said.

"To look for the unknown photographer," I said.

"You are going to look for this girl?" Marie Laure asked.

"Only insofar as she leads me to the guy."

"I see. You are going to look for this girl."

"Well, if you put it that way . . ."

"I will 'elp you," Marie Laure said.

"Don't be ridiculous," I said.

Marie Laure selected one of the photos of the two naked girls. They were not the stolid masseuses of Viennese stone. Wendy was girlish and giggling. *Très americaine*, athletic and adolescent both, with, as Carol had described them, cupcake tits. The other girl was leaner, languid, sipping the liqueur of decadence.

"Don't even think about it," I said. "We don't know what's over there. Stasi. KGB. Secret Police. Smersh."

Marie showed the three-by-five to her mother and indicated which female I was looking for. Her mother looked at me. French women of all ages have very expressive faces. They are supralingual—not confined by the barrier of separate vocabularies and different syntaxes. Then Marie Laure showed the photo to my mother. My mother looked from the photo to me to Marie Laure. Her expression, in Sicilian-American, said much the same thing that the other mother had said in French.

The road to Budapest is through Vienna and straight east. We went, en caravan. Marie and me in the front. Anna, Geneviève, and Anna Geneviève cramped in the back. The trunk loaded with baggage and bags around our feet full of the things we would need to get out hands on en voyage—diapers, mineral *wasser*, pills for her mother, eyedrops for mine, ointments and powder for the baby, tissues, makeup for three, maps, guidebooks, four apples, two bananas, an orange, a half kilo of good French mountain Gruyère, and a loaf of bread as close to French bread as the Austrians can make. Mike Hayakawa's familiar Musashi was comfortably tacked onto the rearview mirror, our excess baggage in his trunk. Behind him, trying manfully to keep out of sight, was Chip Sheen. Obeying an agency directive to rent American, he was now in a lemon-yellow Opel, GM's German subsidiary. It was entirely possible that there were other members of our wagon train, but I didn't spot them.

"*Marie Laure est* a girl *jolie,*" Marie Laure's mother said, throwing the odd word of English in with her French as if it would make her understood. Sometimes it did. "*Comprenez-vous?*"

"Yes, she's very pretty," I said.

"Oh, yes," my mother said. "Very pretty."

"*Arrête de la vous voyer!*" Marie said. "*Tutoyer.*"

"*Pourquoi pas 'vous'?*" her mother said sharply.

"What?" my mother asked.

"There are two forms of *you* in French. *Vous* is formal . . ." I said.

"*Pour les étrangers,*" Marie Laure said pointedly.

". . . *Tu* is more intimate, friendly."

"My mother is being difficult," Marie Laure said.

"*Ma fille* . . ." her mother said.

"Daw-ter," Marie said. "And granddaw-ter."

"*Ma* daw-ter," her mother said. "*Elle est* a good girl."

"Yes," I said, "she is a good girl."

"*Elle est* . . ."

"She is," Marie said.

"She is a *bonne cuisinière.*"

"Yes, she is a good cook."

"*Pourquoi vous ne l'épousez pas?*"

"*Maman,*" Marie said. A warning sound.

"That's a reasonable question," I said, preparing to waffle.

"*Pourquoi pas!*" she said.

"I'm sure," my mother said, patting the other mother-un-in-law, "that the young people have a good reason for doing things the way they are doing them."

Geneviève, Marie Laure's mother, asked Marie Laure what Anna, my mother, had said. Marie Laure translated into French. Geneviève replied. Anna asked what Geneviève had said—which was that I was not fulfilling my responsibilities as a gentleman and that I was a person without honor or that it was a condition without honor. Marie Laure replied to her mother that I was a good man and that she should stay out of it. My mother wanted to know what Marie Laure had said, so she repeated it in English. Anna thanked her for standing by Rick. I said she could say Tony when we were alone. Geneviève pointed out that only criminals don't have names. Anna said that her son was no more criminal than Marie Laure's mother, that in fact my problems occurred only because I was too honorable and that people who did not know the facts should cease slandering me. Marie Laure translated, ponging back and forth like a ball in a game with a net. My mother suggested that perhaps it was Marie Laure who didn't want to get married. Geneviève sat up sharply and asked if that was true and before she got an answer announced that if it were true her daughter was a fool. What is more, her daughter had brought shame on the family and that was why Geneviève was here without her husband, who was at home and would have been contemplating suicide except for the fact that he was in the midst of negotiations with a Belgian food conglomerate who wanted to purchase the family grocery to put in a giant American-style supermarket and multicinema. My mother said that Marie Laure had nothing to be ashamed of, she had produced a beautiful child and should be proud, and that they, as grandmothers, should also be only happy and proud. Marie Laure told my mother not to get between her and her mother. My mother protested that she was only standing up for Marie Laure. I said it's best not to get involved with family squabbles. My mother said to me that though she had refrained from saying so, perhaps it was time that I got married and, whatever reasons I might think I had for not being married, they didn't stand up for one minute to the miracle of my daughter and I better rethink things.

I put on the brakes. I pulled over. "You drive," I said to Marie, "I'll see you all in Budapest." I got out. I flagged down Mike Hayakawa's Musashi. When he pulled over, I got in.

"What's going on?" he said.

"Budapest," I said, pointing.

"Is something wrong?"

I turned on the six-speaker sound system. John, Paul, George, and Ringo were singing "All You Need Is Love" in harmony.

The great cinema images of the Iron Curtain—barbed wire, machine-gun towers, soldiers on patrol in no-man's-land while snarling dogs with droolish fangs strained at their leashes—were all gone. We had two French passports, a baby on its mother's passport, my mother's American passport, Hayakawa's Japanese, Chip and me on false Canadian documents, and we all crossed from Austria to Hungary more quickly and with more civility than if we'd been crossing from the Canadian side to the American at Niagara Falls.

In Budapest Marie and I were reconciled. For two days, at least, it was a family vacation, a kind of honeymoon without sex.

I've driven in New York, Paris, Rome. Anyone who drives his own car in Budapest is mad or owns an East German Wartburg burning gas-oil mix in its two-stroke engine and doesn't care. I parked our car in a lot and left it there. We took trolleys and the metro and lots of cabs. They had meters that calculated in florints. Florints were officialy 68:$1 at the bank, 92:$1 on the black market, and the average fare came out to three dollars. Budapest had all the imperfections that Vienna lacked. Where Vienna's broad avenues seemed to have been a studied attempt to prove that the Hapsburgs were actually imperial, Budapest's reminded me of Upper Broadway. Of home. Buildings were as flamboyant and eccentric as the Ansonia at 73rd Street or the Dakota on Central Park West, where John Lennon lived during his mushroom years.

"I want to go back to New York," Marie Laure said.

I didn't bristle or get my back up. My daughter was sitting on my shoulders, her fingers clutched in my hair. The streets were full of hustle and Romanians and gypsies and long-legged Magyar women who didn't wear brassieres.

"Don't you?" she said.

All of that, plus poverty and stress and embraceable disorder put variety on the faces, just as lack of cash and the peculiar fiscal policy of central planning left facades everywhere in crumbling disrepair.

"Yes," I said. "I want to take you wherever you want to go."

At dinner that night—when we were almost alone, the baby with the grandmothers, Hayakawa discreetly on the other side of the room, Chip Sheen lurking outside in his car—when the gypsy band came to our table their leader looked at us closely and romantically—I don't suppose it was anything but a professional mannerism, but he was good at it—and played a sweet and sad version of "There Is a Rose in Spanish Harlem."

The Hungarians lusted for high-tech sneakers, jeans with labels, and radios that plugged into their ears the way theologians crave proof of God. They lined up outside the Adidas shop like New Yorkers line up for a hit movie and Muscovites queue for food. It didn't matter that almost everything inside cost a month's wages in hard currency. The Big News in town was the opening of the Nike shop—the first twenty-four-hour-a-day store in Europe. Magyars who could speak nothing but their own Hungarian, a language that has neither root nor branch on the tree of Indo-European languages, went around reciting Nike's advertising slogan in English—"Just do it!"

It was Anna Geneviève's kind of town. The Hungarians worshiped babies and respected mothers. Back in America no one loves children. Sometimes not even their own. In Germany and Austria they look at kids the way they look at any other material possession—a car, a pair of skis, or a house. How well made is it? How well turned out is it? Does it look like it cost more than mine?

Chip Sheen insisted on using his lemon Opel to tail us. The Hungarians, like their ubiquitous gypsy violin music, are a romantic people full of melancholia and fate, which affects their driving. Chip had two fender benders in two days. The Opel was a rental car but he still had to stop and exchange paperwork. Exchanging paperwork in Magyar, a language with an agglutinative structure, derived from the Finno-Ugric group, was extremely frustrating for him. He signaled me through our "dead drop" for an emergency meeting. I left my mother and the baby to distract Hayakawa, pretended I was going off for some affectionate interaction with Marie, and met him in his hotel room.

"Use your car," Chip said. "No more taxis." It was an order.

"My mother," I said, "won't let me drive here."

Chip pushed his jacket back so I could see that he was armed. It was the Glock, or a replacement thereof, that had got him in trouble in Vienna. It's very trendy among lower-level drug dealers in Brooklyn and the Bronx—like telephone beepers and gaudy jeeps—because they think it's plastic and can pass through X rays and metal detectors. It's not and it can't.

"Nobody's making you drive that stupid car," I said. "That's not the way you tail someone. Do I have to teach you your job?"

"What's wrong with using your darn car?"

"Why don't you take cabs?" I said.

"Or use the Jap's car. That Musashi is easy to follow."

"So is a cab," I said, "if you use a cab."

"Do what I say for once." He took the Glock out.

"You're going to shoot me to force me not to take taxis?" We both silently agreed that he probably wouldn't. "What difference does it make?"

"I can't expense both the rental car and taxis," he said.

"That's ridiculous," I said. Because it was. Then I understood it. "You have me wired. Hayakawa too," I said.

"No," he said. He was a bad liar. But I let the denial stand.

"All right," I said. "We'll use my car."

"How much longer is this going to take?" he said.

"How do I know?"

"We're losing patience," he said. "We better see some action. Or you're going down the tubes, Cassella. Which would probably make me happy. You're not a patriot."

I went to the parking lot to confirm my suspicion about an electronic device. I found it under the dash, drawing power off of the sound system. It was a Hitachi. Which didn't mean the Japanese put it there. The CIA, I presumed, shops the same places we do. Chip's Opel was parked three cars down from me. I stomped it for spite, right where it would hurt the most, in the recently bashed rear bumper. It was more gratifying than I had any right to expect—I actually bent the bracket more than it was already bent. So I stomped it again and almost broke it. It felt too good to stop so I kept stomping until it snapped.

Then I found the surprise. There was a directional beeper mounted inside his bumper. Someone was following the follower. This one was attached by a magnet and ran off its own battery. A hasty arrangement compared to the practically factory-installed beeper in my car. It was a different brand. This suggested that the two had been done by separate parties. Which was one more party than I knew about.

It was time to make my move. If my family would let me.

"You have to know that I love you," I said to Marie Laure. We were walking along the Danube. We were watched, but at least we weren't being listened to. Which was more than I could hope for in our hotel room.

"Do you?" she said. "I think you do not like the weight of family, baby, *grand-mère, grand-mère,* and me. You would rather be like Paul at Down Under and fucking every new *jeune fille* in St. Anton. I think so."

"You're making me crazy," I said, "but for the first time in my life I know what I'm living for."

"I like to hear that," she said.

"You have to trust me," I said. "You have to let me go now."

"What do you mean?"

I turned her to face me and lifted her face to kiss her mouth, but her lips were still and dry. Her body was stiff.

"I mean that our car is wired with a directional finder—so is Hayakawa's, so is Chip's. I don't even know who all the players are. I just know that they're not on my side. None of them. I also know that I can't do what I have to do with at least six people looking over my shoulder."

"Yes, I know that," she admitted.

"I'm being used," I said. "I'm a pig sniffing for truffles. And whoever the hunters are, they're going to take away whatever I find. So if you want to go to America, we have to cut our deal with Mr. Lime, in writing, through an attorney in Washington or New York, before it goes down."

"You think so?"

"They'll pay what they have to pay and deliver exactly as much as they're forced to. Not a schilling more. Not a dime, not a deutsche mark, not even a florint."

"What about Mike Hayakawa? I think you can trust him."

"I don't want to believe that. If I believe that, I don't know that I can do what I have to do. Unless you're ready to never see the States again. Unless you're ready to live on false papers for the rest of our lives. And what if this patriotic tune that Mr. Lime is playing is for real? What if this *is* in the interests of America? Hey, on some level I can't quite rationalize that away."

"Vraiment?"

"Yeah, truly," I said.

"You talk so cynical. You said it did not matter a good goddamn if you went back or not."

"It doesn't. Unless the skiing here is this bad again next year."

"Why do you do that? The cynicism. The . . . what do you call . . . flippers."

"Flippancy. Flippers is a flounder."

"No," she said, "Flippers was a dolphin. When I was a girl, I watched it. Reruns."

"Will you help me?" I said. I meant—Will you let me get out of here without you?

"Who are you going to make a deal with?" she said. "Which one?"

"I am going to do what makes you happy," I said.

She started to cry. I took her in my arms and she came in close to me. "Since the baby, I am scared and I get angry. I get angry at you and you make me crazy."

"Hush, baby, hush. There's nothing wrong with you at all. I should be more patient."

"I am so scared. Don't let anything happen to you."

"Do I ever?"

"Yes, you do. She kissed me. It was soft and tender and caring.

But there was no ignition. No sex in it. I was disapponted. She knew it. She blamed herself and felt guilt about it. That made her angry at me. But she didn't want the anger. Neither did I. So we held each other. Softly and tightly.

"I love you," she said.

"*Je t'aime. Tu es ma vie,*" I said.

"What do you want me to do?"

"Distract them while I disappear. Then keep things in motion like I haven't left. Then act like I'll be right back."

"With Mike Hayakawa," she said, "I think it is better if you make him part of it."

"No," I said. "Underneath that nice-guy thing he does, he's driven, almost hysterical, and very literal. He has orders to stay with me. He's going to insist on it. He'll get nuts when I'm gone. But show him the beeper in our car. Tell him there's one in his. Tell him that the opposition is planning to rip us off as soon as we find it."

"And Chip Sheen?"

My gut twisted. I wanted to stay close to them to protect them. My worst fear, far more disturbing than any threat to my fate, was that something would happen to Anna Geneviève or Marie. "He and Lime want something," I said. "This disc. They want it bad. Lime, at least, understands that if something happens to you he doesn't get the disc. And Lime controls Chip Sheen. So it should be all right." I believed that with my head. My heart had trouble with it.

Marie Laure looked at me and saw right past the words, into my heart. "Don't worry," she said. "I will handle him."

"You are so very, very smart," I said.

"Don't forget it," she said. "This time if you mess around . . ."

"Who me—mess around?"

"This time, I won't take you back."

"You won't, huh?"

"Where are you going?"

"Where the pictures were taken, of course."

"When do you leave?" she said.

"In the morning," I said.

■

She woke me before dawn. Her teeth were brushed and my stiff cock was in her hand. It was ninety days since my daughter had been born. According to the medical profession the passage was supposed to be ready for love again.

I touched her, she was dry. More than that, her whole body was stiff.

"We don't have to," I said.

"I want to," she said.

I tried to caress her breast. The baby hadn't nursed yet so it was heavy with milk and painful. I knew it was not a sexual area anymore, but I had foolishly reached back into old ways looking for the new ones. She brushed me away before I had a chance to pull back. That made both of us angry, but we tried to continue anyway.

I thought to warm her with my mouth and began with kissing her belly. The lower I got, the more she got rigid rather than yielding. "I think I smell different," she said. "Don't do that. Just put it in me."

I wet myself with saliva and began to rub the head of my penis against her labia. She was so afraid. "I can stop," I said. Though I wanted her to be better and to be able to ram it in again. To take her and have her and make her belong to me, like it used to be.

"Keep going," she said.

"Does it hurt?" I asked, going slow.

"No," she lied.

Then she began to cry.

I held her. "It'll be better next time," I said. I tried to pull out.

"Finish," she said.

I did. It hurt her. I was quick about it.

EIGHTEEN

BOHEMIANS

It's almost impossible to exaggerate the limitations of working out of your own environment. When I worked in New York I knew the game, I knew the people, I knew the law, I knew where traffic was one way, and I could read the street signs. Even in Austria I had a sense of what was going on. But with place names like Salgótarján, Müegyetem Rakpart, Németyvolgyi, the eye ceases to scan, the ear can't hear.

The only thing I had going for me was dollars, which, in the winter of 1990, was the best thing anyone could bring with them to Eastern Europe.

By '91, even, it might be different. Currencies can go hard. Yugoslavia had managed. The dinar, which had been Weimar Republic money through 1989, new values daily, printing bills in ever higher denominations weekly, had been pegged to the deutsche mark at 8:1, just like the Austrian schilling, and it held there.

But in Poland, East Germany, Czechoslovakia, Hungary anything could be had for hard currency. Dollars were favored because on the other side of The Line they were both sentimental and a trifle unsophisticated. They remembered the dollar as the Other Great Power. The one of the shining light. When the world was ripped in half they got the darkness, where nothing grew, neither crops nor industry, where they just changed the locations of the concentration camps instead of tearing them down. And they didn't know that we were a declining power while new powers and old enemies where on the rise. But D marks would certainly do. Also ÖS, £, ¥, FF, SF, lire—real money that would buy Italian shoes, German cars, American jeans, brand-name running shoes, cameras that worked, foreign travel, vegetables in February.

The photographs and where they led were the only edge I had over Sheen and Hayakawa. I meant to use it.

I told Chip Sheen we would be getting an early start and I promised him we would use both cars. That made him happy. I told Mike Hayakawa to follow me in his luxury Élégant, that I wanted to talk to the morning man at the Intercontinental and then at the Hilton. Then we were going to a posh riding resort out in the country that I had been told Tanaka might have visited. Marie Laure drove. I rode in the passenger seat. I would have preferred to leave the baby at home, just this once, but the distance between breast and babe was three hours maximum. I would have preferred to leave the grandmothers behind, but the permissible distance between them and the granddaughter was five meters and in any case, no farther than the other grandmother. Off we went. The wagon train. In truth, the shuffle was going to work better that way anyway.

We pulled up at the Intercontinental. I jumped out. My gang waited. I was inside ten minutes. I came out. We went across the river and up the hill to the Hilton. I jumped out.

I had a stand-in waiting. I got him for ten dollars American. Budapest was like an old-time detective movie where people did things for a deuce, a fin, a dime. He was a student named Miklòs. He spoke English. He wanted to be a banker, make a lot of money, and go shopping in Vienna. He was about my build and height.

He walked out of the Hilton wearing my denim jacket and my cap. He jumped into the passenger seat beside Marie Laure. She drove off. I looked out the front window of the hotel. Mike Hayakawa followed Marie. Chip Sheen followed Hayakawa. I didn't see anyone follow Chip.

I took a cab to the airport. The first flight out was to Munich. It was full. For twenty dollars American, someone got bumped and I got on.

In Munich I rented a car and drove north, past Dachau, and

northeast. The change from West Germany to Czechoslovakia was both more abrupt and more extreme than crossing from Austria to Hungary. It looked different, sounded different, smelled different.

It had a warm and homey aroma, smoky and intimate, like the peat they burn in Ireland. It's soft coal. It makes acid rain. It kills. Trees, animals, people, the soil itself. Not quickly, but you wouldn't want to spend your life breathing it.

There was just one radio station. The music was a very special time warp, as if a box of records had fallen out of the back of an American tank back in 1945 and they hadn't gotten their hands on anything since. I heard Benny Goodman and Big Bill Broonzy and somebody who sounded just like the Andrews Sisters if the Andrews Sisters could sing in Czech.

There were no Western cars. Even the roads were smaller, the pavement was potholed and pitted. No one wore Western clothes. The stores were tiny, few and far between. In winter there were no fresh vegetables at all.

Czechoslovakia in the winter of 1990 was all things that we wanted Eastern Europe to be. Looking backward through its eyes, America was all things we wanted America to be. In Czechovision the U.S.A. was rich, powerful, and the ideal to aspire to. There were three rates for the Czechoslovakian koruna. The low official rate was 14:$1, the "special" official rate—if you stayed at a hotel and used a credit card for your bill, you could then change your cash at the special rate—was 28:$1. The real exchange rate was 42:$1. On the street people would offer you better—100:1, 200:1, even 500:1. But that, of course, was a scam. You would never see a koruna. They might snatch your cash and run. Give you counterfeit. Or you might get zlotys—Polish money—which were worth more than nothing but probably less than counterfeit.

I pulled into town around dusk and began the tedious business of looking for a hotel. If they had a room it was only available for one night, or didn't have a bath, or shared a toilet. Until I showed the desk clerk at the Paris Alexander Hamilton's face. He tipped me the wink. "Yes, sir, room with a private bath, and how long will you be staying?"

"A couple of days, a week," I said, "I have no way of knowing."

"Well, sir, whatever you need, you just see me," he said in German. It is the second language of Eastern Europe. After all, Teutons—as the Holy Roman Empire, Prussia, the Austrian Empire, the Thousand Year Reich—have owned it all or in part throughout the centuries and probably will again.

"I'm looking for a girl," I said.

"No problem, sir—not with hard currency." He tipped me the wink.

"Actually, I'm looking for this girl," I said, and showed him the photo.

He looked and his face worked some changes. "Never seen her," he said.

As sure as Vaclav Havel will never write a play better than his own life, I was that sure the clerk was lying. So I showed him old Ben Franklin. That was 2,100 koruna in a land where 50 koruna paid for dinner; 5 koruna bought a liter of good beer, and two could get you discount brew. He kept on lying.

That scared me.

It scared me so much, I changed hotels. It was another ten bucks to get through the next desk clerk. This time I didn't ask about the girl in the picture. I had a feeling that I should keep my search and my home base separate.

I called Paul at Down Under and I asked him to drop in on Marie Laure, say hello for me, and make sure she and the baby were all right. He didn't ask why, which I thought was very tasteful indeed. I told him I would call back the next day to see how she was.

Then I went out into the night.

It was a time warp. The faces and the clothes belonged to the working people of Brooklyn, Cleveland, Scranton, Chicago the way they were three decades ago. It was like seeing our parents.

The hipsters, the underground, who were now the leading edge, looked like the gang from Café Figaro on the corner of Bleecker and MacDougal the year that Bob Dylan came east, out from Hibbing, Minnesota—the days when we had paperback Kerouacs in our back pockets and Ginsberg was growing his beard and sprouting "Howl," when Ike had just left and Kennedy was just in. These Bohemians were Beatniks. Beards and longish hair, jeans and beat-up tweed jackets. Their drug was beer and their charm was talk. The pubs rang with capital letters. Freedom. God. Revolution. Atheism. Capitalism. Free Markets. Humanism. The Values of Socialism. The Triumph of Art.

As it was in that time, women in public were scarcer than men. Those I did see with my sexist, sexualist, sensualist eye were a disappointment. After the healthy, bouncing, let's-all-go-naked-in-the-sauna spirit of the Germans and Swedes of St. Anton, the long-legged, loose-breasted, erotic presence of the Hungarians, and my aerobicized memories of America, the Czechoslovakian women were drab. A lot like the Brits who'd been left out of Margaret Thatcher's yuppie party: black and shapeless clothes, beer-formed bodies, cigarette-smoking squints, indoor pallor. The girl in the photo should have stood out among them like a diamond in the coal.

I found some people who said they might have seen someone like her. But no one admitted to knowing her.

No one particularly cared. There were so many other things that were important. There was passionate concern over a recent quasi-diplomatic incident. Since I was pegged as an American, I was asked to explain. Why had the American ambassador, Shirley Temple Black, snubbed Frank Zappa? She had even denied knowing his music. Didn't she know how respected and loved Zappa was in Czechoslovakia?

I spoke to Paul. He told me Marie Laure was all right.

"And Anna Geneviève?" I said.

"She'll be skiing by next season," he said.

"Thank you," I said.

Two days and two nights of pub crawling—best beer in the world at the best prices—I began to think I was wrong. The photos had been shot in Prague—there was no doubt of that. But it just didn't seem to be Her home. Perhaps they all—Wendy, Hiroshi, Her, and the unknown man who'd shot the shots—were all just passing through.

Then Vaclav Havel came to town.

He had just wowed them in the States. He was on his way to Russia to see Gorbachev. He was the hottest act on the world circuit. By golly, they turned out for him. The occasion was the anniversary of the death of a student who had died by self-immolation to protest the Soviet tanks that had rolled in back in 1968 to end the Prague Spring. It had been a futile gesture. The troops had come to stay. The experiment called Socialism with a Human Face was terminated. It was now a warm winter, eerily springlike, twenty-two years later. The economy of the Soviet Union was collapsing, the Soviet army had found its Vietnam in the hash and poppy Muslim land of Afghanistan, Havel was on his way to Moscow to negotiate, at last, the removal of that army.

Václavské Námešti, Wenceslas Square, is not a square. It's a five-block-long rectangle, the center planted and green like New York's Park Avenue. It slopes gently down from the national museum at one end to a pedestrian area that enters into the old city at the bottom. It's lined with shops, hotels, restaurants, cafés, and various tourist services.

It was full. As it had been three months earlier during that astonishing week in November when Czechoslovakia walked and talked and sang its way into freedom. There were one or two hundred thousand people there. They were singing.

Then I saw Her. I could have picked the cheekbones alone out of a crowd. She was dressed like the rest of the Central European avant garde. Black was the color of winter. But her clothes had been made in Milan. They hung on her like she'd been designed in Paris and groomed in New York. I swear she looked me in the eye. Her eyes were liquid and they were the kind of blank that invites a man to write his own story into her glance. Her attitude said that she was born to beauty—that was your problem, not hers. Her breasts were small, but there was something about them that suggested there was an inverse relation between their size and how much sensation they would create.

She turned away from me. As she began to move the crowd seemed to part for her and she glided away. When I tried to move the crowd seemed to thicken. I heard a wailing infant and there was a couple trying to squeeze through with a crying child. They couldn't move either. When I looked back the girl from the photo had gone. Then I realized what the crowd was singing.

What they sang, in Czech, was "We Shall Overcome."

No American of my age could fail to be moved by it. No matter whose side you were on, back then, back in the sixties, the diffusion filter of nostalgia puts a Hallmark greeting card sentimentality on our past. It was the song of the time when we were idealistic. When America was grappling with something more interesting than insider trading, junk bonds, and the retrograde voodoo of Reaganomics. It was the time of dreams of Peace and Justice, Freedom and Equality. In spite of my frustration at losing the girl, it held me and it touched me.

Two nights later I found her. Then I went home with her.

NINETEEN

THE DEFENESTRATION OF PRAGUE

The history of Prague is a series of lessons about the stability of illusions and the illusion of stability. Castles and kings, cathedrals and cardinals, communists and governments—all came and went when least expected.

The city is dominated by the castle that sits on a hill rising from the river. It's been there, in one shape or another, for a thousand years. The head of government, frequently a king, makes his home there. Havel is entitled to, but doesn't.

It is where the Thirty Years War started. In the bad old days when there were poisoned popes and antipopes and even three popes at once, Bohemia had a Protestant reformation. While not strong enough to oust the Catholics, the Protestants were strong enough to survive, share in power, and force 150 years of official, though contested, toleration. Matters came to a crisis in 1618. A group of Protestant nobles, upset over the king leaning too far toward Catholicism, decided to express this by attacking two royal appointees. The nobles held an impromptu trial in the castle, declared them guilty of intolerance, and defenestrated them. That is, they threw them out the window.

When it was over the map of Europe was redrawn and Czechoslovakia was Catholic again.

Alongside the castle, still on the bluff above the town, is a park. In the center of the park is a place for a monument. Stalin's statue used to be there. It was so big that, once they decided to take it down, it took two years to destroy it. The demolition budget would have built a small hospital.

I knew all this and other scintillating trivia because my cover was tourist.

My cover was slipping. "Would you be interested if someone were asking questions about you?" the desk clerk said.

"Have some hard currency and tell me about it," I said. I put ten dollars down.

"Are you looking for a girl?" he asked.

"It could be," I said.

"If it were me," he said, "I would look for a different girl."

"Why? What do you know about this girl that I shouldn't be looking for?"

"Nothing," he said. He sounded very sure that that was his answer.

"Who was asking about a man who was looking for a girl?"

"Two men, big men. Like weightlifters," he said. That would be unusual in Prague. It didn't have a muscle beach or a four-page list of aerobic studios in the Yellow Pages. It was a Pilsner and Marlboro kind of town.

"Do they have names?"

"They don't say who they are," he said.

"What does that tell you?" I asked him. I put down another ten.

"State security," he mumbled—hard words to say.

"I thought that was all over," I said. He shrugged. "I read in the *Herald Tribune* that they dissolved the secret police and they were giving newsmen tours of the old headquarters."

"They let go forty thousand," he said.

"That's a lot," I said.

"Do you know how many secret police there were?" he asked.

"No."

"There were a hundred twenty thousand," he said.

"Oh."

"You're very welcome," he said. The last of the ten-dollar bills had disappeared from the desk. I hadn't noticed when it went.

Now I was looking backward as well as forward. I strolled through the Old Town, the New Town, the Jewish Town. There was a Jewish Museum. Much of the collection had been assembled by the Germans. They intended to make Prague the site of the Museum of Extinct Races. Among the exhibits were the drawings and the poems of the children of Terezín, a concentration camp to which 15,000 children were taken. It was where most of them died.

I had a daughter now and she was part Jewish. Not in any sense of religion or heredity or culture or race that I could discover or decipher. Simply in an added fragility. A signpost of the potential insanity of the world into which she had been born. I, as her protector, was to look upon those tragic sketches and crayon scrawls and understand that my responsibility was wider than collecting the coins that came in from my Laundromat in order to buy her bread and blankets and toys.

That night I came upon a rock concert.

I have worked in prisons in New York City. The inmates were bad and sad, full of hate, violence, ignorance, disease, and treachery. Even inside—particularly inside—they stole and lied, oppressed and beat and raped each other. Was it any different in Czechoslovakian prisons? For forty years it was where the best class of people went. Havel had done a five-month stretch seven months before he became president. Before that he'd done four years, 1979 to 1983, and before that, five months in 1977. Along with the other writers, philosophers, singers, and musicians who thought that defiance was a higher form of art than acquiescence or exile. This was their night. The underground was in the open, and the graduates of political prisons were center stage.

The venue was a strange old hall. It was built down, into the ground. It was not a theater with raked seating—rather an open floor with four levels, like balconies, wrapped around the room. From them you could look down to where the bands played. The crowd thronged in front of the temporary stage. Some people danced. I saw Her among them. I made my way through the packs of people, saying, "Excuse me" in German as I pressed past. Most people understood but didn't seem to like me particularly for it. So I switched to American and they didn't understand me but didn't mind.

When I got to the dance floor, she was gone. I began pacing through the hall. Then I saw her again. She was going down one stairway while I was going up another. She looked into my eyes. The way I was certain she had in Wenceslas Square. I smiled at her. She smiled back. I hate it when that happens. I used to like it. I could hook myself on a look like that and reel myself right in between a pair of thighs, just like a hawser pulling a ship up snug to its mooring. I was a daddy—what was I going to do with it?

I turned around and followed her.

"Hello," I said. "You don't know how much I want to meet you."

She said something back in Czech, but we were looking at each other, playing games, so it didn't matter much about the words. Not yet. I tried German. She spoke it some. She asked if I were German. I said I was American. She liked that—she liked Americans. They knew how to dance, she said, and had hard currency.

True love is something that arises in a mother for her baby, in a father toward a child, in a dog to the first person that feeds him regularly. The thing between men and women is about the other things. Money, power, sex, and money. It gets played with varying degrees of honesty and different levels of decency. By and large, men have the money and power in this world. By and large, women sleep with men who have money and power. It may be communicated in the popinjay display of Georgio Armani suits and Porsche cars, vacations by the sea or down payments on the house that can be a home, but the bottom line remains. Very few men are turned on to women because they have money and power. It just isn't what makes a prick stiff. Beauty does. Sex symbology does. We all spend a lot of time insisting that the lies about it are true and that the ought-to-be are realities and crying alone each time we discover that they are not.

She had beauty. The whole Western world is a continuous scream for attention by extraordinary-looking women in magazines and on film. I don't remember when it was exactly, but I remember my incredible relief when I realized that *nobody looks like that.* It takes hairdressers, makeup artists, stylists, retouchers, color labs, lighting technicians, airbrush artists to create women who look like that, and then only from certain angles. They don't come that way out of the box. This one came close. It was the cheekbones mostly. It was the eyes primarily. It was the lean frame and the way she held it. It was her hair. Or it was her teeth.

I told her I had a pocket full of dollars and D marks.

She said, "Let's dance."

We danced. I bought her a beer. She said, "There's something I want—will you buy it for me." It was not a question. So we left and got into a taxi. We wound through downtown Prague and stopped at an old building near Faust's house. She told the cab to wait. We got out. We went down dark stairs to a basement. She rang a buzzer hidden in the shadows. There was no answer. She rang again and again. Then we heard a rustling noise behind the door and someone peered out at us through a peephole. I didn't know what this was—whether we were scoring smack or going to a secret conclave of the last of the Communist Party. A voice from behind the door spoke in Czech. From the tone I guessed that it said, "It's late—go away." The girl spoke back, wheedling and commanding.

With a grudge and creak the thick old door swung open. An old man, more asleep than awake, stood there. She bent down and kissed him on the cheek. He grumbled but led us through a twist of halls, entered a basement room, and turned on the lights. We were in Palmer's East. Racks of lingerie—cotton, silk satin, skimpy, sexy, flannel and comfy hung in this capitalist underground with bare gray stone walls. There was a mirror-topped table with perfumes. I looked around, frankly astonished, and noticed a video camera mounted up in the corner to watch for shoplifters.

The little man came up to me and spoke while she looked around. She was very happy, holding up skimpy things and posing with them in front of the mirror. Touching them and fondling the prices. He asked if I spoke Czech, I suppose. I said, in German, that I spoke English and German.

"I only take dollars and deutsche marks," he said.

"Austrian schillings?"

"At a slight discount," he said, and smiled for the first time.

I looked at the price tags.

"Add fifty percent, sonny," he said. "You're in the East Bloc."

"People could just drive to Vienna," I said, "they can do that now."

"Sure, now," he said. "But this is more romantic. And in Vienna they won't open up in the middle of the night for you."

"That's true," I said.

"In Austria closing time is closing time."

The cadence was more Yiddish than German—the attitude was Orchard Street. That's the strip of New York's Lower East Side that can still pass for a scene in a film about Jewish immigrants. "You're Jewish," I said.

"I'm a tailor," he said. "That's the real secret. I can make it fit. I can fix it if it goes wrong. We do that in the East. We have to. In the West, you just throw it away and get another one."

"I like this," she said, and she held it up in front of her. It was off-white, laces in the front between the breasts, cut high in the thigh. "I have good legs," she said, by way of explanation. She turned sideways to me and lifted her skirt to her waist. She did have good legs. Very long. And a good ass. She dropped her skirt and smiled at me.

"She's not really a good girl," the old man said.

"I got that," I said.

"She's not even what she seems," he said.

"What do you mean?" I asked.

"Are you taking that one?" he asked her.

"Oh, yes," she said, caressing it.

"Chinese silk," he said, "the good old-fashioned kind. An excellent choice. It is like a costume for a great drama."

"I like that," she said.

"I know," the old man said. "Someday you will find a stage that suits you."

She pouted at him, but smiled when I handed him $750. It was the sort of thing I'd really wanted to get for Marie Laure the day we bought the McLaren stroller. Except that for Marie Laure we would have selected an item that featured the breasts more and the length of leg less.

"You kids have a good night," he said as we went out the door. "And mister . . ."

"Yeah?"

"Be careful."

She put her arm through mine. "I like the way you bought that," she said. "I can tell a lot about a man by the way he buys. Some men flinch at prices. Then I know that they are straining themselves, and why should a man have to strain to have me? So I let him go. Some men are eager to show that they can get me more and more, that they have lots of money. That's fun"—she leaned against me—"but vulgar and I cannot tolerate vulgarity for very long. You did very well, so now you take me home."

The cab was waiting and she gave it the new address. It was in the district called Hradčany beside the castle and up on the hill. It had a terrace looking down at the river and the Charles Bridge. She opened the French doors to show me. I'd seen the view before. The last time she had been in Kodacolor, naked in the foreground, nipples popping hard in the winter night. Wendy Tavetian, just as naked, beside her, laughing. Then Hiroshi Tanaka between them. Both of them now dead.

"You must have a regular boyfriend, or lover," I said when I stepped back inside. The house was beautiful. It was a rich man's house. Everything said so. Size. Location. Furnishings. Level of maintenance. The Toshiba TV and VCR. The sound system. The paintings on the wall. Czechoslovakia had rejected communism. But only ten minutes earlier. It seemed too soon for rich entrepreneurs to have emerged. Who had paid for this house? And how? Apparatchik or black marketeer? Buried gold from before the revolution?

"Dance with me," she said. The compact disc player was a Phillips. The rest of the sound system was Pioneer. She played Mark Almond's version of "New York State of Mind," cooler and jazzier than Billy Joel's saxophone, as slow as sex on Sunday morning.

I took her in my arms. The night was warmer than it should have been. The breeze brought in the earthy smell of soft coal from the crooked-chimney landscape of Prague's roofs. It was a town where bartenders carried pitchers of beer out from the pub to the workmen down the street at lunchtime, the way I'd heard they'd done in the days of old New York. Czechoslovakia's present was so like our past. Full of hope and dreams. Simple aspirations.

"Tell me about New York," she said.

I knew she wanted to hear about a New York that looked like Woody Allen's *Manhattan,* that glittered and was as rich as Gershwin tunes. A New York that lit up the night with glamour, not with crack pipes. She wanted to know about limos and Breakfast at Tiffany's—not the stink of a homeless man so foul that the odor emptied a subway car at rush hour and somehow there was no money in all of the U.S.A. to get him a simple shower and change of clothes. It wasn't that the town that held Wall Street ran on greed. That was expected. That was accepted. That was—the whole world had just decided—desirable. It was that the dollar was going down. It was the D mark and the yen on the rise, and the men who were buying art this year were from Germany and especially Japan. She was, after all, original Czech art. She really was.

"Whose house is this?" I asked.

Her head was on my shoulder. "Do you want to see me in your present?" she said, her breath soft and moist on my neck. She leaned back from the waist, her hips pressing against my hips, her eyes playing with my eyes. She let go of me, grabbed the package, and disappeared into another room. The disc ended. I went over to change it. I selected Billie Holliday.

I know two things about sexual fidelity. One is that it is a form of insanity. A social pathology. True commitment and a child had made this more obvious rather then disproving it. I could understand the Muhammadan four-wife concept. No woman can give a child the attention it deserves, a man the attention he wants, and get the rest she needs herself. Or the Italian way—men who are compulsively loyal to their family, attached to their children with bonds of steel, and are expected to try to fuck anything that moves. The Japanese are very old-fashioned in their embrace of the double standard and their separation of family and sex. Especially, Mike Hayakawa had told me, if they can get out of town.

The second thing I knew about sexual fidelity was that the lack of it had ruined every relationship I'd ever had and if I slept with this woman I would either become a liar or lose Marie Laure, likely sooner rather than later.

She came out in her present, a white satin ribbon around her neck, and white spiked heels. She left the front laces loose and untied, so that one side of the thing fell away from a breast. I'd seen her breasts before. In Kodacolor. But that didn't lessen the impact at all. Or eliminate the slight tease of the way the nipple played hide and seek with the fabric. It just made me want to see it as stiff as it had been on the winter night when she'd played whatever she'd played with Wendy Tavetian and Hiroshi Tanaka. The high heels and high cut on the thighs emphasized just how long and elegant her legs were. As she had promised. Billie Holliday sang "Ain't Nobody's Business If I Do." Her voice was hoarse.

"You have to tell me," I said, "who this house belongs to."

"It belongs to the people," she said, like it was a dirty joke. "All the property belongs to the people."

"I know an American girl used to come here," I said. "Her name was Wendy."

"Kiss me," she said. "I feel sweet."

I moved toward her. She came toward me. Her body and her clothes were the lightest colors in the room. The effect was a sex dream that glowed. High heels, rounded calves, the long soft line of her inner thighs running up to the point where the satin between her legs covered her mound. I reached out my hands to hers. She took them and moved slowly to me. I stepped back, to look at her, afraid of her. She smiled. She released my hands and pulled the silk down from her shoulders until both breasts were fully exposed. They were as perfect as a pair out of a guidebook to sin.

I heard the door behind me open.

I turned and looked. Two large men came into the room. The younger one looked like Sylvester Stallone would look if he were

Arnold Schwarzenegger. The older one looked like his father—the same but thicker, going gray, and not so nice. Thor and Odin with short hair on a bad day.

"I hope," I said, "that she isn't your girlfriend. Or wife. Or sister."

They advanced. She retreated. The two musclemen grabbed me. One on each side. They picked me up. Quite easily. They carried me across the room. Then they defenestrated me.

T W E N T Y

DISLOCATION

I landed on a lawyer.

He had been very happy, drunk, wending his way along the streets of Prague. It's astonishing how much detail it's possible to notice even during a short flight. He froze when he heard the glass breaking. He looked up when he heard me shriek. They tossed me out headfirst. With my arms out in front as if I could catch myself or protect myself, I must have looked like an audition for *Superman VI*.

A tree branch went by. I tried to snatch it. I missed.

There is a blank spot around the actual point of contact. When the blank spot was over, I was lying on the sidewalk. He was sitting there, staring at his foot.

"Sorry," I said.

"Ah, you Englisher?" he said.

"No, American," I said.

"Very good. I like American. I am called Jaroslav. I am attorney."

I couldn't remember whether I was Cochrane, the Irish priest, or Applebaum, the Canadian contractor, or Cassella, the American PI. "Call me Tony," I said. I tried to stand up. And made it. But I wasn't standing right. My left side was around toward my front and I was twisted as if I were attempting an imitation of the Hunchfront of Notre Dame.

"I am betrunken," he said.

"*Sprechan ze deutsch?*" I said, because his English sounded very Czech.

"*Ja,* bah," he said.

I wanted very much to be understood. "I need to get to the hospital, I think," I said in German, slowly.

"Talk to me in English," he said. "German is for barbarians. America is a great country. I think so. My English is terrible. I must practice. It is so small, my English."

"Sure," I said. "Hos-pi-tal. Where is hos-pi-tal?"

"Never before has a man flow to me out of sky. Flow to me at my foots. Come we are pub, going. Going or gone?" He started pulling himself up.

"No pub going," I said. "Hos-pi-tal. Go to hospital."

"Ohhhhh," he moaned, and turned pale under his beard. "My foots."

"Hospital?" I said.

"Come," he said.

He hobbled out into the street, favoring one foot. I shuffled, favoring one shoulder. Jaroslav was handling it much better than I was. He was sloshed to the point of anesthesia. I was going into shock, shaking and sweating. He hailed a cab. It was a Skoda. We helped each other to it. It took us to the hospital. A Lincoln Continental or a Rolls-Royce is designed to insulate passengers from the rough and tumble of the world around them. A Skoda is to automobiles what Socialist Realism is to art. Every bump shot up my body into my misplaced shoulder. The two of us clung to each other and moaned over every cobblestone and pothole in Prague. I was begging the driver to go slowly, Jaroslav was screaming for him to go faster.

Jaroslav knew the doctors. He knew the nurses. He spoke to everyone with a drunk's expansive style and injured man's plaintive need. We were seen far faster than I would have been seen in an emergency room in New York and almost as fast as they would have got to me in Austria.

The doctor spotted what was wrong with me from across the room. He spoke only Czech and Russian, but Jaroslav translated. "Good news. First the injection, before you even have to move."

A nurse and the doctor and Jaroslav all helped drag my shirt off me. Every move did violence to my system. When it was off I could see that my arm was hanging in front of my chest instead of from my side.

"Is this your first dislocation?" the doctor asked through Jaroslav.

It was. In a dislocation a bone comes out of its socket. All the muscles, tendons, and ligaments attached to it are stretched out of place, sometimes torn. They try, with all their might, to pull the bone back. But they can't because another bone, in this case a shoulder, is in the way. If pain were a puddle, the puddle had now risen and engulfed me from my feet to mideyeball.

I sat folded over at the middle, letting my arm hang as limp as I could make it. They gave me a shot. A muscle relaxant. I watched my hand as it rested against the floor. I twisted my head sideways, toward Jaroslav. They'd taken his shoe and sock off. His foot was swelling and changing colors.

"The house I came out of . . ." I said to him.

"Yes, where you flow to me," he said.

"Do you know who it belongs to?"

"To the people," he said. He thought that was funny. "Soon private property we are having. All day, new laws. Any day?"

"Every day," I said.

"New laws every day. Will need lawyers, American companies. Yes?"

"Yes, American companies need lawyers."

"To X ray we are gone," he said.

The doctor and nurse were back. I could see their feet. They had a crutch for Jaroslav. The doctor spoke from above in Czech. Jaroslav translated.

"Follow him."

I couldn't straighten up. I slid forward from the chair. I walked like a duck. I was bent double, my arm hanging from the center of my chest, my neck twisted so I could peer forward.

"He wants to know if you can see where you are going," Jaroslav translated.

"Don't worry. I can see all the way up to his ankles," I said.

I followed the doctors' feet down the hall. The treatment for a dislocation is simple. Once an X ray is taken to make sure nothing else is wrong, someone takes hold of the dislocated part and pulls it. They pull it far enough away from the body that it can make its way around the lip of the socket and slip back in. Your muscles are stupid. They don't understand they have to let go in order to get where they want to be. So they fight it all the way. That's what the injection is for and I suppose it would have been even worse without it. Though that is difficult to imagine.

I screamed. Without shame or self-consciousness.

When it goes in, it's over. Someone pulls the plug on the puddle of pain. I don't mean that it didn't hurt. It did. But it was merely hurt. Like a cracked rib or a kick in the head. It wasn't something that enveloped my entire existence and made me walk like a duck.

They gave me a sling. They gave Jaroslav a cast and crutch.

"I am sorry about your foot," I said.

"All about America you will be telling me," he said. "Pub I know—pub still open."

I was already pretty stoned from the muscle relaxant. I am not quite sure why or how, but we ended up back at Jaroslav's socialist workers' paradise apartment. His wife seemed very nice. A tolerant person. I fell asleep on the couch.

When I got up I called Marie Laure directly. I had to hear her voice. Either because I thought it would heal me or because my breakability spoke to me of their fragility and I needed to be reassured.

"I'm alive and virtuous," I said when she answered the phone.

"Anna Geneviève rolled over," she said. "Then she did it again."

"All by herself?" I asked. "You didn't help her?" She swore she hadn't. "And I missed it," I said. Then I asked what happened when Hayakawa found out I was gone.

" 'E throw a fit," Marie Laure said.

"What did he say?"

"I don't know," she said. " 'E throw it in Japanese."

"Is he all right now?"

"Your mother spoke sharply to 'im and made 'im get control of 'imself. Then I showed 'im the electric bug in the car and told 'im 'e 'ad one also. Then we told 'im it was not to trick 'im, but to trick the people following. Then 'e changed 'is anger into admiration for you as a detective. It was all very quick. Quick explosion, quick control. You are right about 'im. Like spring snow. The wrong noise, the wrong freeze, something, and *voilà*—avalanche."

"What about Chip Sheen?"

"You mean Peaches?"

"Yeah," I said.

"Is okay," she said.

"It doesn't sound okay," I said.

" 'E was worse. 'E made the threats."

"What did he say?"

" 'E say I 'ave to tell where you are gone or 'e will take the baby."

"I'll kill him," I said, flush with righteous anger, the best kind.

There are certain things that we imagine would give us full permission to act out our aggression, to lash out with all the resentment and pain we've swallowed in our daily subservience to life. The most popular movies in the world cater specifically to this fantasy—Bronson, Rambo, Schwarzenegger, and the A Team all stomp the villains, survive unharmed, are not indicted, don't even serve thirty days per corpse, and *feel no guilt.* But in real life the only people who normally reach this state of homicidal grace are soldiers, psychopaths, and the deeply religious.

"Your mother," Marie Laure said, "is very smart. She begins to scream. 'Elp! 'Elp! So my mother, she begins to scream, *'Au secours! L'assassin!'* And all the people, they do not comprehend English and Français, but they comprehend. They turn and look at 'im,'e runs away. It was very good."

"What about now?"

"I 'ave spoken with Franz, the gendarme. Also, I am never alone—always with the mothers. St. Anton is not New York. If we yell, people will come. You are not to 'ave worries. We are very fine."

"Be careful, please be careful," I said.

"You too," she said.

"I got hurt," I said. "But I'm okay. Nothing that wouldn't happen skiing."

"What has happened to you?"

"Nothing serious," I said. "Promise me one thing."

"What?"

"When I come home, you'll let me buy you something—something for you, sexy."

"Like from Palmer's?" she said.

"Yes," I said.

"It's so much money," she said. But it wasn't the money.

"Please," I said, "I need to tell you how beautiful you are."

"Thank you. We'll see," she said coolly. It wasn't the money—it was sex that she wanted to say no to.

So Jaroslav and I went to his pub. He wanted to know about America. He wanted to know how much they paid lawyers in America. I tried to explain that they paid lawyers an obscene amount of money in America, but that strange things happened along with it. That they worked obsessively long hours and that they had forgotten to love the children of the world. That lawyers married other lawyers and then they couldn't remember to love their own children and hired Dominicans and Jamaicans to do it for them. I asked if he knew who owned the house where I had been defenestrated. He promised he would find out. I asked if he knew the girl. He said, "Perhaps." And the two strongmen. He said, "Oh, you mean the Bulgarians."

"What do you mean, Bulgarians?" I said.

"Come," he said to a middle-aged man and younger woman who had just walked in, "I want you to meet my friend from America. He flowed to my foots."

They sat down with us. More excellent beer and indistinguishable food arrived. Then some more people sat down with us. Everyone made me welcome. Someone told me that Jaroslav was one of the best lawyers in Czechoslovakia. In his worn corduroy pants, graying white shirt, beard, and over-the-collar hair, he looked like an eternal graduate student from 1957, going from grant to grant, ever ready to recite vigorously unrhymed poetry. He got up to make a phone call.

"How much has he had to drink?" the youngish woman asked me.

"Four beers," I said. "Maybe five."

"Wait till he has six," she said.

"What then?"

"Then," she said, "he will ask you if America penises are bigger than Czechoslovakian ones."

"What do you think?" I said.

"It doesn't matter to me," she said. "I've just been to Vienna and I bought a Japanese vibrator."

"A Hitachi?" I asked.

"A Musashi. I liked the logo. The samurai sword."

"Czechoslovakia is a very surreal place," I said. "Kafka would feel at home here."

"Oh, he did," she said. "I like it now that we're free. Perhaps now the man I love will stay."

"Who is that?" I said.

"I don't know," she said. "In the past they all left too soon."

"Are you sure that was a political problem, not a personal or sexual one?"

Jaroslav came back. He ordered another round.

"When can we find out about the house on the hill?" I asked him.

"After lunch," he said.

"What do you think about artists running a government?" someone else said. "Is it a loss to art?"

"Is it a gain to government?" the youngish woman asked.

"Havel is right," another voice said. A bearded man, but neater than Jaroslav. "What is missing is the moral dimension. The communists made us an immoral country."

"An unmoral one," someone else said.

The youngish woman leaned over to me and said, "You see, we learned very early, as little children in school, that everything they taught us was a lie and that we had to lie back to them. There was no truth. No honesty. It was not even possible. For many of us it is too late. We are corrupted in our brain. Trained to timidity. Broken to hopelessness. But we can save the next generation."

"Cherish this," I said. "Remember this moment. It is your moment. It is your gold. Because when you succeed—democracy, capitalism, department stores, cable TV—you'll see 'I Love Lucy' dubbed into Czech, you'll get Sports Channel so you can watch high school soccer from Romania, MTV, everything. Then there's no more Art, no Truth, and you'll look back and say, 'Why don't we talk anymore, like we did in nineteen ninety?' "

They were, all of them, attorneys and courthouse people. Eventually they rose to return to work. Jaroslav waved for more beer.

"How many have you had?" I asked him.

"Just five," he said, as the waiter put down two more.

I put my hand over the mugs. "Wait. Before you drink it, tell me about the house on the hill."

"Oh, let me drink it," he said. "I'm thirsty."

"No. Then you will start talking about penises and I don't care about them."

"Kvieta told you that?"

"It doesn't matter," I said.

"It would if yours was as short as mine."

"Tell me about the house," I said.

"All right," he said, in German for fluency. "It belongs to Carel Kapek. Like the playwright. You have heard of him? This Kapek is perhaps number-three man in our secret police. He is very powerful—or was. The girl—she is only nineteen. She is his girlfriend. He has a wife. Somewhere. I don't know where. The Bulgarians—they are his golems, his creatures. Sometimes bodyguards. Sometimes they just watch her to keep her in line. She is young. You understand. He is old. Sometimes they are what the movies would call his hit men."

"Does she have a name?"

"Nadia," he said.

"First name or last name?"

"Just Nadia. One name. She thinks very well of herself. Only people who think very well of themselves go by one name."

"Like Madonna or Sting or Paulina," I said.

"Like Stalin and Lenin," he said.

"That's the great thing about capitalism," I said. "The heros are just celebrities and the celebrities are trivial. So they can't do much harm. You'll see. You guys are gonna have fun."

TWENTY-ONE

LAST YEAR IN MARIENBAD

"In America is disability?" Jaroslav said. He said everything with great intensity and a lot of hair. He had the sort of beard that collects crumbs and drama.

"If you speak a language you don't know," I said, "then people don't always understand you." I was in enough pain to be irritable.

"I humbling apologize for the smallness of my English," he said.

"What are you trying to say?"

"I am getting full disability for my foot." He had switched to German, which he spoke in a clear and elegant, though stilted and schoolish, manner. "I don't have to work and I still get money. Isn't communism wonderful. Would I get disability in America?"

"No," I said, swallowing some more aspirin and thinking about something stronger.

"Oh," he said, sounding worried.

"But," I said, "you could sue."

"Sue who?"

"You would sue me."

"Oh, but you are my friend. I would never sue you."

"Yes, you would," I said. "Trust me, you would sue me. You would also sue the goons who threw me out the window, you would sue their employer, and most important you would sue the homeowner."

"Why is the homeowner so important?"

"Because he is the one who is required to have liability insurance. Goons never have liability."

"Because they're Bulgarians?"

"Because they don't have property. What makes a person sueable is property. If it's real estate and they have a mortgage, the mortgage company insists on insurance. That, of course, makes them more sueable. So the more you own, the more you're insured—the more you're insured, the more you get sued for. If you're going to be a lawyer in the new Czechoslovakia you gotta know this stuff. You go after whoever has the most insurance."

"But what if the owner of the house has nothing to do with it? That is unjust. That is unfair."

"That is irrelevant. The notion of liability can be stretched to fit any insured party. Wait till you guys discover medical malpractice."

"I am going to help you," he said. "Yes. I will be your Czech guide and you will tell me about the financial opportunities for a capitalist lawyer."

"What were they under the Communists?"

"Not good. I believe too much. You understand. In things like Justice. So I was always in trouble. Here they appoint the judges to do what they want them to do. So the judge, the prosecutor, the police, the party—they are all one person. The defendant is nobody. The defense lawyer is nobody. Do you have contempt of court in America?"

"Yes."

"We have it here," he said. "It was no good under the Communists."

"Is that why you drink?"

"No," he said, "I drink because I like beer."

She was gone.

The house below the castle was shuttered and locked. No smoke rose from the chimney. The gate was locked. Jaroslav found out Kapek's private phone number from a friend at court. A machine answered. The recording was in Czech, so I didn't understand it, but I recognized the distinctive beep of an Answerfone. I called again and asked Jaroslav to listen and tell me what the recorded voice had to say. "I'm sorry," it said, "I cannot come to the phone right now. Please leave a message at the sound of the tone." I sat on the place for a day and a night. Jaroslav kept me company, on and off. We talked about how change had come to Eastern Europe. And how fast. He told me how bad it had been in the fifties. Those were the days of the knock on the door in the middle of the night. Informers and disappearances. It had been followed by a milder time and the government even began to open things up within the system. Until '68, of course, when the government made the mistake of overestimating the length of the Russian leash. They had been brought up short.

When the tanks came they were greeted with compliance.

"How did the Communists take over in the first place?" I asked him.

"They had a good name, honor, and idealism as antifascists. Who else on this side of Europe stood up to Hitler? The French and the English sold us out. Even the Americans, in a way. They could have liberated all of Czechoslovakia. Your armies were in western Bohemia. But you stopped and left that honor to Stalin," he said. "The shame of it is, we elected them. It was like when you were young and very much wanted to have sex. There was a girl. A good girl, from a good family, and much to your surprise she said yes and lets you between her legs. You do it. She gets pregnant. Then you have to marry her. Then and only then do you find out she is really the wicked Witch of the East, that there is no divorce, and that her four brothers—all of military age and armed—have moved in with you to make sure you stay together. Also, you have to feed them."

"That's your interpretation of how Czechoslovakia went Communist?"

"How the hell do I know? I was a baby. I had nothing to do with it. Nobody talks straight about it. Our parents who hate the Communists don't want to admit that they welcomed them. Just like the Austrians, no one says they welcomed Hitler. But they did. The Hungarians. Did you ever hear a Hungarian brag that they had the first fascist country in Europe? Of course, the people who are Communists, or who were up till last month, call it a triumph of the people. So, that is my interpretation."

"Okay," I said.

"I am a man of great passion," he said passionately, lighting another cigarette. Smoking is even more universal in Czechoslovakia than it used to be in America. And more dramatic. Jaroslav's personal cigarette style was midway between Boyer and Bogart. "I am developing a new passion. To make money. What do you think?"

"Money's a good thing to have."

"Yes, but am I being too trendy?"

"I don't think so," I said.

"But isn't it what everyone is doing?"

"Perhaps it is an idea whose time has come."

"I am the sort of person who wants to be ahead of his time or far behind it. It is a form of vanity." He gestured with his cigarette, a motion similar to a complex Arabic greeting. Ashes spilled across his lap and onto my sling. "Tell me about your baby."

"She can laugh and she can smile," I said. "She can roll over all by herself. At least, that's what Marie Laure said she just did."

"My wife is expecting. I am so excited. We have been trying for years. This will be a baby born free."

"I'll drink to that," I said.

"Okay, you want to go to the pub?"

"No. I'm going to sit here until I'm sure there's no one coming or going."

"And then what?"

"Good question," I said.

"I could get us a beer," he said.

"Sure," I said, "and some aspirin—my shoulder hurts like hell."

"You should be resting," he said. "The doctor said for you to stay in bed for a couple of days."

"No. I want to get this done. I want to get back to Anna Geneviève and Marie Laure."

"She is not your wife?"

"No, she's not my wife."

"You like her?"

"Yeah. A lot. I love her."

"You have passion for her? Strong virile feelings?"

"Yes," I said.

"Is she a nice girl?"

"Yeah, and a good bargain. Usually."

"You should marry her," he said.

He went to get the beer. While he was gone I shuffled through the photos of Nadia, Wendy, and Hiroshi. It was a surprisingly laborious process one-handed. Doing anything one-handed is difficult when you're used to two. Jaroslav returned without the aspirin but with a bartender who carried a full pitcher, two glasses, some bread, and a nameless Czech cheese. The barman even filled the glasses before he put the pitcher on the floor of the car alongside Jaroslav's cast. It was the least inconspicuous stakeout I had ever been on. I clutched the photos in the hand that rested in the sling and the beer in my good hand. Jaroslav tried to hand me some bread, but I had no place to put it.

"Look at these," I said.

He had a beer and a cigarette in one hand, a piece of bread and cheese in the other. He couldn't find a flat surface to balance anything, so he put the bread and cheese in his mouth, like a dog holding a newspaper. Then he took the pictures and put his glass of beer into my hand. He was impressed, as we all had been, by the topless twosome. He asked who the other girl was. I said, "Dead." I asked him if they had all been taken in Prague. Ten of them looked to me like someplace very different. But I didn't know Prague well enough to say they weren't just from a different neighborhood.

"Not Prague," he said, but with the bread and cheese in his mouth he could just as well have been saying *new frog* or *knot grog*.

"Don't speak with your mouth full," I said.

"Not Prague." He balanced the bread on his knee. "Curious, though. In winter? When were these pictures taken?"

"December, judging by the passport—December eighty-nine. Where is it?"

"Mariánské Lázně," he said. "The buildings, the yellow color that is very typically Czech, you know, and the period. But this building I recognize. It is waters for health."

"Where?"

"Marienbad, you call it. Near the border. I will show you." He took his beer back. Since my hand was free, he stuck the pictures back there.

"What about your job, your wife?"

"I have the disability. My wife will be glad that I am not underfoot. If we find this Carel Kapek, who is not the playwright, I will sue him for my foot. How much is a foot worth in America?" He finished his glass of beer. When he went to pour another the bread fell off his knee. He caught it before it hit the floor.

"Well, you have your lost income."

"In Czechoslovakia that is not a great loss."

"Then you have your pain and suffering," I said.

"In my country it would be hubris to call this pain and suffering."

"Then you maybe have your punitive damages."

"Ah. Ah-ha!" he said dramatically. He began to orate. "Ladies and gentlemen of the jury. This one-time agent of state security imagines that in today's democratic Czechoslovakia he is still above the law! Imagine the arrogance. This one-time agent of state security thinks he can have his minions throw people out of his window with no regard whatsoever for innocent bystanders passing below. Once he could hide behind the mask of a totalitarian regime. But no longer. It is up to you, free citizens of a free country, to send a message. You have to look before you defenestrate. How can you send that message? I'll tell you how—six million dollars in punitive damages.

"Like that?"

"Exactly," I said. "That's how we do it in the Free World."

In Europe they believe now, as they have for centuries, in the healing powers of a variety of mineral baths. There are hot springs, sulphur baths, radioactive waters, waters to drink, waters to take home in bottles. Marienbad is one of the most famous and has baths for a wide variety of ailments. Which was a good thing, because we were a fine collection of cripples, me, Jaroslav, and Mr. Lime.

We had checked into one of the five hotels in Mariánské Lázně that catered to Westerners. Jaroslav handled the transaction at the desk.

"We have view of the park," he said.

We walked upstairs—there were neither elevators nor bellmen—and entered our room. Where Lime, who was now John Sebastian just as I was Andy Applebaum, was already waiting in an oversized armchair, a drink in his hand, a boom box on the table.

"What are you doing here?" I said. Though that was obvious. He was waiting for me.

He put the sound track from *The Big Chill* in the portable tape recorder and turned it up loud.

"Why can't you be straight with me?" he said.

"You Make Me Feel Like a Natural Woman" came on. The room was a large airy atrocity. Once upon a time it had probably been, as the exterior still was, full of Mitteleuropa charm. At some point, in a fit of neo-Stalinist delusion, to prove that Soviets were as modern as Americans, a loyal-to-the-party interior decorator had gone abroad and come back with the Best of the West from Miami Beach, circa 1958.

"I barely even know you," I said.

"How bad is the shoulder?" he asked.

"Now that it's in, it's tolerable," I said.

"Physical therapy—that's the thing," he said. "Also, you don't want to let anything happen to it until it's strong again. You don't want to be one of those guys goes to parties and pops his arm out of his shoulder to amuse the kids. That's what happens, you let it get dislocated too many times. That's the down side. The not-so-down side is that it hurts less each time."

"It better," I said. "First time was a monster."

"I bet," he said. "How the hell did you get out of Budapest?"

"How the hell did you find me?" I asked. I looked at Jaroslav.

"Can we order up some beer?" Jaroslav said.

"I thought we had an understanding," Lime said.

"Gerald Yaskowitz," I said.

"Who?"

"Gerald is my attorney."

"Where?" Lime asked.

"New York."

"That's interesting."

"You should know that," I said. "From my file."

"I didn't think it was that important," he said.

"It's not because I don't trust you," I said, "but I sure would like it if you had your people talk to my people. Specifically the New York office of the IRS—or the D.C. office, that's your business—should present a letter to my people—that's Yaskowitz—that says because I found you this disc and turned it over I must be such a good citizen that all that other obstruction-of-justice crap is indeed crap and that there are no criminal charges pending, and et cetera and so forth—you know the drill."

"But you don't have the disc."

"But when I get it," I said.

"Are you going to get it?"

"What do you think?"

"I loved Budapest," Lime said. "Didn't you love Budapest?"

"Budapest was fine," I said.

He put his hand on my shoulder—the good one. "Hungarian women," he said, with more intimacy than I cared to enjoy, "and a strong dollar. That is one hell of a powerful combination. This is a hell of an exciting time, I tell you. You know, a year from now nobody is going to believe you could have a truly prime Magyar girl for twenty dollars. I'm not talking about a quickie blow job in the front seat. I'm talking about doing things right. Scrub your back in the tub. Spend the night. Pour your coffee in the morning. Then give you a quickie blow job."

I looked at Jaroslav. He had to have been working for Lime all along. He let Lime know where we were going so Lime could get there first and get settled in the room that Jaroslav had led me right to. Jaroslav backed up until he bumped into the wall. Then he shuffled sideways, leaning on his crutch. There was a giant armchair in that style called Swedish modern—something we must never forgive the Swedes for. He stumbled against it. Then he sat.

"Is he working for you?" I asked.

"You ever been to Budapest?" Lime said to Jaroslav, switching to German.

"Yes, once for a weekend."

"What'd you think of Hungarian women? Huh, boy?" Lime asked him.

"I'm sure they're fine," Jaroslav said.

"He's self-conscious because he's got a small prick," Lime said, back to English. "But it doesn't matter a good goddamn, does it, Jaro? Women are women the world over and it's the size of your currency that they care about. It's the same in New York, isn't it, Tony?"

"Do we have business to do?" I said.

He put a hand on my bad shoulder and pushed at it gently. I retreated and there was sweat in my armpits, a prickling of moisture on my brow. I looked at his bad knee, measuring the distance. My blood pulsed from the adrenaline hits. My shoulder was so damaged that the increased blood pressure was painful.

"You think I'm just jerking your chain, don't you?" he said.

"Hey, Jaroslav," I said, "you weren't outside by accident when I fell on you, were you? You were following me."

"I was in Nam," Lime said. "Oh, man. Vietnamese women. *Incroyable. Le combination de la français et l'orient—l'eurasienne.*" His French was a made-up franglais. It made him sound more American than ever. "If you like your women big, long legged, big breasted, all right, you got your Hungarians, but for pure femininity, for knowing how to serve a man, the Vietnamese girls were the best. And *the dollar was strong*. You know what a strong currency is? It's the biggest dick, the handsomest face, the best tailored suit, and the slickest line on the block. Guys so dumb and ugly that they couldn't get a pig at a 4-H convention in Iowa were getting shack jobs so gorgeous that you could cry just to look at them. They were getting treated better than their mothers treated them. And if their shack job nagged about money, like an honest-to-God American wife, you gave her ten bucks and it was joyville. You get a lot of these movies—*Platoon, The Deerhunter, Apocalypse Now*—all that crap. All of them are crap. Vietnam was fine. For a lot of folks. Hey, for some grunts up in the jungle who didn't like guns and shit like that, it was a bummer—no question. Rear echelon, intelligence, supply, medical, maintenance—that is, most of your army—stationed in Saigon, Hue—we're talking about Paradise on Earth."

"That's great," I said. "Check *National Geographic.* Find a suitable Third World country, start a new war. Whatever it takes for you to get laid and leave me alone, I'm for it."

"Cassella, you don't get the point."

"I guess I don't."

"I'm talking about America. That's what I'm talking about. I'm a little crude. A little offensive. But how would you like to hear a Japanese or a German talking that way about American girls? 'Cause that's what's going to happen. World War Three is on and it's called Monopoly. The Cold War might be done but the Fiscal War needs to be won. They're buying Rockefeller Center, Columbia Records, Columbia Pictures. Now why the hell do the Japs want Hollywood? To influence our hearts and minds? Maybe. To make money? Surely. Or because they know that the word *producer* is a synonym for *blow job?* You bet.

"These are people who organize sex tours, usually of what they consider second-rate countries. Right now that's the Philippines, Thailand, Singapore, Korea. Like that. But when the yen gets to a hundred to one with the dollar, Fujiyama Tours is going to set up perversion excursions to Los Angeles. You understand, they want to own California. You think I'm crazy. You think I'm exaggerating. But this is what *they* say. And we better goddamn listen to what they say. Like we didn't listen to Hirohito the last time. Like we didn't listen to Hitler."

"Let's say I buy this weirdness," I said. "Let's say I even want to sign up and protect the virtue of American womanhood from yen lust."

"Yeah?"

"Let's say I buy it. What the fuck are we doing in Czechoslovakia?"

"Tell me something, Jaro," Lime said in German. "Who's poised to buy Czechoslovakia?"

"The Germans," Jaroslav said.

Marvin Gaye started singing, "I Heard It Through the Grapevine."

"Have you heard the joke that's making the rounds in Tokyo?" Lime switched back to English. "How will the Japs win World

War Three? They'll join up with the Germans again, but this time they'll leave the Italians out of it."

"What's a source code?" I asked him.

"What's a jet plane?" he said.

"I gone for beer," Jaroslav said.

He hauled himself up out of his seat and went to the door. Lime watched him. When he opened the door, Chip Sheen shoved him back inside. Jaroslav stumbled on his crutch and started to protest. Chip pulled his jacket back and showed him his gun.

Lime turned the music up even louder. Chip shut the door again, with Jaroslav inside with us and himself outside.

"I'm a rock-and-roll kind of guy," I said, "but you're overdoing it."

"Am I? This little country had a hundred twenty thousand people working for the secret police. Now what the hell do you think those people did with their time? They wired every fucking hotel that was clean enough for a foreigner to stay in. Every single room. Now I don't know if someone is listening, but I guarantee the capability is in place."

"You know," I said, pointing at Jaroslav, "he's good. You I never trusted. Chip Sheen I wouldn't send to the grocery for beer. But him I trusted."

"I'm sorry," Jaroslav said. "Now I am gone."

"Stay put," Lime barked.

"Maybe we could go out in the park and talk," I said. There are two parks in Marienbad. The one at the center has been turned into a construction site. No one is quite sure why. "Surely they can't have wired every flower, every tree."

"Surely they can. And this is Kapek's home base. He lives in a fortress up in the hills there. He likes the baths, he believes in them. Herbal remedies and anthroposophic medicine—it ministers to the soul as well as the body. He has one arm and he thinks he'll live forever. Karel is a standard enough name for a Czech male. But in the West it sounds like Carol, the girl's name. He couldn't stand that. These guys—they live by fear, you understand. So he made sure that the opposition, in the West—us, our Germans, the Brits—knew him as Vlad, from Vlad the Impaler, a particularly nasty Transylvanian who was the model for Dracula. So I'm figuring, Vaclav Havel or no Vaclav Havel, the end of communism or the beginning of Mormonism—whatever the fuck is going on—Vlad still has Marienbad sewed up tight, with little ears everywhere. And little eyes. You don't want to be seen with me."

"Tell me what a source code is," I said.

"You know what," he said, sounding relaxed and reasonable, "I want to enlist you, I want to truly get you on our side. Because this is a cause to believe in. I don't care if you're a gung-ho racist marine or a hippie dippie, do-gooding, save-the-whales, and vote-green wimp. Let me tell you what we are up against. The Corporate Society. Do you understand how the Japs beat American industry?"

"Because they build better stuff at a better price," I said. "Because the men who run General Motors are arrogant assholes who thought that little Orientals could never compete and they could keep selling second-rate goods. Drive a Chevy, then drive a Toyota. It was embarrassing ten years ago and it's still embarrassing. And they never noticed. You don't have to enlist me. You just have to cut a deal."

"You're half right," he said. "America is a consumer society. The consumer is right. If the consumer wants to pay for emission controls, we give to it him. If he wants to buy a car from Sweden and send his money overseas, we let him. Japan is the corporate society. The same Sony you buy in the States for four hundred dollars costs eight hundred in Japan. That gives Sony the cushion to undercut anybody in America. If a factory pollutes in the States, the media jumps all over them. It sells more papers, gets more viewers, whatever, and they charge more for the advertising. A company pollutes in Japan, it doesn't make the six o'clock news. Not if they're a big company signed up with Dentsu Advertising that tells the broadcasters what not to say. They pay their people less, and they work them more.

"Japanese banks are real strong. You know why? Because it costs you, the consumer, three to five dollars every time you use a check. Nissan can get a bank loan at three, four percent. General Motors pays the prime rate. Nine to twelve percent. But when you go back to New York I'll bet ten dollars you shop around until you get free checking. You don't want to pay even ten cents a check to subsidize loans to help GM fight Nissan. They have lifetime employment. They're very proud of that. But the flip side of it is that if you quit, you are virtually unemployable. It's a very sophisticated version of owing your soul to the company store. Do you want to live in a society like that?"

"No," I said. "But they do. And that's their business."

"Wrong. Because if we don't compete, they buy California. They buy what's left of Chrysler and General Electric and Con Edison and then Americans have to go to work for them. Their way. By the way, they don't even want to let you work unless you're white, antiunion, and preferably of German ethnic stock. Or in order to compete we decide we better be a producer society instead of a consumer society. To hell with freedom of the press if it makes our corporations less competitive. To hell with consumer pressure if our products don't compete with those of Japan. To hell with the environment if it drags Ford down in its fight with Honda.

"And part of the reason that they are ahead," Lime said, "is that they steal. They stole the microchip by not granting a patent to Texas Instruments for ten years. After they managed to dominate the market through dumping, reverse engineering, and a variety of predatory practices, only then did they recognize TI's patent. What other industry have they targeted? Computers, for one. Hitachi got busted for buying IBM secrets. They knew they were stealing and they were happy to do it. Read the transcripts.

"Now they are buying stolen secrets from a Czechoslovakian spy master. We entered into an arrangement with the Japanese to coproduce an airplane. A fighter plane, based on the F-16, designed and produced by General Dynamics. Good plane. Best in the world at the price. They conned us a little bit. They said they would produce their own. The U.S. is unquestionably number one in the world in aviation and aerospace. No question. No excuse for the Japs to build their own. So we lean on them to buy one of ours. They push codevelopment. Building a new airplane based on the F-16.

"Like I said, we're a consumer society. You gotta make your buck and spend your buck today. So we went for it. Then, thank God, somebody woke up and said, 'Wait a minute.' The Japs have earmarked aviation and aerospace as one of their next targets. Just like they did with automobiles and microchips. Just like they did, before that, with cameras and consumer electronics. They don't give a shit about codevelopment of this plane, except for one thing—to learn how to build them themselves. To learn enough to take on General Dynamics and Boeing. Do you understand that aviation is twenty percent of our export of manufactured goods? Twenty billion dollars a year?

"But we still needed the business. So we modified the deal. The deal was that there are certain things that the Japanese would not have access to. A modern combat jet is a wondrous thing. In point of fact, it just about shouldn't fly. In point of fact, a pilot can't fly it. It needs a computer. It needs a computer that takes in all the incoming information and processes all the possibilities—trim this, adjust that—while it's reading the radar, while it's setting the armaments, while it's running evasion. The secret core of aviation technology is understanding the whole. Both in manufacture and in operations. The heart of the computer software, the program that runs the programs, is called the source code.

"The source code was the number-one thing on the restricted list in this codevelopment deal. Somebody stole it. We don't know who. Once we get a look we might be able to track it back. We now know, through you, that it was stolen by the Czech Intelligence Service. All the Communist spy networks have always been one hundred percent subservient to the KGB. The KGB liked to use them because to somebody who wouldn't betray America to the Russkies, it sounds a lot more innocuous if you sell military secrets to the nice Czechoslovakians or to Poland. It's hard to be afraid of Poland. Also, even the KGB has budget limitations, and this stretches their budget.

"Now, Vlad, who is a very smart man, sees the handwriting on the wall. And he says he maybe needs a new client, because the Soviet Union—they're not cutting it anymore. Vlad is getting to be an old man and Czechoslovakia is changing. Vlad has a problem. Not a problem. Vlad and I have something in common. We like young women. Beautiful young women. Now how, under this new regime, is Vlad going to keep a piece of ass like Nadia. She is something else, isn't she? He keeps her by being rich. How does he get rich? He becomes a capitalist. Instead of giving the source code to Russia in return for power, he decides to sell the source code, the operating language of America's top military aircraft, to Musashi Aerospace, which used to be Musashi Aviation, which made the bombers that bombed Hawaii back in Double-U Double-U Two.

"That, my friend, is a source code."

TWENTY-TWO

VLAD THE IMPALER

Vlad's estate was on top of a hill.

I drove up to it and slowly by. It was protected by a wall topped with glass and barbed wire. There were photoelectric devices on the single approach road. He also had video surveillance, armed guards out front, the Bulgarians—I assumed—inside, and a group of professional canines on the grounds.

"This is very confusing," I said when I got back.

"How's that?" Lime said.

"Well, on TV they said communism was dead. Vaclav Havel, a very nice guy, is now in charge of this whole country."

"Right," Lime said.

"Then how come this guy—this Communist secret policeman, this evil genius of the old regime—is still sitting in that big house on the hill, with Czech army, in uniform, guarding his estate, video and dogs and the whole bit. Is he still in or is he out?"

"Yes," Lime said.

"Cute. But this is no time for cute."

"He's not still in. But he's certainly not out."

"Because what I mean by *in,*" I said, "is a guy who can pop me and nobody will ever even ask where my body went."

"He certainly will be out," Lime said, "if things continue in the direction they're going now. Completely out."

"By the end of the day?" I said.

"Very funny," Chip Sheen said. "He tries to be funny."

"As I've gotten older I've grown soft. I admit it," I said to Lime. "Once I would have distracted the dogs with urine from a bitch in heat, designed a catapult—from common articles available even in a Czechoslovakian supermarket—that would heave me over the wall, evaded the guards by wearing my Ninja outfit, and sickened the Bulgarians by throwing them tainted meat."

"He's being sarcastic," Chip Sheen said. "He does that. I don't think we need him."

"Then, armed with a Mauser or Glock or neoprene laser targeting projectile device, I would have confronted Vlad, taken the disc, forced his confession, and, disguised as Shirley Temple Black, made my escape in a specially modified Shelby-Skoda that looked like a common everyday Czech auto but had a 454 Chrysler Hemi under the hood, mag wheels, and MacPhearson struts." I looked at Chip Sheen and said to Lime, "Don't you have agents to do this shit?"

"If he doesn't have the guts to go for it, I certainly do," Chip said.

"If there is anyone in a position to know all our Apes, Eye-ohs, Uses, and You-asses, it's Vlad," Lime said to me.

"Your what?" I said.

"Sorry. That's spook-speak. AIP's is Agents in Place."

"Like Jaroslav," I said.

"No, he's a 'You-ass,'" Lime said.

"He's a who's ass?"

"HUASS," he said. "Human Asset. And a HUSCE is a Human Source. IO's are Intelligence Officers."

"There is no sanity clause, I knew that," I said. "What's the difference?"

"Intelligence Officers are USNATS, United States Nationals."

"Like Chip Sheen?"

"You better believe it, buddy," Chip Sheen said. He sounded like Radar O'Reilly doing a John Wayne imitation. Looked like it too.

"Right. Works out of the embassy or in some other shallow cover. Now an AIP is deep cover . . ."

"Like a mole?"

"A mole is deep cover but in the enemy's IntServ. Or theirs in ours. A HUSCE is a person we get information from. HUASS is one of their nationals over whom we have some control. Like Jaroslav."

"What control do you have over Jaroslav?" I said. I looked at him.

"Patriotism," Lime said. I watched Jaroslav while Lime spoke. "Hates the Russkies. They put his father in prison—more like a concentration camp. When he came out—well—maybe it would have been better if they'd just kept him. Hates the Germans—they killed his grandmother and grandfather."

"For the job on me?"

"For the job on you, I paid him. He also likes hard currency."

"Do you have any good ideas?" I said.

"What do you mean by *good?*" Lime asked.

"I mean something that'll send me home safe and sound to Marie Laure and my baby. I miss my baby."

"Do you have a picture?" Lime asked.

"No," I said. "I don't."

"You know, it's a funny thing." He reached into his pocket and pulled out his wallet. "When you're single, you laugh at guys walking around with kids' pictures in their wallet. I used to. Until I had 'em. You want to see?"

"Sure," I said. He showed me a photo of two kids—a girl four, a boy about two—both better looking than I would have credited to his DNA. "Very nice. How old are they?"

"The girl's twenty-two," he said, "the boy's twenty. He's at the University of Iowa. On the football team. Big kid. Strong. A real ox."

"Where's the girl?" I asked.

"In drug rehab," he said, "a private clinic in California."

"You've been carrying that picture a long time," I said.

"Yeah," he said. "That's the best age. After that they watch TV and start talking back."

"If we have to shoot our way in, then we have to shoot our way in," Chip Sheen said.

"I guess I'm gonna try to talk my way in," I said.

"That's what I guessed," Lime said.

"How much is this source code worth?" I asked. "Cash value."

"That's an accounting question. It depends on how you measure value. Actual development cost less depreciation? The cost to imitate it? How many years it'll save Musashi Aerospace? What it would be valued at in a merger?"

"What do you figure Musashi is paying for it? That's the bottom line."

"A million bucks," Lime said. "Maybe it saves them ten million, maybe fifty million. It's hard to say. But buying it off the street, like they're doing, I would guess a million. Dollars, that is." Perhaps DM1,000,000 was a bargain for Hayakawa. And perhaps I would never see any such amount. It's so much easier to talk about millions than to produce them.

"Why should we use a guy who's motivated strictly by greed?" Chip Sheen said. "Not by patriotism. That's today's security problem. Our enemies can go into America and just buy people and buy information."

"You used to think Tanaka had it before he died," I said. "What made you think that?"

"He told Hayakawa he was ready to deal. Told him to come to St. Anton. We intercepted a phone call." Chip Sheen looked perturbed that Lime had let me know that. "They were careless. Hayakawa is new to this. His predecessor was the one initiated the deal."

"What happened to his predecessor?"

"He had an accident," Chip said, implying it wasn't.

"Driving too fast," Lime said, and made it sound more accidental. "Tried to pass—in one of those hot new Musashi Élégants, by the way—lost it on a curve in the mountains near St. Moritz."

"Tanaka—he was in this business for a long time?"

"Mostly right on the edge, the gray areas. His head-hunting outfit, that's legit. But it also helped him target dissatisfied executives and scientists. A lot of low-to medium-grade industrial espionage. He understood the stuff, which put him ahead of a lot of people. He had an eye for classified material that got published. A lot of it is. He would read something in the technological literature, then retype it so it looked like it came straight out of the word processor, slap a Top Secret stamp on it, even a limited-circulation number on it, turn around, and sell it sub rosa like he stole it. Man about town in Vienna. Made money. But this—this put him in a whole other league. Now he's messing with national defense."

"Was," I said.

"Yes, was," Chip said. "That's why it's important that the deal go down and we catch Hayakawa dirty. If it's morning in Czechoslovakia, what time is it in America? This case has got to go on the map. So some people in D.C.—they wake up and realize that the Japanese are a real threat. That while we were nose to nose with the Soviets, defending the Free World, a couple of our *friends* were using our inattention to creep up on us. The faster that we learn that they are not our friends, the quicker we can do something about it."

"You know what occurs to me," I said. "It occurs to me that without an enemy you guys are out of jobs."

"I'm in this business because I believe in it," Chip said.

Lime just smiled.

"What if they make up the deficit out of the Intelligence budget?" I asked. "What happens to you? Forced retirement. Or you just languish in grade, no growth, no spaces to promote you to. It's not as if you guys get anything right. Did the CIA say the Berlin Wall was going to fall in eighty-nine? That Havel was the next president of Czecho? That Ceausescu would be shot in time for Christmas? That the Soviet Union would lose in Afghanistan and that when they lost the rebels still wouldn't win? Everyone knows you missed Iran completely. Did you call the Chinese crackdown in Tiananmen Square? Did the CIA predict that the U.S. was going to be the biggest debtor nation in the world and that Japan would be the biggest creditor nation and that the Reagan administration could make that happen in just four short years?"

"You're trying to get my goat," Lime said, smiling. "I understand, it's nerves. It's that tension that comes when it's time to play ball."

"So I figure that what you need," I said, "is proof that the U.S.A. needs a CIA."

"You're a very cynical man," Lime said. "That's good. Go get 'em."

"I'm out of my depth here," I said.

"See? He's out of his depth here," Chip said, ready to volunteer himself.

"Not as much as you would be," Lime said to him. "I don't want another big mistake." Chip blushed. "You'll be just fine," Lime said to me. "Just remember, this is a guy in more trouble than you are. He has a long, long way to fall. This guy, this Vlad Kapek—he's invested his whole life in making it in a particular system. He's climbed damn near the top and he's got everything he wants. Everything anybody wants. Material things. You've been in his house in Prague. That's not socialist worker housing. He's got a better sound system than you or me, video and TV and original art and whatever else he wants to buy. Plus the women. If you've got money and power and you're ruthless about using it, you have, maybe not every broad you want, but close enough for government work. He has power. More power in an absolute sense than anyone in a comparable position in the West. He has respect. People say, 'Yes, sir!' to him. His opinion is valued. His participation requested. All the things that make a man feel good and important, he has achieved.

"Except they just changed the system. He's a man with a Rolls-Royce in a world that just ran out of gas. He's scared. He's looking for someone selling solar power, something, anything that'll keep him rolling."

All of which was the right thing to say. Maybe Lime was not such a bad agent handler after all. I swallowed some aspirin. I was down to two every three hours.

"Do you want something stronger?" Lime asked.

"What I want from you is if I don't come out, I want to know you'll come in and get me."

"Of course we will," he said.

"Sure you will," I said. I didn't ask him how. If I had we would have both had to face the fact that he was lying.

I drove up to the front entrance. Sensors on the road told the guards I was coming. One of them was waiting for me outside the gate, machine pistol hanging loose in his hand. The dogs were inside, eyes glittering, saliva drooling from their fangs. If Vlad was slated to be deposed or defrocked or even defenestrated and stripped of his power and privileges, they certainly hadn't got around to it yet. The gate and the wall were a bright mustard yellow. It was a prewar estate. There was a light breeze and a bright yellow sun. The guard gestured for me to go away.

I leaned out the window. I said, "Tell Vlad Kapek that I am a friend of Hiroshi Tanaka." I spoke in German.

The single eye of a CCTV stared at me from above the guard's head. The guard took a walkie-talkie from his belt and spoke into it.

A second guard arrived and gathered the canines—two Dobies, two shepherds. Then the gate was opened and I was waved in. The drive was a curving quarter mile and lined with trees on either side. Come spring the buds would open and create a shady canopy. The house was stucco over brick, that same shade of yellow as the wall, wooden shutters and wooden door. It was moderately large and sprawling, as well as relaxed and country-looking. An orchard stood beside it. I wondered what bourgeois enemy of the people it had been confiscated from.

If Czechoslovakia produces anything in surplus, it's old women who look like grandmothers are supposed to look. One such, cheeks fat and sweet as a baby's, a babushka on her head and an apron around her waist, opened the door and showed me in. She led me through the living room to an at-home office.

Vlad was no more frightening than the Wizard of Oz. Nor, if I wanted to be technical about it, did he have just one arm. He had two. A good one—the right—and one that had been chopped off halfway between the elbow and the wrist. He was slender and intelligent-looking. If he had been a professor of computer science or musicology I would not have been surprised. He sat at a desk with all the paraphernalia that modern man needs, an Apple with a Sony screen and a modem, a multiline phone, a dictaphone, and a fax machine. Dave Brubeck played "Blue Rondo à la Turk" on an Aiwa CD with an automatic changer.

He spoke in Czech.

"German, please," I said. "Or English."

"Oh, you're American," he said in better-than-fair English.

That was going to make it easier. It's hard to hustle in a foreign tongue. Easy to love and lust, but hard to shuck and jive.

"Once," I said. "No more."

"Why is that?" he said.

"I like to think of myself as a citizen of the world," I said.

"What happened to your arm?"

"It will get better," I said. "A dislocation."

"To lose the use of your arm, even temporarily, is very distressful," he said. "As you can see, I have reason to know that."

"Yes. But in spite of it you're a man of great achievement."

"It is a matter of the will," he said. "Nothing is as great or powerful as the human will. It rises over any handicap. It transforms the world. I am a great believer in the will."

"So was my friend Hiroshi Tanaka," I said, taking a guess—it sounded like a Japanese thing to believe in.

"Not so much as I," Vlad said.

"Oh, really," I said.

"Really," he said, as serious about it as if that were the real subject of our meeting.

"He's dead. Tanaka," I said.

"I know."

"It's put a hitch in a lot of plans," I said.

"Yes," he said, "it has."

"I had an arrangement with Tanaka," I said. "In fact, we were in the middle of what I would call a partnership arrangement with him."

"I never heard about that," he said.

"You wouldn't, would you?" I said. "Until it was finalized. Maybe not even then. You were his ace in the hole."

"I beg your pardon? His what?"

"A gambling term. From stud poker. One card is . . ."

"Yes. Of course. I know poker."

"Yes, you would. Of course," I said. Brubeck went on to "Take Five." "I like the tunes." I said. "You like Brubeck?"

"Do you think I would play music I didn't like? I control my environment. It does not control me." He gestured with his stump. It was unfortunately phallic.

"Anyway, he died, along with Wendy. Do you remember Wendy?"

"Yes. My Nadia liked her very much. I enjoyed her too.

So . . . American. Only Americans can be naive and decadent at the same time. Why do you think that is?"

"It's because we have California, where the sun always shines."

"Mr. Tanaka will be missed," he said.

"Yeah," I said. "He was gonna do a lot of business. It would be a terrible shame if that business did not get done."

"Yes, it would."

"Now, the reason I'm here." I saw that I had his interest, that Lime was right, that Kapek needed Tanaka to keep up the lifestyle he'd become accustomed to. To keep Nadia in the lifestyle she'd become accustomed to. "The reason I'm here is to pick up where Tanaka left off."

"Who did you say you were?"

"My passport says I'm Andy Applebaum. I'm not. I have another passport in the name of Richard Cochrane, Irish passport. Not me either. My real name is Cassella. I come from Brooklyn, New York. I have certain connections. In America and in Italy. I originally connected with Mr. Tanaka because I had obtained certain technical data from an Air Force base in Naples. This data was to pay a debt that could not otherwise be paid by someone with some unfortunate habits. I am in a position to find people with unfortunate habits. Sometimes they are people who appear to have nothing of value. Then it is discovered that they have information or knowledge that, if properly directed and marketed, has a great deal of value. Do I make myself clear?"

"Yes," he said. And smiled. I was on a roll.

"With the loss of Mr. Tanaka," I said, "it appeared that it might be difficult to continue to create that value. A loss to a great many people. Fortunately I was able to make contact with at least a portion of Mr. Tanaka's market . . . I can move the stuff."

"Move the stuff?"

"Sorry," I said. "I'll spell it out. I am in contact with Musashi Company. They want to continue to get the product that Tanaka was supplying. They are willing to deal with me, even if I am *gaijin*. There are representatives of my . . . 'group' in California who have had dealings with certain Japanese groups—Yakuza, they call themselves . . ." I watched my performance in Vlad's face. He was eating it up. Most people love gangsters and think they must be great to deal with. Particularly colorful cinematic ones like the American Mafia and Japanese Yakuza. ". . . who deal with Musashi in Japan. They were able to vouch for me."

"It is all very interesting," he said.

"Now it's my understanding," I said, "that you were to give Hiroshi Tanaka a certain disc. Musashi would like to have this disc . . ."

It was in his face. I'd blown it. I'd had him right up to that point. He picked up a little handbell on his desk. With all that electronic junk, he still summoned his Bulgarian goons with the little handbell.

"Wait a minute," I said, trying to think of something to salvage the situation. "I know he was supposed to have had it. He was supposed to have delivered it to Musashi, right? See, but he died first. Now no one can find it. So I thought maybe it hadn't come in time and you still had it." It was like talking to an obsidian mask. He was done with me. The Bulgarians came in. They recognized me.

"I wasn't gonna touch your girl," I said. "I'm a happily married man. I have a three-month-old daughter. I was looking for you. See, I knew that that was your house and I was hoping to find you." The older, meaner-looking Bulgarian slammed his paw down on my left shoulder. It stayed in, but I moaned. In so far as I could think through the pain, I kept remembering Lime saying, *You don't want to be one of those guys goes to parties and pops his arm out of his shoulder to amuse the kids.*

TWENTY-THREE

ULTRALIGHT

When they took me away, I did not resist.

I don't know if it was the injury to my shoulder or being a father or being a captive in a strange land, but I felt older and frailer than I ever had in my life.

They took me downstairs to the dungeons.

Actually to a basement. It was used primarily for basement things—coal bin, boiler and heating system, cold storage, and wine cellar. But apparently Kapek felt that there would be times when he would need to incarcerate, to interrogate, and to torture without departing from his bucolic retreat. There was an interrogation room and a cell. The cell was small. It had a floor, four walls, a door, a small window—high up—and a bucket.

I hurt.

They didn't beat me. Or use cattle prods or electric jolts to my testicles. They just shoved me along, hitting my shoulder, down the hall, down the stairs, into the cell, and up against the wall. They closed the door and locked it. I was inside. My beloved aspirin was somewhere outside.

Nobody came and nothing happened.

I went around the room. I tested the door. I checked the walls. I stood on the bucket and tried to lift myself to the window with one arm. It was barred. The bars were thick and strong. The lifting was very painful. I sat on the floor with my back to the wall, trying to sit as straight and relaxed as I could. I tried to figure out what story I should tell and what good it would do me. I tried to think of a way out. I couldn't. I tried to believe that Lime and Chip "Peaches" Sheen and the limping Bohemian HU-ASS lawyer would come for me. I believed that as much as I believe in the efficacy of prayer.

I considered myself very stupid for being there. I flagellated myself with self-criticism to get my blood circulating, then cloaked myself in self-pity to stay warm. When I'd been there for several hours, toward sunset, I heard music. Percy Sledge singing "When a Man Loves a Woman." The sound came from outside. I pulled myself up to the window. I couldn't actually hold myself up—I could only get up, fall back, and then sort out what little I'd seen by reviewing the image retained on my retina. Nadia danced alone.

A battery-operated radio hung from the branch of an apple tree. It had rained and the tree bark was particularly black. I knew the trees were budding, but I did not know what I had seen that made me think so. One tree had already blossomed. There was a blur of pink, like a single brushstroke amid the barrenness. The radio shut off abruptly. Shortly thereafter, it grew dark.

I knew what the bucket was for.

I used it and placed it as far away from me as I could. There was no place so far away that I couldn't smell my own waste. It began to get chill. Anna Geneviève and Marie Laure were in St. Anton and this sort of business was for stupid single men who cared for no one and liked to brag about their scars. *If I ever get out of this,* I said, bargaining with a God that I didn't believe in, *there are several things I'll never do again. I'm not sure what they are at the moment, but drop off a list at your convenience. Plus I'll marry Marie Laure and backdate the receipt for the sake of the baby and I'll let both mothers-in-law live with me as long as they like, and I will let poor people wash their clothes at my Laundromat for free.*

I thought as much as I could to distract myself from thinking.

I did not want to think about dying, pain, or being crippled. I did not want to think about not seeing my daughter grow up. She'd been born with hair—spiky funny-looking stuff. She didn't go through a bald stage. The new hair grew right through it and replaced it. Now her hair smelled like a puppy's. A very clean, freshly washed puppy, of course. I did not want to think about Marie Laure finding a new daddy for my daughter. I did not want to think about never standing in the mountains, looking at the sky, wondering what the weather would bring and hoping for fresh snow. Or that I might never again get the chance to turn down an opportunity to be unfaithful.

So I thought about the game we were all playing. Who was telling the truth—Lime or Hayakawa or no one? Was the disc really a source code for an F-16? What had Hiroshi Tanaka really been about? Would Hayakawa come up with a million D marks. Would Lime come through with my pardon? Were Hiroshi Tanaka and Wendy Tavetian murdered?

If the answer was yes, the next question was how? I thought the avalanche had been set. Perhaps with a radio-detonated charge. Perhaps with something exotic—a projectile weapon, a laser, a sound generator. Hans Lantz had been part of the murder. He'd led Tanaka and Tavetian to the spot and then bet on his own abilities to outski the avalanche. I had to respect his—something. Not his intelligence. Not even courage or balls or testosterone. His craziness. The question was why? Why kill Tanaka? I thought Hans Lantz had been murdered. A torn page from Heinrich Heine was hardly proof of suicide. Even in Austria, which is nearly perfect and has the lowest homicide rate in the Western world.

Why was Hans Lantz murdered? That was the single question with a clear answer. He'd been a loose cannon, too ready to brag, to spend, and to kill again. Therefore, likely to lead the police back to whoever had employed him.

That brought me back to question number one—Why kill Hiroshi Tanaka?

It was not a spur-of-the-moment murder. Not a fit of anger. Not a moment of passion. Not a quarrel out of control. To stop him? Who wanted to stop him? Lime? Lime wanted to catch Tanaka, and Hayakawa, dirty. Two Japanese trading U.S. military secrets would be even better than one. Hayakawa? He wanted Tanaka's product. Chip Sheen? Possibly. I could visualize that, at least. A little too eager, too trigger-happy, he takes Tanaka out too soon. Maybe that was "the mistake" that Lime had referred to, that had made Sheen blush.

Where was the product? Vlad Kapek, the source of the source code, was certain that Tanaka had taken delivery. Where was the disc?

Somewhere between midnight and dawn of my first night the Bulgarians came in and got me. They sat me on a stool in the interrogation room. They took away my sling and my jacket. It was cold. And shone a light in my face. Vlad was a voice and a shadow.

"Where is the disc?" Vlad asked me.

"I don't know," I said.

"What are the other names?"

"What other names?" I said.

"Who are you?" Vlad asked me.

I told him the truth. Some more and some less. I left the CIA out of my story. That would only irritate him. I portrayed myself as a sleaze who wanted to scam my way into being an additional middleman. It sounded very plausible to me. I was sure it would to him. We went over it ten or twenty times. I asked for aspirin, food, water. Vlad asked me about Nadia. I said I only approached Nadia because I was looking for him. I even told him my pet theories about infidelity and fidelity and how I thought it might be time for the double standard to make a comeback in America. I told him about the photos and how I'd followed them. The older Bulgarian came around and poked his finger into my shoulder. I fell to my knees and whined and groveled. Then they asked me all the same questions all over again.

When they took me back to my cell the shutters over my little window had been closed. I didn't know if it was still dark or dawn. Without any flow of air the bucket became a doubly dominant force in the room.

They questioned me again, later. I was very much losing track of time. Pain and lack of sleep and lack of food and lack of drink were making things somewhat hallucinogenic. Cravings are funny things. I really wanted a shower, above all. That's what kept filling my mind. A shower. A hot one. With a lot of water. A big shower head, way up high, in a marble stall, like the showers at the New York Athletic Club, a wasteful waterfall pounding down on my shoulder, my back, my neck. I mentioned it during interrogation. One of the Bulgarians hurt me.

They put me back in the cell.

Sometime later they brought me food. A glass of water. A roll. Apparently under communism there is only one type of bread per country. In Czechoslovakia it's a white bread. The roll they have been assigned looks like what a croissant would look like if it appeared in a Polish joke. And an onion, which I ate just like an apple.

They came and got me again.

This third session was a lot like the first two. Except there was more pain. The Bulgarians got into playing a game with my arm. Sort of "what's the most scream I can produce with the least effort."

They put me back. The pail had still not been emptied. This time when I used it, it overflowed.

They came for me again.

This time it was not the Bulgarians, it was a soldier—a Czech—who opened the door. It was all different. He was in a rush and agitated. *"Mach schnell! Mach schnell!"* he cried in a hoarse whisper. I did the best I could, and stumbling, trying to keep my shoulder straight, I followed him, through the basement, up a shallow wooden staircase. He shoved the cellar doors open and pushed me up and through them. *"Mach schnell! Mach schnell!"* I was blinking in the daylight. It was noisy. And there I saw the strangest sight I have ever seen in my life.

I only knew what happened from what they told me. Afterward. Everyone happy and satisfied and smug. When it had already become a story.

"You cannot abandon him," Jaroslav said.

"Heck no," Chip Sheen said. "We have to go in after him. He's a fellow American."

"Yes," Jaroslav said with admiration, "that is the American way."

"By God," Lime said, the idea taking him slowly, "maybe we should."

"All right!" Chip said.

"*Ja,* good," Jaroslav said, nodding, reaching for a beer.

"You know, in all my years in this business we've never gone back in to get an agent. The thing in Iran—but that was so fucked up I'd rather forget it. The thinking in the Company is, Don't do it. Wait a couple of years and we'll come up with a trade. But goddammit, I'm fed up and I don't want to take it anymore. Let's Go Get Him!"

They didn't cheer the decision, but eyes lit up, looks of determination were exchanged, and beer glasses were raised.

"The dirty quarter dozen," Sheen said.

The planning began. The action followed.

The key was Vlad. They had to lure him out of the way.

"His weakness was the woman," Lime said.

"Women make men weak," Chip Sheen said. "Even when they're wives."

"*Der frau* is *der* Trojan Horse," Jaroslav said.

"It was like something out of a World War Two movie. You know—when the GI tells the girl he's a photographer from *Life* Magazine," Lime said. "Well, I put on my best suit, shined the silver top on my cane, got some cards printed up. Then I told her I was from Wilhelmina Modeling Agency in New York City. The agency that represents Paulina. 'Little lady,' I said, 'you have a future. How soon can you get to the Big Apple?' Before she could engage her brain, I said, 'I'm leaving in the morning. If you're interested, come by the hotel.' I put my room number on the card. 'If not,' I said, 'I have been charmed to meet you and I wish you luck and not too many troubles in the coming economic upheavals.'"

"Then I come up to her," Jaroslav said. "You know Czech people are very nice and trusting—except for politics, of course." I could see it. There was something warm, honest, and believable about him. "She tells me about the man from Wilhelmina. 'Could this be real?' she asks. 'How fortunate that I am a lawyer,' I said. 'I will make sure that this offer is legitimate. That it is not idle chat designed to lure guileless and unworldly girls to hotel rooms where foreigners will abuse their Czech virtue.' Such as it was. 'Should I listen to this man?' she asks me. I said to her: 'When opportunity is knocking, let the postman in.'"

"Scene Two," Lime said. "The Virgin, the Hotel Room, the Contract. I actually had a contract ready for her. Thank God she couldn't read English. So she didn't know she was signing a sub-lease on an apartment in Washington."

Someone put down a plate of sliced sausage and cheese and a variety of good Austrian breads. In the West they have more than one bread per country. They have fresh vegetables in winter. There were sliced tomatoes and scallions. I stacked a high and greedy sandwich and started washing it down with *weisbier.*

"Thank God that the copy machine has come to Marienbad. This is the miracle," Jaroslav said. "Without it we could not have manufactured the false documents."

"He just wants credit, and he should have it," Lime said. "He was the one found the Xerox machine . . ."

"It was a Canon copier," Jaroslav said.

"Whatever," Lime said. "Some strategically placed white tape, the rental price and the address disappear, and as long as you didn't know English it could've been a contract for anything. Then you should've seen Jaroslav, like a real lawyer fighting over a real contract—clause by fucking clause. We promised to pick up her airfare to the States. First Class."

"Is not good enough," Jaroslav says. "First-class girls go Concorde."

"Anyway, she's ready to leave with me in the morning," Lime said.

"Meantime, *I* found the soldier," Chip Sheen said. "I was watching the road from the house. The first time I saw this guy, I knew. Weak chin, shifty eyes, dandruff. And tall. If anyone would sell out his country, he was the one. Now I admit it was Jaroslav made the approach. Crude approach if you ask me. Not good tradecraft."

"I said, 'Hey, buddy.' Jaroslav said, 'How would you like to make a hundred United States dollars? Cash. Hard currency. Maybe even five hundred.' 'American dollars?' the guy says. 'American dollars,' I said, and flashed him a hundred-dollar bill.

He wants to see it. I let him. He fondles it, he strokes it. He tastes it. 'Who do I have to kill?' he says."

This was the guard who'd let me out of my cell when the time came.

In the morning Nadia left the house, passport in her pocketbook, ready to ride with Lime to Munich to catch a flight to the Big Apple. She didn't tell Vlad anything. "But I insisted that there be no loose ends, that she had to call and say good-bye," Lime said. "She was afraid, *naturellement*. So I said she could tell him she was going to Vienna. As long as she called. Because, old boy, that was the point."

"I have seen him," Jaroslav said, "where I am waiting. He comes out of the estate so very fast. With the Bulgarians one hundred fifty kilometers per hour. On that little country road."

"Bingo!" Lime said. "We got the head man out. Now we go in."

"Now, you must know," Jaroslav said, and the others were silent because this was his big moment, "what I have been in addition doing. I have gone to the office of the local prosecutor. I have been the lawyer from the Big City. I have needed some forms. He is very nice because nobody knows who is important anymore. Also, here in Czechoslovakia . . ." He paused. He poured another round for all of us, pacing himself, savoring his role. ". . . it is still assumed that if you asked for something you are permitted it. Nobody would dare ask what they are not permitted. We do not yet know that we are free. So I get many papers from him.

"I made up court order for your release. Then I am signing it. I make up a name. A good strong name. Also subpoenas. Never has this been done. To serve legal papers on the Army. This is impossible in Czechoslovakia. It is so crazy that they think maybe it is correct. Maybe I have the right to do this. They do not know—maybe the power of Vlad Kapek is over. Just that I am there, that I dare to be there, with papers, means that Vlad's time is done. The guard at the gate is not sure what to do. So he calls another guard. I give him a subpoena. This he is more frightened of than a poison snake.

"Soon all the guards are there. All paralyzed. Wondering what to do. Except the guard to whom I have give the bribe."

That guard was leading me out of the cellar. There was a coughing roar or a roaring cough and the sound of half a Polski Fiat filled the sky. Coming over the wall in a wide-winged wobble, looking like Rube Goldberg with delusions of being Batman, came Chip Sheen in an ultralight.

An ultralight is the world's smallest heavier-than-air aircraft; A triangle with wheels sits below a pair of wings that look like they've been stolen from the Museum of Natural History's model of a pterodactyl. This triangle has a seat in the middle and a two-stroke engine mounted on the back, a motor that in less adventurous times would power a lawn mower, but here it has a propeller. The person in the seat steers this thing with a crossbar attached to the wings. He very much hopes that there is not too much wind. They were quite popular in Czechoslovakia, but too many people used them to fly over the Iron Curtain and they were banned.

Yapping almost as loudly as the engine and dangling in a basket were two maddened Pekingese. Careening around the orchard, Chip lowered the basket toward the ground. The two Dobies came around the corner from the gate at top speed. The Alsatians followed a moment later.

"That was your idea," Chip said. He felt good about himself for sharing the credit. "But I knew you were being sarcastic and I wasn't sure about just using the urine from bitches in heat so I brought whole dogs. Small ones, of course."

Mad with terror, the Pekingese, who were indeed in heat, jumped out of the basket even before Chip had released the rope.

"Come on, come on," Chip yelled to me. "Jump aboard! You have to run alongside, and get on while I'm still rolling."

As it turned out, only two of the guard dogs were males. The other two went along, as dogs will, just because the first two were running. But once the males caught up with the Pekingese—which didn't take long—and tried to mount them, the female guard dogs saw the males with their pink wet erections and realized that all the fuss was just about chasing bitches. Then they turned around and started chasing me. They were big, they were fast, and they had a great many teeth.

Chip Sheen pulled out an automatic. He had nine shots, but with the ultralight bumping along on the ground and firing one-handed, it would have been remarkable if he shot even one of the dogs and managed to miss me. But he got them both. The Doberman first. The bullet took one of her forelegs right off and she went flopping stomach down onto the dirt. Five shots later he caught the Alsatian in the side. It knocked her over and she whined and whined, blood flowing out of her, scrambling in the dirt and dying.

I struggled onto the ultralight. It bounced, and bounced, and bounced. I was going to need a lot of physical therapy. Then we were airborne.

That was how I dreamed the rescue would be.

The sensation of bouncing came from the throbbing in my shoulder. *Shoulder* is too short a word for it. It went from forearm to my neck, across the left side of my chest, down my back as well.

It was Nadia who came to the door.

"I'm sorry," she whispered. "When I saw it was you, I knew I had to do something."

"But why?" I asked. Stupid question. Who cared why? What if she suddenly realized that there was no good reason.

"You stirred something in me," she said. "Here. Take this." It was a gun. "You don't have to be afraid to kill them. They would kill you. You will be doing a lot of people a favor anyway. I hear them. I must run."

I think I was awake when I dreamed that, which would make it a delirium or a hallucination.

Jaroslav and Lime did come for me. Finally. They appeared at the door with several men unknown to me. Jaroslav was smiling broadly.

"Kapek has been arrested," Lime said. "It took a while for the new regime to catch up with him. He had destroyed the file on himself. But they got around to him. They just took him away."

"Let's get out of here," I said.

"Jesus, it stinks," Lime said.

"We will get you a doctor," Jaroslav said.

But I woke up in my cell again.

The guard came to the door.

"I know where the disc is," I said.

He gestured me to silence. Then he threw a uniform like his own on the floor. "*Schnell,*" he whispered.

I stripped slowly and painfully. He was frustrated and furious watching me. "*Schnell,*" he said again. The uniform stank of whoever had worn it before. Though not so bad as I probably smelled and certainly not so bad as the bucket.

As soon as I was dressed he led me out of the cell, through the basement, up the cellar steps, exiting directly into the orchard without going into the house. It was dark outside. I don't know where the dogs were or whether the odor of my uniform was familiar to them and they were disinterested. We walked a quarter mile, perhaps a half.

"I need food," I whispered. I had a full load of adrenaline running but it wasn't enough. It was making me dizzy and I was trembling.

He looked at me full of incomprehension. It made me angry not to be understood. I gesticulated. Eating is a simple thing to mime. He looked at me in disgust but fished in his pocket and came up with half a grubby Czech chocolate bar. The wall ended. It was replaced by both an electrified fence and barbed wire. The electric wire carried a very light voltage and wasn't really dangerous. The barbed wire was the lethal modern type they use in Manhattan to separate the thieving class from the possessing class. Then we reached a spot where the wires went into the trees and underbrush. There were people waiting on the other side. The guard led me to a spot where I saw that I could cross.

Jaroslav came forward out of the darkness. Followed by my

mother. My mother wanted to call out, Jaroslav gestured her to silence.

My mother gave Jaroslav a wad of money. He gave it to the guard. Some words were exchanged in Czech. Then the guard stepped back and shoved me forward. Jaroslav held the wire up and I crouched down and stepped through.

"Are you all right?" my mother said.

"Yes," I said.

"Come," Jaroslav said.

"What did I cost?" I asked.

"Five thousand dollars," my mother said, very annoyed. Close to tears in fact.

"Where are Lime and Chip Sheen?"

"Gone," Jaroslav said. "Quiet, we go to car."

The car was a hundred yards away. I got in the passenger seat, my mother got in the back. Jaroslav drove.

"How did you get here?" I asked.

"He had your phone number from your things, at the hotel," my mother said. "He called for Marie Laure. But I answered. He said that you were in trouble. He was very difficult to understand. Very difficult. He said that he found a way to get you out. But it would cost five thousand dollars."

"My English is so small," Jaroslav said. "I am making apology."

"I cashed all my traveler's checks, then got a cash advance on my VISA card. I didn't know if I should trust him. I said I wouldn't pay until I saw you."

"Thank you, Mom."

"I wish . . ." she said.

"You wish what, Mom?"

"I wish you had finished law school."

"Thanks for coming to get me, Mother. I love you. It's good to know I can depend on you. I'll pay you back. But don't mention law school again. That's a long time ago."

"After all, it was Yale," she said.

"I'll get you back the $5,000."

"It's not the money," she said.

"I know that," I said.

"You're too old to be doing things like this. You have a

wife and baby now. You should not need your mother to help you. Also I'm very frightened and I don't like feeling frightened."

"Do you happen to have aspirin?" I said.

"I have Tylenol," my mother said.

"Jaroslav," I said, "I have to thank you."

"No mention of it," he said.

"How come you stayed when they left?"

"I am very upset when they are gone. When they abandon you," he said. "When I became a human asset for American intelligence, that was not the America I imagined."

TWENTY-FOUR

MOTHERS AND OTHER STRANGERS

I expected to be treated like a wounded lion. To lie around, look handsome and impressive, yet hurt and vulnerable, be fed and cared for and pampered by my harem of females, each one intent on pleasing the king of beasts.

This was not the case.

When I was six and did something that frightened my mother, she got angry with me. As she did when I was fifteen, twenty, twenty-five, thirty. And she did so now.

Anita—my ski bum—was angry because receipts at the Laundromat were down, she hadn't made what she had anticipated, and probably could not afford her return ticket to Australia.

Geneviève, Marie Laure's mother, was mad because receipts at the Laundromat were down and Marie Laure was dipping into savings. She pointed out that if there had been a wedding there would have been wedding gifts—lingerie to kitchen ware—and she would never have to buy a thing again. If she had been married she could have come home and there would have been baby showers—bassinettes to booties—and she would never have to buy a baby thing.

Marie Laure was angry at me because her mother and my mother were angry at me. This put her in the uncomfortable position of having to agree with them or defend me. Actually, she didn't mind agreeing with my mother. It was agreeing with her own that she found difficult. She wasn't relying solely on secondhand reasons—she had her own reasons to be annoyed with me. For leaving her alone to deal with the mothers, for not calling from Marienbad, for getting hurt when I should be invulnerable, and because Glenda, the woman that I was living with when we met, had called. Twice. Marie Laure was annoyed that all I wanted was hot baths, straight aspirin, sleep, and to be waited on. Also, she was angry with me because I dared to resent her being angry at me and got angry with her. Clearly we had evolved from being merely lovers to having a real relationship.

Anna Geneviève was not angry. But she didn't seem to recognize me, which was worse.

And they were all of them angry—excluding Anna Geneviève—because I had not solved the mystery of the missing disc, scored the money, cut a deal, and legitimized myself to become a citizen with a country and a real passport.

To hell with them all. I sulked in my bed. I soaked in the tub.

The doctor said I was an idiot, but that after a week of total inertia I could begin physical therapy combined with massage.

My mother announced that Guido was well enough to travel. He was on his way. I still don't know what their relationship is. That is a euphemism meaning that I don't know if they have sex. He's a priest whose God has failed him and he's an excellent cook. He would defrock himself, no doubt, but he knows no nonclerical way to make a living.

Glenda called again. She was calling on Wayne's behalf, she said. That made it okay, of course. She wanted to know how I was and, parenthetically, who I was with. Was it the same one? Which same one, since there had been several during my years with Glenda? The same one that I'd left her for, she said. I said I hadn't left her for anyone. I had left America because they were going to put me in jail if I stayed. "I would have come with you," she said, "if you had asked." Who wanted to open that can of worms. The apartment, she said, was fine. The bubble of Manhattan real estate had not burst but it had deflated somewhat. Naturally we had bought at about the top of the market. Anyway, it was about Wayne. Who needed both adventure and direction and might benefit from a summer in Europe. I asked what was wrong. She said nothing was wrong. "Teach him about girls. I mean from a man's point of view," she said. I asked her what that meant, but she didn't make it clear. I said that there were several problems. It was not that I had a new baby. "Oh," she said as if she didn't know, but she did because I had written Wayne about it. It was that things appeared to be coming apart, and I didn't really know where I would be and if I would be in a situation where I could have guests. "You're still not married, are you?" she asked. I admitted that I was not. "Wayne needs you," she said. Sitting, sullen, in my bedroom, with more family than I ever wanted or needed or could use surrounding me, I said, "Yes. Wherever I am, which might be back in the States, he can come." She said she would bring him to Austria herself. It would be nice to spend a day or two with me.

Yeah, we were all going to enjoy that.

Mike Hayakawa came to the house the day after I got home, while I was at the doctor's. My mother, who enjoyed him very much, invited him to dinner. I thought that was a great idea in that everyone was much more civil when an outsider was around.

Anna Geneviève remembered Mike Hayakawa. She cooed and gurgled for him. He adored her back.

Geneviève had done the cooking. We had an onion soup for a starter. Good soup, not the kind with the wad of stretchy cheese on top.

Once upon a time, I suppose, when someone from Japan came to dinner, an exotic after all, the conversation might have turned to Zen, haiku, flower symbology, Shinto. Now we spoke about money. Yen versus dollars. GM versus Toyota. Hitachi versus IBM.

"Americans are very funny," Mike Hayakawa said. "They apply a double standard. They describe us as economic predators. Not very long ago the United States had every advantage—capital, markets, skills, technology, research. Even with all those advantages, you used the CIA and your armed forces to make the world safe for American multinational corporations. If a country threatened to nationalize property, the United States of America overthrew that government. That's a fact. In Iran, the Congo, Greece, Lebanon, Chile, Guatemala, Nicaragua, all over Southeast Asia.

It is not a secret that America was making the world safe for United Fruit, ITT, Exxon, Chase Manhattan.

"Please don't misunderstand me. I am not criticizing the United States for this in any way. This makes sense. This is admirable," he said, and he meant it. "I am a capitalist, all the way, not a Communist. My point is that when all Japan does is sell well-made products for a good price, we are accused of bad conduct."

The main course was duck cooked into a pie, braised vegetables on the side. Hayakawa held my daughter while Marie Laure helped her mother serve. "You have a very nice granddaughter," he said, nodding to both grandmothers. I had bought the wine. Geneviève found it unacceptable. When it was served she forced Marie Laure to announce that she had not selected it, that it was the only wine in the house, and that someone else was at fault. She was right. It did not live up to the cooking.

Hayakawa said that one thing that separates the Japanese from the rest of the universe is the formation of groups as emotionally connected as a family. The company was such a group, as was the nation. All for one, one for all. He had enjoyed America, but he could not understand how Americans could endure their isolation and differences. The disconnectedness. Like many Japanese, and many Americans for that matter, it seemed self-evident to him—though he understood how impolitic it was to say so—that certain minorities were dragging America down. It was they who committed the crime, used the drugs, spread disease, and hurt our educational system.

My mother told him that this didn't make the Japanese special. Ethnic exclusivity—us against the outsiders—was extremely common. She got the *Herald Tribune* and opened it right across Hayakawa's duck. Romanians were fighting Hungarians. Russian troops were trying to prevent Azerbaijanis from killing Armenians, Iraqis were gassing Kurds. Geneviève, in silent fury over the insult to her food, slid the plate out from under the newspaper as my mother turned the pages. Italian thugs beat some African immigrants to death. Then there were Lebanese, Israelis, Palestinians; tribal conflicts in Africa; white against black in South Africa. The standard day's news.

"Ethnic purity is the source," Anna said, "of misery, bloodshed, and pain. The Japanese should be ashamed of it. Not proud of it. Even if you think it helps you sell Nikon cameras and Hitachi cars."

"Hitachi does not make cars," Hayakawa said. I thought he was furious under his polite face. He was a driven man with very good manners.

"The diversity of America—even the blacks and Latins that you don't think well of—is an advance for humanity," my mother said.

"Even in Brooklyn," I said, as a joke. Nineteen ninety was not a great year for race relations in Brooklyn.

"This business of racial purity," my mother said, "is a step backward."

By golly, my mother makes me proud sometimes.

If Hayakawa had been lectured as sharply about racial attitudes by anyone but an older person, and especially a grandmother, I think he would have reacted very strongly. As it was, he swallowed it. Perhaps he turned a slightly whiter shade of pale.

Marie Laure and I—with my stunted "franglais" that I'd learned mostly in bed and on a few selected Alps—tried to keep up a rough-running translation for Geneviève. She now spoke up. French civilization, she said, was *the* unique civilization. Far more advanced than the Japanese. Look at the cooking. The Japanese ate everything raw. Now that the Japanese had money and wanted good things, where were they going? To France, for Luis Vuitton, Chanel, Yves St. Laurent, and for a decent glass of wine.

Dessert was fresh fruit and sorbet.

After dinner Hayakawa pulled me aside. "The disc?"

"I don't have it. Yet."

"What do you mean 'yet?' " he said.

"The cash. Do you have it?"

"No, not yet," he said. "But I can get it."

"That's what I mean by yet," I said. "Same thing you do."

"Then you do have it?"

"How long will it take you to put together the money?" I asked him.

"Four days," he said.

"Then in four days I will get it. I don't want to sit with it. I don't need that much exposure."

"You are positive you can get it?"

"You know, I've been kidnapped, imprisoned, dislocated, and defenestrated looking for this disc for you. I haven't seen deutsche mark number one, let alone a million deutsche marks. I haven't seen your letter of credit, your checking account statement, your savings bank passbook. Nothing. I believe in the deutsche marks as much as you believe in the disc."

"Musashi Corporation always honors its contracts. Always," he said. "See to it that you do too. I will not accept betrayal."

That night I had a dream. It was a rock-and-roll dream.

St. John Belushi led a Children's Crusade. He was outfitted as a Blues Brother, in an ill-fitting suit, porkpie hat, and sunglasses. He had the blues in his left hand, cocaine in his right, the drumstick of a chicken sticking out of his pocket, and barbecue sauce on his mind. He was followed by generations of Eastern European immigrants—Ukrainians, Poles, Letts and Litvaks, Serbians, Dalmatians, Czechs, and Slovaks—all from Chicago in red, white, and blue. They boogied down the avenue. The cops were German and the firemen wore buttons that said KISS ME I'M IRISH. Kareem Abdul Jabbar was by his side in a Watusi outfit that embarrassed him no end because he is a gentleman of refinement and class. He had a bodyguard of genuine Italian hoodlums who had their shoes shined, their silk suits shiny, and their chrome gleaming. They rode in Cadillacs, MADE IN DETROIT stamped on their hoods, MADE IN CONNECTICUT stamped on their Colt firearms. Hassidim danced to the "Theme from Peter Gunn" while a team of Vietnamese played saxophones.

Harry Lime was there. He pushed Larry Flynt, publisher and creator of *Hustler*, in his wheelchair. He carried a sign that said I REPRESENT THE RACIST SALACIOUS SUBCONSCIOUS OF AMERICA—AND I'M PROUD OF IT. They were with a contingent of *Cosmopolitan* girls from Queens and Brooklyn who had all taken off from their secretarial jobs, at great personal expense, to be at the parade. Bengali vendors sold rice, hawked newspapers, and figured out how to become merchant bankers. A Chinese kid stepped up to the microphone and said, "This is just my high school science project." Ronald Reagan said, "Have a good time, kids," and, smiling genially: "You don't mind if I work for the Japanese. They like me." Nancy Reagan said, "I *like* the Beach Boys." Shirley Temple Black sucked on Frank Zappa's reefer. Vaclav Havel did a duet with Milos Forman, singing "Dancing in the Street."

Marie Laure clung to my arm and said, "Is this America or am I in Hillbilly Heaven?"

"The party's over—it's time to call it a day," the policeman said.

"We're so glad to see so many of you here tonight," St. Belushi cried. "I'm here to preach a sermon. I'm here to say that 'everybody needs somebody to love.'"

A bunch of Japanese police were sent in. They attacked in riot-control formation wearing helmets by Hitachi, plastic shields by Toshiba, and swinging batons by Musashi.

Then Ray Charles came out with a mariachi band and we all danced to "Let the Good Times Roll."

When I awoke Harry Lime and Chip Sheen were at my front door.

"Eat shit and die," I said.

"Won't we please come in," Lime said.

"No," I said.

"Well, son," Lime said, "I sure am glad you got out of old Czecho. Did Jaroslav help you out like I instructed him?"

I tried to close the door. Chip stepped in to block it. What a nice thing to do. I was, after all, only incapacitated on my left side. I hit him with a short right as hard as I could. I got some snap in the punch and weight behind it. I caught him flush in the face. It hurt both of us. He went flying across the hall. I went to my knees as the shock wave traveled back up my other arm. He came up and clawed for his gun. That created enough anger that I practically stopped hurting.

"Go ahead, shoot me, you stupid motherfucker," I said. Actually I snarled and spittle spewed from my mouth.

The baby was awake and crying. Marie Laure called out to ask what was going on. My mother, whose room was down the hall, came padding out in slippers and a housecoat.

"Now, now, boys, calm down," Lime said, as if he were the neutral and the spat was between Chip and me.

"What's going on?" my mother said.

"Get the fuck out of here," I said, but not to my mother.

"I'm going to get you," Chip Sheen said. "Man to man, one on one. You'll see. Don't underestimate me because I'm small and a Mormon."

"Lime, if you and your dog aren't out of here in ten seconds, I'm going to get my shotgun and blow you out of here."

"Just do me one favor," he said. "Look in your wife's makeup bag. Think about what you find."

"She's not even his wife," Chip Sheen said.

"I'll be back in an hour," Lime said.

I closed the door on them. There was a knock almost immediately. It was my mother. I let her in and closed the door behind her. "What was that about?" she said.

There was a knock on the door. I opened it. Geneviève came in.

Marie Laure came out of the bathroom with her makeup kit. "What is this?" she said, and held up a Baggie of white powder.

"Shit," I said.

Marie Laure looked at me with disapproval. "My mother," she said.

"Sorry," I said.

"What is that?" my mother said. "Why did they want you to look in there?"

"To tell me that I am vulnerable," I said. "I assume it's drugs. I'm going to kill him."

Geneviève started speaking in very rapid, intense French. It was something about using *drugs*—an international word—and her daughter and her granddaughter and me, the bum that hadn't married Marie. Marie told her mother to please be quiet.

"What is this?" Marie Laure said to me.

"It's a message. First, they're telling me that they know I'm back. Then, they're saying they can get in and out of our apartment at will. Finally, they're making a threat. Instead of telling us about the drugs, they could have gone to the police."

Marie Laure translated for her mother. Her mother said that since Marie Laure wasn't married it was all right if she left me. Even though her father was upset about the baby, she could come home. Marie Laure told her mother to stop it, that she was not going to leave me.

"Let's go to the police, now," my mother said. "We can show them the drugs. Tell them that someone is trying to plant them on you. This horrible Lime man. Let the police deal with it."

"Sometimes you're very American," I said.

"I am an American," my mother said.

There was an exchange between Marie Laure and her mother.

"What did she say?" my mother said.

"She said she will make the coffee," Marie Laure said, "and wants Tony to go get croissants. How can one think before breakfast?"

"I'll have decaf," my mother said. "Instant will do."

"Oh, no, no, we will brew it," Marie Laure said.

"Actually, I prefer the instant," my mother replied, as she did each morning. And went into the kitchen.

"There's no point in going to the police, even to Franz, the gendarme," I said. "It doesn't solve the basic problem. Which is my legal status. We have to figure out what we really want."

"Are you willing to deal with these people?" Marie Laure said.

"You want me to fix things so I have a real passport, don't you? No more running and hiding. You know it's a big world and there's more to it than skiing. We could switch to windsurfing and sailing. That way we could live in the Seychelles, Sri Lanka, Brazil."

She didn't think that was funny, but all she said was, "I don't want you to do anything that you can't live with. You have to do what is right for you."

"I have to know what you really want," I said.

"I would like you to be Anthony Michael Cassella of New York again. An American. Free to go anywhere. But I do not want you to be in prison or hurt or hurt inside from doing what is not right."

"I love you," I said.

"Say it in French," she said.

"*Je t'aime,*" I said.

"I think you're cute," she said, and kissed me. The kiss got very open and wet and involved tongues, the pressing of body parts, and an erection. "Come into the bedroom, quick," she said.

"I don't want to hurt you," I said.

"You won't," she said, "I'm going to suck you and drink you. But you better not make a sound. If our mothers hear I will die."

It sounded far too good to ruin it by telling her the apartment was wired. It had to be. That's how Lime knew I was back. He'd heard me reconfirm my deal with Hayakawa. That's why he had gone to the trouble of proving he could frame me. Perhaps I should have been even angry about him listening to my private life, but it seemed like a small detail compared to the stress of having two mothers-in-law in the house when you're not even married.

When Lime returned I was in a much better frame of mind.

"Can you get the disc?" he asked just as urgently as Hayakawa had.

"Did you get that letter to my lawyer?" I asked.

"I knew we could work together," he said.

"As soon as it's in writing."

"Well, I don't know how quickly I can get it done. Channels are channels and New York is far away."

"Fuck you, Lime," I said, genially.

"Can I at least see the disc before I get the whole agency in an uproar?"

"No," I said.

"How do I know I can trust you?" he said.

"I know that I can't trust you," I said. "Isn't that sufficient?"

"You're pretty friendly with Mike Hayakawa," he said. "Are you sure you know what side you're on?"

"Same side I've always been on. Mine, Marie Laure's, Anna Geneviève's. I know what you can do to me. Don't bother with the drug thing, or threatening my daughter."

"I don't think you appreciate the full subtlety of the setup. We get you," he said, "because your passport is a fake and you're wanted for obstruction of justice and tax evasion in the States. Then we get the French girl on drugs. I wanted you to actually see that we could plant the stuff on her. What's nice about that is she gets labeled an unfit mother and they take the kid away. Don't cross me."

"Something happens to them," I said, just as quietly, "I'll kneecap you." I picked up his cane. I tapped his good knee with it. "A lot of punks when they're getting sent up, they make threats, 'I'm gonna get you.' Shit like that. To the judge, the prosecutor. Nobody worries about it. But *you* have to worry about *me*. If you need me to show you that I'll hurt you, I'll hurt you right now."

"I'll get that letter to the attorney," he said.

"Do that," I said.

"Four days?" he said.

"Why leave it till the last minute?" I said. "If you want good planning, give me some room. If I were you, I'd have the thing done in two days, three at the most."

"Do you have the disc now? Come on, you can tell me."

"Lime, you left me there. In Vlad Kapek's basement. With his Bulgarian goons. Jaroslav . . ."

"I told Jaroslav . . ."

"We both know you didn't," I said. "Jaroslav and my mother got me out. So the deal is just what we always said it would be. Hayakawa gets the disc, I get Hayakawa's money and the pardon . . ."

"Not exactly a pardon. A plea bargain."

"A plea bargain down to a noncriminal offense, no time, and an affordable settlement. Very affordable. You get the opportunity to take Hayakawa with the disc."

"What do you mean, the opportunity?"

"I'll set him up," I said.

He nodded. He stood up. He held out his hand to shake. "Done," he said.

If I was wrong, again, about the disc, at least I had stalled for four more days. The world keeps turning, there are avalanches and road accidents, bureaucrats get transferred, papers get lost, and even women change their minds. I didn't shake hands with him.

TWENTY-FIVE

DOWN UNDER

"Please help me," Robert Tavetian said. "She's out of control."

"What?" I said. The Bulgarian band was back. They were louder than ever. Doing a disco version of "New York, New York." The time warp was swallowed by the culture warp. Only St. Belushi could've explained it to the beer-crazed Swedes and he was dead.

"Look at her," he said.

She was on the dance floor. She was not the only woman in her late forties I've ever seen rocking like she was twenty with tight pants and a tight bra to make what was soft look firm and a lot of makeup and a general air of manic despair. Actually she was more typical this way than when she'd arrived as a suburban mother, neatly shapeless and formlessly attractive.

"Do you know who killed our daughter?" he said. "That might stop Arlene."

"An avalanche killed Wendy—ten tons of snow and gravity."

"No, no," he said. "Somebody did it. They were after that Japanese man who was with Wendy."

"Maybe," I admitted.

"Tell me who," he pleaded, clinging to my sling.

"If I find out, I promise I will."

"Was it that American, the little Mormon, or the Japanese guy? Do you think it's one of those two?"

"Robert, the best thing you could do is go home."

"Do you . . . do you know . . . do you know what she is doing? Arlene?"

"No," I said.

"She's f-f-f-fucking anybody she thinks our daughter had sex with. Then she tells me about it. She . . . that ski instructor. And another one, Luis. I thought I would be jealous of him the most. He's so good-looking. She's insane and she's my wife. I have to stand-stand-stand by her. I have to stand by her. The Japanese man."

"Mike Hayakawa?"

"Yes. She did it with-with him also. With him. He's the only Japanese here. To find out why Wendy was with a Japanese. She only wants to understand. It can't be understood though, can it. It is the way of-of-of God. You know, of fate. Or is it an accident? Do you know why our daughter was selected to be the one to be with the man who was murdered in an avalanche all the way across an ocean from where she was born? Do you know . . . do you know . . . what will be done to your daughter by-by whatever did this to us."

"I'm sorry," I said, pulling away.

"Stop her—please stop her before she does something really bad," he said. But I don't think he really thought I could.

I found Paul in back, watching the room, mentally counting his money. Chip Sheen, who had followed me in, was near the entrance, keeping guard and testing his Mormon soul with beer.

"Have you noticed," Paul said to me, "that nothing ever happens in St. Anton anymore. I'm bloody bored. How about you?"

"Well, it's been a bad season,"

"What happened to your arm? Ski accident? Happens to the best of us."

"No," I said. "Defenestration."

"Oh, yeah," he said. "That can be tough."

"I'm looking for Carol," I said.

"I'm thinking of selling out," he said. "You interested in being a saloonkeeper? There's a lot of money in it. I'll tell you what, mate. I could retire tomorrow and buy the biggest sheep ranch in

New South Wales. Be a gentleman rancher. Fly over to New Zealand for heli-skiing."

"I might be moving on myself," I said.

"Bloody boring town," he said. "Not what it used to be. But you know what I'm going do? I'm heading for the land of opportunity. You might be interested."

"Carol, is she still working for you?"

"Dishwasher girl? Yeah, sure, mate. I want you to look at this." He held out a brochure. "This is the future: the Soviet Union. They've got mountains that've never been skied. Heli-skiing. Miles and miles of it. No bloody Greens to tell you heli-skiing is bad for the environment."

"Is she around?" I asked him.

"No, it's her night off," he said. "This is one place that won't be too crowded to ski on the weekends. No lift lines. When you get powder it won't get skied to death in four hours. Plus the opportunity—I guarantee you they need people who understand capitalism. There never was a Marxist-Leninist knew how to run a decent disco. Come with me. The punters'll need Laundromats."

"This is in the Caucasus," I said.

"You got to hand it to Gorbachev," he said. "He's the first world leader to open up an entire new mountain range to skiing."

"There's a war there—the Azerbaijanis and the Armenians."

"Yeah, but we're skiers. They won't bother us."

"Of course not," I said. "I'd like to take another look at Carol's room. You mind giving me the key?"

"She was pissed last time," he said.

"I'll be discreet," I said.

"Right, then," he said. "You should think about it. Mount Elbrus, highest peak in Europe, five thousand six hundred thirty-three meters." He gave me the key. I glanced over at Chip Sheen. When he was distracted, I walked into the kitchen and out the back door.

Women masturbate in a variety of positions.

Carol, on this occasion at least, lay on her side, covered from the hips down by her blanket. I could tell by the shape beneath that her top leg was drawn up, the bottom leg stretched out. One hand was hidden. Her other hand was at her face. She touched her cheek and her lips with light, wondering fingers, the way she might want a lover to touch her. On the floor beside the bed, where she had dropped it, was the page that had been torn out of the *manga,* Hiroshi Tanaka's Japanese comic for adults.

It was one of the climactic scenes of the story and a single picture filled the page. The heroine was tied down, spread-eagled, naked. Her pubis was hairless. The villain held a razor to her throat. He had made a shallow cut. The thin trickle of blood dripped in an artistic minimalist Japanese pattern suggestive of fine calligraphy. The villainess, a large-breasted, fatty, Western-looking woman with a lot of hair in her crotch, clutched the heroine's thighs and leered.

"Wendy, Wendy, Wendy," Carol called out. The *manga* heroine, I now saw, did indeed look like the cartoon version of a generic Wendy.

When Carol reached her orgasm she buried her head in the pillow to muffle her noises. When it was over she rolled over onto her back and opened her eyes.

"You motherfucker," she said. "Get out of here!"

"Take it easy," I said.

"I'll holler. I'll holler rape. I'll scream."

"You're at Down Under," I said. "They couldn't hear it if there were ten of you screaming rape."

"You stole my photographs, you motherfucker."

"I'll give them back," I said. "But you have to give me something."

"No. Don't touch me."

"I won't touch you," I said.

"I don't believe you. If you try to rape me, I have a knife—I'll use it."

"Get dressed if you want," I said.

"I just want you out of here!"

I picked up a T-shirt from the pile on the chair and tossed it to her. "The night Wendy died," I said, "you went over to Hiroshi Tanaka's apartment. There were some private things you had over there. Some letters maybe. You were in love with her, weren't you?"

"None of your fucking business."

"It's okay. Loving is good. I hope she loved you back."

"No," she said. "It's none of your fucking business."

"I know that."

"She was wonderful. I loved her. I'm not ashamed of that."

"You shouldn't be," I said. "But you went into Tanaka's apartment. You had the key. You were the first one there. You wanted some mementos. Did she really look like the pictures in the comic book?"

"Yes, sort of," Carol said.

"Did she shave?"

"Yeah, she did. For Hiroshi. He wanted her even younger than she was. I loved her just the way she was. But she was exciting this way."

"That's when you picked up the photos with Nadia and Wendy and Hiroshi. You tore out the page from the comic and maybe by accident you picked up something else, a computer disc. Right?"

"Why should I tell you?"

"Let's not fight. I don't want to search. I don't want to make trouble for you. I just want the disc."

"It's in the closet," she said. Then she picked up the T-shirt and covered her face with it and began to sob. "I miss her so much. I never loved anyone like I loved her," she said through the cotton and the tears. It was the same one she'd worn the first time I'd met her, the one that said JUST BECAUSE I SLEPT WITH YOU LAST NIGHT DOESN'T MEAN I'LL SKI WITH YOU IN THE MORNING. The disc was in a paper sleeve. There were five names handwritten on it. Vlad Kapek was one. I didn't recognize the other four, but if I had to guess, one was German, one Polish, one Hungarian, and the last was written in Cyrillic. I took the disc and left.

TWENTY-SIX

FATHER GUIDO

Goddamn Guido had to arrive in his clerical collar.

He couldn't travel like a normal person in jeans and a T-shirt or in ski clothes or in a suit and tie.

Since my mother was going to the train to meet him it just seemed natural for me to go with her, Marie to go with me, and Anna Geneviève to go with Marie. Geneviève came with everyone else.

I may not have been sure what Guido's relationship to my mother was, but Geneviève was certain. So this was my mother's "companion." Her "special friend." The French do a lot of reading between the lines—they regard it as a higher truth.

Guido hugged my mother fondly.

Geneviève was aghast. *"Mais c'est scandaleux."*

Guido hugged me, like a fond uncle. Or stepfather. "Let me see the baby," he said. Marie Laure handed the infant to him. He beamed. Like a step-grandfather.

"Ce n'est pas bien, ça," Geneviève said.

"Did you have to wear the fucking collar?" I said.

"I get a clerical discount," he said. "And they treat me better."

"C'est une abomination," Geneviève said. Cloaking herself in darkness, she turned away and began a march through the town, back toward our *pension*. Her daughter ran after her.

"Oh, dear," Guido said, handing me the baby, "what have I done?"

"I thought she was Jewish," my mother said. "Didn't she say that in Vienna?"

"She said," I said, "that her mother was Jewish by birth. But she was raised Catholic. In Algeria. Didn't you notice her going to mass on Sunday?"

"I thought that was for the music," my mother, who is usually so smart, said. She was being willfully ignorant, as if that would take any blame for the fuss away from Guido, who continued to apologize.

Now we had to organize the luggage. I only had one arm and that was holding Anna Geneviève. I thought it made sense for my mother to take the baby and me to carry the two suitcases. But there was still snow on the ground and my mother was afraid she would slip. So they each took one, but they were really too heavy for people that old and we made a sorry procession. There was much resting and more denying that there was a problem. Finally I made them stop and got a taxi to take us the six blocks or so.

When we reached the house, Geneviève and Marie Laure were on the street yelling at each other. Geneviève had packed and was putting her suitcase into the red and black Citroën 2CV6.

"Please don't go," my mother said.

"Oh, dear, have I upset you?" Guido said.

"You are a stupid old woman," Marie Laure said, in French.

"The acorn does not fall far from the tree," Geneviève said, in French.

"What seems to be the problem?" Guido asked. He didn't look that good actually. Thin and hospital pale.

"I think there's a misunderstanding," my mother said.

"No wonder you are raising a bastard," Geneviève said, in French.

"You are a narrow-minded bourgeois," said Marie Laure. "Go home! Go back to France! To your narrow-minded bourgeois friends and their petty stupidities."

And she did.

T W E N T Y - S E V E N

DENOUEMENT

When Anna Geneviève smiled and laughed and shrieked with delight, the whole world lit up. She loved to stand, and if I held her up she thought she was. She was beginning to have conversations. Not with words that any of us were familiar with—and among us we had English, French, German, Italian, and Latin—but with the rhythm and the attitude of language nonetheless. Nor did she yet distinguish between listener and nonlistener. One of her most extended lectures was to my shoe. She had the build of the Michelin tire man, rolls and rolls of happy fat, all of it pure breast milk. Her cheeks were as round as a trumpet player's. To my surprise, that wasn't fat—it was muscle. She was the best of all those babies that show up in Renaissance paintings as cherubs.

When Marie Laure was tense or unhappy it darkened my whole life. But no matter what bothered her, she was always Perfect Mom to Anna Geneviève. She still never got angry when the baby woke her at night, which she did several times every night. Anna Geneviève had done well for herself.

I wanted them happy. Safe. Secure.

As the clock ticked down and the four days passed, I kept looking at that feeling and playing with the baby to find the answers to what I was going to do. I guess I kept looking because the answer was both apparent and not what I wanted it to be.

I liked Mike Hayakawa. He was opinionated, clever, fun, didn't lie to me too very much, and had saved my daughter's life. I did not like Harry Lime and Chip Sheen. They were blackmailing and bullying me. They'd left me to languish or perish without thinking twice.

I liked the idea of being an exile, expatriate, outlaw, small-scale Byronic ski bum, and laundry scammer. I did not like the image of myself as family man, a careful-to-cross-the-street can't-afford-to-be-out-of-work da-da doing what the mommy wants in life. Pussy-whipped we used to call it back in Brooklyn when we were young and macho studs.

I liked the idea of going home—if I ever went home—on my terms, not theirs. I wanted someone to apologize and admit I'd been framed. This was childish in the extreme and I knew it. It didn't carry a lot of weight with me. Not intellectually, anyway.

I liked the idea of paying my debts—which meant doing right by Hayakawa and doing harm to Lime and Sheen.

But if Hayakawa came through with the money and Lime came through with the letter to my lawyer, it was going to go down the way Lime wanted it to. Because Marie Laure wanted it that way. Because my daughter deserved it that way. There was no way of looking at them and seeing any other answer. They had filled up the place in me that was full of shifting values and relative choices, they were as close to an absolute as I could get, and Anna Geneviève was my lucky star.

Guido wanted to know what was going on.

I told him, keeping in mind that there was a microphone in the room. I was certain that my listener was Lime because Lime acted on what we said and Hayakawa did not. The distant follower who I had sensed following Chip Sheen, following me, and who might have been the one to put the directional beeper on Sheen's car had not reappeared. Perhaps the beeper had something to do with Hungary. After all, they still had some sort of police and secret police and their intelligence agency who could well have picked him out as CIA and wanted to keep tabs on him, even if the world was changing.

In the version of the story that I told Guido I had not yet picked up the disc, but I had seen it, was certain it existed, and would pick it up just before the exchange. I said this so that Lime, who was listening, would not try to hijack me and cut me out of the action. It wasn't in the apartment either. It was stashed near where I'd found it, Down Under.

I could hear Mike Hayakawa through the door before I knocked. He was working out. When he opened the door his hairless torso had a nice sheen of sweat. Half naked and pumped up with exercise, he looked driven and intense. Not the somewhat ineffectual character he appeared to be when he wore his exactly correct brand-name clothes and masked his eyes with brown-rimmed glasses, a self-deprecating disguise, partly personal and partly a cultural affectation.

"You have good news?" he asked.

"Do you have the money?"

His eyes appraised me, wondering who could take who if he said, "Yes, there's a million deutsche marks in the room." He noted my sling—I was a one-wing bird—but Americans are always running around with guns. "At the bank. Here in town," he said.

"Tomorrow," I said.

"Really?"

"Really."

"What time? Where?"

"It's tricky," I said. "I'd like to trust you. I'd like to think I could hand you the disc and you would hand me the money and we could turn around and walk away. Not even look back over our shoulders."

"You can trust me," he said. "I want something and I am willing to pay for it. What do I care?" He giggled. Sort of. "It's company money. Expense account."

"It's easy for you," I said. "You take back the deutsche marks, you have a million deutsche marks. I hold on to the disc, I have nothing."

"You pick the place," he said. "I want you to be comfortable."

"I'll pick a place we can both go in, look around, make sure we're alone, unarmed. Then you get your money from wherever you want. When the money comes in, I go bring the disc. Is that all right?"

"That's fine. Where?"

"I don't know yet," I said. "I'll tell you tomorrow. After we meet at the bank and you show me that you have the money. I want to see it. Otherwise no meet, no nothing."

"I understand. I am sorry that there is so little trust."

"Me too," I said.

As I went out the door he was already back to his exercises. It was a martial arts series with exploding breaths and simulated blows. He did it with the floor-length mirror, admiring himself, seeing another Bruce Lee in the definition of his own muscles. We all do that—see tough guys in the mirror.

Chip Sheen all but leapt upon me as I came out. His eye was in terrible condition—green and brown and puffy where I'd hit him. I'd split the skin and he had a little butterfly Band-Aid on the break.

"You got him set up?" he said.

"Why don't you make yourself a little bit obvious?"

"You got him set up?"

"I haven't heard from my lawyer yet."

"I wish you understood how important this was. We were in a war. Communism was the anti-Christ. That was easy to understand. They were godless atheism, we had God on our side. That's why we won. But God does not want us to rest, to forget our mission to instruct and lead. God wants us to be tested. So He has risen up a new enemy—The Godless Orient. Shinto and Buddhism are other names for pagan atheism. We are very lucky, because America needs enemies. Our enemies make us strong."

"Listen, bow-wow, I have a deal with your master. It includes a letter to my lawyer. No tickee, no laundry, no diskee, no Hayakawee."

"You are out of line, mister."

"Listen to me, Sheen. I didn't walk into your toy store—you walked into mine. I didn't threaten your existence—you messed with mine. Go tell the man."

"If it were up to people like you, America would go down the tubes. You have no spiritual dimension."

■

At 11:00 P.M. in St. Anton it was 5:00 P.M. in New York and the day was done. We had cleared away the dishes long ago, had our after-dinner tea, and digested. My mother and Guido had gone to bed. The baby was asleep. There had been no phone call from the States. No message from my lawyer—no Gerald Yaskowitz saying the Feds say, "Come home, all is forgiven."

I took Marie Laure by the hand. I said, "Let's go look at the moon."

She said, "But the baby."

I said, "I need some air. Let's go outside."

She shook her head. "You go," she said.

"For once, just once in our post-baby life, do what I say, just because I ask."

That pissed her off, but she threw on a jacket and stomped out.

"Listen to me," I said, "I want you to be prepared for this. If I had my choice we would go with Lime. Set up Hayakawa. But it doesn't look like the CIA or whoever the hell he's with is coming through for us. I want you to understand that if they don't, our one choice just may be to take the money and run."

"I do not understand," she said.

"Let's say that Lime really is a CIA agent and this is a real CIA operation and he really can make a deal for me with the Justice Department. He will only do that in order to get the disc and nail Hayakawa. He will not do it afterward, out of honor or gratitude. What he might do afterward is turn me in to the IRS anyway—for extra brownie points. That is the nature of the beast. That is the law of the jungle.

"It's time to face things. I don't see it coming through—a verifiable deal, in writing. What I see is we take the money. Then we have two chances. One is we go underground again. Different country, different names—like I said, maybe a different sport. I mean if we're underground we might as well be having a good time. Or we take the money and go to the States. We hire a high-powered, connected law firm and let them fight it down to the wire—six hundred thousand dollars' worth. Maybe we can win."

"You don't think they will send the letter?"

"No," I said.

She was very sad. Neither of us slept well. We were both tossing and turning. My shoulder throbbed and there seemed to be no comfortable position for it. Finally at 3:00 A.M. I fell asleep. At four the phone rang.

"Tony, Tony, is that you, Tony?" Gerald Yaskowitz yelled.

"Yeah," I mumbled.

"Can you hear me?" he screamed.

"I hear you fine," I said.

"Wow. All the way across the Atlantic Ocean and you hear me fine. That's great."

"Softly, Gerry, softly."

"I can't get over it. How the hell are you?"

"Fine, Gerry, and you? You got the letter?"

"You know about the letter? How the hell do you know about the letter? I call him all the way across the Atlantic Ocean with news about something that just this one minute happened. I'm talking not sixty seconds ago the messenger—he walked out the door of my home—and he already knows. Telepathy. I'm telling you, telepathy. Next you're gonna tell me what's in it? Right?"

"Go ahead, read it to me, Gerry," I said.

"It says . . . uh . . . 'To whom it may concern, Anthony Michael Cassella is in the process of doing a major service to his country. On the completion of this service and upon the verbal confirmation of same by this office, this office will require and recommend that any outstanding criminal or judicial charges involving Mr. Cassella be terminated as a matter of National Security. . . .' Whaddaya think about that? I'm impressed—you and Ollie North. To continue . . . 'The agency will appear as amicus curiae to speak for Mr. Cassella in any judicial proceeding.' It's signed by Jeffrey MacFarlane the Third at something called the Office of Economic Research, Central Intelligence Agency. Well, whaddaya know about that?"

"It looks like I'm coming home," I said.

"It looks like you're coming home," Gerry said.

"It looks like we are going home?" Marie Laure asked, stirring beside me.

"Yeah, I guess so," I said to her.

"Wow, all the way across the Atlantic Ocean and he already knows."

I had a flash of paranoia. "Gerry, you do me a favor—you call this guy and you find out if this letter is real."

"You think it might not be real?"

"Gerry, do you know what time it is here?"

"About lunchtime? Right?"

"It's about four in the morning."

"Hey, gee, I'm sorry, but it's such great news."

"Yes, Gerry, good night. Thank you."

"I want a gun," I said to Lime.

"I can't give you a gun," he said.

"Give me his." I pointed at Chip.

"What for?" Lime said.

"I'm going to make this as simple as I can, but it's very fucking complicated, and if you fuck it up and it goes wrong I want a sense of security."

"Is that what you call it?"

"That's what I call it," I said.

"I'm not giving up my piece," Chip said.

"You have the disc?" Lime asked.

"Does a bear shit in the woods? Do Austrians ski? Was George Bush head of the CIA? What are we sitting here talking for?"

"Okay, I got it. Give him the gun."

"Mr. Lime . . ."

"We'll find you another one," Lime said.

I held out my hand. Chip slowly and reluctantly gave up his Glock. I took it. It was loaded. I put it in my pocket. Getting Sheen's gun away from him was the point of my request. There was something fanatic and erratic about him and I had the feeling that the final confrontation might be a lot smoother if he was unarmed.

"We will meet," I told Lime, "at Down Under. They close early tonight. Two o'clock. I meet Hayakawa there at three. We each get to look around. If all is well and all is quiet, he goes and gets the money. This should take no more than five, ten minutes.

Once the money is there I'm supposed to go get the disc. At three fifteen I step outside, you see me. When I go back in, you give me a minute, maybe two. That gives me time to give him the disc and put some distance between us. One of you comes in the front door. The other comes in the back. Do it quiet. Or bring the cops. I don't know what kind of deal you have with the Austrian police, or what their neutrality means when it comes to arresting someone with stolen U.S. property. That's your business."

"What if he's faster about bringing the money?"

"I can stall by counting it. Or by taking longer to get the disc. The point of making it three fifteen is that when he checks the place out he doesn't stumble over you."

"Not bad," Lime said. "Maybe not airtight, but not bad. Tell me something—where did you find the disc?"

"Tell me something," I said. "Who killed Hiroshi Tanaka and Wendy Tavetian?"

"I can only make an educated guess," he said.

"Too bad," I said.

"I'll see you at three fifteen."

"Don't rush things," I said.

"Why am I letting you use my place?" Paul asked. "Remind me."

I gave him ten thousand shillings. About $850.

"Right, mate, now I remember."

"You do some hunting, don't you?"

"Not too often," he said.

"You use a shotgun?"

"Shotgun, rifle—depends what I'm after."

"Lend me the shotgun."

"Lend you the shotgun?"

"If I use it, I'll kick in another ten thousand. I don't expect to use it."

"Bloody fucking Americans. You're all bloody mad. You think the world's a show on the telly and you can go around blowing each other away. Five thousand whether you use it or not. If you use it, just say you stole it."

"Done."

"Don't lose those keys, mate, they're the only extra set."

"Before you close up," I said, "you put the shotgun up there, next to the animal heads. Like it was part of the hunting exhibit. Except make sure it's loaded."

"You are a television show, aren't you? I'll do it now."

While he did that, I went and checked the disc behind the cases of beer where I'd left it. It was still there. I took it out of its dusty old sleeve and put it in a brand-new envelope with some cardboard for stiffening, wrapped it all in plastic, and taped it shut.

I met Mike Hayakawa at the bank. He had an attaché case and there was a lot of money in it. I told him the version of the plan he was supposed to hear. He thought it sounded reasonable. He agreed to it.

I went home. I rubbed my shoulder with Arnica ointment. It was supposed to encourage healing. The doctor said it worked but couldn't explain how. Then I did my first set of physical therapy exercises. It involved rotating my arm in a circle. Then resting. Four times. It was stressful. I thought the list of names on the sleeve that had held the disc were important. I copied them over and hid the sleeve under the rug. Then I took a long hot bath, soaking my shoulder and arm. At least it had happened at the end of the season, not the beginning—and a bad season at that.

After dinner I called Gerald Yaskowitz at the office and at home. He was out. Then I told Marie Laure the deal was going down that night, or rather early the next morning. She asked me where and when. I knew the place was wired, but since all the principals already knew where and when it didn't matter who was listening. So I told her. She asked me if I knew who had killed Wendy Tavetian.

"Her poor mother," she said, "I would go mad if anything happened to our Anna Geneviève. Absolutely insane. I would kill myself, I think."

"My best guess," I said, "is Chip Sheen. Because he's a fanatic and not real competent. So I figure he had orders to stop Tanaka from making delivery. Or he misinterpreted his orders. Anyway, he stopped him. But he didn't secure the disc first. Or after. So then, when Hayakawa showed up, Lime got the bright idea of making sure that the Japanese and the espionage are connected, unless, like I said, that was the idea in the first place, and Chip jumped the gun. Nothing else makes sense. Does it?"

I got to Down Under early. I stashed the automatic in the cash register, a round in the chamber and the safety off. I didn't expect to use it. But if I wanted it, it seemed like a good place to have it.

At three, on the dot, Mike Hayakawa came in. He was tense, not as affable as usual. Me too.

"I guess I should look around and search and make sure you're unarmed?"

"You should," I said. "It's the prudent thing to do."

"This has been fun," Mike said. "Working with you. You are so independent and resourceful. I was really at a loss until you came along."

He walked around the room, looking under tables, up at the roofbeams, behind the Austrian stove. He looked right at the shotgun on the wall between the stuffed heads of the chamois. It was so much in plain sight he didn't see it. Then he came over to me. I raised my arms and spread my legs and let him pat me down.

"I have been empowered," he said when he was done, "to offer you a job. If the disc is correct and everything. Musashi intends to make a very major investment in Europe. You could work here. Musashi pays very, very well and also has excellent benefits. This is something to consider now that you have a child and are perhaps planning another."

"Thank you," I said. "I'll talk it over with Marie Laure."

"I will go get the money now," he said.

He was back, according to my watch, which is an eighteen-dollar Casio, at three ten.

"Let me look," I said.

He opened the attaché case. The deutsche marks were stacked

thick and solid and rich-looking. There's something about money—cash money—that gets the stomach churning, the blood flowing, the greed going.

"Do you want to count it?"

"No. I want to get this over with," I said.

"Me too," he said.

"I'll be back in two minutes," I said.

I went through the kitchen and outside. I stood there. I breathed the alpine air. I said an unbeliever's prayer and watched the moonlight of a quarter moon play with the snow and the peaks. Then I went inside, got the envelope from behind the beer bottles, and gave it to Mike.

I took the attaché case and headed for the bar. "You want a beer?" I asked Hayakawa.

He was tearing the envelope apart. He took out the disc. He looked at it.

"Where's the list?" he screamed. He was livid.

"What list?"

"The list!" he screamed. "The list! Where is the list!"

"You wanted a disc," I said "Not a list. You got a disc."

"Freeze, partner," Harry Lime said, standing in the doorway, his gun pointed at Hayakawa.

Hayakawa froze.

"What's this, Tony? No list?" Lime said.

"What list are you talking about? The two of you have been raving about a disc. Now you're screaming about a list. Don't you know what you want?"

I saw Lime's face fall and fill with loss. Then I looked where he was looking, as did Hayakawa. The body of Chip Sheen, dripping blood, hanging limp, was moving into the room. The wider body of one of Vlad Kapek's Bulgarians was behind him, holding him up. I looked back at Lime and before I could cry out the other Bulgarian, the younger one, had grabbed him from behind. He squeezed Lime until he turned pale and dropped the gun.

"Is this yours?" the Bulgarian holding Chip Sheen asked in German.

"Oh, what did you have to kill him for?" Lime said.

The Bulgarian shrugged. "This is the way we found him," he said. Chip's body was soaked from the stomach on down. He'd been knifed in the belly, stabbed over and over. The Bulgarian dropped him.

"I want the list," Hayakawa said.

"There is no list that I know of," I said as calmly as I could.

Hayakawa gestured to the Bulgarian holding Lime. The Bulgarian lifted Lime in a bear hug from behind like a kid carrying a big dolly and dragged him over beside me, in front of the bar. He let Lime go and moved over to Hayakawa, the three of them watching the two of us.

"If he says there is no list, then he didn't find it," Lime said.

The door opened. We all turned and looked.

It was Marie Laure and Guido. She came rushing in, the old man following more slowly behind. "Tony, Tony," she cried. Lime thought that Mike and the Bulgarians were distracted enough. He reached down for the gun in his ankle holster. But he was slow. The Bulgarians were faster. One swung toward Marie Laure and Guido and pulled his gun out. I watched in total terror. The other outdrew Lime and fired first. There was just one shot and we all froze.

"Oh, shit," Lime said, sad and sinking. "Gut shot," he said, "fucking gut shot."

"Where is the list?" Hayakawa asked again.

"What is the list?" I said. Though by now I knew. I just wanted to slow things down. Calm things and figure a way out.

Lime laughed and choked. "The list is what it's all about."

"Not the disc?"

"The disc is just proof. Of ability. The list is . . . fuckin' funny."

"What's funny," I said.

"Unemployed secret . . . ha . . . ha . . . agents. All over East Europe. Going private. Get it. It's all industrial these days, anyway. All about . . . money and high tech. Tanaka was taking all of East Europe's spies and going private."

Five names. One each from Czechoslovakia, Poland, Hungary, East Germany. One in Cyrillic.

"To the highest bidder. The fuckin' Japs. Musashi Company.

The disc was just proof they could get good stuff. Then . . . then money to go private. How much was Musashi going for . . . twenty million up front?"

"Yes. Twenty million for the greatest industrial espionage network in the world," Hayakawa said.

"Dollars?" I asked.

"Dollars."

"What if I could get you the list?" I said.

"Don't give him the satisfaction," Lime said. "No satisfaction. I'm gonna die. Motherfucker. I been one bad motherfucker."

"You let them go," I said, pointing to Guido and Marie Laure, "and I'll find you the list."

"Don't do it," Lime said. "Then he has to kill you anyway. Don't you?"

"Shut up," Mike said. "Shut up." He grabbed a gun from one of the Bulgarians and marched forward, the gun outstretched, pointing at Lime's head.

"I almost outbid him . . . didn't I, Mike? With, with Germans, SpeerGruppen. Don't give him the list. He'll kill you . . ."

Mike fired. He wasn't more than two feet away by then. The back of Lime's head blew away. It splattered and scattered, spewing brain and blood and bits of bone. Marie Laure began to scream and scream. Guido put his arms around her and held her. She sobbed into him. I tried to move toward her, but Mike swung the gun around and pointed it at me.

"Wait a minute. Take it slow," I said.

"I am very sorry," he said. "Very sorry. I like you, Tony. Like your mother. Nothing personal. But you are a witness."

"I'd lie for you, Mike. Any time," I said.

"I don't think so," he said. "You set me up. I am not angry with you for that. After all, you pursued your first loyalty and that is right. Do you pray?" he asked. "No," he answered for me. "I don't think so. But I would let you before you die if you did."

"Mike, let Marie go. We have a new baby. Think about your baby, and leaving her an orphan, no mother . . ."

"Tony, don't plead. Have dignity. Your daughter has her grandmother. I will send money. I promise."

"Mike, I'm begging you . . ."

"Have dignity," he snapped at me, and aimed the gun.

"Okay, sure, no pleading. Mike, for our friendship, there is one thing I would ask," I said. Anything to stall. Something to stall. Until maybe I could get the shotgun or the automatic in the cash register.

"What is it, Tony?"

"The lady, Marie Laure, I want to marry her. I don't want my daughter to be illegitimate. That's important to me."

"You want what?"

"The old man—he's a priest. He could marry us, before you . . . you know."

"Are you serious?" Mike said.

"Oh, Tony," Marie Laure said, tears streaming down her face. Not tears of happiness at being wed at last. Tears of fear and worry for her baby. I knew I was going to go after Hayakawa. If I ate a bullet doing it, then so be it. I just needed to break the rhythm, break his attention and get close to the shotgun.

"You, priest," he said.

"Yes," Guido said.

"You make this real fast," Mike said.

"I will," Guido said.

"Two minutes, no more," he said.

I started walking toward Marie Laure, toward the shotgun as well. I gestured her to come toward me. "I got to thank you for this, Mike. I really do. It's a special kindness."

"It is," Marie Laure said. "Thank you. It will give me a chance to tell him how much I love him."

"I love you too," I said, my eyes filling with tears and sentiment. "I really do."

"*Je t'aime,*" she said.

"*Je t'aime,*" I said.

"Are you ready?" Mike said.

I was standing under the shotgun. "Yes," I said. "Father, why don't you stand there," I said, pointing to a spot that would put him partly between Hayakawa and me. While he shuffled into position I said, "Let me ask you something else, Mike, just out of curiosity. Who did hire Hans Lantz to kill Tanaka?"

"I did," he said.

"What the hell for?"

"He was disloyal. He was working for Musashi! Then Harry Lime came to him with a deal from another group. SpeerGruppen. Germans. He was going to deal with them."

"So he had the list and you killed him and you were going to take the list and put together the network yourself."

"But I have failed."

"You know," I said, "I still think I could get you the list."

"Yes, but if you know the list, and your loyalty is to America, what good is it? You will give it to the CIA and they will eliminate all of them."

"You overestimate the CIA, Mike. Why think they're any better than General Motors?"

"You are a witness, I have to kill. You better get married quick," he said.

"All right," I said. "Go on, Guido."

"I guess I better keep it short," Guido said.

"Yeah," I said.

"Marie Laure, are you ready?" Guido asked.

"Yes, Father," she said. "Thank you for this, Tony."

A banshee screamed and two figures ran, yelling, into the room. They came at Hayakawa waving knives. I shoved Marie to the floor. I reached up and grabbed the shotgun. Hayakawa and the Bulgarians were firing into the screamers, who just swallowed up the bullets and kept on coming. They staggered like the undead from a bad zombie movie, losing bits and pieces while they came.

I fired twice in rapid succession. The Bulgarians and Hayakawa were in a group and the shotgun blast took them all. The older Bulgarian turned toward me. He was still standing. He aimed at me. Arlene Tavetian, more dead than alive, fell into him, the big kitchen knife held in front of her, and stabbed into his gut. Marie Laure and Guido were both down, crawling behind tables. I ran for the bar. I hit the cash register. Someone was still shooting. The drawer popped open, I grabbed the gun, turned.

The younger Bulgarian was standing. His hand was over his face, blood streaming from his eyes. He was blind. But still shooting. I shot him. Mike Hayakawa was on the floor. I shot him.

Then, it was quiet.

T W E N T Y - E I G H T

PAYMENTS

I had the presence of mind to send Marie Laure away with the deutsche marks. That was fortunate because it cost me DM500,000—that is, $333,000, plus Rick's American Laundromat, to get Franz, the gendarme, to make a palatable story out of the insane massacre. Austria is not America. Everything is perfect in Austria. They have the lowest murder rate in the world. It's expensive to cover up a killing there. It wasn't like he got to keep it all—he had to spread some around. I understood that.

The official version was that Lime had a shootout with Hayakawa and the Bulgarians. He handled all the guns. I wasn't even there. Nor was Marie Laure, nor was Guido. The Bulgarians were blamed for Sheen, though that wasn't who killed him. Arlene Tavetian had. And I was an accomplice in a way. The Tavetians were there, in the official story. But no one was going to blame the Tavetians, who only had knives, for attacking men who had guns. Particularly since Hayakawa had murdered Wendy.

The reason Marie Laure and Guido had showed up was that Guido had discovered a microphone and thought he should warn me that someone must have listened in. When we went back we discovered two sets of microphones. A day and a half later, Robert Tavetian was well enough to talk. Fortunately he would only talk to me.

"Tried to warn you she was crazy," he said.

"Was that your microphone?" I asked. "In my house?"

"Got it mail order. From Spy Inc. catalog, Miami."

"Did you put a beeper on Chip Sheen's car? Follow him to Budapest?"

"Yeah. Arlene. Obsessed. Sorry."

"Mail order?"

He nodded yes.

"Did she kill Chip Sheen?"

He nodded. "Heard you say . . . him."

"Sorry about that," I said.

"Not your fault," he said.

"Don't mention it," I said. "We already blamed it on the Bulgarians."

He nodded. "Arlene," he said, "gonna make it?"

"Maybe," I said, "but not in real good shape."

That was all he could take. Tears rolled down his cheeks and he looked away from me, at the wall.

I married Marie Laure under my real name. Guido performed the service. My mother and Franz, the gendarme, were the witnesses.

Gerald Yaskowitz called. He said that there was no such guy at the CIA as had signed my letter. It was a phony. That was more or less what I had expected.

Hiroshi Tanaka had had a fairly brilliant idea. One of the few things the Eastern Europeans had really developed to the point where they were competitive with the West was espionage. In recent years, rather than political or military, it had become primarily technical and industrial espionage, which made it even more marketable. All it needed was a packager—someone to realize the potential of the networks already in place, take them commercial, and bring their services to the people with real money to spend.

Viewing it from the other side, the buyer's, it was also a great idea. An established, working spy network already in place. It would do far more for the Japanese, for example, than it had ever done for the Russians, because the Communists didn't know how to utilize the information. The production and engineering capabilities of Toshiba or Musashi—for that matter of a Hyundai or Mercedes—coupled with the information-gathering capabilities of

Stasi, the KGB, the Czech, Hungarian, and Polish security services would be fearsome indeed. It could be the alliance that tipped the balance in the economic wars of the coming century. Assuming that the balance has not yet tipped.

Harry Lime was an old man with a taste for young women and intrigue who was facing a gimpy retirement on a government pension based on dollars in a decade where that currency was the wrong place to be. I thought he actually was CIA. As such, he got wind of Tanaka's idea and decided to take it over. He was able to use some official sources and resources. He was even willing to use some personnel, like Chip Sheen, because Sheen was both very eager and not too swift, a boy scout with a gun who thought God was on his side. And Jaroslav, the Czech lawyer. But not too many people could know about it. Because Harry Lime was not going to turn the result of his operation over to the CIA. He was going to take Tanaka's place and go private. Lime had lined up a German consortium, SpeerGruppen, to bid against Musashi. That's why he was so eager to use me. I was unconnected, dispensable, disposable.

At least, that's what I think happened. Based on what people did, rather than what they said, since everyone was lying all the time. Why shouldn't they? I didn't really care about The Truth or making the world safe for General Motors or even about the Tavetians too terribly much. I cared about making Marie Laure happy and keeping Anna Geneviève safe.

"I have half a million deutsche marks to fight my case," I said to Gerald Yaskowitz.

"How much is that in real money?" he asked me.

I also had the names of five leading East European spy masters ready to go commercial and take their operations with them. That was an additional bargaining chip.

On the flight home I read the first copy of the *New York Times* I'd seen in years. It sounded like the Mets were going to blow it again. There was a story in the financial section about Musashi Aerospace. It said that they were going to coventure aeronautics research with SpeerGruppen of West Germany.